Dawn of Chaos

Volume One of the

Sanctum of the Archmage Saga

by Tony Andarian

Edited by Samantha Rosalbo
Cover Art by Alex Perkins

Dawn of Chaos is a "compilation volume" that includes previously published titles. Unless otherwise noted, they were originally released in 2017 by Andarian Publishing as an e-book on Amazon Kindle under the title *Dawn of Chaos*. This represents the updated 3rd edition of that book.

Rogue Wizard, The World of Kalara, and *The Legend of the Defender* were released in 2014 under the title *Dawn of Chaos.* The title was changed to *Prologue to Chaos* in 2015.

Inquisition on Trial was published in 2019 in *Prologue to Chaos, 5th edition. The Ambassador's Daughter* was published in 2021 in *Prologue to Chaos, 6th edition. The Warning* and *The Muster of the Elves* were published in 2021 in *Aftermath, 1st edition.*

Dawn of Chaos was re-released in 2022 by Andarian Publishing as a trilogy under the following titles. This book combines that trilogy into a single volume.

Prologue to Chaos (6th edition), Hell Gate, and Aftermath

Hell Gate was released in 2021 by Andarian Publishing as a four novella serial under the following titles.

Hell Gate I - The Return of the Horde
Hell Gate II - The Ring of the Killravens
Hell Gate III - The Massacre of Lannamon
Hell Gate IV - The End of the Beginning

To Stacey, my soulmate and the love of my life

Table of Contents

DAWN OF CHAOS, BOOK 1

PROLOGUE TO CHAOS

Introduction - The World of the Sanctum

The Lands of the Children

The world of the *Sanctum of the Archmage Saga* is known as *Kalara*. The reasons lie within its oldest traditions and legends.

Kalara's many peoples all retain a remarkably cohesive origin story. In one form or another they tell of a prehistorical golden age, or *Age of Legends*, in which they were brought from other worlds to live in harmony with a race of beneficent deities. These gods cared for and watched over them, until their idyllic paradise was shattered by an invasion from the hell-realms of the demons.

The *Great War* ravaged Kalara — but in the end, the gods prevailed. The power of the demon armies was broken, and their survivors were driven to the far corners of the world. And although they eventually left to return to their homes in the heavens, the gods rewarded the people for their loyalty. Their gift in the elder tongue is called *A'lessa Kalar*, the *Covenant of the Children*.

It is this covenant, which lay at the heart of Kalaran religion for thousands of years, that inspired the name by which the world has come to be known. *Kalara*, in the elder language of the elves, means the *Land of the Children*.

The name is often used to refer to the world as a whole, as opposed to the nameless worlds from which its people were once thought to have come, or from the heaven and hell worlds of the gods and the demons. Yet it is also used to refer to the great *continent* of Kalara. It spans the known lands between the Adaran Ocean to the east and south, and the Walls of the World to the west.

Kalara is home to many diverse cultures and a striking variety of sentient races. Dragons, giants, and other fantastical creatures, both friendly and malevolent, all vie with men and elves for dominance over its lands. And while legend holds that the demon lords were driven from the world, not all of their servants shared that fate. Though long banished to the harsh mountains and wastes of the far north and west, these terrible fiends present a never-ending threat to the Children of the Covenant.

Chapter 1

Rogue Wizard

The Ninth of Winterfall, in the Year 1642 of the Taming

Gerard Killraven stepped through the door from the Wizard's Tower and into the Great Hall. It was the height of the Yule season in the Kingdom of Carlissa, and the walls and arches of the royal palace were strung with magical lights and decked with garlands of mistletoe and holly. The cheery ambiance provided a stark contrast to his sense of dread at the summons that had brought him down from his research.

He saw his brother Aron closing the door to the conference room at the far end of the hall. Aron waved, and then strode purposefully to meet him. *Right in character*, Gerard reflected. Everything his brother did was laced with a sense of purpose, from the way he fought — the elder prince was already notorious as one of Carlissa's finest fencers — to the way he moved and spoke.

The expression he wore now, though, was grim. Whatever was happening, it was serious.

"I came down as soon as I got the message from Grandfather," Gerard said. They met in the center of the hall and briefly clasped arms, a gesture of greeting and salute that had become habitual between the two princes.

He glanced over Aron's shoulder at the conference room door. It was locked and guarded by a dozen men at arms.

"It doesn't take a diviner to tell there's a crisis brewing," he added. "What's going on?"

Aron put a hand on his shoulder and gently steered him toward the gate to the courtyard. "Not here," he said.

Gerard grinned at the sound. The rich baritone of his brother's voice had become one of the elder prince's signature features. It never failed to instill him with reassurance.

"Let's take a walk outside and I'll fill you in. Father's ordered the Great Hall to be cleared, so it's best if we don't stay here, anyway."

Gerard nodded and fell into step beside him. He knew better than to ask questions. Despite the many differences between them — Aron was a warrior and a statesman, Gerard a wizard and scholar — they shared an uncanny intuition for each other's thoughts and moods. He waited patiently until they were well outside, walking along the south parapet of the courtyard, and far from where prying ears could overhear.

"There's been another incident with the Inquisition," Aron said at last.

Gerard sighed. "I should have guessed. Who is it this time?"

"There have been three arrests so far. All of them are instructors in the Grand Academy's Department of Society and Culture."

"Hardin is getting out of control. How much longer is Father going to allow this to continue?"

"There's more to it than that, Gerard. This one's serious. So serious, in fact, that the high priest is supervising it personally."

They came to a stop by a corner of the parapet. The face of Mount Cascade towered above the palace behind them, looming like a great wall over the Carlissan capital of Lannamon. The last rays of the westering sun touched the mountain's massive shoulder as they shone into the valley, bathing the city below in a soft, golden light.

Gerard turned to look carefully at his brother. "You studied in that department during your time at the academy," he said. "Did you know the instructors who were taken?"

Aron nodded. "All of them. That's why you saw me coming out of the conference room. I was in there for almost half an hour. Father and Grandfather were grilling me for everything I could tell them. What were they like, what did they teach, what ideas did they advocate, and so on."

"That's a lot of trouble to go through for a handful of academics. I take it there's another shoe to the story? One that you haven't let drop yet?"

Aron smiled. "A rock giant's boot. All the instructors arrested were close colleagues of a highly placed academy fellow. The Church is bringing charges of blasphemy and heresy against the entire group."

"So this fellow is someone important," Gerard mused. "Someone Hardin needs to tread cautiously with. Probably someone you studied under ..."

His eyes went wide as he made the connection.

"Oh, Light," he breathed. "Not Lord Zomoran of Westreach?"

Aron nodded. "Zomoran's a member of the High Council, so Hardin didn't dare try to arrest him as well."

He paused when Gerard looked at him quizzically. "The legal tradition allowing the Church to prosecute heresy cases doesn't extend to members of the civil government," he explained. "It would have been taken as an attack on the Crown."

Gerard nodded. "Of course. Knowing the high priest, though, he's not going to just leave it at that."

Aron grimaced. "No, he's not. Even as the warrior-priests arrested his alleged conspirators, Hardin was bringing his accusation directly to the academy regents. They met today, and he presented a detailed case against Zomoran for 'crimes against the Covenant.'

"And they voted to expel him, Gerard. The entire board. The vote was unanimous."

Gerard gasped. "Even Grandfather?"

Aron cocked his head back toward the now heavily guarded palace.

"Hence, the crisis atmosphere. The case must have been rock solid. Grandfather would never have gone along with it otherwise."

"He wasn't actually preaching heresy, though, was he?" Gerard asked. His voice was incredulous. "From a fellow's chair, and protected by a seat on the High Council? With no one noticing until the high priest accused him?"

Aron shrugged. "Grandfather didn't share the details. It wasn't hard to work out the gist of the case, though, from his questions about

Zomoran's lectures and research. What's frightening is that it actually sounds plausible. He and his group were known for some pretty radical ideas."

"Radical ideas? Like what?"

"Well, Zomoran's the academy's leading demonology scholar. No one knows more about those cultures that still practice the demonic religions than he does. His *Essays on Hellman Society* were full of weird insights about how elements of their social structure could be adapted to our own. That's just an example, but you get the idea. I had always dismissed them as impractical academic speculation. But some of the other students seemed quite taken by them."

Gerard pursed his lips. "You think he may actually be a closet demon worshipper?"

Aron shrugged. "I honestly don't know. Based on what I know of him, I can see it either way."

Gerard raised an eyebrow. "Care to elaborate?"

"Well, he's not the most personable instructor I've ever had, if that counts for anything. He's arrogant and self-important, in that extreme kind of way that only the truly brilliant and powerful can get away with. And Light help you if you dared try to disagree with him. His invective could be brutal. If you weren't on his level — and almost no one ever was — he'd humiliate you without a second thought."

Gerard laughed. "Yes, I know what you mean."

Aron looked surprised. "That sounds like the voice of experience," he ventured.

The young wizard nodded. "He's not just a cultural scholar. He's a full magus as well. I had him as an instructor for my studies in conjuration."

Aron nodded in return. "So you know what I'm talking about, then."

They lapsed into a long silence. The sun had disappeared below the shoulder of Mount Cascade, and shadows were growing from it like fingers reaching into the valley below. Fading orange fire still sparked from the towers and buildings of the Upper City on the ridges to the north and south.

"So Zomoran's been expelled from the Grand Academy," Gerard said finally. "Is that going to be the end of it?"

"With the high priest?" Aron grimaced. "Of course not. He sits on the council too, and he's already called a meeting tomorrow to present his case there as well. He hasn't shown all his cards yet, but Father's convinced he intends to demand Zomoran's removal."

"That still won't allow him to be arrested, though. Will it?"

"No, there's more to it than that. Even without his seat on the council to protect him, he's still the Lord of Westreach. But Hardin's strategy seems pretty clear: isolate Zomoran from any sources of support, and build a growing and very public case for him to be taken by the Inquisition. If he's expelled not only from the Grand Academy but from the High Council as well, then that gambit will likely succeed, at least eventually."

Gerard whistled.

"I can see why Father and Grandfather are locked away trying to figure out what to do," he said. "If the evidence was strong enough for Grandfather to actually vote with the other regents, then it must be pretty damning. I don't see how they'll be able to let him keep his seat on the council."

Aron nodded. "And if they expel him, it sets the stage for his eventual arrest — and probably, execution — for heresy. Such a high-profile prosecution will give the Inquisition greater influence with the people, and with the lesser nobility. That, at a time when the Crown has been working to try to institute more liberal reforms.

"Father's cross, to put it mildly. He's not sure if this is a subtle attempt to head off the reform movement, or a power grab by the Inquisition, or an earnest prosecution, and Zomoran really is as dangerous as Hardin says. Maybe it's all of them at the same time. However you take it, though —"

A bright flash interrupted him. A shock ran through the stonework of the inner bailey, followed a few seconds later by a thunderous boom. Gerard looked down from the palisade in surprise.

The Cathedral grounds in the High City below were in chaos. Part of a building had erupted suddenly into the air, spraying chunks of stone in all directions. Bodies lay strewn around a gaping hole in one wall.

"It's the Cathedral prison!" Gerard yelled over the sudden pandemonium. Cries and horns from the palace walls responded to the unexpected blast, sounding frantically to spread the alarm.

The Two Princes by Charles Imbro

Aron looked down, and his sword rang as it cleared its scabbard. The weapon glowed with a soft, white light. *Flamebane* was a famous blade, a gift to him from his grandmother, and enchanted to protect its wielder from all but the hottest of fires.

"Jailbreak!" Aron cried. "The damned fools — they've pushed Zomoran too far! Come on! We've got to get down there to help!"

Gerard gripped Aron's arm as his brother turned toward the barbican.

"Zomoran is one of the most powerful wizards alive," he said loudly, struggling to be heard over the din. "If he's actually desperate enough to attack the Cathedral, then running in to confront him will be very dangerous!"

Aron grinned and clapped him on the shoulder. "Not to worry, Brother," he said. His voice was laced with lighthearted charm. "You'll be there to deal with him!"

Gerard rolled his eyes as Aron sprinted toward the gate, but he followed right behind. "I was actually going to suggest waiting for Grandfather," he yelled. "I guess you've decided that's out of the question?"

"Entirely," Aron shouted in response.

Gerard kept running and didn't press the matter. Heroism came naturally to the elder prince — a bit too naturally for his own good, his brother sometimes thought — and he knew there would be no dissuading him.

They came to the end of the palisade where it overlooked the main gate. A wall rose in front of them. The stairs down to the High City were on the far side.

Aron looked around, and his gaze settled on a coiled length of rope atop the wall. It was tied to a metal ring driven into the stone. With an almost casual leap, he vaulted onto the parapet, grasped the line, and backtracked along the narrow ledge to pay it out.

"See you below!" he cried cheerily, and leaped into space.
Gerard scrambled to the edge in time to watch him swing down along the palace wall. The elder prince moved in an almost perfect arc that carried him over the road and set him down on the roof of the gatehouse. Gerard saw that a quick bound and a roll would take him the rest of the way to the ground. In moments, he would be up and running again along the road to the Church compound.

"Reckless idiot," Gerard muttered with an affectionate grin. He didn't try to copy his brother's move, nor did he run the long way around to the stairs. He knew the right spell for the occasion. His approach would be a little less dramatic, but no less effective.

His mind reached out, summoning the Magic. Quickly, he wove what he needed: a levitation spell. Then he climbed on top of the parapet, turned to face the road to the south, and jumped.

The gate road ran east from the palace. Aron's swing had taken him across it to the north. While his brother was climbing down the gatehouse and cutting back along the road, Gerard simply stood, riding the air. Carried forward by the momentum of his leap, he descended to the ground at a gentle but constant speed.

He landed in the middle of the road to the Cathedral, the *Divine Way*. He arrived with just enough time to draw his wand and turn as his brother came running up to meet him.

"What kept you?" he asked. There was just a hint of mischief in his characteristically serious voice.

Aron laughed as he sprinted toward the commotion on the hill below. "Well played," he called over his shoulder. "You'll have to teach me that sometime!"

"I have tried," Gerard responded drily.

The wizard prince extended his spell to cover them both. Lightened by its magic, they ran toward the Cathedral with remarkable speed. It was over a mile from the palace to the Church compound, but they covered it in only a handful of minutes.

The road ran through an entrance in the compound's outer wall. Guards lay on the ground in and around the gatehouse. Some were still, while others were groaning and moving feebly. The gates themselves had been thrown open in a ruin of twisted iron. A healer was running frantically between the stricken soldiers, doing what he could to help.

Several other soldiers stood with their weapons drawn, looking around wildly, as though expecting an attack from any direction. When they saw the two princes, they set themselves into a defensive stance.

"Strangers! Identify yourselves!" one yelled. His voice was shaky and his weapon trembled. His eyes were wide with panic.

"Aron and Gerard Killraven, princes of the realm," Aron called back. He kept his voice calm and his rich baritone soothing. It seemed to have the desired effect, and a look of relief washed over the guard's face. "What happened?"

"Thank the Light you're here, Your Highnesses!" the man gasped. Gerard noted with alarm that he didn't lower his weapon. "The Church is under attack! A man dressed in black, surrounded by some kind of huge, black cats." He shuddered. "With red eyes and bodies dark as pitch. Swords went through them, but their claws rent like a lion's. I know it sounds crazy, but it's true!"

"Shadowcats," Gerard said, when Aron gave him a questioning look. "It's a conjuration spell. An advanced one, too. Not within the capabilities of your average, run-of-the-mill wizard."

He turned to the guard. "They generate an aura of fear," he explained. "That's why you're feeling so spooked. It's a magical effect. Just take a deep breath and relax. That's it. Now, are there more of them about?"

"I don't know," the guard replied. The knowledge that his fright had come from a spell seemed to calm him, and he finally lowered his weapon. "We're not the gate guard."

He turned, gesturing to the fallen soldiers. "That's them, over there. We were at the barracks when we heard a commotion and came running. Whoever the man in black was, they were challenging him. Then the — shadowcats, they came out of nowhere, and the other guards were all dying or running and screaming. Then he pointed his staff at the gates, and they just twisted apart and fell open like they were made of putty."

"It's got to be Zomoran," Gerard said. "There are only a handful of wizards who could perform all of those castings. And who else would have a motive to attack the Church today?"

"It *was* Zomoran," one of the fallen guards moaned feebly.

They turned to look at him, and the healer rushed to his side. The man's face had been badly mauled. Gerard could see a commander's insignia on his shoulder.

"We were on watch," he continued weakly. "We'd been warned that he might come, to try to see the Lord Inquisitor. We were told to refuse him entrance."

"Apparently, he didn't take kindly to that," Gerard observed.

Aron looked around. "Guards, we have work to do," he said loudly. The ones still standing snapped immediately to attention.

"Your compound is under attack by the Magus Zomoran of Westreach," he continued. "We believe that he may be here to free his collaborators from the Grand Academy, who were taken into custody by the Inquisition earlier today. My brother and I were on the palace walls when we saw the prison building blasted and came to help. Zomoran is a powerful mage and stopping him will not be easy — but stop him, we will."

He pointed to one of the guards. "Remain here and watch over the healer and the wounded. Tell anyone who comes what has happened." He pointed to another. "Run back along the road to the palace. You should find a force on their way here to investigate. Tell them that the princes Killraven have gone on to the prison to try to stop the attack. Tell them to send their fastest runner to alert my grandfather, the Archmage. They'll find him in the council room of the palace.

"The rest of you: with me!"

Aron dashed off along the road, and Gerard fell in beside him. Shouted cries of "To the Princes!" rang out as the guards followed behind.

Gerard marveled at his brother's ability to rally men who, only moments before, had been quaking in fear. He wasn't surprised; he'd seen it before. Aron had inherited the power of their mother's voice, and it never failed him in times of need.

The road ran through a thickly wooded section of the compound. Darkness seemed to close in menacingly beneath its dense eaves as the light ebbed around them in the deepening dusk.

Gerard saw a fork in the road ahead. The main way continued toward the Great Cathedral of Lannamon, but a side path turned to the right and began climbing steeply into a knot of hills. At its end, in a clearing nestled into the foot of Mount Cascade, stood the prison building. Screams echoed from the sheer face of the mountain behind it, and fires burned in and around a huge rent in its north wall.

Gerard suddenly felt the hairs rise on the nape of his neck. Dark patches of vaguely feline shadow loomed along the darkening road before them. Tiny pairs of red lights turned to face them as they approached.

The guards faltered when they saw the creatures that had attacked them earlier blocking the way, but the princes didn't. Gerard's wand flicked the air in a complex gesture, and a ball of bright light emerged from its tip and floated forward. The monsters shrank back, their shadowy outlines becoming suddenly clear and distinct in the unexpected luminescence.

Aron's voice rang as he charged to meet them. "For the Light!" he cried. "Guards, to me! To me, my brother!"

One of the shadows padded cautiously toward him. Flamebane swept out in a graceful arc as Aron feinted to one side, and the enchanted blade scythed through the creature's neck. With a bloodcurdling howl, the shadowcat exploded in a cloud of black smoke and vanished.

The battle that followed was brief. The shadowcats' aura of terror evaporated at the sound of Aron's voice, and the guards, emboldened once again by the elder prince's call, rushed to attack. Gerard's spell seemed to negate the monsters' shadow defense, and the soldiers' blades bit fully on the feline shapes under its light. No match for the ferocity of the assault, the creatures had all soon been cut down — vanishing, howling, into clouds of dark vapor.

Again, the princes ran forward, the guards close behind. The road left the trees and opened into a clearing. More soldiers, all in the livery of the warrior priests of the Divine, lay strewn along the path. There was no stopping to render assistance; these were the elite soldiers of the Church, and they had fought to the death. Several had been mauled, and others charred or dismembered by blasts of flame or magic.

A reddish light shone in a gaping hole in a wall of the prison building. Gerard held his arms out in a gesture of restraint as they approached it.

"Careful," he said quietly. "That light isn't natural. There's someone — or something — in there."

Aron nodded as the group slowed. "My brother's right," he said, pointing to the building with his sword. "Whoever blasted their way into the dungeon is coming out again. Surround that hole. We will not let them get away."

The guards fanned out to form a semicircle around the riven side of the building. The light grew quickly as they watched and waited.

The leading edge of a sphere of shimmering red magic passed through the opening, followed by a tall, thin man dressed in black. He wore a suit of dark leather armor, and carried a staff of polished obsidian. A billowing cloak of black flapped around him in the mountain breeze, and a salt and pepper beard ending in a neatly trimmed Van Dyke framed a face that seemed hard as stone. Huddled closely behind him, and within the protection of the warding spell, walked three prisoners: two men and a woman. They were naked except for blankets that had been thrown around their shoulders.

Lord Zomoran of Westreach stepped out into the twilight air and tapped his staff once on the ground. A flare of red magic, like a fireworks rocket, erupted from its tip and sailed into the sky. Then, a calculating rage burning in his eyes, he turned his attention to the guards, and to the two brothers at their head.

"The princes Killraven," he said. His voice was thick with mockery. "Here to stop my rampage, I presume. And too witless to realize they're doing the high priest's dirty work for him. I'll be generous and offer you a chance to live. Walk away now and don't interfere."

Gerard raised his wand in a gesture of warding, and Aron did the same with his sword.

"You know it can't happen like that, Zomoran," Aron called loudly.

The elder prince's gaze flicked to the three figures standing behind the magus. The woman's hand was dripping blood. His eyes widened when he saw that two of her fingernails were missing.

"And I'm no puppet of the Church in this," he continued. "If there is cause, then the Inquisition will answer to the Crown for its actions today. But so must you. Stand down before more innocents are killed. Your case will get a fair hearing and a fair trial. You have my word on it."

Zomoran laughed. He stepped out into the field beside the building. The tip of his staff moved casually in the air before him, like the head of a snake preparing to strike.

"A pretty speech, whelp," he said. His voice was thick with derision and contempt. "But it's too little, too late, and very much beside the point. Do you really think there's any going back for me now? I wouldn't want it if you could offer it to me. Which you can't, and you know it."

Gerard shook his head. "It doesn't have to end like this, Professor."

"Yes, it does," Zomoran said. "Because I'm done with you. Done with years of trying to bring wisdom and progress to this intellectually barren kingdom. Done with appealing to fools, aided only by a handful of friends who understood — who saw the brilliant society we could engineer, if only we could order things as they need to be. Done with writing and speaking to classes of empty minds, who lack the inspiration and courage to see and dare the truth."

His gaze came to rest on Aron, and a strange anger blazed in his eyes.

"Done with puppets of the ruling class, too busy tiptoeing around zealots, and dancing on the strings pulled by an old man behind the scenes. The only other great mind in this entire besotted nation, but without the ambition to guide it into the embrace of history.

"Oddly enough, I may owe Salmanor Hardin a debt for opening my eyes today. I see now that this society is decadent beyond redemption. It is time for it to be purged in fire and rebuilt from the ashes."

Aron's eyes hardened as he returned the magus's acid glare.

"The people of Carlissa are not toys or machines, Zomoran," he said, "to be 'engineered' to suit your view of the way things should be. They are individuals, with rights and dignity. Too often in the past have we made that mistake. It's time to try a better way."

Zomoran shook his head and laughed again.

"So parrots the puppet," he mocked. "Your grandfather's ideals are a delusion, boy. A nation of sheep cannot govern itself. It needs to be led, by those with the knowledge and spirit to understand what is best for them. Or do I truly have to lecture a princeling of the realm on the meaning of *noblesse oblige?*"

His free arm reached behind him. He drew the woman with the bloody hand into a protective embrace.

"Would a great man allow his best minds to be given over to torture and the threat of a heretic's fire?" he demanded. "For the mere crime of thinking bold thoughts? Or would he lead and protect them? And if others lacked the wisdom to follow of their own accord, would he not shepherd them? By force, if necessary? For their own good?"

"A great man doesn't concern himself with his own greatness," Aron replied firmly. "Empty minds, you say? I was more attentive to your lessons, Professor, *and* to your example, than you realize. You stand there, sheltering a colleague whose devotion feeds your vanity, and you leave a trail of dead and broken bodies in your wake to do it. And you presume to lecture me about the meaning of *noblesse oblige?* Whose needs do you truly serve, Lord of Westreach?"

Zomoran regarded him icily, but with a look of sudden wariness.

"You are clever, princeling," he said. "More so than I gave you credit for. You're stalling, trying to keep me talking and arguing, while you wait for reinforcements from the palace. Yes, I know that the Archmage is there. And as much as I would relish the opportunity to test myself against him, that is not my plan for today."

Without warning, he raised his staff and then struck its base upon the ground. A concussion of force erupted from the edge of his protective sphere, and the guards were thrown from their feet by the blast. Aron staggered backward, arms pinwheeling to try to keep his balance. Zomoran raised his staff again, and then lowered the tip to point directly at the elder prince's heart.

Gerard had been quietly preparing himself while the others spoke. Now he leaped into action. Zomoran's spell broke like a wave around a coruscating sphere of silver that bloomed suddenly into form around him. He threw himself between the magus and his brother, and raised his wand in a warding gesture as a bolt of livid blue lightning erupted from the staff. Gerard's shield flared brilliantly where it was struck, but it held — and some of the bolt reflected back toward the caster. Zomoran's shield flared too at the contact, and dwindling arcs of electricity shot back and forth between the globes until the sparks had finally discharged.

The magus blinked in surprise, trying to recover from the blinding afterimage. The young wizard ran toward him, trying to press his momentary advantage. The shields of silver and red collided and flared brilliantly where they met. Motes of multicolored light sparked around the contact point as the two spells fought, trying to drain each other of power. Then, with a flash and a loud thumping sound, the silver shield winked out of existence. Gerard stumbled backward and fell to his knees.

Zomoran blinked again and looked around. The younger prince was struggling to recreate his defenses and was, at least for the moment, no longer a threat. But now Aron was striding forward, his eyes hard and unforgiving.

"You can't win, Zomoran," he said. He reached the edge of the magus' shield, which was visibly weakened from Gerard's attack. He placed the tip of the enchanted blade against the surface, as if preparing to try to plunge it through. "The Archmage, the King, and half the palace guard will be here in moments. Even if you defeat us, there's no escape."

Zomoran smiled. "Wrong again, dear boy," he said smugly.

Gerard surged to his feet and charged. He caught Aron around the waist with one arm and raised his wand with the other. The sphere of silver magic flickered weakly around them again, lighting his face, pale with sudden desperation.

"Guards! Run!" he cried.

He looked up, and the others followed his gaze. An enormous dragon was flattening its descent and bearing down on them. A trail of flame ran behind it where it had flown over the shoulder of the mountain, hugging its slope to fall on them from almost directly above.

Zomoran stepped back, laughing, as the monster's jaws opened, brimming with fire. Aron, too, raised his sword over his head. As the princes watched death descend upon them, he clasped Gerard's shoulder and whispered, "I love you, Brother."

The dragon's wings beat harshly to slow it as it swept in, and it came to a crashing halt atop the prison building. The structure collapsed under its weight, and the monster rode the cascading rubble downward in a spray of broken stone and splintering wood. A gout of white-hot flame exploded from its maw as it struck the ground before the two princes, and they were engulfed in a terrifying inferno.

Further back, and still recovering from Zomoran's first attack, the guards fled. The blossoming edge of the firestorm pursued them. One guard was too slow, and it caught him. He ran, aflame and screaming, into the deepening night.

Zomoran turned his back on them. He waved his staff once more, and he and his companions floated upward as the dragon's breath ebbed. It turned toward them and reared, reaching out with its monstrous foreclaws. It grasped the two male prisoners in one, and the woman and the magus in the other. Then, driven by its powerful hind legs, it surged again into the air. Beating its wings, it rose slowly into the sky, flying away to the south and west.

Gerard looked out from under the hood of his cloak. The brothers had drawn theirs grimly over their bowed heads as the dragon landed, hoping desperately to somehow survive the attack. The shimmering aura of frosty white that surrounded them faded, leaving behind only the icy glow of the elder prince's sword. Their clothing was scorched and burned, and he suspected that he would find ash where parts of his beard and eyebrows had been. But they were alive.

"What magic!" Aron cried, turning toward him. "And against a dragon's breath, no less! Grandfather is going to be *very* impressed."

Gerard shook his head. He saw the dragon ascending into the sky, already disappearing over the southern arm of the Eldar Mountains.

"It wasn't me," he said. "My spell protected us for a few seconds, but then it collapsed."

Aron's eyes widened. "Then how — ?"

Gerard nodded at his brother's sword.

"It was Flamebane that saved us. I knew it was spelled against fire, but I had no idea that the dweomer was so powerful!"

Aron gazed with a look of renewed appreciation at the enchanted blade. "Thank you, Grandmother," he said earnestly.

Then he clapped Gerard soundly on the shoulder. "What a battle! We will have to ask Randia to compose a ballad for us. Is it not as I've always said? The princes Killraven! Shoulder to shoulder against the greatest of evils, and no foe can defeat us!"

Gerard grinned at him. "Ever the optimist," he observed drily.

A horn sounded, and the pair turned. A company of the palace guard was running onto the grounds, swords and shields raised. Behind them strode the King, his powerful voice angrily bellowing orders.

"Better late than never," Gerard laughed. "Come on. Let's see what can be done to help the wounded. And Father will want to know everything that's happened. Somehow, I think his worries about the Inquisition are about to be overshadowed by other concerns."

Chapter 2

Inquisition on Trial

Salmanor Hardin's eyes swept the throne room with an angry glare. "This questioning is a waste of time," he said imperiously.

The high priest's words hung in the silence that followed. When King Danor finally spoke, his voice was cool with disapproval.

"Do you truly regard your Inquisition as so above the law, Salmanor," he began slowly, "that you have no obligation to answer to the Crown for your actions?"

Hardin's eyes widened. "Answer for my actions?" he asked indignantly. "Are you serious?"

"Very," the King replied.

Danor leaned forward on the Carlissan throne. He waited, eyes fixed on the high priest's face. The moments stretched on into another angry, awkward silence.

The King's appearance matched his reputation as the most formidable warrior in Carlissa. He was tall and powerfully built, with a neatly kempt mane and beard of auburn hair. They framed a face with dark eyes and hard features that were handsome, but not overly so. It was the nose — just a little too large, and a bit too hooked — that kept them from true beauty. His manner was commanding, and he exuded an aura of visceral masculinity.

"What is there to answer for, Your Majesty?" Hardin demanded at last. "I thought I had been asked to appear before you to give aid and counsel in the crisis that faces us. To receive thanks, not endure accusations. You speak as if the Inquisition had done something wrong in ferreting out a dangerous blasphemer from among the highest ranks of Carlissan nobility. You dare call it to account for fulfilling its holy duty to defend the Covenant?"

"So you say," Danor said evenly. "Omitting, of course, that the accused *also* happens to be a lord of the realm of Carlissa."

"And a member of its high council," Aron added. He stood beside the throne, at the King's right hand, and Gerard was at his side. The brothers had cleaned up as best they could from their battle, but still wore their scorched cloaks. The elder prince's blond beard had been hopelessly singed by the dragon's fire, and he had shaven it completely. The hard, angular lines of his now exposed face were set in an angry expression as Hardin turned his gaze on him.

"You of all people should understand, Your Highness," the inquisitor said. "You and your brother. You confronted that demon worshipping traitor in an act of bravery rarely seen even in the storied history of this land — and he tried to murder you in cold blood. Surely you don't question the Inquisition's case against him?"

"I do question it," Aron countered. "You brought your accusations in secret and in surprise, Salmanor. Behind the accused's back, when he wasn't even present to defend himself."

Hardin waved a hand in dismissal. "Zomoran would have had a chance to answer the charges tomorrow before the council. Instead, he and his conspirators chose to run. And even your grandfather voted with the other regents to expel him from the Grand Academy."

Danor's eyes narrowed. "He did so only after securing their commitment to hear Zomoran's appeal," he said tightly. "Emil had a right to face his accusers, and to answer their accusations, however damning."

"We all respect the seriousness of the charges you've presented, Salmanor," Aleanne said soothingly. "But you must admit that the way you've handled this case raises questions."

The others turned to her. A woman of middle years with brown hair and dressed in a flowing blue robe, her kind expression contrasted starkly with the tall man at her side. He wore chainmail armor of shining bluesteel. His face was proud, and he looked at the inquisitor with hard eyes.

"Your presence at this meeting was not requested and is not

required, Lady A'Venna," Hardin said sternly. "Nor was yours, General Darren. Return to your duties at the Cathedral at once. That is an order."

"They are here on *my* orders, Salmanor," Danor cut in, before either could respond. "As High Priestess of the Order of the Lady and Captain General of the Order of Light, they are, after yourself, the two highest ranking members of the clergy in Lannamon. They are here because I intend to find out whether your inquisition acted alone in this move against the Crown, or if the Church as a whole was involved."

The inquisitor looked at the King in shock. Gerard broke the awkward silence that followed.

"I take it, Your Grace," he said, turning to Aleanne, "That your order was not a party to this?"

"No," she said. "I knew nothing of the case against Emil until earlier today."

The King nodded. "As I suspected. Augustus?"

The armored man shook his head. "We were both kept in the dark."

He turned his gaze on the High Priest, and his proud eyes flared angrily.

"And *had* I known, I would have opposed the decision," he added. "I don't deny that this evidence against Zomoran is damning, but the law on this is clear. The Crown should have been involved in any case brought against a member of the civil government. To do otherwise courts chaos and violence — as we saw this very evening."

Hardin glared at the Captain-General defiantly.

"And if the Magus had allies in that government?" he challenged. "Co-conspirators, as he did at the Grand Academy? How many dragons would have descended on the city this night, had he received warning that he was about to be exposed?"

"Do you have evidence of that?" Lord Rugon asked intently. The head of the High Council of Carlissa, he stood beside the throne to the King's left. "That Zomoran had allies in sedition? On the council itself?"

The High Priest smiled. "We were working to secure that evidence when the magus attacked."

Gerard barked an angry laugh. "That much was obvious," he said. His voice was bitter, and the others turned to him in surprise.

"What do you mean, Your Highness?" General Banderman asked. The commander of Lannamon's elite guard, he stood at Lord Rugon's side. "What was obvious?"

"What my brother means, General," Aron said firmly, "Is that we had a chance to speak with Zomoran before he fled. *And* to see the prisoners he freed."

He faced the King. "They had been tortured, Father."

Aleanne's face went white, and Danor's eyes widened. "Are you certain?" the King asked.

Aron nodded. "The woman's hand was bloody and missing fingernails. There were signs on the others as well."

Augustus Darren spun on the inquisitor.

"There are protocols for authorizing torture, Salmanor," he said angrily. "They are strict, and for damned good reason. You know the kingdom's history, and the Church's role in it. What were you thinking? To do such a thing without sanction not only from the Crown, but even the senior clergy?"

"There was no time for discussion or debate," Hardin told him coldly. "Or to coddle squeamish sensibilities when bold action was needed."

His gaze swept around, holding each of them in turn.

"In your zeal to second-guess the Inquisition," he said forcefully, "you all seem to have forgotten what has actually happened. A full magus, a lord of the realm of Carlissa and a member of its high council, has been revealed as a demon worshipper. You know the events of this night. There is no doubt about this. He *attacked* the Church. He killed seventeen guards and injured a dozen more. He summoned a dragon to the city, and came within a hair's breadth of murdering both princes."

"That's not the point, Salmanor —" Aleanne began.

"It *is* the point," he retorted hotly. "You all stand there, protesting about how your prim little views of 'due process' weren't followed — *in unmasking a traitor to the Covenant on the High Council.* Does that truly matter now? The Inquisition was — and has been proven — *right* about him. And the civil government you're trying to protect is likely infested with other cells of demonic acolytes. Instead of bickering, we should be planning further investigations to root them out."

A shocked silence followed. Lord Rugon nodded reluctantly. Aleanne looked at the floor. General Banderman sighed with a note of grim acceptance.

Then Aron stepped forward. He walked up to the high priest and looked levelly into his eyes. His expression was confident and uncompromising, and he shook his head.

"No," he said.

Hardin met his gaze evenly. When he spoke, his voice was a mixture of sadness and condescension.

"Such foolishness," he said, "displays a serious lack of responsibility and vision. It is unbecoming in the heir to the throne of Carlissa."

Danor rose to his feet. "Guard your words, Lord Inquisitor —" he began icily.

Aron held up a hand. "No, Father," he said sternly. "I will handle this. Gerard and I were there. The high priest was not. I believe that his understanding of Zomoran's fall is gravely mistaken, and I need to explain why."

The King sat down. His eyes were proud as he nodded to his son.

"Very well," he said. "We will hear your testimony, and your argument."

Aron looked around. His resonant baritone carried forcefully across the room as he spoke.

"Emil Zomoran was once a great man," he said. "A brilliant leader, scholar, and wizard, his loss is a terrible tragedy. As the high priest's evidence makes clear, he was certainly being seduced by evil. Our words with him tonight only confirm this. And they lead me to believe that his soul has been on this journey for some time."

He glanced at Gerard, who nodded reluctantly. The high priest smiled with a look of satisfaction.

"So I agree that the Inquisition has shown," Aron continued, "that Zomoran held — and regrettably, taught — ideas that are repugnant to the Church. What it has *not* shown, however, is proof that he intended rebellion against the kingdom or harm to its people."

"Ridiculous," Hardin countered imperiously. "Have you read the charges? His sympathies are well-documented. His intentions were clear: to undercut the morals of Carlissan society and lead the people into the darkness of demon worship."

"And therein lies the nub of the Inquisition's case, my friends," Aron replied earnestly. "Zomoran dared to *disagree* with church doctrine, you see. So of course he *must* be a dangerous traitor intending rebellion against the kingdom and its people. But does blasphemy equal treason? And if not, then should a man fear to lose his life for it? Does not the inquisitor's premise *equate* Church and state — and in a way that has not been acceptable in this kingdom for many years?"

"Are you referring to the Codex War?" Darren asked cautiously. Aron nodded.

"We must not forget our own land's history," the prince continued. "How the Church tried to murder Aldran, first of the Killraven kings of Carlissa and my family's own ancestor, for attempting to bring the ancient knowledge of Janthala back to the world. Had the adventurer mage and his allies not won the resulting civil war, the last two centuries of flourishing and enlightenment would never have happened."

"That was different," Hardin said. "Whatever his flaws, Aldran was no demon worshipper."

"You'd never know that from the accusations leveled at him by the Church," Aron countered. "And he certainly *was* accused of blasphemy, and threatened with death, for spreading ideas that defied church doctrine of the time. And when we examine the evidence against Lord Zomoran, is there proof that he did more than this?"

"Is that not enough?" Hardin scoffed.

"No," Aron said firmly. "*I* say that it is not. It may suffice to expel him from the Grand Academy, or even the High Council. Sympathy for the demonic religions is no virtue, and those august bodies would be well within their rights to no longer accept him. But we speak here not of ostracism, but of execution. Of crimes of *speech* for which the ancient penalty is death."

"Then let it be carried out," Hardin declared. "That is the law."

"But should it be?" Aron asked. "Should a man face execution not for threatening his fellow men, but for disagreeing with them? Is ending that injustice not one of many reforms long overdue in our land?"

Augustus Darren shook his head.

"You are saying that Zomoran was not a threat to the kingdom," he said. His voice was skeptical. "That is not what history teaches us to expect from those who preach demonology."

Aron sighed. "And I fear that die is now cast," he said. "Whatever his intentions before, the events of the last day have forever turned Zomoran from the Light. But it did not need to be so."

"And what do you base that on?" Darren pursued.

Aron turned to Gerard. "Do you remember his words, Brother?"

Gerard nodded. "I do. He said, 'I may actually owe Salmanor Hardin a debt for opening my eyes today. I see now that this society is decadent beyond redemption. It is time for it to be purged in fire and rebuilt from the ashes.'"

Aron nodded. "That is what I heard as well. Those words came only *after* the Church had provoked him into desperate retaliation — by imprisoning and *torturing* his associates, and threatening him with execution for heresy. And what they tell *me* is that he did *not* turn on his people until he believed that *they* had turned on *him*."

He spun on the high priest.

"And for that, I blame the Inquisition," he continued accusingly. "Why was this case brought to the Crown only *after* arrests were made, and Zomoran publicly humiliated before the regents of the Grand Academy? Is it not clear that this was done to gain political advantage, rather than out of concern for the consequences of provoking a full magus into open rebellion?"

"There was no time —" Hardin began.

"Of course there was time," Aron countered. "You did not stumble on this evidence overnight. What you lacked was not time, but *trust*. Trust in the Crown to work with you for the good of the kingdom. Because your *true* agenda was not to prosecute a prominent heretic, but to use the opportunity he presented to strengthen the Inquisition's hand in its ongoing debate over the reform movement."

"That is a serious accusation, Your Highness," Lord Rugon said cautiously.

"Nevertheless, I do make it," Aron said forcefully. "And make no mistake. The consequences of the high priest's reckless political scheming today are serious. Not only has he forfeited any hope of turning Zomoran back to the Light, but he has earned the kingdom a powerful and relentless enemy that it did not have before."

He turned to Aleanne. Her eyes were wet and gleaming as she met his gaze.

"Could not a compassionate church, Your Grace," he asked gently, "one that truly believed in the teachings of Lady Tianth, have at least *tried* to do better?"

She closed her eyes. "Yes," she whispered. "It could have."

Salmanor Hardin glared at Aron. His face was a mask of undisguised fury.

"You display a stubborn naiveté about the seductive dangers of demonology, Prince Aron," he said icily. "It will be your downfall, and the kingdom will one day come to regret it."

He spun on his heel and walked from the room. The others watched him go with looks of astonishment.

Augustus Darren turned to the King. "Where is the Archmage?" he asked. "Should we not hear his counsel in this matter as well?"

"He is with the Queen," Danor replied. "At the summit of the palace tower. They are working their magic to track the magus' flight."

"I fear they will be unsuccessful, though," Gerard said.

Danor looked disappointed. "I had hoped that together they could locate him."

Gerard sighed and shook his head.

"Zomoran will have cast a cloaking spell by now. And he's a master of that kind of magic. Even Mother and Grandfather, with all their skill, would have to scry close to his exact location before piercing it. They might get lucky, but it'll be like trying to find a needle in a haystack."

Lord Rugon frowned. "And even if they do, will we be able to apprehend him?"

Aron turned to his father. "We will have to ask Grandfather Acheron for help," he said.

"The Peregrine King?" General Banderman asked.

"Yes," Danor said. There was a note of reluctance in his voice. "My father-in-law is not the easiest one to ask for favors, but he would do it. And there is nowhere in all Kalara that Zomoran would be safe from the pegasus warriors of Mount Cassandra."

A long silence followed. Lord Rugon finally broke it.

"What happens now, Your Majesty?" he asked tentatively.

Danor sighed. "Salmanor will press his case," he said. "And my son will press his."

"We both will," Gerard said firmly. "I stand with Aron in this."

"And I with my sons," Danor affirmed. "I fear that this will lead to a very public confrontation between the Inquisition and the royal family."

Lord Rugon nodded reluctantly. "Then the High Council will have to decide where it stands," he said, "when it meets tomorrow to hear the high priest's case."

"As will the Church," Aleanne agreed. "The Captain-General and I must confer with the senior clergy. The inquisitor's zeal to defend the Covenant is admirable, but his conduct in this matter is troubling. May we have permission to withdraw, Your Majesty?"

Danor nodded and stood.

"You may. This audience is concluded for now. We all have much to do, and much to prepare for in the days ahead."

Chapter 3 - The City of Rainbows

Randia's View

The Sixth of Floren, in the Year 1643 of the Taming (Six Months Later)

Randia Killraven looked down with a mischievous smile on the City of Rainbows.

She stood, naked, at the edge of the mountain bluff. The cliffs around her ran like a pair of great arms thrust down from the feet of the Eldar Mountains to the west. The city seemed to nestle between them in the valley below, as though held in their protective embrace.

A stiff wind blew across the ledge. Usually, her hair was a cascade of loose locks — gold, with just a hint of red — that reached past her shoulders. Now those locks seemed to float, like shining wisps, hovering around her head in the moving airs. She brushed them back impatiently with a slender hand as her blue eyes gazed eagerly at the vista before her. *This is a magnificent morning to see the city,* she thought, with the sun shining brightly in a nearly cloudless azure sky. She didn't want to miss any of it.

She looked across the valley. Hills ascended from the docks and ports around the tip of the long Firth of Fajang. The hills were terraced, cut into the arms of the bluff like steps for an enormous giant. They rose in levels, connected by ramped streets and staired walkways, until they met the sheer face of the cliff-wall that shielded the city to the north. The southern side below her looked much the same, nearly a mirror image of its northern partner.

She looked to her right. There, the ring of cliffs was finally broken by the narrow waters of the firth. The bluffs descended gradually from the mountains to surround the great inlet, eventually disappearing into the plains of northern Carlissa. The shining water continued into the distance toward the Nyan Sea many leagues away.

She glanced along the line of cliffs beside her. There she saw the terraces of the southern arm of the Upper City come to a sudden end. Where they did, the halls and tower of the Silver Star Adventurer's Academy shone brightly in the mid-morning sun.

The sun. That reminded her of why she had wanted to come here today. *Okay, one of the reasons*, she amended quickly, thinking with a smile of Stefan as he set out blankets by the pool for their swim in the little glade behind her. She turned to where the sun's rays fell onto the western end of the valley, and her breath caught at the sight.

This is why they call it the City of Rainbows, she thought in wonder. The shoulder of Mount Cascade loomed above the bluffs, its heights descending in a face of jagged cliffs. And there, their courses as if severed by the stroke of a giant axe, the high waters that flowed through the last peak of the Eldar Mountains rushed over the brink and into the valley below.

Waterfalls too numerous to count fell from the mountain cliffs above Lannamon, City of Rainbows, capital of the Kingdom of Carlissa. A rainbow could always be seen in the mist from those falls on days when the sun shone, an enormous arc of color appearing above the valley with the morning's first rays.

The sun cleared the top of the cliffs behind her, and she saw the scene as she had for the first time many years ago. From here, and for only a few minutes, the rainbow hovered above the ground as a full ring encircling the westward cliffs. It framed the High City, the palace, and the waterfalls, like a picture set in an enormous locket of prismatic light.

She gazed for a long minute at the sight, savoring the view.

Her eyes moved to the palace, and she smiled fondly. She had grown up there, and knew it well. It was built into the shoulder of the mountain, surrounded by falling water on all sides. A broad road wound up toward it like a snake from below, ending at its main gate. At its center, a great tower soared into the sky.

Her eyes followed the road from the palace toward the firth and the docks. Her gaze swept past the great amphitheater and descended into the center of the valley. There, far beneath the waterfalls and between the surrounding cliffs and terraces, lay the heart of Lannamon. At least, *she* thought of it as its heart, and had for a long time.

The firth was ringed with great docks and shipyards. The land around it was a mazework of streets with homes, shops, and apartments. This was the Lower City, home to most of Lannamon's people. More importantly, to her, it was home to its best inns, taverns, and playhouses.

She grinned at the thought. The theaters of the Upper City were magnificent, and the Great Hall of the Bard's College beyond compare in all the Eastern Continent. She still loved them and relished attending when she had the chance. For all their grandeur, though, they had become stale and formulaic. More and more she was seeing the creative energies of her art expressed, not by the court musicians of the Upper and High Cities, but in the makeshift venues of the Lower. The bards were freer there, not bound by the stuffy classical traditions that still dominated the halls of the nobles. She relished slipping away from the palace to perform with them, to the raucous cheering and earthy humor of the crowds — and not infrequently, the chagrin of the guards who would be sent out to find her.

A pair of strong arms encircled her waist, and she felt Stefan's body press against her from behind. She leaned back contentedly into his embrace. His lips nuzzled her neck as he looked over her shoulder.

"You weren't exaggerating," he murmured appreciatively. "Thank you for bringing me here. What a sight! A circular rainbow, suspended like a ring of color over the city. I will simply have to paint it."

"Don't you dare!" she cried.

She spun in his arms to face him. He held her firmly against his lean body, their faces inches apart and lips nearly touching.

Stefan Arokkan was a gifted artist and musician. The City of Rainbows was famous as a center of culture and learning, and its Bard's College renowned as the finest in all the lands of the Eastern Continent. A prince of Thressa — though only a nephew of its king, and several times removed from its throne — he had insisted on pursuing his studies in the capital of Carlissa.

Their relationship had begun with an intense rivalry. Stefan was a charismatic performer, and they had quickly developed a reputation as the college's two most gifted students. They'd competed relentlessly for awards and honors, and Randia had quickly developed a stubborn obsession with besting him at everything they did. He'd taken up their rivalry with an easy confidence and a knowing, mocking smile that maddened her, which only drove her on to compete with him more fiercely.

That rivalry had eventually given way to an equally intense bond of love and admiration. They were to be married in the fall.

Their engagement had finally blunted the nobility's disapproval over her attending the Bard's College. They had frowned on her failure to attend to the many suitors that had sought the hand of the only daughter of King Danor Killraven and Queen Elena Starlight. Her lack of interest in receiving the noblest of Carlissa's blue bloods had led to talk, and to raised eyebrows in the High City. That gossip had finally shifted with news of their engagement to discussion of alliances and trade with the western kingdom, and plans for their wedding.

Randia gave the gossip little thought. What mattered to her was that she was going to build a life with a charming and talented man she admired, who shared her life-consuming passion for music and the arts.

"You mustn't paint it!" she continued, pleading. "You'll give away my secret glade! Any idiot will be able to work out the location. They'll come looking for it!"

Stefan smiled. "Perhaps I could be persuaded to imagine a different viewpoint," he mused. One of his arms slid around her back as she looked mischievously into his eyes. "That is, if milady were to offer a suitable incentive ..."

"Why, you scoundrel!" she exclaimed indignantly. There was just a hint of mockery in her voice; she recognized the line from a comedy they had seen at a theater in the Lower City. She fell at once to playacting with him, as they would often do, and with the ease of slipping on a glove.

"Would you hold my secret ransom to satisfy your beastly desires, sirrah?" she asked.

"Not mine, milady — yours," he quoted back with a grin. Then they kissed as they stood together on the bluff overlooking the city —

their game, the rainbow, and everything else forgotten.

He swept her into his arms, and they laughed as he carried her into the glade behind them. The entrance was little more than a crack among the rocks, almost completely hidden from view. In it lay a small lagoon, shrouded by stone and trees, but open to the sky above.

"Come, my love," he said, setting her down on a blanket by the edge of the pool. His voice had a smoky tone as he looked deeply into her eyes. "We have water for our swim, and a comfortable spot for us to dally after."

"Dally first, I think," she replied. Then she kissed him again and drew him with her to the ground.

The Ambassador's Daughter

Diana Dal Meara stepped into the library of her family's home on Brightstar Street.

She saw her tutor, and stopped. She had always found him sitting when she arrived for her morning lesson, his attention on a set of notes laid out on his desk. Today, he was standing in the center of the room.

Something is up, she thought to herself.

She felt a sudden thrill of anticipation, but did nothing to betray her excitement. Instead of closing the door as she usually did, she came a few paces into the room and stopped.

"Good morning, Master Edgar," she said. "I am here for my lesson on Dorian civics."

Master Edgar bowed to her. "There has been a change of plan, my child," he said curtly. "The ambassador has instructed that we join him immediately in his office."

He gestured toward the doorway behind her, and her eyebrows arched. There was a note of tension in his voice. Whatever was going on, he clearly did not approve of it.

He followed as she walked from the library, through the sitting room, and down a hallway. The door to her father's office was open when she arrived. He stood inside, looking out a window. He made no move as Diana entered and dropped into a formal curtsey.

"I have brought your daughter, as ordered, Your Excellency," she heard Master Edgar say.

There was a long pause. She held her curtsey, head bowed, waiting for her father's voice. *That was protocol.* And protocol was something that one did *not* fail to observe in the presence of Damien Dal Meara.

"Thank you, Edgar," her father said finally. "Please close the door and remain to attend our discussion. You may rise, my daughter."

Diana lifted her head and stood at attention. "Good morning, Father," she said.

She smiled as he stepped toward her. He took her shoulders in his hands and briefly kissed her forehead. She smiled as he stepped back, looking at him with disciplined affection.

"Good morning, Diana," he said. "Are you well today?"

Protocol, again. She knew what was expected. There was no hesitation in her reply.

"I am well, Father," she said. "Is there something that you require of me?"

He nodded. "Yes. I've asked Master Edgar to bring you to me to discuss a matter relating to your education."

A flicker of uncertainty passed through her. Had she received a poor mark from one of her instructors?

"I hope that my performance has been satisfactory?" she asked cautiously.

The ambassador's eyes turned to look behind her. "Master Edgar?" he asked.

"Lady Diana's instructors all report that she is doing well in her studies," Master Edgar said.

The ambassador nodded. "As expected," he said.

He picked up a letter from his desk and handed it to her. "Please read this aloud," he ordered.

Diana opened the letter and looked at it. It was written in Carlissan, using the northern dialect common in and near the capital city of Lannamon. She recognized the seal of the Grand Academy.

"'Your Excellency,'" she began, "'I have received your letter of Floren the third, and its inquiry about enrolling your daughter in the academy's new junior scholar's program. Please accept and convey our compliments to her on the very impressive transcripts that you provided.

"'After a careful review of Lady Diana's academic credentials, and having made the appropriate inquiries through Dame Marjeune's office at the palace, I am pleased to inform you that she has been accepted into the program. It will begin with an introductory course on the subject of philosophy. The first lecture will be held on Floren the sixth at ten o'clock.

"'Given the shortness of the notice, I have directed that this letter be brought to you by courier immediately. Please make arrangements with Dame Marjeune for Lady Diana to join her entourage from the palace in the morning. We look forward to having her as a student at the academy.

"'Sincerely, Alfred Lander, Dean of the School of Philosophy, The Grand Academy of Lannamon.'"

A rush of excitement ran through her. She was to attend a course at the Grand Academy! And not only that, but she was going to study the philosophy of this wonderful land that her father had brought them to!

She fought to control her breathing as she looked up, to keep her expression carefully controlled. She knew her father's expectations. An overt display of emotion at this time would be ... frowned upon.

"This letter is dated yesterday," she said carefully. "The class it describes is today."

"Yes," her father said. "I sent Bran with a note to Dame Marjeune to expect you. Karl will escort you to meet them as they come down the palace road." He lifted the timepiece that hung from a short chain at his belt and glanced at it. "You will need to be ready to leave in ten minutes."

She nodded. She fought to keep the eagerness from her voice when she spoke.

"As you wish, Father. I will need only a few minutes to fetch my pen and a notebook, and to brush my hair."

She waited for the expected dismissal, but it didn't come. Instead, her father's eyes moved to where Master Edgar stood behind her.

"Your tutor does not approve of this assignment," he continued. She was surprised to hear that her father's tone had become conversational, almost amused. "Is that not correct, Edgar?"

There was an intake of breath behind her. When her tutor spoke, however, his voice was measured and controlled. *Of course*, Diana thought. *That was protocol.*

"No, Your Excellency," he said firmly. "I do not."

Her father's eyes returned to her, and he smiled.

"Master Edgar and I have observed in your demeanor an unusual ... fascination, shall we say, with Carlissan culture," he explained. "He thinks that it should not be encouraged, and has advised an increased emphasis in your studies on the ways of our Dorian homeland. To help remind you who your people truly are."

A flush of dread washed over Diana's skin. She knew that the color in her face was betraying her emotions, and that it was not protocol — but she could not stop it.

"I see," she said slowly. "Is this why I have been allowed so little time at the palace as of late?"

He nodded. "Such fascinations are understandable in a girl who has spent much of her youth in foreign lands. It may, however, indicate the need for an adjustment in your education."

"Then why send her to attend classes that expose her even more to such foreign ways of thinking?" Master Edgar asked.

The ambassador shook his head. "You give my daughter insufficient credit, Edgar," he said. "She has the discipline — and, as it turns out, the opportunity — to place this interest of hers in the service of her people."

Diana struggled with her emotions. Her father's compliment was an unprecedented break in his normally severe manner. She fought to slow her racing heart, and to control the pride that she was certain now colored her cheeks.

"I don't understand," Master Edgar said.

"No, I would imagine not," the ambassador said. His voice held just a hint of amusement. "Tell me, Edgar. Under whose guidance are these courses being prepared and taught?"

"The Grand Academy of Lannamon," Edgar replied cautiously. "More than that, I do not know."

"Yes, well, fortunately, I do. Their involvement is behind the scenes, but the program is being spearheaded by the royal family. Prince Aron in particular, and through him, the Archmage."

A light went on in Diana's mind. "The reform movement," she said.

"Very good, Daughter. That is why we did not return to our homeland last year, after my term as ambassador to Rayche. The Inner Circle is concerned about the significant cultural and political changes occurring in Carlissa. They needed someone to report on them. To assess their meaning, and whether they could pose a threat to our people. I was sent because I could be relied on to carry out that mission effectively."

"What does that have to do with Lady Diana, and these courses?" Edgar pursued.

The ambassador turned to her. "Demonstrate your cleverness, Daughter," he ordered.

Diana understood, now. The heat drained from her face, and she held herself with an air of confidence as she spoke.

"The Archmage is widely understood to be the architect of the reform movement," she explained. "He seeks to guide Carlissa toward a new way, and to change many of its most ancient institutions. Some factions oppose him, but King Danor and Prince Aron share his vision. If these courses were developed under their guidance, then a student could provide valuable insights into understanding that vision."

The ambassador nodded. "Full marks," he said.

"So I am to report on what I learn in these classes?"

"Yes, in detail. You will attend in particular to how these new ideas contrast to the ways of our own land. You will write a bi-weekly essay that we will meet to discuss, and that I will grade personally."

She nodded. Her green eyes were shining. "Yes, Father," she said.

He walked to her. To her astonishment, he placed his hands again on her shoulders, and looked into her eyes.

"You are now seventeen years of age, my daughter. And I think it is time that you were given — and trusted with — a new responsibility to your people." He glanced over her shoulder at Master Edgar. "To help remind you who you truly are."

She merely nodded. She didn't trust herself to speak.

He stepped back and checked his watch again.

"You may go," he said. "You have only three minutes left to prepare, and to meet Karl at the front gate, so you will need to hurry."

She curtsied. When she rose, she turned and strode from the room — as fast as protocol would allow.

The Grand Academy

Orion Deneri strode briskly down the marbled corridor in the Hall of Philosophy. His face was calm, but beneath his carefully controlled expression he was thinking: *This is going to be the start of something wonderful.*

It was his first day as an instructor at the Grand Academy of Lannamon. He held a small writing book in his left hand, but carried nothing else. The book contained a set of carefully written notes and an outline for the class that he was to conduct that morning. He had gone over those notes a dozen times during the last few days, carefully editing them again and again, until he could see no way to improve them.

I'm sure I will after the first lesson, though, he thought wryly. His mind flashed back to his time as a student at the Silver Star Adventurer's Academy. He saw the face of his instructor, and fondly remembered the Archmage's words. *Nothing ever goes exactly as you plan. Adapting to that fact is the first rule of a successful adventurer.*

Or a successful life. It was the same principle, he reflected. It just had a little more immediacy if you were fighting monsters in a ruin filled with ancient magic.

Not that he had ever done anything like that. His year as a freshman adventurer at the Silver Star had been wholly theoretical. He still thought of his studies there as the high point of his young life, even though in the end he had chosen to pursue a different career.

That had been a great relief to his family. They'd been horrified at his decision to enroll at the Silver Star. He'd graduated from the Grand Academy with highest honors the year before, and they had expected him to finally put an end to his studies and take up his long overdue position in the family business.

Though far from the nobility, the Deneris were a leading family of the Carlissan Trade Guild. And as he'd grown to adulthood, their impatience with his interest in scholarship had become a source of friction between them. He had a keen mind and an unusual aptitude for finance, and they couldn't understand his reluctance to settle down and apply it to the needs of the *Deneri Trade and Import Company*. They had told themselves that his odd flirtations with philosophy and history — and then, adventuring, of all things — were just a phase. An eminently sensible boy in other respects, he would eventually outgrow them to focus on the important things in life.

Those, of course, were money and status.

He hadn't understood, at first, why he'd decided to accept his unexpected offer to apply to the Silver Star. It was an act of rebellion, he'd finally realized, a subtle gesture of defiance against the expectations of his family. It wasn't that he disliked business, per se. Quite the contrary; he'd always had a healthy appreciation for wealth, honestly earned. The *honestly earned* part had never seemed quite the priority with his family that it was with him, though. Perhaps that was part of the reason he'd chosen to remain a student for so many years. Books and learning seemed so much cleaner than what he'd seen of life in the Trade Guild.

Recent events, though, had led him to leave his studies at the Silver Star. Those events had started with a letter from one of his old professors at the Grand Academy. Dean Lander was head of the philosophy department, which was sponsoring a new academic program. It needed junior faculty with the right training, and Orion had distinguished himself as a student there.

The idea, the letter explained, was to provide courses for some of the more gifted of the young lords and ladies of the nobility. They wouldn't be part of the official curriculum, but they would be held at the academy itself. They would bear its imprimatur and carry its prestige. And the pay would, *finally*, give him the option of a career away from the family business.

That had been three weeks ago. It had been followed by a blur of interviews and applications, and a rush of sleepless nights to develop a curriculum for his appointment as *Junior Special Instructor of Philosophy*. Now he was on his way to teach his first class.

No, he had arrived, he corrected himself, as he stopped before the door to the lecture hall. It was one of the rooms that bordered the garden, with an outer wall of panels removed for open-air use. The sun was shining brightly, and the garden was in full bloom. He couldn't imagine a more perfect setting for his first day of teaching.

"Ah, Orion! There you are," a voice called.

He saw the familiar face of Dean Lander coming toward him along the corridor. Orion stepped forward to meet him, and bowed in greeting.

"Good Morning, Dean Lander," Orion said respectfully. "How goes your day, so far?"

"Correct and deferential, as always, Orion," the dean replied. "But also quite unnecessary. You're one of us now. James will do, I think."

"That will take some getting used to — James," Orion admitted with a dry smile. "But I shall apply myself to the task, as always."

Dean Lander clapped him on the shoulder.

"No doubt you will. So, are you ready for your first day of class? I read the lesson plan you submitted. Impressive. Unorthodox, to be sure. But innovative as well. The review committee had quite a debate over it, as you might imagine."

Orion's eyebrows rose slightly. "I wasn't aware that it had generated controversy," he said slowly.

Lander shook his head dismissively. "Nothing to be worried about. Professors of the more traditional school are always leery of deviation from the standard lecture format. But these classes themselves are an innovation. They called for a new approach, and you gave them one. Some of us saw what you were trying to do and pointed it out."

"I'm glad to hear that. So they understood my emphasis on motivation as a factor in designing the curriculum?"

Lander nodded. "As you observed in your proposal, students admitted to the formal programs have already made a commitment to scholarship. But this program is intended to *stimulate* such interest. To encourage those with the aptitude to appreciate the value of academic training. That required more than just a straight presentation of content. In the end, it led to less debate than your appointment to the faculty."

Orion's eyebrows rose again. There was a long pause.

"I didn't know that, either," he said finally. "Should I be concerned that my tenure here seems to have been accompanied by so much controversy?"

"Not at all," the dean said hastily. "Your qualifications were excellent, and never a cause for concern."

He paused, as though debating with himself. When he spoke again, it was in a hushed tone.

"That concern came from another matter," he said. "One that we should discuss more privately."

He gestured toward the lecture room, and Orion led the way in. Lander continued once they were inside and had closed the door.

"This is something I've debated talking with you about. Deliberations on faculty assignments are privileged, as you know. However, this concerns something that I suspect you knew nothing about — and if not, then I think you should. I trust that I can count on you to keep this conversation in confidence?"

Orion nodded quietly. He kept his face composed, struggling to control a growing sense of dread.

"Your appointment became controversial because of an attempt to influence one of the regents on your behalf," the dean explained. "It appears that your mother requested an audience with Lord Oster, and used it to speak in support of your application. Did you know that?"

Orion's blood ran cold. His family was notorious for its extensive contacts in the Trade Guild, as well as among the lesser nobility. And it was equally notorious for its success in using them to curry favor.

He tried to understand their motive. They had never understood his interest in scholarship, but they *had*, at least, accepted his decision to attend the Grand Academy. It was something they could parlay into a source of status, and they took advantage of every opportunity to brag about it.

Enrolling at the Silver Star had been another matter entirely. Traditional Kalaran culture had looked askance on *adventuring*, as a profession, for thousands of years. Despite the many benefits it had brought to the world — such as the discoveries of ancient knowledge and artifacts from before the Grim Times — it had always carried something of a social stigma, particularly to the more provincially minded.

"No," he said emphatically. "I did *not* know she did that. It was certainly without my consent or approval. And I am deeply disturbed to learn it. A faculty appointment should be based on academic merit, not on the exercise of personal influence. If this is why I was chosen, then I must, and with regret, tender my immediate resignation. I will stay on until you can find a replacement, of course. But it would be inappropriate to remain in my position, given these circumstances."

Lander shook his head. "Just the reaction I was expecting. And no, Orion, I won't be accepting your resignation. Please put that thought out of your mind right now."

Orion looked at him in confusion.

"You misunderstand," Lander continued. "Lord Oster was not your sponsor, and your mother's attempt at favor-currying didn't help your application. Instead, it nearly killed it. You got the job despite the questions and misgivings it raised. Because your record spoke for itself, and because your sponsor spoke forcefully in your defense."

Orion closed his eyes, feeling a mixture of anger and gratitude. Gratitude toward his sponsor, who, of course, he assumed all along had been Dean Lander himself — and anger at his family for sullying his achievement with their machinations.

His mind raced, struggling to make sense of what they'd done. When he'd enrolled at the Silver Star, they had threatened to cut him off and throw him out of their home. And for the first time in his life, he had openly defied them. He would attend, he said, taking nothing with him if necessary but the clothes on his back.

They had given in, but their pressure to change his mind and leave the Star had been intense and relentless. Was *that* why they'd tried to help with his application to the Grand Academy? Certainly they would have thought it a more respectable alternative, but ...

Then he understood. A post instructing young nobles would offer him the opportunity to make important contacts. Contacts that he could eventually be persuaded to use to help the family business ...

"Thank you for letting me know about this," he said quietly. "I will need to think carefully on what to do about it."

"Quite so," Lander agreed. "Your sponsor was able to save you this time, but in the future, you may not be so fortunate. He convinced the committee — with some help from me, I'm proud to say — that you were an honorable man who would have never countenanced such meddling. Moreover, he seemed to know quite a bit about your family's regrettable habit of favor-currying, and didn't hesitate to educate the others about it. Lord Oster was particularly mortified."

Orion looked at him in surprise. So his old professor *hadn't* been his sponsor. Who had? He found himself suddenly consumed with curiosity, but he also knew that this was not something he could ask the man to reveal.

"I won't presume to advise you on how to handle this matter," the dean continued gently. "But such meddling by your family can only hurt your career. You will need to protect yourself from it. Indeed, it may end up hurting their own position as well, and more than they realize. Political sentiments are changing in Carlissa, and things will likely be very different for them under King Danor's new reforms."

King Danor's new reforms. Orion could feel the tumblers falling into place in his mind at those words, unlocking the answer to his question. The city had been awash for weeks in rumors about the new laws that the King and the High Council were preparing to proclaim. And it was no secret that the King's father had been involved in drafting them.

"The Archmage," Orion said suddenly. "He was my instructor at the Star this past semester, for my course in magical theory. He spoke highly of my work. *He* was my sponsor."

Lander grinned. "You didn't hear it from me, dear boy," he said, his eyes twinkling with amusement.

A sharp knock at the door ended their conversation. It opened before they could respond, and they saw a woman with gray hair that was tied into a tight bun. Her manner was brisk and no-nonsense. She stepped quickly into the room and delivered a flawlessly efficient curtsy.

"Dean Lander," she said. "The students are here for their first lecture." She turned to Orion. "I assume this is Instructor Deneri?"

The dean nodded and made introductions. "Dame Marjeune is Mistress of Lessons at the royal palace," he explained. "She has been assigned to coordinate attendance for your class."

The matron stepped out of the doorway, and two armed palace guards entered the room. Orion saw them look around, expertly doing a rapid threat assessment, and then choose posts near the open walls to the garden.

"You may enter now," Dame Marjeune called.

The students began filing in. As expected, he counted sixteen of them, boys and girls of varying ages spanning their teenage years. He waited until they had taken their seats, and a third guard had closed and assumed his post by the door.

"Young lords and ladies," Dame Marjeune began. "You are here today at the Grand Academy of Lannamon to begin a course of academic instruction in the subject of philosophy. The Grand Academy is the finest institution of learning on the Eastern Continent, and some of the noblest of the aristocracy — including Prince Aron himself — have numbered among its students. To study here is an honor."

Orion saw several faces in the class turn to look at him. Not everyone seemed convinced by Dame Marjeune's words. They knew he was not of the nobility, and a few of the haughtier students would object to being instructed by him. His authority would be challenged, and he would have to be prepared for that ...

He turned as he heard Lander speak his name. Dame Marjeune had finished her admonishments and given the dean the floor to complete his introduction.

"Instructor Deneri will be your lecturer for this course," Lander explained. "He is a recent graduate of the academy and one of my most accomplished students. You may also find it of interest that he is a journeyman adventurer, and has studied metaphysics at the Silver Star under Lenard the Archmage himself."

A startled murmur rippled through the class, and Orion smiled inwardly. The statement had thrown the students' preconceptions about him into disarray. That *could* make his job easier ...

"He carries the academy's full authority to conduct the class and to administer and grade examinations, so you would be well-advised to attend him. I leave you now in his care."

The dean turned and bowed to Orion, then to Dame Marjeune, and then strode from the room. She took a seat by the door, and Orion stepped up beside the podium to begin.

A thrill of excitement ran through him. His preparations had been thorough, and he saw the lesson in his mind now like a map laid out before him — with all the topics like places to visit, clearly marked. He had earned his position despite all odds, and had been recommended by the Archmage himself!

Even news of his family's clumsy interference could not dim his enthusiasm. It was the last straw in their deteriorating relationship, and he would have to deal with it when the time came. For now, though, he was finally ready to begin his new life as a teacher and a scholar.

"Good morning, class," he said. The sun shone brightly in the garden outside, and a susurrus of birds twittering lent a fittingly cheerful background to his triumphant mood.

"Before one can undertake the study of any subject, one must first answer three fundamental questions. What is it? How do I know that? And why should I care?"

Orion smiled as a murmur of quiet laughter went through the room. "That last has no doubt occurred to many of you, and we will give it special attention. As we do, we will find that those three questions hold a special significance. Indeed, they are, in essence, the very subject of philosophy itself ..."

Chapter 4 - The Calm Before the Storm

The High Council

Lord Rugon paced before the balcony of the palace conference room. "Your Highness, I must once again respectfully protest this precipitous course of action," he said.

"And I must once again insist on my resolve in undertaking it," King Danor answered patiently.

The lord paused to look at him. For all his dignified manner — the royal advisor was meticulous about maintaining it, no matter the circumstances — he was beginning to look like a trapped animal. The balcony was open to face the mountainside, and it framed him in the view of the High Council. The way the ground dropped suddenly away from the railing around it only reinforced the impression.

Nowhere to run, Queen Elena mused, naming the thought to herself.

Danor forced himself not to nod. Her magic had allowed them to develop a mental bond over the years that let them share each other's thoughts and feelings. Few outside their family knew of it, and its advantages encouraged them to keep it that way.

He's been doing everything he can to delay this, she continued. *But now he's run out of options. And he knows it.*

Danor spared a glance at her. She sat to his right at the great bronzewood conference table. The seating was deliberate; she had been his partner in ruling the Kingdom of Carlissa since their marriage twenty-eight years earlier.

Elena's rosy skin, high cheekbones and elegant bearing betrayed her lineage from the elven royalty of the Eastern Continent. Her shining hair was tied into a long golden braid that reached to the small of her back. The daughter of Queen Talina of Elde and the Peregrine King of Mount Cassandra, she was beautiful even by the already high standards of her people. Her deep blue eyes watched the lord's consternation with just a hint of amusement.

The King shifted in his seat, and the muscles of his upper body flexed visibly beneath his ornate cape. He had chosen it to give added formality to the meeting, and to signal his determination to move forward with his plan. Lord Rugon, whose political subtlety was second to none, had not missed the gesture.

Danor's sword lay at the center of the conference table. *Guardian* was an enchanted blade, a large, two-handed weapon of nearly pure bluesteel that had been handed down in his family for generations. It was a tradition of the High Council for the King to lay his weapon on the table before them, a symbol of the Crown setting aside force in favor of reason and persuasion in its deliberations.

"And these steps are not being taken precipitously," Danor continued. "Your wise counsel has helped to ensure that. Thanks to your suggestions, we have amended the new constitution so that some of its changes will be introduced more gradually."

Lord Rugon started to respond, but the King cut him off. "Even my father, the Archmage, was swayed by the prudence of your words about 'avoiding social upheaval,' as you so eloquently put it. Great time and care has been taken to address those concerns, but that work is now done. The time has come to review the document's final editing, and to prepare it for proclamation."

"It's just that ..." Lord Rugon began. He paused, appearing flustered, groping for words.

"I'm concerned that these proposals need more study," he continued at last. "With respect, my liege, customs and social institutions should not be changed without grave care! They developed over the course of centuries, and have stood the tests of time. These new ideas ... they are bold, to be sure, and some perhaps would seem to have merit in thought and on paper. But they are so untried! If you would hear my counsel, it would be to take the time to test them out first. One at a time, and in a limited way, under carefully controlled conditions ..."

Danor held up his hand. "Haven't we already had this conversation, Cyrus? Nigh on a dozen times, I think, though I've long since stopped counting. Your trepidation has been noted. To the extent that it has been deemed prudent, allowance has been made for it. Further delay is unwarranted, unless we are to bring the new constitution's principles again under question. And to that, I say we are not. We have debated, and the decision has been made. The vote of the High Council has spoken."

Lord Rugon looked around the room. More than a dozen faces regarded him from their seats at the massive conference table. A few wore expressions of support and empathy. These included Salmanor Hardin, the high priest and Lord Inquisitor of the Church of the Divine in Carlissa. The majority, however, were clearly in sympathy with the King. A few — Prince Aron in particular, Danor's eldest son and heir to the throne — were openly hostile. He would not find support to delay the proclamation any longer.

Slowly, and with an air of resignation, he bowed. "Very well, Your Highness. It is as you say. Whatever my counsel, I remain your faithful servant, in this and in all things. If the Council is determined to proceed, then I recommend that each article of the new constitution be read aloud as review. It should then be confirmed with a yea or nay vote to publish it as written."

The room seemed to relax, and Danor nodded his approval. "I agree. Aron, my son, will you do us the honor of reading the articles for confirmation?"

"Of course, Father," the prince replied.

Several parchments were laid out before him. He took one, and without pause, began to read.

"Let it be known that these are the words of the King and of the High Council of Carlissa, in proclamation this day, the sixth of Floren, in the year 1643 of the Taming.

"There are times when an evolution of thought among men of learning, of conscience, and of good will impels them to undertake a reform of the very institutions by which they order their lives. Such an evolution faces us today, in the form of a growing recognition of the rights of reasoning beings, and of the freedoms to which they are by their nature entitled. It calls us to respond with this *Constitution of the Kingdom of Carlissa*, which is hereby proclaimed. Let all who hear or read it know that its articles shall not only have the force of law, but shall henceforth be the very basis of law in our land."

Aron paused for a response. No one spoke, but a few heads nodded absently. This was just the preamble, and no one seemed to think it needed a vote.

"'Article One. The practice of involuntary servitude is hereby outlawed in the land of Carlissa. All slaves and indentured servants are immediately declared free. Anyone attempting henceforth to keep or traffic in slaves in any form or manner within the borders of the kingdom shall be prosecuted for the crime of kidnapping.

"'Section One. Any person entering the borders of Carlissa, if they be declared slave in another land, shall upon request immediately be granted sanctuary. Anyone attempting to interfere by force with such a request within the borders of the kingdom shall be prosecuted for the crime of kidnapping.

"'Section Two. No claim for compensation to former slave-owners from the consequences of this article shall be upheld or enforced by any court or branch of the government of Carlissa.'

"That's the full text of the article. All in favor, raise your hand and say 'Aye.'"

The assembled lords all signaled their agreement. No one was surprised; the article outlawing slavery had been the least controversial of the new constitution's proposals. The sale of slaves had been prohibited by decree since the old Archmage had assumed the throne years ago, and few vestiges of the institution remained. Travelers bringing them across Carlissa's borders, however, had posed a lingering problem. It had led to diplomatic incidents, especially with the Kingdom of Rayche, which still practiced it in its southern cities near the Tiberax Archipelago. The second section was intended to warn travelers not to bring slaves with them to Carlissa, and to take a clear stand with other nations that any who entered the kingdom would *not* be returned.

"'Article Two. The Kingdom of Carlissa recognizes the right of all people to the peaceful exercise of freedom of speech, and of association. The government of Carlissa shall enact no law, nor shall those who administer its powers take any action, to prohibit the peaceful exercise of these fundamental liberties.

"'Section One. This article shall not be construed to protect *non-*

peaceful speech and association. Speech in support of violent crimes or aggression against the people of Carlissa shall be considered and punished as accessory to, and conspiracy to commit, said crimes and aggression.

"'Section Two. This article shall not be construed to establish a prohibition of any kind on the peaceful expression of *disagreement* with the speech of others, or any refusal to associate with them. Non-violent ostracism and other acts of social disapproval shall be recognized as expressions of free speech and association under the meaning of this act.'

"All in favor, raise your hand and say 'Aye.'"

This one was more controversial, and it was reflected in the vote. Salmanor Hardin made a deliberate show of folding his arms across his chest and glaring at the prince in defiance. Everyone understood that this measure would restrict the power of the Church by neutering the blasphemy laws. Chaos and evil would reign, Hardin had raged in their debates, if demon worshippers were allowed to preach their sacrilege without fear of a warrior-priest's sword. Yes, the Church had been known at times for an excess of zeal in such prosecutions, and a few had been put to the fire that were later shown to be innocent. But the right way to address these problems was through safeguards, ones that the high priest would be happy to oversee personally.

Other hands remained lowered. Lady Rayne, recently appointed chancellor of the Bard's College, was an outspoken opponent of the rebellion against the traditional arts that was growing in the land's taverns and alehouses. It needed to be outlawed before it could spread further, she had argued, not given such an explicit sanction. Lord Desmond, the Marquis of Seacrest, had disciplined commoners for impertinence on several occasions. Baronet Kuhl, representative of the Carlissan Trade Guild, had opposed nearly every article of the new constitution, and this one was no exception.

They were, however, the only dissenters. The article was quickly approved with no need to count the vote.

"'Article Three. The granting of royal monopolies, including those over participation in trade and commerce, is hereby abolished ...'"

The morning wore on as the High Council approved the provisions of the new constitution. The result had been known ahead of time by everyone present. The most controversial proposals, which had proved too liberal even for most reformers on the council, had already been set aside, and the rest reworked until they could command the needed support. Whether they thought it for good or for ill, everyone in the room knew that the winds of a profound change were stirring in the Kingdom of Carlissa.

The Secret Glade

Randia climbed to the top of the stones. They were flat, and had been placed along the back wall of the glade to form a set of makeshift stairs. A spring gushed next to them, a streaming rivulet that splashed noisily into the little pool from above. It was one of hundreds of tiny waterfalls that fell from the shoulders of Mount Cascade. Their courses meandered through the gaps and channels in the cliff-face, eventually making their way to the firth far below.

Stefan was lying on a blanket nearby. He watched her naked form with appreciation as she sprang nimbly to the top stone, and then, without a pause, dove headfirst into the pool. Her body knifed cleanly into the water, making barely a ripple in the calm surface.

She was under for a long time. He clapped and laughed when she finally reappeared.

"I'm glad I never had to compete with you at swimming," he said. "Are you certain you're not part merwoman? It would explain much."

Randia shook her head, grinning. Her wet locks sprayed droplets in all directions.

"Bah," she told him. "You're impressed by that? It's only ten feet. I need to bring you to the sea cliffs along the north side of the firth. The water's deep enough there for a *real* dive."

He shook his head. "I think I'm going to let you be the daredevil in the family. The pool here's more to my liking — cool, relaxing, private, and conspicuously lacking in hundred foot drops onto rock-laced surf."

Randia swam across the lagoon. She climbed out of the water and lay next to him.

"Oh, you can trust that I'll get you up there to dive the cliff with me," she said, mischievously tracing her finger along the line of his arm. "I'm going to show you all sorts of things that'll make your heart race, Stefan Arokkan — once we put our wedding behind us and have a chance to relax."

She grinned and stuck out her tongue at the look of mock consternation that came over his face.

"I'm glad you like my little glade, though," she continued. "We can come here more often if you like. There's nowhere in the city we can go for this kind of privacy." She snuggled toward him, and added, "I'm finding that I really like that."

He slipped an arm around her and nodded.

"As do I. We can't start disappearing too often, though, or for too long. People will notice, and we want to avoid suspicion. Does anyone else know about this place?"

Randia tilted her head upward. Her blue eyes flicked briefly toward the sky.

"Just Windheart. She's been bringing me up here for years. And she'd never tell on us."

Stefan smiled. "Your rapport with her is remarkable. Having a winged steed ready to carry you wherever you want to go must — well, save a lot of time, among other things."

Randia shook her head.

"Not everywhere," she said. "She'd fly into a storm of fire to rescue me if I ever needed it, but you do *not* take a pegasus for granted. I'm sure she'd leave me stranded on a mountain peak for a few days if I ever tried, just to teach me a lesson."

"You're obviously quite close, though. I almost feel a little jealous."

"That's just the way it is with us. We've been bonded since I was a child, and we've always been great friends."

"I was glad to finally meet her. And the flight was ... stimulating."

She looked into his eyes and grinned again.

"She likes you, too. She's being coy and trying not to let on about it, but she does. She would never have agreed to carry you up here if she didn't."

"Coy, eh? That sounds familiar."

Randia nodded. "We're actually very much alike." She frowned. "Well, alike in spirit, anyway. As much as a winged horse and a half-elf can be."

"You do both seem to have a bit of a mischievous streak."

She laughed. "Oh. Do you mean the loop? She was just teasing you. I hope you weren't frightened. She would never have let you fall."

"I know. Tell me — is it true that you can sense each other's thoughts?"

Randia nodded. "When we're flying together, yes. It's part of the magic that comes with a pegasus choosing you as her rider."

She paused, looking thoughtful. "It's not just your thoughts, though," she said at last. "It's kind of hard to describe. Your senses and ... *instincts* merge, too. While we're flying, I can feel the air under her wings, and she can feel the wind on my face. It's almost like becoming two parts of one whole, thinking and feeling and reacting together like a single being."

"That's remarkable. I've heard of the pegasus bond, but we have few of them in the mountains of Thressa. Is it common here?"

"Occasionally a pegasus will bond with a human, but not often. It's much more prevalent among the elves. Especially in southern Carlissa, where they live together among the peaks of the Nurian Mountains."

"Where the Peregrine King rules," Stefan said, nodding. "Your grandfather. I shouldn't wonder that you have a pegasus friend. It probably runs in the family."

Randia nodded. "It does. We're all pegasus riders. Father, Aron, Gerard. Mother and Grandmother, of course. And Grandfather Killraven."

Stefan chuckled.

"The Archmage. You do have a rather intimidating family tree. Is there anyone important in the eastern realms that you're not related to?"

Randia rolled her eyes at him.

"Don't remind me. And don't get me wrong. I love them all dearly. But having the rulers of three different kingdoms for parents and grandparents ... All I can say is thank the Divine I'm the youngest, and no one seems to be expecting me to help with that."

She stood up, looking toward the sky above.

"We should have our picnic," she said. "The morning's wearing on, and Windheart will be back soon to pick us up."

She stopped abruptly, her head turning toward the exit from the little glade. She squinted, shielding her eyes, looking more intently. Stefan rolled over to follow her gaze.

"What is it?" he asked.

Randia pointed. "There. Do you see that? It looks like a cloud rising over the city."

Stefan frowned. "That doesn't sound good. Could there be a fire?"

Instructor Deneri

"So we can see that there are two kinds of fundamental truths," Orion said. "There are truths of the outer world, which we may call 'existence,' and of the inner world, which we may call 'awareness.' This much we can know by simply opening our eyes on the one hand, or attending to our own thoughts on the other."

Orion looked out over the class. A few wore pensive expressions, and some were dutifully taking notes in their assignment books. He saw that there were few quills and inkwells. Most of the students were using the new magical pens that he had heard about. It wasn't surprising. They were all of the nobility, and their families could afford the expense.

At least they had settled down. The challenges had come in the first few minutes, as he'd expected, and mainly from the girls. The form had been teasing, trying to embarrass him and throw him off balance.

"He's too pretty to be a scholar," a raven-haired beauty had opined aloud, in response to a jibe from one of her classmates. She was an older girl, and one of those who had been watching him before the lesson. She'd seen him look hastily away, then. *A shy boy who could be made to blush at a pretty girl's attention*, he'd guessed at her thoughts, as she openly looked him up and down in front of the class.

He'd turned to her and smiled. To everyone's astonishment, he'd responded by executing a flawless court bow with all the flourishes.

"I daresay that no man could but speak the same of you, My Lady," he had replied. "Though I warrant there is indeed more to you than meets the eye, as well." His own glance of appraisal had been too brief to mistake for presumption, but not quite brief enough to avoid notice.

The unexpected boldness had had the desired effect. She'd flushed crimson, and the class' laughter had turned on her. Orion had let out a barely concealed sigh of relief when he saw that they all seemed to approve of the jest.

One girl in particular, with a long shock of chestnut hair, had looked right at him as she laughed. There was an intelligent glint in her bright green eyes. He'd met her gaze for a few moments, and she'd nodded to him with a wide grin.

Dame Marjeune had leaped to her feet, sternly clapping her hands for order. Orion had allowed the laughter to continue for a few moments, and then raised his own hand in a call for silence. The room had quieted immediately. He'd had little trouble with the class acting up after that.

"But what is the relationship between existence and awareness?" he continued. "Are they equal, or does one come from the other? Does our inner world *create* our experience of the outer world, or does it merely observe it? These are the basic questions not only of philosophy, but of religion as well. And they are crucially important, because they will tell us how to look for answers to the *rest* of our questions."

He noticed some confused looks, and paused. He needed to get them to see how ideas actually *mattered* in their lives. If they heard them merely as words, they would never appreciate their true meaning and power. He knew accomplished scholars who had never really understood that, who treated philosophy as a kind of game with no practical importance. He wanted to do better in his first experience as a teacher.

"Let's take an example," he said. "Lady Hawthorne, perhaps you would be good enough to assist us by answering a question. Have you ever wished upon a star?"

Lady Hawthorne looked up. Her expression was surprised, as though her mind had been wandering. "Why, yes, of course," she said quickly.

Star-wishing was a Carlissan folk custom with a long history, so Orion wasn't surprised at her response. "And have such wishes ever come true?" he continued.

"Well, sometimes," she answered. "If they're modest, of course.

You can't expect really greedy or outlandish wishes to come true, after all."

A flutter of smiles rippled through the class. Orion opened his mouth to continue, but was suddenly interrupted by one of the young lords.

"But that's just having a prayer answered," he said stubbornly. He was one of the quieter and more sensitive boys, and the vehemence of his interjection seemed strangely out of character. "I mean, isn't it? The gods live among the stars, and sometimes they hear our prayers. Don't they?"

Orion smiled. "Many priests would agree with that," he said. "The Order of Light, for example, holds precisely that view. Others in the Church consider it an appeal directly to the Divine for guidance or favor. Other scholars think it a subtle manifestation of the Magic. And there are some who deride both wishes *and* prayers as a superstition that imbues simple coincidence with unwarranted meaning."

There was a rustle of whispers as the class digested his words. He had purposely used an example about which they would likely have been taught differing views. He could see that many of them were realizing it for the first time. He waited for their reaction to die down.

"The question 'what should we do' pervades our understanding not only of philosophy and religion, but of life as well," he continued. "Even the simple query, 'should we wish upon a star,' is fraught with philosophical import. And the answer depends on the kind of world we live in. Is it a world in which wishes are granted by communion with the Divine? In which our prayers to the gods are heard and answered? In which magic can answer the call of our minds, and not merely the spells of mages? Or are miracles merely examples of coincidence, in a world that is what it is without ..."

His voice trailed off. A commotion was becoming audible from over the wall at the far end of the garden. It bordered the streets of the High City north of the firth, and of the central marketplace. The students shifted, looking around. The guards were instantly on alert.

"That sounds like screaming in the distance," one of the students said.

Orion nodded. He turned, gesturing for silence.

"Quiet, please. The guards and I will need to find out what's causing this commotion, and if any action on our part is required."

One of the guards nodded, looking at the scholar with renewed respect. It was clear that he was the officer in charge, and that he'd just remembered it.

"Instructor Deneri is right," he said, pointing to one of his soldiers. "Trevane, go out to the streets and see what's happening. Report back here immediately."

Chapter 5 - The Storm Breaks

Constitution's Promise

"I'm going to need a nice, stiff brandy when this is over," Lord Rugon said.

He stood before the balcony doors of the palace conference room. The view overlooked the shoulder of Mount Cascade and the bluffs on the north side of the valley. Rapids fell along the sheer rock-face and into pools that fed the city's aqueducts. Their waters ran from them in elaborate channels and arcades, racing like rapids to feed the palace and city below.

"I think I'll join you in that drink," Danor offered. He looked out at the morning sunlight shining on the mountain and the falls, and put a hand on the lord's shoulder. "If you don't mind the company."

Lord Rugon turned to look at him. "I will always be honored to drink with you, my liege," he said quietly.

"I'm glad, Cyrus," Danor replied. There was a hint of gratitude in his voice, and Lord Rugon smiled weakly and nodded. He had instructed the King as a boy in the art of proper conduct at court, and he understood the gesture and its meaning.

"Thank you, Your Majesty," he said. "This has been trying for us all. I regret that we have so often been on opposite sides of this debate."

"As do I, my old friend," the King agreed. "I will not forget your loyalty despite our disagreements. And I will need your help and your wise counsel now more than ever."

The pair lapsed into a reflective silence. The conflict arising from Lord Zomoran's attack on the Church six months earlier was still fresh in their minds. The debate and recriminations that followed had polarized the kingdom and lead to the morning's events.

Salmanor Hardin had declared that the attack vindicated his accusations against the Lord of Westreach. Danor had rejected that claim, and his harsh rebuke of the Inquisition had stunned the Church and its supporters. A division had quickly appeared among the people as they took sides in the conflict.

Few defended Zomoran, but many supported the growing reform movement. The Archmage himself had begun those reforms when he'd sat on the throne, and his son Danor was determined to continue his work. Others had defended the Inquisition, saying that its sometimes harsh prosecutions were necessary to defend the kingdom from evil. Opposing factions that had been developing for years beneath the surface of Carlissan society had been forced suddenly out into the open.

Lord Rugon's eyes moved across the room to settle on Aron. The elder prince was talking earnestly with several of the other council members. His powerful voice resonated confidently across the chamber. The King turned to follow the lord's gaze, and a proud smile touched his lips.

It was Aron who had tipped the scales in favor of the King and his supporters. The story of how he and Gerard had fought the magus and his dragon had spread through the city like wildfire, and the two princes had become instant heroes. Princess Randia had even composed a popular ballad extolling their exploits. Already widely admired, the elder prince's role in facing down the Lord of Westreach had given him great credibility with both sides. And he had argued his case with notorious passion and eloquence.

Many on the High Council were already angry at the Inquisition's ruthlessness in prosecuting one of their own. Aron's speech had secured their support and fractured Hardin's within the Church. The controversy had compromised the moral high ground the high priest had expected to claim, helping the Crown to finally press its case for reform.

"Most will see things as I do, Your Highness," Lord Rugon said carefully, ending the long pause in their conversation. His eyes moved to where Baronet Kuhl and Lady Rayne stood at the far end of the room. Salmanor Hardin stood apart from them in a corner, talking with one of the serving maids. "A few may not. You will need to be watchful."

The King followed his gaze. Kuhl and Rayne were whispering quietly together. That wasn't cause for concern in itself, but it wasn't a good sign, either.

Danor's eyes moved to the high priest. He couldn't hear what Hardin was saying to the girl, but she appeared raptly attentive to his words. She was strikingly attractive, with an air of young innocence that made her seem strangely sensual at the same time. *She must be new to the palace staff,* he thought, and made a mental note to ask the steward to speak to her. Hardin's motives might be a trifle less spiritual than the young ingénue expected, and she was just his type.

"Kuhl and Hardin have been thorns in my side nearly every step of the way," the King agreed. "But do you think their opposition might extend to disloyalty?"

Lord Rugon sniffed. "The high priest's loyalties are to the Church, not to the Crown," he said dismissively. "And Kuhl's are to his next opportunity to acquire wealth and power. This new constitution strikes at the heart of their sources of prestige and influence. Repealing the blasphemy laws will encourage some to defy Church doctrine, and ending the royal monopolies will hurt the Trade Guild. Whatever their merits, these changes will earn you enemies that you did not have before."

Danor sighed and turned toward the balcony. He looked out again at the sunlit morning on the mountainside.

"Then I will have to be prepared for that ..." he began with resignation.

His voice trailed off. A shadow had fallen across the cliff-wall outside the window. It looked like the silhouette of great wings wheeling above the palace, cast on the mountainside by the morning sun.

Lord Rugon smiled. "Perhaps your daughter is out flying with her pegasus again today," he offered.

The King shook his head.

"I know what pegasus wings look like. That's something else."

Another shadow fell across the bluff, and then another, and

another ...

And then the sound of a horn from the palace battlement pierced the air.

The Marketplace

"Surely you do not mean to give offense with such an offer? I am merely a poor and humble jewelry merchant. What would my wife say if I returned to her tonight not with a profit, but a loss? A loss! And a loss, no less, on an item of such dazzling beauty as this?"

He held up the amulet to sparkle in the morning sun. "See how the silver is worked in such an intricate pattern," he said. "And laced with a delicate filigree of bluesteel tracing ..."

The lady smiled. The merchant had managed the improbable task of looking both offended and pathetic at the same time. Then he'd returned to his sales pitch without batting an eye.

"Perhaps ten percent purity," she countered dismissively. That wasn't true, of course, and she knew it. It didn't hold up to his exaggerated claims, but the alloy *was* at least twenty percent pure. It was spell grade bluesteel for certain, and the design was definitely a dweomer matrix. A moderately competent artificer could easily get the dainty amulet to hold an enchantment, and she was more than moderately competent.

She looked at the merchant and arched an eyebrow. Nothing in her carefully cultivated manner or dress hinted at being a craftmage. Hunting through the market for unidentified artifacts could be quite profitable, especially when she wasn't marked for her profession. Wearing her finest outfit and pretending to be a haughty noblewoman did bring the price up a bit, but much less than giving away the *actual* reason for her interest.

The central marketplace of Lannamon bustled around them with late morning activity. Wheeled stalls were scattered throughout the huge plaza in a carefully ordered pattern. They were laid out expertly to allow for a free flow of patrons, while still allowing plenty of space for shoppers to stop and browse their wares.

A main road ran through the center of the plaza. It ascended into the hills and terraces of the Upper City, both to the north and to the south. Many smaller roads branched off from those two great arteries, most of them curving to follow the long line of the firth to the east. The nearer ones disappeared into the streets of the Lower City, running through a maze of docks, shops and homes.

The marketplace itself was divided into sections for different products. It ended to the east at the tip of the firth in an elevated pier that provided a magnificent view of the water. Restaurants were scattered along its edge and down short runs of stairs that descended to the level of the docks. Stalls of fruits and vegetables and butchers' stations hung with fresh cuts lined that side of the plaza, and the smells of cooking meat and exotic spices filled the air. Boats and ships of all kinds bobbed on the firth itself, their many colored sails dotting a background of deep sea-blue.

The western end of the marketplace adjoined the great amphitheater, which sat at the foot of the High City to its west. The amphitheater was shaped like a long, shallow bowl, and a raised dais at its center served as a stage. The ground around it was covered with a lushly tended lawn of vibrant grass suitable for seating on blankets and chairs. It had been created for public events, from performances of plays and music to lectures, debates, and speeches.

The King also used it to address the people of the city, or to issue royal proclamations and decrees. A small group of clerks and heralds from the palace had arrived and were preparing for just such an event. Stands for distributing printed copies of the new constitution were being set up all around the dais.

The western edge of the marketplace was where its most expensive goods could be found. These included fine weapons, jewelry, and magically enchanted items. It was also where the merchant's booth had been set up. The haggling pair stood near the amphitheater's east gate.

"It is a pretty piece, though," the lady mage continued nonchalantly. "I'll give you twenty-five sovereigns for it." The amulet would be worth over three times that when enchanted.

The merchant smiled. "While that is more reasonable, My Lady," he said, "it is still surely too little for an item of such magnificent quality. I might be persuaded to come down as low as forty-five —"

His voice was cut off by a sudden movement of air. A stiff wind had come out of nowhere. It swirled around them, blowing their hair over their faces. The merchant lunged for his cart to secure some of its lighter items.

The lady mage looked around in annoyance — and then frowned. The wind seemed much stronger within the amphitheater. She could see the clerks setting up for the afternoon proclamation rushing around wildly. Tables and chairs had tipped over, and some of them were skidding across the ground. A box full of printed sheets had been blown open, and its papers were already being carried high into the air.

Her frown deepened. The sheets seemed to be following a circular pattern, as though the wind were forming a vortex about the amphitheater's central stage. They swirled around, only to break suddenly free near the edge of the bowl and sail out over the city in random directions. There wasn't a cloud in the sky to account for it, and it didn't look natural.

She turned back to the cart and cursed. The amulet was glowing! Its filigree of fine bluesteel lines was now shining with a faint bluish light. It was spell-grade alloy, all right, and better than she'd thought. It was so good that it was actually resonating with nearby magic. Someone was literally conjuring up a storm, and their reckless casting was going to tip the merchant off to the item's true value. If she didn't act quickly she was going to lose a very profitable purchase.

The merchant had finished securing his stall. "Truly, you do know your trade, my good sir," she said, as he turned to look at her again. She hastily palmed the amulet to cover its glowing face and smiled awkwardly at him. "Forty-five sovereigns it is."

She slipped the amulet into the pocket of her skirt and took out and opened her purse. She heard the wind pick up behind her, and the shouts of the clerks rising with it. She tried to keep calm as she carefully counted out the coins. She wanted to get the transaction done with quickly and to get away as soon as possible.

She was at forty when she realized that the merchant wasn't watching her any longer. He was looking over her shoulder, and his eyes were wide. She turned — and gasped.

An electric haze had settled over the amphitheater, a hemisphere of eerie light that darkened with each passing moment. The wind was a howl around them now. The rising commotion of the crowd behind them was barely audible above the din.

"Forty is good," the merchant said abruptly. He scooped the coins she had placed on the counter into a leather bag with an expert sweep of his hand. Then he turned brusquely and kicked out the wheel-blocks on his cart.

"Thank you very much for your business," he said. "I'm closing my stand for the day."

She nodded, barely noticing his words. She was still staring at the menacing dome forming over the amphitheater.

"What do you think it is?" asked a woman beside her. She was young, and didn't seem disturbed by the developing phenomenon. "I heard there was going to be a big proclamation from the King and the High Council today. Do you think the Archmage could be preparing some kind of show to herald it?"

Had she been less distracted, the lady mage might have laughed. That Lenard the Archmage would turn his immense power to the creation of a magic show — well, that was just absurd. He had much more important things to do. Still, the spell building in the amphitheater *was* stronger than anything she'd encountered before. Could anyone else *have* cast it?

"I have no idea," she told the girl honestly.

She noticed a sudden uncomfortable warmth growing at her hip. She looked down and saw with horror that the light from the amulet was shining through the fabric of her dress. She slipped a hand into her pocket and nearly scalded it on the hot metal. She hastily produced a handkerchief and used it to take out the talisman. It dangled from its chain, blazing in her hand like a star.

She wasn't alone. A quick look around confirmed that several other items in the stalls of the magic vendors nearby had begun to glow with the same bluish light. All bluesteel matrices, she guessed, and all with weak or no enchantments on them to damp their resonance with the magic building in the amphitheater. That she had never even *heard* of a spell powerful enough to do *that* sent a chill up her spine like nothing she'd felt before.

"Hey! Is that amulet I sold you magical?" the jewelry vendor demanded indignantly.

She paused at the absurdity of the complaint, torn between competing urges. She wanted to snap an angry retort, to stare with fascination at the frighteningly building spell, and to dash like mad to get away. The last urge took only a few seconds to win out, but those seconds proved fateful. Even as she hiked up her skirts to run, she felt the spell build to a climax and engage.

A wave of force erupted from the darkening hemisphere. It struck her with a sound like a dull thud, throwing her and the young woman backward as though shoved by an enormous hand. They landed on the ground, stunned. The vendor's cart shielded him from the brunt of the blast, but it toppled over, spilling its wares. Its owner desperately tried to leap aside but failed; he was caught beneath it as it fell.

The mage forced herself back to her feet. The young woman lay on the ground next to her, whimpering hysterically. The vendor was staring in slack-jawed pain at the darkening sky, his legs pinned beneath his fallen cart. Scattered gems and jewelry lay on his chest and on the cobbled street around him. The entire western end of the marketplace was strewn with fallen people, carts, and wares.

The mage looked back toward the amphitheater. A translucent dome of hazy purple magic had settled over it. It was enormous, covering about half the arena's diameter. Outside its boundary, clerks, tables, and boxes of proclamations lay scattered across the grass like leaves tossed by a gale.

With a gasp of horror, she saw that everything within that dome had been crushed — impressed into the grass of the arena as though stomped on by a giant boot. One man appeared to have been right at its edge. His torso lay outside, struggling feebly, his broken lower body lost within it.

A point of scarlet light appeared at the dome's apex. It spread rapidly, its leading edge a circle of fire that rushed along the surface toward the base of the hemisphere. It continued into the earth, severing anything in its fiery path. It put the maimed man out of his misery as it passed, parting his torso as though sliced by the blade of an impossibly sharp knife.

A strange vista appeared within the glowing magic. It was like looking into a gigantic lens in which everything nearby was blurred and out of focus, but the panorama behind could be seen clearly. It was a blasted landscape, barren, rocky, and mountainous, lying beneath a sky dark with clouds. Drifts of ash lay everywhere, tinting the scene with an ominous, gray cast.

A great peak dominated the background. Little licks of flame danced around a river of lava that ran from its riven summit and down its side. Winged creatures wheeled in the distance. They were too far to make out, but they looked almost like giant bats or insects hovering and circling in the smoke-filled air.

"Is that — Hell?" a voice squeaked beside her. The girl had stopped whimpering and climbed to her feet. Her eyes were fixed on the vision within the dome, and she was shaking. "And is something ... *moving* in there?"

The mage dropped her gaze to the blurry foreground. The girl was right. She still couldn't make it out, but whatever it was, it was definitely in motion. A blurry mass seemed to be surging toward them in waves, growing larger and more distinct with each passing moment ...

With a stab of insight and horror, she realized what was happening. It was impossible, unbelievable — a thing out of legend — but nothing else could explain it.

"Hellgate," she whispered.

A figure emerged from the roiling background. She stared at it, eyes wide. A part of her mind screamed that she should run, *now*, but she didn't seem to be able to move her legs. Its appearance sharpened into focus as it stepped through the edge of the dome and into the city.

It stood about twelve feet in height. It was man-shaped, walking upright on two legs, and wore what looked like a harness of red, leathered straps. A heavily muscled body of jet black skin gleamed as though wet in the bright morning sun.

Gigantic wings covered with black feathers shrouded it like a cloak. They came unfurled as it walked, reaching out to either side, and beat the air menacingly. As they did, they revealed two arms carrying an enormous axe with a viciously serrated edge. The axe shone with an evil red light.

The creature strode boldly across the amphitheater. It stopped halfway between the edge of the dome and the marketplace. It turned, surveying the city and its people. Then it unfurled its wings to their full extent, threw back its head, and laughed.

"I am Incanus Thad," the demon's voice boomed. "Captain of the Horde of Zomoran, the Black Magus. Behold me, mortals, and despair — and die!"

The girl standing next to her screamed once, and fainted. The sound seemed to snap the craftmage out of her paralysis. She turned and ran from the scene, blindly, as fast as her legs would carry her.

HELL GATE

Prologue

The Legend of the Defender

From <u>Tales of the Covenant</u> by Edgar Tran, a compendium of Carlissan children's stories.

Many thousands of years ago, a great war between the Gods and the Demons came to the world. The Demons had opened a door from the realms of Hell itself, and their armies threatened to overrun the earth.

In those ancient times, most of Kalara was wild and unsettled, except for two great centers of civilization. Humans ruled the Kingdom of Nuracinth (now the Northern Plains), while the elves and faeries shared the realm of Eldacinth (now the lands of Elde and Carlissa). The world then was still under the active protection of the Gods, and the Army of Heaven prepared to meet the Hordes of Hell in battle.

The Gods asked the races of the time to fulfill their oaths of obedience, and to stand beside them in the Great War. Although men have long forgotten them, the elves still remember the Faeries, who commanded powerful magic but refused the Gods' call. They retreated to the land of Faerie and wove the sparkling curtain around it, forever cutting themselves off from the rest of the world.

The other races were afraid and hesitated to fight. The Horde ravaged their lands and many were killed, until the goddess Tianth finally saw and took pity on their fears. She appeared to Calindra, a simple warrior woman from Rayche whose spirit was true to the

Gods and filled with courage and faith in the Divine. She spoke words of hope to her, and gave her the *Shield of the Defender*, forged from a shard of the goddess' own heart.

Inspired, Calindra rallied the elves and men of the time to stand with the Army of Heaven, and they met the Horde in the heart of Nuracinth. The kingdom was devastated by the war and remained barren for a thousand years, and even now, only the hardiest of nomads can survive there. But the Army of Heaven prevailed, and Calindra — protected by the magic of the shield — herself slew the Captain of the Horde. Thus, the demon lords were driven forever from the face of the earth.

In the years that followed, the Gods left the world to return to the Heavens. But before they left, they established the Church of the Divine as a covenant with those who had shown their faith by standing with them in the Great War. The Gods promised they would always hear and answer the prayers of their priests, who, to this day, wield the magic of the Divine in their name. Because of this covenant, the races of men and elves have become known as the *Children of the Gods*, or simply *The Children* for short.

The Kingdom of men had been devastated by the final battle. In its aftermath, the rulers of the realms that remained vied for dominance. Calindra had become a hero among the Children, and she tried to use her influence to help unite them into a new, great kingdom. But the leaders and statesmen of ancient Nuracinth were gone, and the rulers who remained were men of lesser stature. They tried to use Calindra to expand their power by drawing her into their petty wars and intrigues.

Dismayed, Calindra left them to return to her homeland of Rayche, there to wander the countryside as an adventurer. She vanished from the knowledge of history, her final fate unknown, and the shield vanished with her. But according to legend, it still lies somewhere in the world, in the last resting place of Calindra the Defender. And it waits for the day when its power will be called upon once again to strengthen the hearts of the people against a great evil.

Chapter 1 - The Return of the Horde

The Invasion Begins

The demon ignored the screams and turned its back on the crowd in the marketplace. It lifted its axe with one hand and pointed it toward the hellgate. A beam of red light shot from it and vanished into the glowing dome.

The roiling mass inside surged forward. It too now came into focus, resolving itself into rank upon rank of hellish soldiers in red and black armor. Some were human sized, with horns and skin the color of lava, carrying shields, swords and spears. Others were great battle demons, eyes burning with yellow flame and bearing wicked axes and mauls. The latter were large, some ten feet tall or more, with bestial features of all kinds. Some were ursine, some canine, some insectoid, and some looked like nothing the people of Carlissa had ever seen.

They marched through the surface of the dome with military precision. As they did, a dense fog grew around them that darkened the sky and blotted out the sun. They chanted menacingly in a guttural tongue and raised their weapons against the people of the City of Rainbows.

Everyone who could, ran. A few of the guards and clerks in the amphitheater were too slow; the advancing soldiers scythed them down like wheat. With frightening speed, the hellish troops formed a ring around the dome, and around their captain.

More creatures marched into the city to fill their ranks, and winged demons emerged from the top of the dome. They flew in a tight circle around the growing army. Most of them were smaller than the battle demons that gathered below, but no less grotesque in appearance.

A new group emerged from the shimmering hemisphere. Two figures flanked a tall, thin man in a black cape and armor, carrying an ebon staff. A guard of the smaller, red-skinned invaders surrounded them.

Incanus Thad waited for them as another winged demon descended to join them. The Horde Captain faced the man and then looked from him to the demon at his right. He clapped one closed claw to the opposite shoulder in salute.

"The beachhead has been established, My Lords," he said in a booming voice. "There has been no resistance so far. None is yet developing."

The demon to the man's right nodded absently. It was smaller than Incanus Thad, not much over seven feet in height, and had an enormous, serpentine head perched atop a long, sinuous neck. A single menacing eye looked out from a bony, ridged forehead.

"That will change quickly enough," it said, in a voice thick with menace. It turned to the winged demon that had joined them. "Lieutenant Usnaroth, what is your report?"

Usnaroth repeated his captain's salute. It was larger than the other flying demons, and nearly as tall as Incanus Thad. It had a bat-like head and a powerful, ursine body.

"A few guards witnessed the formation of the gate, My Lord Borr," it replied. "They have been slain, and no alarm has sounded. We have the element of surprise for now."

"Let us not waste it," the man in black said. "Captain, is your strike force ready?"

Incanus Thad looked up. His eyes scanned the demons that circled the dome, and he nodded. "They wait only to follow my lead, Warlord Zomoran."

"Then let it be as we planned," Zomoran said. His voice and face were hard as stone, and there was no trace of compassion or pity in either. "Captain, you will take the elite winged demons to the palace to kill the royal family: the King, the Queen, and their three brats. And do make a point to give the elder prince my greetings when you slay him."

He turned to Usnaroth. "Lieutenant, you will take the rest of the airborne force to scout the city and establish a perimeter. Look for pockets of resistance forming and destroy them before they can become rallying points. The Crimson Slayer will march a battalion of battle demons to the Silver Star to deal with the Archmage."

Usnaroth and Incanus Thad saluted, claw to shoulder, and took to the air. The flying demons split into two groups and swarmed into their wakes. Their wings beat with a deafening noise, blotting out the sun like a host of enormous bats.

Unlike the others, the demon at Zomoran's left was largely human in appearance. A tall man dressed all in red, he wore a long sword at his belt, and an ostentatious cavalier hat that sported a crimson plume. His face disappeared in shadow under the brim of that hat, so that none of his features were visible beneath it.

He drew his sword. The blade glowed with evil runes in the waning light. His left hand was ungloved, skeletal, and burned with an impossibly white-hot flame.

"You will be rid of your archmage," the creature called the Crimson Slayer said. "And remember our bargain, magus. One hundred souls for my blade to feast upon, plus any I may harvest from the battle."

"You may sate yourself upon the people of the city," Zomoran agreed. "The rest of your price will be paid on proof of Lenard Killraven's death."

The Slayer pointed to the massing troops, and a line of the gathering battle demons stepped forward. Without another word, he strode away toward the southern arch of the amphitheater. The enormous creatures fell into lumbering step behind him.

"That leaves the two of us," Borr hissed. "As we agreed, I will remain here at the gate to command the invasion. I assume your plans remain unchanged?"

Zomoran raised an arm, and a company of the lava-skinned soldiers behind him snapped immediately to attention. "No change," he concurred.

He turned to the nearest of the soldiers. It promptly drew a flaming sword and knelt before him.

"We will be paying a visit to the Grand Academy," Lord Zomoran explained. "The regents are meeting there this morning, and I have unfinished business with them." A hint of amusement flickered briefly across his face. "I believe that some changes in the administration, and in the faculty, will be in order after today."

He made a rising gesture with his hands. The officer came to his feet, face hot with anticipation.

"And mercy shall not be required, Colonel Y'Thra," he added. "Your Hellmen may take spoils as you please."

The Craftmage's Flight

The craftmage ran. An icy wave of fear coursed through her as she sprinted toward the gate to the north road. She didn't look back.

The crowd milled around her in fright and confusion. Some bolted toward the gates as well, and she had to fight not to be shoved aside or trampled. Others watched in horrified fascination at the events unfolding in the amphitheater.

Hellgate, her mind repeated in numb terror. She knew what was about to come through that dome, and what would happen to anyone nearby when it did. She was determined *not* to be one of them.

She ran through the gate and onto the north road. The streets of Lannamon fanned out before her, curving away from the marketplace into a series of terraced lines to the north and east. They paralleled the firth at ever-increasing heights that rose toward the cliffs surrounding the city.

She took the clearest way she could find to escape. That proved to be the road that rose most steeply into the Upper City to the north. She kept running, heedless of the growing fire in her legs and lungs as she climbed the difficult slope.

She hadn't gone far before she heard the confusion behind her escalate into panic. Again, she didn't look back. She knew what she would see if she did: a horde of infernal monsters emerging from the dome to attack the city. Her fears were confirmed when she heard the harsh, militaristic cries and marching of the demonic soldiers. And she heard the screams of gawkers as they finally realized what was happening — and they, too, tried to flee.

She heard a loud buzzing. A winged demon passed overhead, a grisly insectoid figure with mandibles like giant pincers. It veered aside before she could react, turning to fly in a protective ring around the mustering army. She kept running.

A grey fog had formed around the center of the city as the hellgate took shape. Now, as she climbed the sloping road to the north, she ran suddenly through its edge. She blinked as the sun shone brightly around her once again.

The next few minutes merged into a desperate blur. She dodged frantically around startled riders, carriages, and passersby. When she reached the line of the terraces, she raced up the staired walkway into the Upper City.

She ran for as long as she could. When at last she couldn't continue, she collapsed to the ground. Her chest heaved in great gasps as she tried to catch her breath.

She finally risked a look back. In her mad rush, she had climbed over a hundred and fifty feet above the shore of the firth. She should have had a clear view of the docks and the marketplace below. Instead, she saw a darkening cloud of mist that hung low to the ground, obscuring the amphitheater and everything around it. She thought she could make out the glow from the hellgate shimmering deep within it.

"Miss, are you all right?"

She looked around. She found that she was lying on the steps before the main gate of the Grand Academy of Lannamon. A palace guard was kneeling at her side. He was a young man with a brusque manner, but the concern in his voice sounded genuine.

A dozen people stood nearby. A few were looking at her, while others were staring into the city below. The guard glanced down at the firth and then back to her.

"Did you run all the way up here from the Lower City?" he asked. "Do you know what's happening down there?"

She nodded helplessly, her chest heaving as she gasped for breath. She tried to rise, but her legs gave out beneath her. She fell into a sitting position, leaning hard against the guard's side. He looked startled and a little abashed by the unexpected contact, but caught her shoulder with a strong hand to steady her. A crowd began gathering around them.

"Attack," she gasped. "D-demons."

A woman standing nearby shrieked.

"That's absurd," a man snorted derisively. He wore a purple suit of a kind that had become fashionable among the lesser nobility in the last year. "The woman's addled. There hasn't been a demon attack in Carlissa in centuries."

"What do you think it is, then?" another man asked.

He looked down at the cloud below and affected a look of critical evaluation.

"Must be a fire in the marketplace," he said at last. "They'll have it put out in no time. Nothing for us to worry about up here."

The craftmage shook her head. "I'm — I'm not — not addled," she gasped.

She looked back toward the Lower City. People were running out of the cloud in panic. The distant screams were growing louder.

"Baron Geld is right," a woman chimed in. She wore the formal robes of an academy professor, and, if possible, her manner was even more disdainful and supercilious than his. "The demons are nearly extinct. There may be a few left, holed up somewhere in the Walls, or in the frozen wastes of Narr-Venn. But that's thousands of miles away."

Baron Geld nodded in agreement. "Besides, they couldn't have approached the city without warning."

The guard turned to face him. "What about the dragon that attacked the Cathedral a few months ago?" he asked thoughtfully. "There was no warning of that either, and it nearly killed the two princes. If a dragon could sneak up on the city, why not a demon?"

The craftmage shook her head. "It's not just one," she said.

The fire in her lungs had finally subsided, and she discovered with relief that she could speak again. She struggled to get up, and with the guard's support, she rose shakily to her feet.

"And they didn't need to sneak up on the city," she added. "They formed a hellgate in the amphitheater."

"Ridiculous," the professor countered. "Do you understand what you're saying? What kind of magic that would require?"

The craftmage glared at her. "Fully," she retorted.

She held up her left hand and waved it angrily. It was still clutching the amulet she'd bought in the marketplace, its chain wrapped tightly around her singed palm and fingers. Although not as brightly, the bluesteel design shone with the same light as before.

"I'm a craftmage," she said hotly. "Do you understand what *this* means?"

"That you've got a magic light trinket?" Baron Geld replied derisively.

"It's preposterous," the professor repeated. She was looking at the amulet, but her tone had suddenly become uncertain. "Who could summon that kind of magic? Who would want to?"

Icy realization closed like a claw around the craftmage's heart. The color drained from her face.

"Zomoran," she whispered. "The demon said it served Zomoran."

She turned to look at the inscribed lintel above the entrance to the Grand Academy. Her eyes widened.

"Oh, my god," she said, in a voice of dawning horror. "They'll come here!"

Renewed panic cut through her exhaustion. She tore herself free from the guard's supporting hands and stumbled again into the street. She made her way down the road to the east, running as fast as her trembling legs could manage.

The guard started to follow, but then stopped. His orders had been to find out what was going on, and to report back to his lieutenant. He looked after her for a few moments, his face conflicted by indecision. Then he reluctantly made his way back up the stairs and through the academy gate.

Orion's Caution

The growing commotion outside seemed to be testing even Dame Marjeune's ability to maintain discipline. A buzz of excited conversations filled the classroom by the garden, but they died abruptly as the guard stepped back in through the door. The lieutenant turned to meet him.

"Something is going on in the city center, down by the amphitheater," he reported. "A dark cloud's formed around it, so it's impossible to see anything clearly. People are running out of it and screaming in panic."

The lieutenant nodded. "Sounds like a fire in the marketplace," he said.

"It does," the guard concurred. "Except for one thing. It was very odd. I met a woman who was running up the street from the disturbance. She collapsed in front of the academy gate. I tried to help her. She looked terrified, and said she was running from a demon attack."

An explosion of laughter ran through the room. Dame Marjeune, face darkening like a storm cloud, turned to the students and admonished them sternly.

The lieutenant waved his hand in dismissal. "Sounds like a crazy woman. Demons in the city center! What an imagination! Did they just drop in out of the sky?"

The guard shrugged. "She said something about a hellgate," he continued. "She was carrying some kind of glowing talisman, too. Seemed to think it meant the whole city was about to come under attack."

Orion's head snapped sharply around. His eyes fell hard onto the guard's, who returned his suddenly intense gaze with uncertain surprise.

"Tell me everything you saw and heard," Orion ordered. "Don't leave anything out."

The lieutenant turned to him, clearly annoyed. "It's only a fire —" he began.

Orion held up a hand. "Most likely," he interrupted. "But please humor me for now." He allowed a self-deprecating smile to touch his lips. "If it turns out I'm just being overly cautious, then I'll buy you and your men a round later to make up for it."

The lieutenant looked at him with disapproval. Finally, he nodded.

"All right," he said reluctantly. "Seeing as you're a scholar who studied under the Archmage and all. And I could do with a pint once we get off duty. Just remember that I'm in command here, not you. If any orders are to be given, they come from me. Clear?"

"Clear," Orion agreed. "And you're right, of course, Lieutenant. I didn't mean to challenge your authority."

He turned back to the guard. "What kind of talisman was it? Was it bluesteel, by any chance, and glowing with a bluish light?"

"Yes, it was," the guard replied. The lieutenant's eyebrows arched in surprise. "It was an amulet, with some kind of bluesteel design on it. Shining just like you said. Her hand was burned where she was holding it. She said she was a craftmage, and that it proved what she was saying."

"What exactly did she say it proved?" Orion persisted. "To whom?"

"One of the professors. She said a hellgate had appeared in the amphitheater, inside the cloud. They were arguing about whether that was possible and how much magic it would take."

Orion took a deep breath. "What else did she say?" he asked carefully.

"She said she saw a demon, and that it said it served Zomoran."

"Lord Zomoran of Westreach?" the lieutenant blurted. "The one the Inquisition tried to take for heresy? Who summoned a dragon to attack the Cathedral, and nearly killed the princes?"

The guard shrugged. "I assume so. Anyway, she bolted off again in panic."

Orion nodded. "She could be suffering from delusions, of course. Light, I hope so. But her story actually makes some sense."

The lieutenant looked puzzled. "How's that?"

"A bluesteel matrix with no dweomer imprinted on it will resonate with nearby magic," Orion explained. "It's a primitive magic detection charm. To glow so brightly, though — to say nothing of burning someone's hand — it would have to be reacting to an incredibly powerful spell."

The guard gaped at him. "You don't think her story's actually true, do you?"

Orion shrugged. "I admit it seems far-fetched," he said. "But whatever is going on involves powerful magic. The glowing amulet proves that, at least. And Zomoran has the power and motive to be behind it."

"We need eyes on the Lower City," the lieutenant decided. "Trevane, go back outside and keep watch. If anything new develops, come back here immediately and let us know."

"Wait," Orion said, before the guard could salute and run off. "We can do better than that."

The others turned to him expectantly. He pointed through the open doors to the garden outside the classroom.

"That wall to the south. The academy lawn is right on the other side. I've climbed it many times. You can get an excellent view of the city from the top."

The lieutenant nodded. "Good idea. You and I will go up and get a look at what's going on. Trevane, you and Jenkins stay on watch down here."

The guard nodded. "Yes, Lieutenant Caldor," he said.

The three looked around the room. The class had remained rowdy and distracted after its outburst, and Dame Marjeune seemed to be having little success in quieting them. Some students were joking loudly at the idea of demons appearing in the capital city of Carlissa, while others had resumed their banter and flirting. The noise had allowed Orion and the two guards to continue their conversation uninterrupted, and without being overheard.

"Clever woman," Orion remarked suddenly.

Trevane frowned. "What do you mean?"

"Dame Marjeune. She's not really trying to get them under control. She's just making a show of it so they don't get suspicious. She's letting them distract themselves while we figure out what's going on."

Caldor grinned. "Good. That'll keep them out of trouble for now. Let's get up on that wall and see what we can see."

He walked toward the garden, and Orion fell into step behind him. Dame Marjeune spared them a momentary glance and an almost imperceptible nod. None of the students seemed to take notice of their nonchalant exit.

The View from the Wall

Orion slipped the toe of one boot into a crevice in the garden wall. He grasped a sturdy vine that ran down its length in one hand and used it to keep his balance. He was familiar with the handholds from his time as a student, and he climbed swiftly. Lacking that knowledge and weighed down by his armor, Lieutenant Caldor labored a good distance below.

The stone wall was fifteen feet high, and he was near the end of his climb. The lip of the wall should be just above him. He reached over his head to grab it.

To his surprise, he felt a hand reach down to grasp his. It was slender but strong, and it helped draw him up. With its aid, he scrambled onto the flat summit of the wall, and turned to look at his unexpected companion.

He saw a tall girl with a long tress of chestnut hair. She wore a knee-length brown skirt of fine material but simple design. It was hiked up around her thighs. She was sitting on the wall's edge, looking out over the city and kicking her feet absently. Orion was startled to realize that it was the green-eyed student he'd seen earlier.

"About time someone else thought of coming up here," she said cheerily. She pointed down and to her right. "The wall has a much better view than you can get from the entrance."

Orion balanced himself to sit next to her. "How long have you been here?" he asked.

"About five minutes. I was curious to see what was going on, and getting impatient for the guard to come back and report. I saw the wall here in the garden, so I sneaked out to climb it."

Orion studied her. She sat with ease on the narrow ledge. The simple cut of her dress emphasized the lines of a long-limbed, muscular physique. She spoke with just a hint of an unfamiliar and exotic accent.

"Private Trevane left only a few minutes before you came up here," Orion observed. A hint of a smile touched his lips. "You become impatient very quickly, it seems."

The girl grinned at him. "Oh, have you noticed that?"

Orion heard a scrabbling noise, and saw Lieutenant Caldor clamber awkwardly on top of the wall beside them. He gripped the stone with white-knuckled hands.

"Hello, Kieran," the girl said with a teasing grin. "Feeling a bit of vertigo?"

His eyes shot up to look at her, mortified. "What are you doing up here?"

"Apparently, she got our idea before we did," Orion observed drily. "She's been watching the city for a few minutes."

"You shouldn't be up here, Lady Dal Meara," Caldor said. His voice was heavy with disapproval.

The girl frowned at him and turned to Orion. "The guards are always so formal and protective around us," she explained. "Maybe I can get *you* to call me Diana?"

"All right," Caldor said impatiently. He nodded his head toward the center of the city. "Since you've been up here, let's have your report. What have you seen?"

Diana turned to follow his gaze. A thick grey pall had settled over the amphitheater, extending around it to cover the marketplace and nearby roads.

"Mostly that," she said, pointing. "The cloud was already there when I came up here. People have started running out of it, looking really panicked."

Orion squinted toward the center of the city. His eyesight wasn't especially strong at a distance, and years of book-reading hadn't helped to sharpen it.

"The guard said that people on the street thought it was from a fire," he noted. "What do you make of it?"

"That's what I thought at first, too," she replied. "But it's just sitting there, churning in a slow circle around the tip of the firth. It's not moving or spreading, and there's no sign of a flame anywhere. It's like a storm cloud, hugging the ground over the amphitheater. And there's some kind of purple glow at its center. You can see it through the mist every once in a while."

"No demons, though?" Caldor asked. Diana arched an eyebrow at him.

"A woman ran by just after I got up here, shouting something about demons," she said skeptically. "I assumed she was addled." She turned back to the center of the city, staring intently at it. "You don't think ..."

"That's what she told Trevane," Caldor explained. "Something about a hellgate and a demon horde serving Lord Zomoran."

Diana grabbed Orion's shoulder. "Look!" she said, pointing.

"What is it?"

"There are figures circling inside the cloud now. Lots of them.

Figures with wings. Something's happening."

Orion looked. Even with his modest eyesight — Diana's seemed a lot sharper than his own — he could see that she was right. Winged figures were flying out of the brume now in all directions, circling into the city in ever widening arcs.

He gasped as a mass of them emerged from the western side of the cloud. It quickly formed into a line, moving with frightening speed toward the palace.

Demons had faded into legend in Kalara over the centuries, but everyone knew the tales and images from the past. There was no doubt what they were seeing.

Orion stole a glance at Diana. Her playful demeanor had vanished, and her green eyes were wide with horror.

"So the woman was right," Caldor said. His voice sounded weak, as though he were about to be sick. "It's a demon attack."

"Yes," Orion agreed. He fought to keep his voice flat. He didn't trust himself to let any of the emotion he was feeling into it.

"And the cloud's finally dissipating," he added. "It must have been summoned by magic. To cloak the creatures as they arrived."

Caldor turned to Diana. "You've got sharp eyes," he said. "Now that the mist is thinning, can you make out how many there are?"

"There's a dome of purple magic in the middle of the amphitheater," she said. Her voice sounded numb. "I can see ranks of creatures already lined up in formation around it. Hundreds of them, maybe thousands. And more keep coming out of it."

She pointed. "There's a group of them marching along the south road. Big creatures, most of them, right out of a nightmare. Mostly in red and black armor. And there's another group taking the north road toward us."

"Lady of Compassion preserve us," Caldor whispered.

Screams echoed around them as others saw the scene unfold. A horn brayed nearby, followed by the frantic clanging of the academy's tower bell.

"This isn't just an attack," Orion said grimly. "A demon force like this hasn't been seen on the eastern continent since the Taming."

"We need to get down to warn the others," Caldor said. "There must be defended areas in the academy. We'll need to regroup there with the staff for protection."

He swung his legs over the inner side of the wall. Without waiting for an answer, he grasped the vine and began to climb down. He made much better time on his descent than he had on the way up.

Orion turned to Diana. "You should go next."

"Someone has to stay up here," she said. "At least a few minutes longer, to watch their movements. I've got good eyes. I can do it."

He shook his head. He pointed to the winged demons that had emerged from the evaporating cloud.

"Those creatures are spiraling out in a rising and widening pattern," he said. "They'll be flying passes over the Upper City in a few minutes. It's not safe to stay up here. You'll be a target."

"So when they do, I'll come down," she replied stubbornly.

She laid herself, prone, on the top of the wall. "I'll keep a low profile in the meantime," she added. "Now get moving! I like Kieran, but he's not exactly the sharpest blade in the armory. You'll need to be there to keep him from doing anything stupid."

He raised an eyebrow at her and grinned. "You don't mince words, do you?"

She shook her head. "We don't have time for it. Now go!"

"All right," he said. "But be careful. And come down at the first hint of danger."

She chuckled. "Oh, I will. Trust me."

Orion nodded. Then he swung his legs over the wall's inner lip and climbed swiftly back down into the garden.

Chapter 2 - The King's Magic

Attack on the Palace

The resonant blare of a horn pierced the air over the palace. Danor recognized it immediately. An alarm was being sounded from the battlement. The same alert had sounded months earlier, when Zomoran's dragon had appeared. Before that, it hadn't been heard in decades.

A short burst rang out, followed by two more just like it. As they did, more of the winged shadows fell across the mountainside. Whatever they were, they were converging on the north side of the palace.

"'Ware!" the King cried. "Guards, to me!"

He raced through the balcony doors. The guard posted there turned to him in surprise. He had been watching the city below and hadn't yet noticed the shadows.

"What is it, my liege?" the guard asked, drawing his sword.

"There," the King replied curtly, pointing. "Coming out of the sun to blind us to their approach."

The two looked up, squinting against the bright light. A flight of winged creatures was racing toward the palace with terrifying speed. The flight split into two groups as they watched. One group plunged toward the main gate. The other banked directly toward the balcony they were standing on.

The color drained from the guard's face. "They're coming right for us!" he blurted.

"What is it?" a voice asked from behind. Aron had sprinted across the room at the sound of his father's call. His sword, Flamebane, was already in his hand, the bluesteel of its enchanted blade gleaming brightly in the morning sun.

"Winged demons!" the King called out. He turned, pushing the prince and the guard back into the room ahead of him. Then he swung the balcony doors closed and dropped the bar to seal them.

"Everyone, away from the outer walls and windows!" he cried. "The palace is under attack! Retreat to the Great Hall! We mustn't be cut off!"

By tradition, ten soldiers were arrayed throughout the room to protect the High Council when it was in session. They were the elite of the palace guard, and they obeyed the orders without hesitation. Four of them formed around the King and the prince as screams of panic erupted throughout the conference room.

Two more guards fell in at the Queen's side. Elena had ignored Danor's order to retreat and was rushing forward to join him. Lord Rugon and several of the councilors had followed her example, drawing their weapons. The remaining guards arrayed themselves to protect the others as they stampeded toward the exit.

The ceiling near the east wall exploded in a concussion of fire and lightning. Stone sprayed through the air and crushed the refreshment table set near it. The blast knocked the councilors racing for the exit from their feet.

Demons, one after another, flew in through the opening. They flanked the fallen councilors and drove a wedge between them and the royal family. In moments, they had cut the two groups off not only from each other, but from the exit as well.

Another explosion tore the balcony doors off their hinges. Their remains flew into the room in shards of splintered wood. The King and his group were right in the blast's line, but it didn't strike any of them. A shimmering barrier of sky blue flared suddenly in the air before them, deflecting the debris and blunting the concussion.

Aron grinned. "Nicely done, Mother," he said simply.

A massive figure with jet-black skin stood framed in the ruin of the doorway. It wore a harness of red leather straps for armor, and held a great axe in one hand. It slowly furled its enormous wings, and, stooping to accommodate its great height, stepped through the opening and into the room. More demons swarmed in behind the creature as it strode forward, finally coming to a stop before the wall of shimmering blue magic.

It appraised the barrier briefly, and then looked around the room. The felled councilors had staggered to their feet or been dragged into the corner of the chamber. The high priest stood between them and the advancing demons, another wall of magic shimmering in the air before him.

The monster's gaze returned to the King. He lifted his massive axe.

"I am Incanus Thad," his voice boomed. "Wielder of Destruction, and Captain of the Horde of Warlord Zomoran, the Black Magus. He rules in Carlissa now. Prepare for death, because your line ends today."

Danor stared at the enormous demon. His eyes narrowed dangerously.

"So, you and your master think to slay me and my family?" he demanded. "And to so easily conquer the kingdom I have sworn to protect?" He swept an arm around in a gesture of mockery. "You will need more demons than this to make good on such a boast!"

He raised his left hand. A gold ring with a blue gemstone appeared suddenly on its third finger, and began to burn with a bright yellow flame. With a flash, that flame spread to envelop his entire body, like armor, in a sheath of fiery magic.

He gestured to his sword where it lay at the center of the conference table. Guardian leaped from its scabbard. It, too, burned with golden fire as it flew across the room and into his hands. One demon stood in its way; it scythed through the creature's midsection, cutting it in half.

The King lifted the enchanted blade over his head, and then pointed it at Incanus Thad. His body blazed as though he had become a being of living fire. When he spoke, his voice echoed like the sound of a god returning from the Age of Legends.

"And *I* am Danor Killraven," he declared. "Descendant of Aldran, and son of Lenard the Archmage. You face the power of my family's magic, monster. Defend yourself!"

The Queen watched the scene unfold with a determined expression. Everyone else in the room stared at the King in undisguised shock. Danor was renowned as a great warrior — but unlike his father, he had never shown more than a meager skill for wizardry. Clearly, none of them, the demons included, had expected this display of magical power from him.

Incanus Thad bared his fangs and roared at Danor's challenge. The blue shield parted to either side of him like a curtain as he leaped to attack. His axe, Destruction, fell upon the King's incandescent form with a powerful stroke that carried the great creature's full strength behind it.

Danor braced himself, and Guardian swept upward in response. The two weapons met with a deafening ring and a blinding flash of fire and magic. The concussion knocked the demons standing before the King backward, and staggered the Captain of the Horde. His axe flew up, nearly torn from his grasp.

There was a moment of quiet as the two recovered from the violent exchange. Incanus Thad brought Destruction before him in a defensive stance, and the other demons quickly followed his example. Their arrogant bravado now gone, they regarded the King with cautious hostility.

Danor stepped back, seemed to waver for just an instant, and then planted his feet firmly on the ground. Guardian swept around once more to point, flaming, at the Captain of the Horde. The blue shield firmed again. It formed two barriers now, one to either side of the King, protecting those who guarded his flanks.

The moment of quiet stretched on as everyone struggled to grasp what they had just seen. The demons — and indeed, most of their prey — had expected an easy slaughter. The King had just shown them the error of their presumption.

It was Aron who seized the moment and the opportunity it presented. He dropped into a fencer's stance and, Flamebane's point extended before him, lunged at the nearest demon. The creature leaped back as the tip penetrated easily through the blue shield. The enchanted blade caught it in the leg and opened a gash that dripped with black ichor.

"For Danor the Defender!" he cried.

His resonant challenge echoed through the room, and the power of his voice roused the hearts of the others. Cries of "Danor the Defender! For King and Carlissa!" rang out in its wake. Emboldened by Aron's example, they surged to attack.

Danor's sword spun in an arc of fire, slashing the air around him until it became almost a fiery shield itself. Lord Rugon fell in at his left, and Aron his right. The rest of the guards, and the lords that stood with them, formed a wedge behind him. The Queen stood at their center, protecting them with barriers of magic.

The demons held their ground. Incanus Thad roared, his axe striking again and again at the King, trying to beat him down by sheer force. Wicked steel, claws and demon fire lashed at the defenders, parried by weapon and shield or blunted by Elena's magic. The blades of the King's men struck, reaching easily through the protective aura that surrounded them.

And nothing seemed to be able to touch Danor. His immolated form drove relentlessly against the Captain of the Horde, countering his every stroke, his sword moving to block any attempt to close with him and his people.

Aron spared a glance to take in the situation around them. The conference room was spacious and designed with high ceilings, but not so large that it could easily accommodate over two dozen men and as many powerful demons. The monsters were having trouble flanking them. Several attackers turned to threaten the second group of councilors where it was trapped at the far end of the room. The high priest's own shield of magic was keeping them at bay.

He felt his mother linking his mind with hers, and with the King's.

Salmanor Hardin is protecting the rest of the council, he thought to them. *I think they're safe, at least for now.*

Remarkable, Elena replied. There was a note of surprise in her mental voice. *I didn't think he had it in him.*

One of the smaller demons tried to leap on Lord Rugon, claws outstretched. The blue aura before him flared brilliantly and the creature stopped in mid-air, as though it had run headlong into a wall. The lord's weapon lashed out, slashing the monster across the midsection. A hint of the azure magic lingered on the blade for a moment as it passed through. The creature sprang back with a howl of pain, and a shallow gash across its belly.

How are you holding up? Danor asked, concern edging his thoughts.

Elena's reply seemed strained. *Not well. The demons are powerful, and there are a lot of them. These shields are taking all of my strength. I won't be able to keep them up for long.*

A creature with a spiked flail charged a guard on their flank. The weapon's head glowed with an eerie black aura, and it passed through the azure ward. The soldier tried to parry the attack, but his sword and arm were shattered by the blow. A quick back-swipe from the glowing weapon crushed his skull.

Aron lunged through the barrier to plunge Flamebane into the demon's throat. It stumbled away, coughing dark ichor.

They're starting to counter my defenses! Elena thought in alarm.

We can't last much longer like this. No one except father and I really seem to be able to hurt them.

Demon hide is resistant to non-magical weapons. Thank the Light Mother gave you that blade of yours!

Stand fast! Danor thought. *We have to hold until reinforcements arrive!*

A demon hit the King from one side. His fiery armor absorbed the blow, and he turned and struck off the creature's arm with a swift stroke of his sword. Incanus Thad followed with a killing strike from his axe. Guardian was almost too late in coming around to parry it.

We don't have time! Elena thought desperately, as another demon tore through her shields. Insectoid mandibles ripped out the throat of a second guard. *We need a new strategy!*

The blue aura surrounding them vanished as Elena turned to the demon. The guard's neck was still caught in its jaws, and his head lolled lifelessly from side to side. With a violent twist, the monster hurled the body away and faced her. For the moment, no one stood between them.

Aron spun in panic. "Mother!" he cried.

He stepped out of position at Danor's flank and ran toward the demon. The move left his rear undefended, and another demon lunged forward to strike at him with a long, scorpion-like tail. Danor pivoted to bring his sword around to defend him, and his stroke sliced through the appendage. It fell, thrashing like a snake, onto the marble floor.

Incanus Thad's face twisted in a monstrous grin. He backed away, allowing two other demons to take his place in fighting the King.

A sweet, metallic odor assaulted Aron's nostrils. His hair stood suddenly on end as Elena, body glowing with a nimbus of bright blue, gestured at the monster that was charging her. A bolt of lightning sprang from her outstretched hands. It struck the insect demon in the thorax with a brilliant flash and a deafening concussion. The creature flew backward, slamming into and scattering a group of monsters behind it. The prince's ears rang from the thunderous report as the Queen spun toward the defenders' left flank.

Another creature was rearing up before Lord Rugon, preparing to crush him. The councilor stood, braced for the attack, his sword held desperately before him. Elena gestured again, and a vortex of flame formed around the monster. The column of fire enveloped it before it could strike, lifting it into the air and hurling it away.

A shadow fell on the Queen, and she turned to face Incanus Thad. The demon stood before her, wings extended to their full span. He held Destruction before him like a shield.

"Impressive magic, elf-bitch," he growled. "Let's see you try it on me."

Elena gestured. Another bolt of lightning sprang from her outstretched hand, striking the creature's axe. With a humming and crackling sound, it vanished as quickly as it had appeared.

Danor turned, seeing his wife's peril. He tried to move to her side, but the defenders' line was broken. Without Aron to guard his flank, demons had surged around him to bar his way. He struck out in desperation, but they parried his blows, holding him back. In horror, he realized he would not be able to reach her in time.

Elena's eyes widened as Incanus Thad drove toward her with a roar of triumph. Her azure shield sprang desperately into form again between them. It caught him in mid-strike, wrapping around him like a net, trying to force him back. He struggled, hacking at the rippling curtain of magic, trying to sever it with his axe.

Aron leaped into the space between them and struck. Flamebane's tip slashed the creature's arm. With a bellow of pain and surprising agility, the demon leaped backward and into the air. His wings beat to catch him in flight, and he landed quickly on his feet.

He turned to regard the prince. A smile of long, gleaming fangs broke out on his face.

"Very well," he mocked. "My master bade me to convey his regards to you in particular, princeling, before I slew you. It's time I delivered his greeting."

"Back, monster!" Aron cried, stepping forward. "You will not touch her!"

Attackers were coming at the group from all sides. A blow from a demon fist sent Lord Rugon sprawling a dozen feet across the room to lie crumpled against the west wall. Another of the guards was lifted into the air, screaming, by a demon that seemed to be composed mostly of claws; they tore him in half. Elena spun barely in time, summoning a gout of fire that blasted a demon coming at her from behind. Danor struggled to reach her, slashing at the burning and howling monsters that grappled his incandescent form, trying to drag him down.

Aron circled his foe, his enchanted blade held out cautiously before him. Incanus Thad turned with him. There were no other demons near the pair; the massive form of the Horde Captain, with his wings extended, was blocking their advance. A rivulet of black ichor ran down his arm and onto the hilt of his axe, which glowed as though red with anger.

The pair exchanged blows, testing each other's defenses. Then the demon struck.

He feinted again with his axe, and then extended his other hand. A blast of fire erupted from his outstretched fingers, engulfing Aron in a blossoming inferno.

Aron held Flamebane before him, blade outward. The sword's magic flared brilliantly as the torrent of fire reached it. The prince stood firm as the flames parted at the saber's edge and flowed harmlessly around him. Then he lunged, and the enchanted weapon slipped below the surprised demon's guard. The point pierced his thigh, opening another wound that flowed with black ichor.

Incanus Thad roared again in pain and anger. He swung his axe down; Aron launched himself into a backward somersault, leaping out of his way. The strike shattered the marble floor where he had stood only moments before. He slashed at the prince again, and then again, Destruction spinning around his body in a red blur.

Aron was renowned throughout the kingdom for his speed and agility as a fighter. Now he was forced to call on all of that skill and finesse. As fast and as powerful as Incanus Thad's strokes were, he could not score a hit on his prey. In desperation, the prince spun, dodged, and leaped to evade the enraged strikes. Unlike his father, he knew he could not parry a blow from the enormous weapon. A single hit would be his end.

When it came, it looked like just another wild stroke of the demon's axe. Aron dodged it easily with a spinning leap to the side. One of the demon's wings dipped as the prince launched himself into his move, sweeping toward where he had committed himself to land.

In a split second of horror, Aron realized his mistake. He tried to twist away from the wing, but it was too late. It slammed into him in mid-air, hurling him back into the path of the descending axe, and the blade passed cleanly through his neck. His severed head flew spinning across the room to land next to where Lord Rugon lay collapsed against the wall.

Incanus Thad threw back his head to roar in triumph — but to his surprise, no sound escaped his lips. Instead, his great body spasmed uncontrollably. His cry of victory was choked off and replaced by a scream of agony.

He wrenched his head around to face the Queen.

Fury and despair raged on Elena's face as she stared at him. Her eyes were blazing with blue magic. Shining azure tears ran freely down her cheeks.

"Killer!" she shrieked. "Murderer!"

The power in her eyes built until the demons could no longer stand its radiance. All around her, they recoiled from its menacing light. Danor slammed through their startled ranks to come to his wife's side and raised his sword to guard her. Shock and determination at what had just happened to his son mixed in his incandescent face like an alloy of molten golden metal.

"Die, demon!" Elena cried. "I will have your life, even if it costs me my own! You face the daughter of the Peregrine King, and your soul is forfeit!"

Pain lanced through the monster's skull as the Queen's consciousness burned into his mind. Her grief and rage became a weapon of pure thought that tore into his brain like wildfire. He felt her seize his psyche as though it were a physical thing, straining with all her will to tear it apart.

Incanus Thad was the Captain of the Horde of the demon lord Borr. He had the size and strength of a giant, and commanded magic that few beings could match. But through a haze of agony and with the last of his vanishing thought, he knew with cold certainty that he was no match for the Queen's attack. Elena's mind was more powerful than any that had ever challenged him, save that of his master itself.

She used that power now to rip the demon's consciousness apart. She attacked with abandon, heedless of the toll on her own mind and strength. He knew she meant to kill him at all costs. In her despair, she truly did not care if the effort cost her own life as well.

The monster staggered back. Destruction slashed back and forth blindly as he fled, sweeping aside anything that stood in his path. One demon was too slow and found itself parted at the waist. The others leaped wildly out of his way.

He reached the outer wall and began smashing at it with his axe. The vicious blade tore through, shearing away slabs of stone that fell with a thunderous crash down the mountainside below. Then he hurled himself through the opening. His great wings unfurled to beat wildly, carrying him away from the palace.

Elena sagged like a puppet whose strings had been cut. Danor caught her with one arm, holding her limp form firmly against his side. His fiery golden aura spread to envelop her as well, but it had dimmed visibly since the start of the battle. She was exhausted and helpless, and the King had spent most of whatever reserve of power he had drawn on. Now only his waning strength stood against the remaining creatures.

The demons surrounded them. One of their blades slashed cautiously, and Danor staggered as he parried it. He waved Guardian with his free hand, trying futilely to warn them off.

His gaze moved across the council chamber. "Hardin!" he cried. "For the Light's sake, help us! You're the only one left!"

Salmanor Hardin stood before the group of councilors at the far end of the room. He had stayed there throughout the battle, maintaining his shield of power to protect them. A few of the demons had tested it with bursts of fire and lightning. Most, however, had concentrated their assault on the royal family and their guards.

The high priest shook his head. "I must defend the council," he said flatly. His tone was cold and hostile. "The house of Killraven has brought this scourge upon itself. Now it must pay the price."

Danor suppressed an oath as the demons rushed him. Guardian slashed, more slowly than before, trying desperately to parry their attacks. Bursts of magic washed again and again over the King's fading aura of fire.

One bear-like demon wrapped an ursine appendage around the King's sword arm. It grappled him, slowly forcing him toward the floor. Danor went to one knee, trying to turn his weapon back to hack at the creature. With only one arm free, he couldn't. And if he used his other arm, the Queen would fall from his grasp, defenseless.

Do it, Elena's voice said weakly in his mind. *Do what you can to save yourself, my love. You cannot save us both.*

That will not happen, my starlight princess, Danor replied. He clasped her fiercely to his chest. *We live or die together. That is how it has always been with us, and it will not change now.*

Elena surrendered, resting her head on her husband's shoulder. Ursine jaws slowly forced themselves toward the King's throat. He braced himself, his fiery armor now all but gone, and waited for the end.

A flash of silver magic streaked over his shoulder. The demonic fangs abruptly halted their descent. The bear-demon's head reared back in a ruin of scorched hair and flesh.

With the last of his strength, Danor threw the monster off and staggered backward. More flashes of silver and scarlet magic streaked by him. The fusillade slammed into the attacking demons, driving them, howling, toward the ruined wall of the chamber.

Then soldiers were racing past him on either side. They were fresh, and the points of their spears and the blades of their swords glinted with the characteristic gleam of bluesteel alloy. They surrounded the King and Queen, throwing their armored bodies between them and the demons. Reinforcements had finally arrived, and they had armed themselves with enchanted weapons from the palace arsenal.

Danor turned and stumbled toward the doors to the great hall. They were thrown wide, and a company of soldiers was streaming through them. On one side of the entrance stood the court mage, Palanad Lantar, staff in hand; on the other stood Prince Gerard with his wand. The pair sent bursts of magic flying at the invading monsters with deadly precision. A line of archers beside them fired a hail of bluesteel arrows.

The surviving demons were wounded and spent, while the two wizards and their guards were fresh and well-armed. And the invaders' leader had been driven in humiliation from the field. As if at a silent command, they turned and fled. They leaped through the breaches in the walls and ceiling, their wings beating back toward the center of the city.

The remnants of the King's fiery armor vanished. He sagged, dazed with exhaustion, the Queen still held in the crook of his arm. Guardian fell from his hand to clatter on the floor. Gerard raced to their side and embraced them fiercely.

"Your Majesties ..." a voice said tentatively.

Gerard looked up. Lord Rugon stood unsteadily before them. Blood flowed along one side of his face from a gash on his head. His shirt was wet from another wound in his side.

He carried the severed head of Aron Killraven. Tears streaming down his face, he slowly dropped to his knees, and set it with gentle reverence beside the elder prince's body.

The King bowed his head. His shoulders shuddered with sobs that he could no longer contain. The Queen began to weep uncontrollably.

Gerard stared in uncomprehending horror at his brother's lifeless form. The three of them sat on the floor for a long time, tears flowing down their faces as they embraced, their grief finally overtaking them.

Chapter 3 - The Better Part of Valor

Exposed on the Cliffs

Randia and Stefan ran from the shelter of the little glade and into the open sunlight. They came to a stop at the edge of the bluff and stood together, gazing out at the valley. The distance and the whine of the wind made it impossible to hear anything from the city below, but they could see the roiling cloud over the amphitheater. It was dense and grey, like an enormous thunderhead that had settled itself on the ground near the mouth of the firth.

"That doesn't look like a fire to me," Stefan ventured.

"Not to me, either," Randia said. "It looks more like a steam or a vapor. It's almost like an actual rain cloud, hovering over the center of the city."

"I've seen fogs like this here by the mountains," he said, nodding. "But there are no other clouds out. The sun is strong, and it should be burning this away."

Randia pursed her lips thoughtfully. "I think it's a spell," she ventured at last.

Stefan frowned. "Why would anyone want to cast a cloud over the amphitheater?" he asked. "Is there going to be a surprise there today? Something they would want to hide until it's ready?"

"Father does have an announcement planned for this afternoon," she answered uncertainly. "But there'd be no reason to cover it up. And it wouldn't be like him. He's never been one for theatrics."

He laughed. "That's more your style than his."

She grinned. "Yes, Father and I are rather different in that way, aren't we? Aron can put on a show when he wants, but he doesn't have the skill with magic for this."

She looked intently at the cloud, shading her eyes from the sun with a slender hand.

"I think I can make out something moving inside it," she said at last. "Like figures flying around, circling the center. Mostly black and red. They're hard to make out, though."

"Could they be pegasi?" he asked.

She shook her head again. "The colors are all wrong. And pegasi would be even less likely to pull a stunt like this than Father."

Stefan pointed. "There's a violet glow tinging the cloud. Can you see it?"

A group of figures emerged from the edge of the brume. Enormous wings beat furiously around them, gleaming evilly in the light of the morning sun. They were far away, but Randia could make out their shapes plainly enough. She gave a cry, and the back of her hand rose to cover her mouth. Her mind reeled in disbelief as she saw them fly toward the mountain.

"Are those what I think they are?" Stefan asked. His normally vibrant voice was weak with shock. His arm slipped instinctively around her. She noticed it was trembling.

"Demons!" she gasped. "A whole flight of them! By the Light, Stefan! The city is under attack!"

The lovers watched numbly as more demons appeared. They emerged from the cloud, launching themselves into the city in all directions, circling it in a relentlessly expanding spiral.

"There must be scores of them already," she said shakily. "And they keep coming. But how? Why?"

Stefan's eyes narrowed. "You said you thought there was a spell involved. Doesn't that make the question 'who?'"

Randia nodded in sudden understanding.

"Of course," she said angrily. "A spell to summon a cloud, to conceal the arrival of attacking demons. This is Emil Zomoran's work. It has to be."

Stefan pointed to the first group. It had settled into a formation racing westward, like the head of a broad-bladed spear. "That flight," he said. "It's headed straight for the palace."

Randia's eyes went wide. "They're after my family!" she screamed.

She twisted, looking around wildly, as though searching for a way to rush down to the city to warn them. Stefan tightened his grip around her.

"It's no good, Randi," he said, holding her firmly. "We're too far away, and they're almost there already. There's nothing we can do."

She sagged into his arms, crying.

They stared helplessly as the demons reached the palace walls. Flashes of red and blue sprang from the head of the spear-point. A portion of the battlement erupted into the air in a shower of glowing fragments.

"Lightning and demon fire," Stefan said. "Some of them are sweeping the battlements on the north side. What do you think they're after?"

"The conference room," Randia sobbed. "Where the High Council deliberates. Aron told me they were meeting there today. To vote on the new constitution."

"This is a surgical strike," he said grimly. "They're trying to take out the Council and the Crown together in a surprise attack."

He pointed down toward the amphitheater. The cloud was finally dissipating. They saw the shimmering dome clearly through the thinning mist now, along with the true extent of the massing army.

"That thing — it's like the hellgate from the legends of the Great War," he whispered. "This isn't just an attack, Randi. It's an invasion."

As if to underscore his words, they heard a booming series of distant explosions. The sounds of the attack on the palace had finally reached them on the cliffs.

Randia's face was pale and she was shaking, but she had stopped sobbing. "We have to get down there," she said firmly.

Stefan shook his head. "Not you," he insisted. "You have to get to safety. When Windheart returns, you need to take her and head straight out along the firth to the east."

Randia's blue eyes flamed in defiance as she turned to face him. "And where do you think *you're* going?"

"I'll go down to the city. To do what I can to help."

"Not without me, you won't," she said obstinately. She grabbed the arm holding her and pushed herself forcefully out of its grasp. Stefan pointed angrily at the city.

"Look at that, Randi," he said. "Take a *good* look. That's not just dozens. It's hundreds already, if not thousands. And they're still coming. You're the princess of Carlissa. And from the look of it, you may be the only member of the royal family not caught in the attack. *We have to get you out of here.* And someone has to get away to warn the rest of the kingdom."

Randia nodded numbly, blinking back a new spurt of tears. "All right," she said. "But I'm not going without you."

He shook his head. "If Windheart has to carry us both, it will slow you down."

"*No, Stefan!* I'm *not* leaving you here!"

He looked into her eyes, his face tortured. Then he turned to look down at the city.

"I don't want to leave you, either," he said. "But I need to do what I can to help."

To his surprise, she smiled suddenly at him. She leaned in and kissed him.

"Oh, my dear, sweet prince," she said, stroking his cheek. "I understand you. The thought of fleeing shames me as well. But can you truly ask *me* to run, if you are unwilling to do the same?"

He closed his eyes, his expression pained. Finally, he nodded.

"You're right," he said. "And I suppose we need to be honest with ourselves about this, you and I. We are performers. Singers, artists. Bards. That's the choice we made for our lives. We've spent them learning music and poetry, not wizardry and combat. We can fence passably for a stage production, but we're no warriors. If we go down there to fight, we'll almost certainly be killed. And our sacrifice will be for nothing."

She nodded reluctantly.

"The best we can do now is escape to warn others," he continued. "We'll ask Windheart to bear us east until we're far from the city. Then you'll set me down in a town on the south shore of the firth. Ironsbridge should do. I'll rouse the countryside and get them to spread the alarm."

"And then?" she asked.

"And then *you* will continue on to safety in the Elven Citadel," he concluded forcefully. "And to warn Queen Talina."

"All right," she agreed. "If anyone could send help in time, it's Grandmother. If I fly hard, I should make it to Elde before nightfall."

Stefan nodded, looking relieved. He turned again to look down at the city.

Then he grabbed Randia by the arms and threw her to the ground. The breath blew out of her lungs as she struck the rough earth behind a patch of thin scrub. Stefan landed beside her a moment later.

"Quiet," he whispered. "Don't move, and don't make a sound."

She looked at him in bewilderment. He placed his lips against her ear.

"We were fools," he breathed. "Standing out there in the open and talking about what to do, while winged demons circled out over the city. There's a group of them flying along the cliff just below us. One of them was looking our way and rising toward the glade. I think it may have spotted us."

Panic washed through Randia like a wave, and she felt her skin grow clammy with fear. She glanced around. The bushes afforded little cover, and there was nothing better to be found near them where they lay at the edge of the cliff. "What do we do?" she whispered.

He shook his head silently, and she nodded in terrified understanding. She tried to still her ragged breathing, to stop her body from shaking. Her hammering heart sounded loudly in her ears.

They heard the beat of wings, and a creature rose into view a few dozen feet from the cliff. They couldn't see it clearly through their cover of underbrush, but it wasn't large. The size of a tall man, it was surprisingly human looking. It wore a jerkin of black leather, and its feathered wings and skin were tinged a deep red. In one hand, it carried a wickedly curved scimitar.

A half-demon, Randia decided in a fugue of detached fascination. *The rare offspring of an elven or human woman taken by an incubus.* She had heard of them, but those stories were more rumor and legend than known fact in the modern age of Kalara. At least they were in the civilized world, far from the remnants of the demon armies of the past that still lived in the lands far to the north and west.

Yet here they were now. A horde of them was massing right in the capital of Carlissa.

The half-demon hovered, looking around uncertainly. Randia held her breath. Had it seen them standing together at the edge of the bluff, or heard their voices? The wind was loud and it might have masked them. Perhaps it would miss them and move on ...

The creature's eyes settled on the cliff-face behind them. With a shiver of fright, she realized that it had spied the narrow opening to her glade. It began to rise and move forward, clearly intending to investigate. In moments, it would see their hiding place ...

A blur of white fell on the half-demon from above. It dropped right out of the sun with a sudden roar of wind. The creature's eyes squinted at the blinding sunlight as it looked up in surprise.

A harsh war-whinny sounded its challenge over the cliffs as Windheart attacked. The pegasus' great wings unfurled to beat the air, and its body spun as it dove in to strike. Its powerful hind legs lashed out, and its hooves caught the creature squarely in the face. The demon's head snapped backward in a spray of black gore. It toppled from the cliff, its body limp, and fell out of sight.

Randia's heart sang as the pegasus flew by. She reached out to Windheart through their bond as her friend's presence once again flooded her mind. She would run to her, leaping from the cliff and onto her back. It was a dangerous stunt they had practiced many times, riding together among the peaks of the Nurian Mountains. Then they would circle back for Stefan and escape over the ridge, flying away to the south and east.

She started to rise. Stefan grabbed her around the waist and pulled her back down behind their meager cover.

"Are you out of your mind?" he whispered harshly. "They'll see you!"

Randia struggled to break free. "No!" she whispered hotly. Somehow, she kept the presence of mind not to raise her voice. "Now's our chance to escape!"

When she looked again, though, she saw Stefan was right. Windheart hadn't come around for them. The pegasus was flying directly away from their hiding place on the ridge. Randia felt their bond weakening as the distance between them increased.

"She can't come back for us," Stefan whispered. "The demons have spread out too quickly, and it's too late to escape by flying. She's leading them away, giving us time to flee without being spotted."

The full realization of what was about to happen came to her in a burst of horror and loss. She reached out to Windheart desperately through their bond, screaming at her friend not to do what she intended. No creature in all of Kalara could match the speed of an unburdened pegasus of the Nurian Mountains. There was still a chance that she could outpace the monsters that were converging on her as she flew out over the city.

Don't do it! she pleaded. *Get away while you can!*

But if she did, Randia realized in despair, the demons scouting along the ridge would return too quickly to their search. They would find the lovers before they could escape.

The pegasus reached out to her, touching her mind for the last time.

You must live on, my friend. You and your new stallion. Find new life together, and remember me to your foals.

No! she thought, weeping. *No, No!*

The bond between pegasus and rider extended not only to the sharing of thoughts, but of sensations, perceptions, and emotions. Randia could see the city through Windheart's eyes. She could feel the warmth of the sun on her mane and the rush of the wind under her wings. She could feel the winged steed's fierce loyalty, and her determination to save her friend's life at all costs.

The pegasus tried to release their weakening bond as it raced away. In panic, Randia struggled with all of her will to hold on to it — and succeeded.

Their minds melded with a rush of magic that she didn't know she could command. Her hiding place on the bluff faded from her awareness. She was one with the winged horse, lost in its thoughts and feelings, as it soared over the city.

"We have to move now, Randi," Stefan whispered firmly in her ear. "You told me there was a path down to the city from here. You have to lead the way."

Randia couldn't hear him. She was seeing the world through the pegasus' far-vision. Flying demons had established a perimeter around the city. They were converging on her winged form, swarming in from all sides to cut off her escape.

Stefan tried to drag her with him as he crawled slowly away from the ledge and back toward the glade.

"You have to get a grip on yourself, Randi," he pleaded. "If we delay, we won't make it. I can't lead you. You're the only one who knows the way!"

Randia felt the wind under her wings as she wheeled and dodged. Arrows whined through the sky around her. She galloped on the air in the way of her kind, evading the demons that clawed and swiped at her with their weapons. Her agility and grace made them look slow and clumsy by comparison. Her heart sang with pride.

The net of enemies drew in around her.

Stefan managed to get one shoulder under Randia's body. He rose into an awkward crouch and staggered toward the glade. He carried her, knees bent, keeping low to stay out of sight.

A stab of searing pain pierced her flank. She looked down to see the shaft of an arrow protruding from her left shoulder. She stumbled, her foreleg going numb. In desperation, she banked, and began a steep dive toward the palace.

Yes, her mind sobbed. *Go there. Mother will protect us.*

Stefan staggered through the opening and into the glade. He carried Randia's naked form into the pool and held her there in his arms.

She looked down at the palace. Demons were crawling all over the bailey, keeping the guards from regrouping to defend the inner gates. The conference room was cut off.

It is time, Windheart's voice wept in her mind. *You must let go of me now!*

No! I won't let you die alone!

Stefan splashed water on her face. "Randi, snap out of it!" he insisted. His voice was frantic.

Five winged demons appeared in the air between her and the palace. Three of them held enormous bows, nocked and drawn. They loosed.

Another arrow pierced her flank, and then another, and another. She writhed in agony as the barbed heads ripped into her side and neck. Stefan clapped his hand over Randia's mouth in desperation to muffle her screams.

She pitched to the side and began to fall from the sky. A vulture demon descended on her, its huge claws outstretched. They raked across her belly. Through a haze of searing pain, she felt a gush of liquid running down her legs, and the wet slap of ropey flesh striking her thighs.

Stefan dunked Randia's head beneath the water and then pulled it back up again. She spluttered and gasped. "Come back to me, Randi!" he pleaded.

A wyvern slammed into her from the other side. Its claws tore into her flesh like hooks, holding her fast. Its jaws closed around her neck.

Goodbye, my princess. Her vision dimmed, and blackness swallowed her.

I love you, my Windheart. Go now into the embrace of the Divine.

"She's giving her life for you," Stefan whispered angrily. He took Randia by the shoulders and shook her. "If we don't go now, her sacrifice will have been for nothing!"

Stefan's words finally reached her. Through a haze of pain and despair, she forced herself to look again through her own eyes. She saw where they stood in the pool and felt the water dripping from her face and hair. Windheart's death throes faded from her mind. She was herself again.

Stefan looked into her eyes. Worry furrowed his brow. "Are you all right?" he asked.

She nodded. Her expression was strangely blank and detached, but when she spoke, her voice carried a new note of determination.

"Get our clothes and throw them in my pack," she said quietly. "We'll need them, but we can't dress now. That'll have to wait until we're away from here."

Stefan sprang out of the pool and ran to where they had left their things. Randia waded to its far end, next to where it was fed by the little waterfall.

"What about my pack? And the picnic basket?" he asked.

"Leave them," she said. "Our footprints are all over the glade. There's no time to erase signs that we were here."

"What if the demons track us? Won't they be able to follow our scent?"

She shook her head. "I wouldn't worry about that."

She dove under the water. Stefan finished gathering their things and waded in after her. After a minute, her head broke the surface again.

"It's still where I remember it," she said. She looked relieved.

"What's still where you remember it?"

She pointed.

"There's a small opening behind a rock under the water right here. It leads to a submerged channel. It's narrow, but you should be able to squeeze through it. How long can you hold your breath?"

"Does it matter?"

"I suppose not. Give me my pack. I'll take it and follow you through."

He looked at her obstinately.

"You know I'm a better swimmer than you," she said. Her voice was insistent. "I can hold my breath for a long time. And I know the way."

"All right," he said reluctantly. "What do I do?"

Randia took the pack and slung it over her shoulders. There was a metal insignia in the shape of an eight-pointed star stitched into the leather flap just above the buckle. She twisted it with her fingers, and it turned like a dial. There was a brief sighing sound, and the pack's straps tightened visibly.

"Breathe deeply to charge your lungs," she told him. "Once you're under, go right into the opening. You'll be in a narrow, rocky channel that's about forty feet long. It turns a little, so keep your hands ahead of you to feel your way. Use them to pull yourself forward and kick your legs to keep moving. Don't pause or stop."

"How far should I go?"

"When you can't feel the walls around you anymore, swim for the surface. You'll find yourself in an underground lagoon inside the bluff."

"How long has it been since you used it? What if it's blocked?"

"If it's blocked, we're dead," she said simply. "There's no other way out except trying to scale the cliff."

He looked at her carefully. Only minutes ago, she had been weeping in pain and despair. Now she was planning their escape with purposeful efficiency. Her manner seemed strangely flat, without affect. It was as though a switch had been thrown inside her.

"Randi, are you all right?" he asked tentatively.

She shook her head. "No time for that," she said curtly. "Go on now. I'll be right behind you."

He nodded reluctantly, and breathed deeply, in and out. Randia nodded, doing the same. After a dozen breaths, he dove under the water. She waited for a few seconds and then followed him.

Flight from the Academy

Orion stepped from the garden back into the classroom. It was already in an uproar. The students were all talking over each other, and Dame Marjeune was shouting to try to quiet them down. Lieutenant Caldor was barking rapid orders at the other two guards. Private Trevane looked like he was about to be sick, and the other one, Jenkins, was shaking his head in disbelief.

The room quieted abruptly as he entered. Frightened and skeptical faces alike turned toward him, as though waiting for him to speak. He nodded in understanding.

"It's true," he said loudly. "A large force of demons has appeared and is attacking the city. We're still trying to understand how, but they seem to be entering through some kind of magical gateway that manifested in the amphitheater."

"Oh, come on," one boy replied, rolling his eyes. "How gullible do you think we are?"

"It must be some kind of weird philosophy lesson," a girl said. "They want to see how we react to a fake crisis!"

Orion looked around. At least half of the students wore openly skeptical expressions.

"I don't blame you," he said. "It sounds crazy to me, too. I wouldn't have believed it either, if I hadn't seen it for myself."

Then his eyes hardened.

"Unfortunately, we don't have time for a discussion," he continued. "Our lives may depend on quick action. So I'm going to *show* you. Everyone outside. Now."

He had expected an argument. To his surprise, there was none.

The students fell quickly in line and moved toward the garden, Dame Marjeune expertly herding them along. There was still some laughing and chatter, and most of them still looked skeptical — but they were moving.

Caldor came to his side with the other two guards. "Can you see the demons already?" he asked.

"It won't be long before some of the fliers pass overhead," Orion replied. "The commotion in the street's getting pretty loud, too. I'm hoping that'll be enough to get the students in line."

Caldor looked around. "Where's Diana?" he asked.

"She stayed on the wall to keep watch. She promised to come down as soon as the flying demons got close."

Caldor's face twisted in anger. "Why did you let her do that?" he barked. "It's dangerous! She could be killed — or taken!"

Orion followed the students out into the garden. He looked carefully at the lieutenant.

"I'm going to guess you've had some experience with trying to tell that girl what to do," he said calmly. Trevane put a hand over his mouth and chuckled. "I didn't think trying to wrestle her down from a fifteen-foot wall was a good use of our limited time to prepare for — whatever's coming. Besides, she was right. We needed someone to stay on lookout. I believed her when she said she'd be careful."

Dame Marjeune assembled the students along a path that led through the garden. Brightly colored flowers bloomed in the sunshine and they saw bees everywhere, going about their business.

The cries of panic in the streets outside the academy were unmistakable now as screams — not ordinary screams, but the blood-curdling shrieks of people fleeing in mortal terror. Then, in the distance, faintly at first but slowly getting louder, they heard a martial chant. Soldiers with harsh voices were marching through the city, and they were coming their way.

A swift blur of brown caught Orion's eye. Diana was descending the wall, climbing hand over hand down the vine as though it were a rope. He had a moment to marvel at her agility before her feet hit the ground. She ran up to him and nodded.

"They're coming," she said. "Straight up the road from the marketplace, less than a quarter of a mile away. A column of soldiers in red and black armor. Human sized, but with red skin, almost like lava. A tall man in black with a staff is leading the way. They're chanting something as they march. I don't know the language, but it doesn't sound friendly."

Orion nodded. "Hellmen," he explained. "The song is their Slaver's Chant. The wizard leading them will be Zomoran of Westreach."

A figure circled into view above the garden. Orion looked up to see a large, winged demon with a scaly green hide, carrying a glowing red sword. Its wings beat steadily as it arced around them, rising slowly into the air above the Upper City.

One of the students screamed. Dame Marjeune put her face in her hands and began to sob.

"I told you this was no joke," Caldor said harshly, through the numb silence that followed. "These things are real. And it's my job to keep you safe until the army can drive them off. For that, we'll need discipline. So no more acting up. Clear?"

"What do we do, then?" one of the students asked. His voice was quavering and uncertain. "Run for the palace?"

Orion shook his head. "We'd never make it," he said. "We'd have to go right through the part of the city that's already thick with demons. And the palace itself is under attack. It's not safe to return there."

"Then what do we do?" Trevane asked.

"We can't go south or west," Orion replied. "And if we go north, we'll just end up pinned against the cliff wall. If we bolt, it'll have to be east, along the line of the firth. And we'll have to do it now, before that way is cut off as well."

"No one is running," Caldor declared harshly. The others turned to look at him in surprise.

"We're not going out into a city that's filling up with rampaging demons," he continued. "We'll stay at the Grand Academy. It's well defended by guards, and there are scholars here schooled in magic. It's the safest place for us to wait out the attack."

Diana gripped Orion's arm. When she spoke, her voice was suddenly panicked.

"Wait. Did you say that Lord Zomoran was leading them? Lord Zomoran of Westreach?"

"Yes," Trevane said. "That's what the lady mage running up from the marketplace said, too."

Diana looked directly into Orion's eyes. "You realize that means they'll come here, don't you?"

Orion's face went white. "Oh, no," he breathed.

"The mage said the same thing before she ran off," Trevane said, bewildered. "What does it mean?"

"Lord Zomoran was expelled from the Grand Academy the day of his rampage at the Cathedral," Orion explained. "And the same regents who expelled him are meeting here today. Right now, in fact. If he's back, he's out for revenge. And the academy will be his first target."

"We have to get out of here!" Diana cried. "Make a run for it along the east road, like you said!"

"*No!*" Caldor barked. "You don't *know* that they're coming here. And even if they are, it's still our best chance of safety. Running off into the undefended streets is suicide!"

"I'll take those odds," Diana countered. Her eyes flashed with defiance. "Who's with me?"

Orion turned to the lieutenant. He tried to keep his voice calm.

"I agree with Diana," he said. "My vote is to run while we still have time."

Caldor grabbed him by the shirt. He thrust his face directly into Orion's.

"You don't get a vote," he said flatly. "I'm the ranking officer here, and we do this as I say. Clear?"

Orion's eyes narrowed. "I'm not under your command," he told him carefully.

"You are now," Caldor replied menacingly. "I'm an officer of the guard, and I have conscription authority. I'm using it."

"Oh, for Light's sake, Kieran!" Diana yelled. "We don't have time for a bull-rutting contest!"

The lieutenant ignored her. "You're going to stick with us and help protect the students," he continued, still looking at Orion. "Now, where's the best defended position in the academy? Where will the rest of the staff go?"

Orion took a deep breath, trying to hold down his anger. He pointed to a tall building that looked like a fortress.

"The Deans' Library," he said at last. "There's an exit into the courtyard at the far end of the garden. From there, you can't miss it."

Caldor nodded to the two guards. "Orion and I will lead the way. Trevane, Jenkins, bring up the rear. The rest of you, double time it!"

Diana stepped up to him. She slapped him, hard, across the face.

"You idiot!" she screamed. "You're going to get us all killed!"

Before he could react, she turned and bolted across the lawn. She was halfway to the wall before Caldor had even raised his hand to his cheek in shock, and scaling it before he started to move after her in pursuit.

"You'll never catch her," Orion said.

The lieutenant stopped. Diana was using the vine like a rope, grasping it with both hands and walking up the wall with her knees bent.

"Not in that armor, anyway," Orion added. "She's too fast for you, and you know it."

Caldor looked at him acidly.

"Then you get her," he ordered. "Bring her to the Deans' Library. Knock her out and carry her if you have to, but bring her back." He looked menacingly again into Orion's eyes. "If you don't, I *will* see you in the dungeons when this is over. Do you understand me?"

Orion took another deep breath. He nodded.

"I understand you perfectly, Lieutenant Caldor," he said tightly.

He turned and ran toward the wall. Dame Marjeune at his side, Caldor led the rest of the group toward the exit from the garden.

Diana was already on top of the wall by the time Orion started his ascent. She was racing along it to the east, looking for a place to climb down. He scaled it quickly and was soon running after her.

She heard him and turned. She stopped, waiting for him to catch up.

"Quick — what's the best way down to the street?" she asked.

"Caldor ordered me to bring you back," he said quietly. "I'm risking prison if I don't."

Diana glanced down into the garden to see the others running through the exit and into the courtyard. Then she turned back to Orion. Her green eyes met his brown ones and held them for a long moment.

"You know we're right," she said at last.

She looked down into the city and pointed. "They're heading straight for us. If we don't go right now, we'll be cut off. If we go back, we'll be killed. And that's if we're lucky and aren't captured. You know as well as I do that no one's going to get here in time to save us."

He followed her gaze. He saw the line of Hellmen coming up the road. There was no mistaking the figure of Lord Zomoran now, walking at the head of the column. One of the fire elves marched close at his side.

"What is it that Hellmen do to prisoners, Instructor Deneri?" she asked. "I've heard stories, but a scholar and a journeyman adventurer must know them in gruesome detail. Do you want that to happen to *us*?"

Orion sighed. He shook his head and pointed in the direction she had been running.

"Keep going. There's a tree near the wall up ahead. We can jump to its branches and climb down from there."

Diana smiled. "Then let's go."

A minute later, they were sprinting across a road that led further into the Upper City. There were estates on either side of them, surrounded by low hedges. They hopped over one and cut across the lawn. After a short time, they emerged on a street that led east, parallel to the firth.

As they did, the first lines of the Hellman force ran up the road from the Lower City. With ruthless efficiency, they surrounded the Grand Academy.

Chapter 4 - The Hunt Begins

The Hunter

The ground shuddered with the heavy *thud* of Gorath's feet as it lumbered up the palace road. Behind it, a second wave of demons rushed forward to block escape from the High City.

An agonized roar keened through the air above. It looked up to see the enormous form of Incanus Thad flying toward the hellgate, its great wings beating frantically away from the palace.

Gorath threw back its head and laughed. As with most of the larger and more powerful demons, its voice was loud, and it reverberated menacingly. It had a grating edge that made it difficult to listen to, like the sound of nails being raked across a chalkboard.

"So, the royals aren't so soft after all," it said aloud. "And once again you overestimate yourself, *Captain of the Horde*. I don't know what Lord Borr sees in you. Without that axe of yours, you're just a second-rate *Deman* with pretty feathers."

It turned toward the palace, and what it saw made its eyes narrow dangerously. The remnants of the winged strike force were being driven back by a disciplined line of soldiers with gleaming pikes. A fusillade of arrows rained down on them from the upper walls. Alchemical bombs and bursts of magic launched from the tower above exploded in their midst. Many of the monsters were already leaping from the lower walls to escape. The attack was quickly turning into a rout.

"So much for the 'decapitation strike,'" it growled angrily. "Thad's fleeing and we're losing the bailey. It won't be long before the rest come limping out as well."

It was quickly proven right. Demons appeared around the corner from the north side of the castle, where the walls and ceiling of the conference room had been breached. Some were so badly wounded that they could barely fly. The rest of the attackers took to the air as well. They fled the palace, wings beating away from it to the east.

Gorath raised a scaly hand. A burst of flame erupted from it and flew into the sky. Some of the demons immediately banked toward it. Before long, many of them had landed nearby, regrouping around it.

One of the larger creatures stepped toward it with a salute. Gorath did not return it.

"Report, Barzoun," Gorath ordered.

Barzoun bowed, eyes lowered. "The strike force has been repelled, Captain Gorath," it said.

Gorath grabbed the demon's head and slammed it into the ground. It grunted in surprise and pain as its face struck, hard, against the paved stone of the roadway.

"Do not tell me what I can plainly see for myself, worm-brain," it growled. "Tell me what I do not know. And tell it quickly, lest I become even more displeased with you for wasting my time. What resistance did you encounter, that forced you to withdraw, instead of readying the palace for my forces to secure?"

Barzoun was among the demons that had assaulted the conference room. Face held in the stone and dirt of the palace road, it explained what had happened, up to the arrival of the rescuers. It told the story with remarkable speed and conciseness.

Gorath released the monster's head when it had finished, and it rose unsteadily to its feet. By then, more of the creatures had landed around them. Others had run up along the road from behind.

"Barrier formation," Gorath ordered. "Form a line across the valley here. Nothing gets out of the High City."

"Should we send fliers to surround the palace on all sides?" one of the winged demons asked.

"No. The cliffs and the mountain will keep them in."

"What about the pegasi?" the demon countered.

Gorath turned to glare at it. "Explain," it demanded impatiently.

"We slew a pegasus in the air above the palace," it said in a suddenly shaky voice. "We thought it might have arrived to carry off some of the royals."

Gorath smiled with interest. "You saw only one, then?" it queried. "And it wasn't mounted?"

"No. It came in over the ridge to the south and slew one of our scouts."

"And then flew right to the palace?" Gorath demanded. Its grating voice was incredulous. "While it was being attacked by your force?"

"Yes," the creature replied.

"Bring me one of the wyverns to serve as steed," Gorath ordered. "You will show me where it attacked this scout."

It turned to one of the others as the demon flew off.

"Nagoth, you will remain here," it commanded. "Carry out my orders while I investigate this incident."

Nagoth grinned. "Just the blockade?" it asked.

"Just the blockade," Gorath confirmed. "Any attempt to escape by flight has already been accounted for in Lord Borr's plan."

Chaos in the Streets

Orion and Diana ran along the road to the east. This part of the city was dominated by homes, mainly for the capital's more affluent citizens. High hedges blocked their view of an estate as they sprinted past it on their right.

The panic in the marketplace had reached the Upper City. Terrified shrieks and wails rose around them. To their left they could see people looking out of windows, or standing on porches and lawns, staring into the air and pointing in horror.

Winged shapes circled above, laughing and mocking them with fell war-cries. Occasionally an arrow or a ball of fire would arc down, striking an unwary soul or igniting a conflagration. Flames were spreading as the people ran for cover, afraid to come out into the open to fight them.

For the moment, though, the demons were making no concerted attack on the city. Aside from the force moving on the academy, they seemed content simply to spread fear and panic.

A bow twanged to their right, and an arrow shot up from behind the hedge. It flew true, striking a demon as it passed overhead. There was a harsh cry as one of the creature's wings twisted awkwardly, and it fell toward the ground.

A cheer went up all around them, but the celebration was short-lived. The demon spread its injured pinion, arrested its descent, and yanked out the arrow with a clawed hand. Black ichor dripped from the air as another demon circling nearby turned to join it, and the pair banked toward the source of the shot.

Twin balls of fire rocketed down and exploded with a deafening roar behind the hedge as Orion and Diana ran past it. The verdure absorbed the brunt of the blast, but the concussion still staggered them. Shrieks of death rose from behind it as demon-fire rained again and again on the grounds within.

"They're sending a message," Orion gasped. "Resist, and die."

Diana huffed agreement. "We can't keep running in the open like this. We need to find cover!"

"Not here," he said. "We're still too close to those troops coming for the academy. We need to get further away."

She spared a glance to their right. The burning hedge ended as their road curved toward the edge of the terrace. They were running past the lawn of a small park now, and the Lower City was once again in full view.

She pointed. "Trouble," she panted.

Orion looked. Small groups of Hellmen were running east along the streets on the terrace below them.

"They're making for the road from the docks," he huffed. "If we don't get there first, they'll cut us off!"

"It's all or nothing, then!" Diana cried. "Run for it!"

They sprinted down the road along the ledge of the terrace. The ground to their right fell away in a forty-foot drop, and they could plainly see the chaos in the Lower City below. Screaming people were running, most of them away from the amphitheater along the line of the firth. Smoke and fires dotted the marketplace and the docks. The sky was thick with winged demons.

The next few minutes faded into a haze of pain and terror. Orion once again found himself grateful for his time at the Silver Star. He would never have been able to run as fast or as far before his adventurer's training, with its strict regimen of physical conditioning. Yet Diana was still outstripping his pace. She held her skirt hiked up above her knees, her athletic legs pumping as she ran. She pulled ahead of him despite his efforts to keep up.

A fork appeared in the road before them. One way ascended steeply to their left, rising to the next level of the Upper City. The other descended in a switchback that wound down over the lip of the terrace to their right.

Diana came to a stop and turned, heaving huge gulps of air. She tried to speak as Orion caught up with her, but barely got out the words.

"Wha — wha — way?" she whuffed.

He raised his hand to point to the right. He didn't even try to speak.

Diana nodded. Her green eyes were wide with a look of desperate trust. She fell in at his side as he turned onto the fork.

The intersection was halfway up the terraces on the north side of the city. The road dropped away in a series of winding coils that traveled all the way down to the docks and the firth. The first level of the Upper City cut across it below them. Flights of stairs ran down the center of the switchback.

Diana pointed as they reached them. On the level below, a group of Hellmen was jogging in their direction. They were about to be cut off.

Orion didn't hesitate. He ran along the length of the first switchback to its far side. Then he turned, vaulted over the low railing, and launched himself into space.

The jump was nearly eight feet to the next curve of the road below. He hit the ground hard and rolled, coming back to stand in a single, fluid motion. He turned to help or catch Diana as she followed, but there was no need; she had already landed on her feet beside him. They ran wordlessly together across the road and jumped again. Orion held his breath as they repeated the dangerous move, knowing that one bad leap and landing would finish them.

They made it. Three times they jumped and rolled, crossed the street, and jumped again. In less than a minute, they'd descended most of the way to the terrace below.

After their last jump, he caught her arm and turned to the left. They ran a short distance and stepped over another guardrail. On the far side they saw a steeply descending hill that ended in a ledge.

They looked down. A copse of trees grew along the face of a sheer rock-wall that lay beneath them. Twenty feet below they could see the yard of a house nestled under the shoulder of the terrace. The boughs of several trees were within jumping distance.

Diana nodded and raced ahead. She clambered recklessly down the slope and leaped, grasping wildly for the nearest branches. For a moment she fell, suspended in space. Then, one of the boughs caught under her arm. It held, and her body swung. One of her legs landed on another branch, and she came to a painful halt amid the leafy limbs.

She looked back at Orion. He'd stopped at the ledge and was looking carefully at the branches. His eyes settled on one, and then he leaped to follow her. He landed neatly in the nook between it and the bole of the tree.

They descended quickly out of view from the road. The yells of the Hellmen grew louder, along with the harsh sound of boots on the roadway. They stopped and waited, desperately trying to quiet their labored breathing. Long, tense seconds passed until the noise receded, clattering up the stairway to the terrace above.

They climbed the rest of the way down and dropped to the ground. Then they ran together across the yard. They didn't hear any sounds of pursuit.

Eventually, they reached a gate. Dizzy with exhaustion, they climbed over it. They saw that the little wood ended there, and that a series of densely packed buildings blocked their way forward. They followed the cobbles of an alley that ran to their right. When it ended, they found themselves on Tribute Street, a main road running east.

Orion looked around. They were on the lowest level of the Upper City, in a commercial neighborhood dominated by shops and peddlers' stands. The carts were abandoned and there was no one in sight. Outside the cover of the trees, he could once again see demons circling in the air above.

"Hey! You!" a voice hissed.

They turned, startled. The door of the building next to them was slightly ajar, and a hand was gesturing to them through the crack. Above it hung a sign that read: *The Smiling Nymph Inn and Tavern.*

"Come in off the street!" the voice called softly. It sounded panicked. "The monsters are killing anyone they see in the open. If they spot you, you'll bring them here!"

Orion and Diana exchanged glances.

"It's as good a place as any," Diana breathed. Her lungs were heaving, and Orion saw her sway unsteadily. "My legs are like lead and I'm about to collapse."

He nodded. He took her arm protectively to support her, and they stepped together toward the door.

The Sky Chamber

Palanad Lantar knelt at the King's side and laid a hand on his shoulder. "Your Majesty," he said gently. "We need to see to the defense of the palace."

Danor looked up through tear-stained eyes. Slowly, he released his wife and surviving son. He rose unsteadily to his feet, still swaying with exhaustion.

The court mage slipped a shoulder under his arm. "Are you injured, my liege?" he asked. "I can provide you with healing if you require it."

Danor shook his head. Gerard rose beside him and helped his mother to stand as well. The Queen looked broken and exhausted. She had difficulty staying on her feet without leaning on him.

"Thank you, Palanad," the King said gratefully. Then he turned to his son.

"And you too, Gerard. Never in history did a rescue arrive so in the nick of time."

Gerard shook his head.

"I'm glad we could save you and Mother," the prince said simply. He looked down at his brother's body. "But in the nick of time? I can't call it that."

Danor nodded. "I know. But not now. There'll be time enough for grief later."

He turned to an officer that stood next to him and took a deep breath. "Report, General Banderman," he ordered.

"The demons have retreated for now," the general replied with a salute. "But they remain nearby, and they've cut us off from the rest of the city."

"A second flight struck at the gates and drove into the great hall," Gerard added. "They blocked reinforcements to the conference room until Palanad and I arrived with the general and broke through. There weren't enough of them to hold it against us."

"Then you and the council were the primary targets of the attack," the court mage opined.

Danor nodded. "I suspected as much. They intended to cut off the head —" He stopped abruptly, stricken by the analogy that had come unconsciously to his mind. "To eliminate the leadership of the Carlissan government," he corrected himself. "They had only a limited window of time to accomplish that before the palace defenses were mobilized."

"The Captain of the Horde said they were here to kill the royal family," Elena said thoughtfully. "Whether they intended to kill the council or merely capture them, we still don't know. They focused nearly all their attacks on us."

"So they gave up once they realized they'd lost the element of surprise?" Gerard offered.

"Perhaps," Danor mused, frowning. "But I still think we're missing something. It's clear they didn't expect the strength of our resistance. Had they defeated us, they would have swept through the conference room and into the rest of the palace. Your force would have been overwhelmed."

"And they would have succeeded, had it not been for your magnificent stand against them, my liege," Lord Rugon put in. He was sitting on one of the few chairs that hadn't been smashed during the battle; a medic was fussing over him, dressing his wounds. "And the Queen, and Prince Aron, may his soul rest in the Light of the Divine. It was like a scene out of the Age of Legends. The Defender herself could not have matched what you did here today."

Palanad Lantar's eyebrows rose. "What are you talking about?" he asked. "What happened?"

"Yes, I'd like to know that too," Gerard said. "I sensed an eruption of magic here, unlike anything I've ever experienced. Mother is strong, but even she couldn't have done this by herself."

He paused to look around the decimated room. Soldiers were busy heaving the enormous bodies of the slain demons toward the riven openings in the wall, dumping them out and down the mountainside.

"I agree their plan seems to have been based on speed and surprise, and that they didn't expect to be driven off," Gerard continued. "Whatever was unleashed here killed a dozen elite demons, and gave their strike force such a bloody nose that they actually ran when we came to your aid."

"That was the King's doing," Lord Rugon said.

"So I gather," Gerard said. "When the door opened, Father, I half expected to see the Archmage himself standing here in pitched battle. Instead I saw you, immolated in magical fire."

The court mage frowned. "I can see that some powerful sorcery was at work here," he said. "But I didn't sense any magic except the Queen's, and the high priest's."

The King shook his head. "You wouldn't have," he said reluctantly. "Only another of my bloodline could."

"Danor," Elena interrupted. Her face was still pale, and it wore a concerned expression.

He turned to her, looking surprised. "What is it, my Queen?" he asked.

"I think explanations about that can wait," she replied. "We need to see to the defense of the palace, and to find Randia. And we should get out of this conference room. Much of the outer wall and ceiling are gone, and the enemy has archers and spell casters."

"I concur, Your Majesty," General Banderman said. "My officers are already fortifying our position and searching for the princess. We can do little with this room, though. It's not safe to remain here."

"Yes, let us be away from this place," another voice agreed.

The group turned to see Salmanor Hardin approaching them. Many of the other lords of the council stood with him. The serving girl he'd been speaking with earlier was at his side, clinging to his arm.

"We must find a more defensible position for the lords of the council during this crisis," the high priest said.

Lord Rugon regarded him with open loathing. He spat on the ground at his feet.

"You betrayed the Crown, Hardin," he said. "You left the King and Queen to die."

"What?" Gerard exclaimed. His eyes narrowed in surprise and suspicion.

"That's treason," Palanad Lantar said coldly.

"No," Danor interrupted. He reached out to place a hand on his chief councilor's arm.

"I understand your anger, my friend, but we cannot afford the luxury of infighting right now. We must stand united against the threat we face." He turned a stern gaze on Salmanor Hardin. "The high priest and I will discuss his failure to come to my aid when I called for it, but we will do that later."

"My power was needed to defend the council," Hardin replied haughtily.

"The demons were after the King!" Lord Rugon said hotly. "They barely noticed the rest of the council!"

"Because they saw they were under my protection," Hardin countered. His tone was acid. "Had I left them to come to the King's aid, they would have been slaughtered."

"Enough!" Danor yelled. "We will not fight with each other while demons attack the city! Is that clear?"

The King's command struck their voices into silence. Lord Rugon executed a shaky bow.

"As you wish, my liege," he said.

"I may disagree with the high priest's tactical assessment of the battle," the King continued, "But he does have a point. His power will be needed to help protect both the palace and the council."

He turned to Hardin.

"Since it appears that I can trust you with that duty, your grace, and with little else, you may take it as my command. General Banderman will fortify our position, and bring the rest of the council to the safest place in the keep that he can find. He will bring the princess there as well, and send word *immediately* to let me know, as soon as he has found her. You will help as you can to defend the palace, and fall back to protect the council if it is breached."

Hardin opened his mouth to reply as the general saluted the King's orders. Danor turned his back on him.

"Palanad, I want you to come with us. Gerard, the Queen, and I will accompany you to your laboratories at the top of the tower. I want any spells or magical items that we can use in the coming battle made ready. Nothing is to be held back."

He glanced through the room's ruined windows. "I also want to get a good look at what's happening in the rest of the city. There's nowhere better to do that than from the sky dome."

He strode through the doors, and the others followed quickly behind. They crossed the great hall and stepped onto a platform at the base of the stairs to the palace tower. There, a shaft surrounded by a circular stairway rose through the center of the citadel. The court mage spoke a word of command, and the platform began to ascend rapidly through the shaft. Palace guards and workers rushed along the stairs around them, most of them carrying weapons, food, or other items.

Elena turned to Gerard. "This was *your* work, wasn't it?" she asked.

Gerard nodded. "For my studies in magical crafting. It was my final project."

Palanad grinned. "It earned him highest marks, too. He invented an entirely new dweomer to construct it. We're studying the design now to see how it can be adapted for other uses."

The Queen beamed at her son. "You have a gift for this, Gerard," she said. Her voice was proud. The prince colored slightly in embarrassment.

The lift reached the laboratory, and they stepped onto a porch by the entrance. The doors were wide open. Young men and women in apprentice grey were running in and out of them, carrying items up or down the stairs.

"I anticipated your order, Your Majesty," he explained. "Anything that can be used to combat the demons, no matter how experimental, is being put into play."

Danor nodded. "Good work," he said.

"Most of the apprentices, and a good number of wizards as well, were in the palace when the attack began," Palanad continued. "With your leave, I'll join them in organizing our magical defenses."

"You have our permission to do so, Mage Lantar," the King replied formally. "Gerard can lead us the rest of the way."

The court mage bowed and strode off. "Alanon!" he cried to one of the other wizards. "How much Mage's Fire do we have on hand? We'll want to collect all of it for loading in ..."

Gerard gestured with one hand. "This way, Father," he said.

The prince led them through a narrow passage and into another stairwell. This one had no lift, and the three had to climb the rest of the way up. Danor seemed to have recovered his strength, but Elena still appeared weak. The King lifted her easily into his arms and carried her. She protested at first, and then subsided, resting her head on his shoulder.

"Thank you, my love," she whispered.

The stairs opened onto a wide, circular platform. They stepped onto it, and Danor set the Queen on her feet.

The top of the mage's tower was the highest point in the city. The platform was open to the sky, and a magical ward surrounded it like a dome of shimmering glass. They felt only a slight breeze. The barrier allowed fresh air to penetrate, but otherwise protected it from rain, wind, or intrusion by matter or magic.

Danor strode to the eastern edge and looked out over the valley. Chaos met his gaze.

The dome of the hellgate glowed in the center of the amphitheater. Endless ranks of demons in military formation surrounded it, and more were marching through its surface. Flying creatures dotted the air, circling as far out as the cliff-wall. A barrier of them hovered and wheeled around the palace, surrounding it, though at a respectable distance.

The King looked around the city. Two more groups of demons were marching along the roads to the north and south. The southern group seemed to be composed of especially large and powerful creatures. It had already swept around the tip of the firth, and was making its way along its shore to the east. There were more in the northern group, though its soldiers were smaller. Their skin and armor glinted in shades of red and black.

"Lady of Compassion protect us," Danor said quietly.

"There must be thousands of them already," Gerard said numbly.

The King pointed to the shimmering violet dome. "That's what they're using to enter."

"It's like a scene from the legend of the Great War," Elena breathed.

She turned to her husband. There was a look of horror in her eyes.

"This isn't just an attack on the city, Danor. It's something much greater. It's an invasion of our whole world."

He looked down to the palace road. Scores of battle demons were running along it and fanning into the surrounding streets. More were following from behind.

"No getting out that way," Gerard said grimly. "We're cut off."

"They're still marshaling," Danor observed. "Whoever is directing this battle is an experienced general. He's doing nothing gratuitous, taking no chances for effect or emotional self-indulgence. He's making sure that he has an overwhelming force built around his gate before launching his main attack. We've barely seen the beginning of this."

"What about the groups marching through the city?" Gerard asked.

Danor pointed. "Strategic positioning," he replied. "The one coming up the road toward us is setting up to prevent our escape."

He pointed again. "And if I read it right, that big group to the south will be heading for the Silver Star. My guess is that their commander is probably risking a second strike force, like the one they sent against us. He knows better than to try to take your grandfather by surprise, so he's coming after the Adventurer's Academy with a slower but stronger force."

"It's led by some kind of fire demon," Elena said. They looked at her, startled, only to find her staring with a faraway expression on her face. "Small and remarkably human-like, but incredibly powerful. Stronger even than the Captain of the Horde."

"Be careful, Mother," Gerard cautioned. "The demons may sense you scrying them."

The Queen waved a hand in dismissal. "Of course I'll be careful, Gerard," she scolded. "I'm no amateur at this, you know. Besides, the tower ward will protect me."

"Are you strong enough to link our minds again?" Danor asked. "It would help us if we could see what you do."

"Yes," she agreed. "I can."

A moment later, it was done. Danor and Gerard found their awareness projected suddenly above the city, as though they were flying over it and through the air. For a moment, everything around them became a blur. Then they settled above a force marching north into the city. It was a brigade of Hellmen warriors, Zomoran striding at its head.

Predictable, Elena thought. *They're making for the Grand Academy. Just the vanity I would expect from Emil.*

"Excuse me, Your Majesty?" a querulous voice asked.

Their shared viewpoint blurred again, and then settled behind them on the entrance to the sky dome. A young guard was standing there nervously, trying to attract their attention.

The King turned to face her, the sight of his own eyes abruptly re-asserting itself. "Yes, soldier?" he said.

"The general sent me with a message," she answered cautiously. "He said you would want to hear it right away."

Danor nodded impatiently. "Your report, then?" he asked.

The guard swallowed.

"We've conducted a thorough search," she replied. "We found the remains of a pegasus, fallen onto the ramparts. The general believes it is Princess Randia's steed. The demons appear to have attacked and killed it in flight.

"There is no sign of the princess. We cannot find her anywhere in the palace."

Chapter 5 - A Brief Respite

The Road Through the Cliffs

Randia's lungs heaved as her head broke the surface of the water. She was in a dark, high cavern with little light. The only illumination came from an opening in the vault far down the length of the cave. There, streaming sunlight shone into the darkness, reflecting weakly on the wet stone of its walls.

She blinked. Her eyes made out a few glints from the pool she had emerged in. She saw the faint outlines of shadowy shapes around her, but little else.

One of the shadows moved toward her. "Randi, is that you?" it asked.

She heard Stefan's voice and breathed a sigh of relief. He had made it safely through the submerged passage.

She swam to meet him and grasped the shadowy arm that reached out to her. It drew her out of the water. She fell onto her side on the bank.

"Are you all right?" he asked.

"Yes," she said. She took a minute to breathe deeply, trying to catch her breath.

"You were a long time," he told her anxiously. "I was beginning to think you'd gotten stuck, or caught."

She waved a shadowy hand of her own in dismissal.

"Nothing to worry about," she said softly. "I tried to hide the opening behind us. There was a large stone and some underwater plants nearby that did the trick. There was no room to turn around after, though, so I ended up having to go through the passage backwards."

She heard Stefan sigh. "You didn't leave yourself much of a margin for error," he admonished.

She shrugged. The movement was barely visible in the dim light.

"Perhaps not," she said. "But it was enough."

She slipped back into the water. "We need to get away from here," she continued. "We'll follow the cavern toward that light. The pool leads to a stream that leaves the cave there. Then it runs along a ravine between the cliff walls. Try to stay in the water as much as possible, so we don't leave a trail or a scent to follow."

"Are you sure you don't need more time to catch your breath?" he asked. His voice was still anxious.

"We don't have time for that," she said impatiently. "The demons might still find a way to follow us. I want to be well away from here if that happens."

Stefan followed her into the water. "All right," he said reluctantly. "Let's go."

They swam toward the light at the end of the cave. The pool was wide but not deep, and it wasn't long before they were wading through it toward the ravine.

The light grew steadily as they progressed. A long, narrow crack was opening in the cavern's roof. Before long, they saw the sky come into view, and could see each other again.

Stefan pointed upward. "Could the demons spot us from there, if they fly over the cliffs?"

"They might," Randia agreed. "That's one reason we need to be quick about moving on, before they give up on the pool and start searching the area. There's a whole network of ravines through this part of the cliffs. To see them, though, they'd need to fly up over the southern bluffs."

"That should buy us some time," Stefan offered. He sounded relieved.

"And this one's harder to see than the others," she agreed. "The trees and brush are thick at the top, so they'd have to be looking almost straight down. It took Windheart a while to spot it, and she has much sharper eyes than any demon."

Randia's voice caught, and she fell silent. They were wading along the center of a stream now. Lines of trees ran along the bank to either side, becoming steadily taller as they progressed. Soon they were obscuring their view of the sky above.

"*Had,*" she finally corrected herself. Her voice was barely audible. "She *had* sharper eyes."

Stefan reached out to take her hand. "Randia, I am so sorry," he said gently.

She squeezed his hand tightly. "I know," she whispered. "Thank you."

"The way she came down and attacked the demons, drawing them away from us ..." He paused, and she realized he was crying. "It was the bravest thing I've ever seen. It deserves to be commemorated in song."

"You write it," she said. "I don't think I'll ever have the heart."

"I will," he promised.

Randia picked a few pieces of fruit from the trees as they walked. She bent to wash them in the stream, and then handed one to Stefan.

"We never got to our picnic meal," she said simply. "We should eat something."

Stefan took it with a nod of thanks. It was a *leron,* a large orange fruit with a sweet and sour pulp common to northern Carlissa and Elde. He sniffed it, and then bit into it with relish. It was soft and ripe, just the way he liked them. They walked together in silence for a while as they ate.

By the time Randia led them out of the water, their view of the sky had disappeared. They were completely hidden now by a thick canopy of trees that grew around the stream. A dim light scattered through the leaves above them, illuminating their way in soft hues of brown and green. A rough path of earth and stone ran along the bottom of the ravine wall. They followed it.

The gurgling of the water faded as the stream turned away from them to their right. They continued along the rock wall on their left until they came to a shallow indentation in the cliff. Randia turned into it, and soon they were walking into a cave. She stopped them after they had gone a short way inside.

"This is the spot I was making for," she said. "We should rest here for a bit where there's still some light, and get dressed."

Stefan nodded with a wry smile. They had become so comfortable with each other's bodies during their courtship that it had slipped his mind that they were both still naked.

"We've had it easy so far," she continued. "But some of the terrain ahead is pretty rough. Without shoes and clothes, it'll be difficult and painful to get through."

She turned the device on her pack's buckle again, this time in the other direction. The straps loosened with the sighing sound of air rushing through fabric. She slipped it off her shoulders and set it on the ground.

"Let me carry that from now on," he offered.

She shook her head. "It's not that heavy. And it's about to get a lot lighter, anyway."

She drew out the clothes that Stefan had stuffed into it earlier. They were all dry, protected from the water by the buckle's enchantment. They dressed quickly and in silence.

"This cave looks very dark," Stefan offered, when they were ready to go on. "Could we use a light? Wrap some brush around a branch and make a torch?"

"We might," she said thoughtfully. She had withdrawn a small hunting knife from her pack and was attaching the strap of its sheath to her belt. "It would make us easy to spot in the darkness, though. And we can get through the cave without a light by hugging the wall on the left."

"All right," he agreed.

He looked around, took a few steps to the side, and bent down. He came up with a stout wooden branch. It was green enough not to have become brittle, and still had some small twigs extending from it.

"I'll take this anyway, just in case," he said. "It might come in handy."

She nodded and took his hand. Reaching out to touch the wall, she slowly led them deeper into the cave.

The Smiling Nymph

Orion blinked, trying to adjust his eyes to the dim illumination. It was dark in the tavern despite the bright sun outside. All the windows had been closed and shuttered, and the curtains were drawn. A scattering of candles and lanterns provided the only light in the Smiling Nymph Inn and Tavern.

He stepped out of the vestibule and glanced around. The inn was well-kept, and had the look of a prosperous business. Beams of rich, dark brown supported the walls and crossed the ceiling of the large common room. Some of them were inlaid with intricate carvings and designs. Rows of shelves occupied part of one wall, loaded with a display of ornately painted beer steins. A small stage for performers at the far corner was empty.

A group of patrons sat or stood in the room. Orion estimated nearly two dozen at a quick glance. They stared numbly at the pair as they entered, and he tried to gauge their mood. Most looked haunted or fearful, and some were quietly praying with fervent intensity.

A large, oval bar occupied the center of the room. He saw a nondescript man in a blue suit come out from behind it to meet them. The one who had let them in closed and re-bolted the door.

"Were you seen?" the man from the bar whispered.

"I don't think so," Orion answered quietly. "We came down the lane from out of the woods. They gave us cover until we reached your inn."

The man — the innkeeper, Orion guessed — didn't seem to be addressing them. He looked pointedly at the one who had opened the door.

"No," the man answered. "The sky was clear. I checked first."

The innkeeper let out a breath of relief. "Thank the gods," he said in a low voice. "Be careful, Cooper. You saw what happened to the bakery down the road when they were spotted gawking at the monsters. We don't want to end up like that."

"I *was* careful," Cooper replied quietly. Like the innkeeper he kept his voice low, despite the obvious heat in it. "I'm not a complete fool, you know. But we can't leave people out in the streets to die in this — attack, or whatever it is. It wouldn't be right."

The innkeeper sighed. "We'll do what we can. Let's just try not to get killed in the process."

He turned to Orion and Diana and held out his hand. "Jameson

Rivers, owner and proprietor of the Smiling Nymph Inn and Tavern."

Orion took his hand and shook it. "Instructor Orion Deneri," he replied. "This is Diana, one of my students. We fled into the streets when we saw a force of Hellmen advancing on the Grand Academy."

"Diana Dal Meara," Diana elaborated. She gave the innkeeper a quick curtsy.

Several patrons in the common room perked up at their introduction. A young man who had been sitting alone at a table with a large stein of ale stood up and strode forward.

"You were at the academy?" he asked. His face was bright with interest. "And it was attacked? Were you able to see what's going on in the city?"

"Some of it," Orion acknowledged. "Not much once we bolted, though. We were too busy running."

The man offered his hand to Orion. "I'm Davin Ross," he explained. "A second-year student. My family lives on Bayes Drive just down the road. I was passing the inn on my way to class when I saw the monsters flying over the city, and ducked in here."

Orion took his hand. "Good decision, Davin. If you'd kept on, you would have been caught."

"What's going on, Instructor Deneri?" an elderly woman asked querulously. Orion noted that she was dressed in conservative business attire. A shopkeeper from the street, he concluded. She was shaking, and her eyes were streaming with tears. "What are these creatures? What do they want?"

"It's a demon attack," Diana said impatiently. "They're overrunning the city. Presumably, they want to conquer it."

Another man slammed his hand on the table. "I *told* you they were demons, Jamie," he barked. His voice had a note of triumph. The innkeeper turned to look at him, and then back at Orion.

"The demons are a myth," he said stubbornly. "Fables and stories to scare children. They're not *real*."

Orion shook his head. "I'm afraid they're quite real. I don't know where this army is coming from, but it's entering the city through some kind of magical gateway."

Another man laughed bitterly. "The people have forgotten the Covenant, Jameson," he growled. "Just like you have. And this is our punishment. The gods have withdrawn their protection over the Children. We're all going to be killed because of your lack of faith."

"Now just a minute, Henry —" the innkeeper began.

"Stop it," Diana said forcefully. Her tone startled the two men, and they turned to face her.

"Arguing won't help," she said firmly, her voice low. "We need to keep calm and figure out what we can do."

"Did you actually see this gate you're talking about?" Davin asked tentatively. Diana nodded.

"It appeared in the amphitheater. A big dome of purple magic. The demons are walking and flying out of it."

"But why?" the innkeeper pursued. "Where did it come from?"

"The Hellmen marching on the academy are led by Lord Zomoran of Westreach," Orion said.

A ripple of gasps and exclamations met his words. He waited for them to subside before he continued.

"You've all heard the story about his confrontation with the princes, and the accusations that he's a demon worshipper. We think he may be the one who opened this hellgate."

The merchant woman put her head in her hands. "Where is the King?" she sobbed. "And the Queen? And the soldiers? They should be protecting us!"

"I'm sure they're doing the best they can, Else," the innkeeper said.

"We saw a large force fly toward the palace," Orion said. "I think we're on our own, at least for now."

"The Archmage can close this gate and stop them," another woman said. She looked up at Orion, her eyes pleading. "Can't he?"

"I don't know," he said. His words were gentle, but his face was grim. "I hope he can. And I'm sure he's working to find a way. If he can't, I dread to think what will happen to the city — and to us."

"So what can we do?" one of the others asked.

"For now, I would say, nothing," Orion replied. "Keep in here, safe and out of sight, as you've been doing."

"We also need to keep an eye on the city," Diana added. "Arm yourselves as best you can. And be prepared to act if something develops."

Orion nodded and turned to the innkeeper. "I agree. Master

Rivers, is there a window on your upper floor with a good view? Where we can take turns as lookout?"

"There is," Jameson said cautiously. "But it's dangerous. If we're spotted, these … demons … could decide to attack the inn."

"I'll go," Cooper put in. "I'll stay out of sight."

"I'll join you," Davin agreed. "We should keep watch in pairs. None of us should be alone in this."

Cooper nodded. The two of them moved off toward a door at the back of the room.

Diana stepped up to the bar and took a seat. She turned to Orion and patted the stool next to her.

"We may be in for a long wait," she said. "Care to buy a girl a drink in the meantime?"

Finding the Trail

Gorath rose after examining the body. It was a mere half-demon, one of the weakest of their army. It lay, broken, on an outcropping of rock that jutted from the side of the bluff. Its head had been shattered by a blow to its face.

A huge reptilian creature with membranous wings stood at its side. It stamped about restlessly on two wickedly clawed feet. Several of the flying demons that had given their reports stood around it, waiting for orders.

The demon captain looked up the slope. There were signs that the body had struck the rock wall repeatedly as it fell. Its gaze followed the line of scrapes and gore to another narrow shelf in the cliff.

It turned to one of the creatures and pointed to the spot. "That ledge up there," it demanded. "Did you search it?"

"No," it replied. "We saw no need, and we were busy trying to take down the pegasus."

"Fool," Gorath replied. It bounded onto the winged creature's back and grasped it by the neck. The steed reared in fright, but quickly settled down under the ruthless ministrations of the demon's claws.

"Follow me," it ordered.

The demon captain was large, and the wyvern labored to carry its great bulk up the slope. Gorath used the slow, spiraling ascent both to scan the cliff-side, and to survey the city. Nagoth had carried out its orders faithfully, blocking off every line of egress from the palace. The wall of demons had turned back or killed the few intrepid enough to try to flee.

It saw other signs of resistance developing. Warrior priests of the Divine were running across the church compound, desperately trying to muster their forces. Usnaroth had sent some of his winged troops to harry them. That seemed to be hampering their efforts, but it wasn't stopping them. Clerics wielding the Magic of the Covenant were striking back at the attackers. A shield of shimmering white had formed over the Cathedral, and blasts of power rising from the marshaling forces were forcing the demons to withdraw.

Gorath looked to the east. The battle demons led by the Crimson Slayer were rising through the streets and terraces of the Upper City South, destroying everything in their path. Screams echoed along the cliff-walls as the people fled before them. From beyond, he heard horns sounding from the towers of the Silver Star. The adventurers could see what was coming and were preparing themselves.

It smiled. *Let the Carlissans think they had a chance to resist. It will all be for nothing when Lord Borr springs its trap.*

The wyvern finally came level with the ledge. Gorath jumped from its back and landed in a crouch by the edge. The creature reared, beating its wings and backing away. The other demons circled or hovered nearby.

Gorath lowered its great head to the grass and inhaled — and immediately caught the odor it had expected. It moved toward the rock wall, following the scent. With satisfaction, it noted tracks in the undergrowth along the way.

The trail led to a small stand of young trees and brush growing along the edge of the cliff. It rose to its full height and forced its way through the copse. Demonic muscles rippled as it tore one of the saplings out by the roots and tossed it aside. Behind them, it saw a narrow opening in the rock.

"The pegasus was a diversion," it said harshly. "To lead you away from your true quarry, hiding in here."

The opening proved too narrow to accommodate the demon captain's great size. Instead, it grasped the rock with its powerful fingers, and began to climb. Before long, it had found the partially open roof to the glade. It jumped in, landing with a splash in the little pool.

The other demons followed and began to search. They found signs of the two lovers' presence all over the little glade: footprints, an abandoned picnic lunch, and a lute.

"As I suspected," Gorath said. "A male and a female. Human and half-elf. The glade is thick with the stink of their rutting."

It paused as it picked up the lute. "One of the royals. Probably the princess. But they're not here now, and there's no sign or scent of where they went."

The skin on the back of the demon captain's neck suddenly prickled. It turned in surprise, and a broad grin opened on its features.

Chapter 6 - The Ring of the Killravens

Blinded

"Are you sure my daughter is not in the palace?" Danor asked the messenger. Surprise and worry lined his face, and an edge of harshness had crept into his voice. The guard winced.

"Yes, Your Majesty. Her pegasus was seen flying over the palace early this morning. And her fiancé, Prince Stefan, is missing as well. No one has seen either of them since."

"That sounds like she may have gone out flying," Gerard mused. "But Stefan?"

"They took him with them," Elena said.

The others turned to her. New lines of worry had appeared on her face.

"Windheart flew off with the two of them earlier," she continued. "I was hoping they were still out of the city, and fled when they saw the attack."

Gerard's eyes widened. "She got Windheart to carry them *both*?"

"You know how convincing Randia can be when she's wheedling for something," Elena said. There was a note of gentle affection in her voice. "Windheart was becoming jealous of Stefan. Randia was trying to get her to warm up to him."

The prince nodded. "I suppose that explains how they got out of the palace without the guards marking their exit."

Elena shook her head firmly.

"Don't underestimate your sister, Gerard. She can be quite the sneak when she puts her mind to it. I'm sure she knows plenty of ways to get in and out of the palace without being seen."

The King's face settled into an angry frown. "Why didn't you tell me about this?" he demanded.

"Oh, for Light's sake, Danor," she said. Her voice was exasperated. "Your daughter was trysting with her betrothed lover. It's not the sort of thing she'd want to tell her father about. And don't look at me like that. You know perfectly well that we did the same, and *we* weren't even engaged yet."

The King subsided, coloring visibly at her rebuke. The guard went scarlet to the ears.

"How did *you* know about it then, Mother?" Gerard asked. He looked suddenly uncomfortable.

"Windheart and I had an understanding," Elena explained. "I *am* still the princess of Mount Cassandra, and heir to the Peregrine Throne. She told me just enough about Randia's activities to assuage a mother's need to know that her daughter was safe."

"Do you know where she went, then?" Danor pursued.

Instead of answering, Elena turned to the guard.

"Thank you, Daria," she said. "Tell General Banderman to keep an eye out for the princess and her fiancé. Have him send word to us immediately if there is any sign of them. You may go."

The guard saluted with fist to heart and hurried quickly away.

"Oh, and Daria?" the Queen added. The guard froze at the top of the stairs.

"Let's not mention that part about my family's … *activities*," she said gently. "I don't think anyone else needs to know about it. Wouldn't you agree?"

Daria flushed an even deeper shade of red. She nodded vigorously.

"Of course, Your Majesty," she gushed, looking mortified. "Of course!"

Elena nodded. "Thank you. Off you go, now."

She turned back to the others as Daria disappeared down the stairs. "I don't want to speak openly about where Randia might be," she explained. "The tower ward should protect us from eavesdropping, but that may not be enough. I'm going to link our minds and erect a barrier to keep anyone from reading them. We need to be certain that our deliberations are secure."

"Why, Mother?" Gerard asked. "Are you concerned about spies?"

"Yes. I sensed someone earlier trying to skim my thoughts. Furtive and cautious, and extremely skilled at the art. It's doing nothing to give itself away."

"One of the demons?" Danor queried. "The Horde Captain?"

Elena shook her head. "It might be a demon, but it's definitely not him. I know the touch of his mind from our battle. Incanus Thad is all brute force and rage. This one is much more subtle."

Gerard felt the mental ward form as the Queen completed her spell. He turned to face the King.

"All right," he said firmly. "Now that we have some extra privacy, Father, do you have something that you want to tell me? About what happened in the conference room?"

Danor looked down for a moment, and then back into his son's eyes. "Yes, Gerard," he said. There was a note of regret in his voice. "I do."

He took a deep breath. "It's a secret that your grandfather and I have kept for many years," he continued. "I was forced to reveal it to defend against the attack. Lord Rugon was right. If I had not called on its power, we would have all died there today."

He raised his left hand. The golden ring appeared once again on his third finger, its rich blue gemstone gleaming in the sunlight. He removed and held it before Gerard's astonished eyes.

"This is the Ring of the Killravens," Danor said.

Gerard examined it with fascination. "I've never heard of it before," he replied. "What does it do?"

"It is an artifact of power," Danor explained. "And it has been passed down from monarch to monarch since the beginning of our family's dynasty. Aldran himself found it in the ruins of Janthala, and tamed its power to serve our line. None but a Killraven can wield it."

"A Janthalan artifact!" the prince exclaimed. "And you used it to defeat the demons?"

"Defeat?" Danor asked. His voice was bitter. "Hardly. You saw yourself when you arrived that we were within moments of being killed. But it did give me the strength to hold them off — long enough, fortunately, for you to rally the palace defenses." A wry smile appeared briefly on his lips as he placed the ring back on his finger. "And to deliver that 'bloody nose' you mentioned earlier."

"We need to find Randia," Elena interrupted. "I'm going to scry for her."

"Yes, please do that," Danor agreed. He walked back to the edge of the platform and looked out again to the east. "While you search, I'll try to evaluate our tactical situation. Gerard, will you help me? My command of the tower's enchantment is crude at best."

"Of course," the prince replied. "I'm not nearly as skilled as Mother, but I'll do what I can."

Gerard strode to his father's side. He drew his wand, and its tip began to glow with a soft, silver magic. He swept it before him in a wide arc. The shimmering dome flared brightly where the wand passed over it, describing a large circle on its surface.

When he was done, the inscribed section of the dome shimmered. The view of the city within it blurred, and then seemed to rush forward. The image settled on the glowing hellgate, and the legions of demons still marching through it.

The King nodded in approval. At his request, the prince shifted the scene displayed in the silver portal, moving it about the city. Danor's face fell when he saw what it had to reveal.

Elena turned away. Gerard's conjuring would suffice for the King's need. Her ability to use the tower's scrying dweomer was greater than her son's, and she would need every bit of it to find her daughter. Only the spell's creator — the Archmage himself — was her equal at wielding its power.

Once again her eyes took on their faraway look, and, once again, she experienced a rushing shift of viewpoint. She found herself looking down at the palace from above.

A broken equine body lay on the palisade. The guards had covered it as best they could with a shroud of blankets, but she could see the outline of the pegasus' mangled wings beneath its contours. The cover was soaked through with blood and gore.

There's no sign of Randia and Stefan, she thought. *They couldn't have been riding her when she was killed. Unless the demons took them? But why? The enemy was out to kill the royal family, not capture it. And Windheart would never have carried them into a flight of demons. No, something else is going on here …*

She pursed her lips, frowning. *Why was Windheart here at all? She had to have seen the demons before she approached. The pegasus could have outrun them and escaped, but she didn't. She was clearly killed above the palace, but she would never have left Randia and Stefan when there was such danger at hand. Unless she had no other choice …*

Of course. That has to be it. Oh, my poor, brave Windheart!

I think Randia and Stefan are somewhere in or near the city, she said through the bond. *Too near for Windheart to have picked them up and fled, or she would have done so. Her death must have been a diversion, to draw the flying demons away from wherever they were hiding.*

She felt a surge of shock and horror from the King and the prince. *Yes, that makes sense,* Danor finally agreed.

They wouldn't have taken Windheart just to go down to the city, though, Gerard thought.

No, they wouldn't, Elena concurred. *They would have gone somewhere else. Somewhere more private.*

The Queen's sight rocketed dizzyingly along the face of Mount Cascade. *Somewhere high up, where they might have been more easily spotted by flying demons,* she thought. *Somewhere in the bluffs or up the mountain, perhaps?*

The King looked at his son. "Your mother will find her," he said.

Gerard could tell that his father's voice was trying to project reassurance. He nodded, and the two of them returned their attention to the scrying portal.

"I'm sorry that I never told you about the ring," Danor volunteered suddenly, without warning.

Gerard looked at him in surprise. He had expressed no resentment over the matter. Only now that the King mentioned it did he realize how stung he had felt at being excluded from the secret. His father had read him better than he had himself.

"Did Aron know?" he asked tentatively.

"No," the King replied. "Only your mother and grandfather knew. Your grandfather, because he is the one who gave it to me." His voice took on a note of amusement. "And your mother, because it is impossible for me to keep a secret from her. Literally."

"But you would have told him, eventually?" Gerard pursued.

"I would have passed it down to your brother in time," Danor agreed. "That responsibility must now fall to you."

Gerard started in shock. Amid the crisis of dealing with the attack, there had been no time to think about the future. Now the full meaning of Aron's death finally hit home. Not only had he lost the older brother that he had idolized since childhood, but he was going to have to take his place. *He* was now heir to the throne of Carlissa.

"Your grandfather insisted on keeping it hidden," Danor continued. "And it was hard to argue with his caution. Its existence was the most closely guarded secret of our dynasty. It was instrumental to Aldran's rise to the throne two hundred years ago."

"How does it work?" Gerard asked.

"It is an amplifier," Danor explained. "It magnifies the wielder's power, and in keeping with his particular strengths and skills."

Gerard frowned. "What do you mean?"

"Well, in my case, our family's magic manifested itself not in a skill for wizardry, but in prowess as a warrior. It would have done much the same for Aron. For you, it will undoubtedly increase your abilities with magic, and by many times."

"Was the ring the source of Grandfather's power, then?" Gerard asked. "Is it what made him the Archmage?"

"No," the King said. His voice was suddenly filled with a profound respect. "Your grandfather's mastery of the ring was unparalleled, but he rarely used it — at least, not to my knowledge. And he never did so openly. He became Archmage on his own merits. None of the works that earned him that title were achieved through its power."

Gerard nodded. The two of them fell silent and returned to their grim survey of the city.

Elena's sight was racing along the line of bluffs on the southern side of the valley. *Perhaps somewhere here?* she thought.

Flying demons patrolled the air above the city and before the cliff-wall, but she saw nothing that looked out of the ordinary. Except ... was that a knot of them, hovering over one section of the bluff? And did it look like they were searching for something?

Her mind's vision blurred again, and suddenly she was floating among the creatures. Scrying so close to them risked detection, she knew, but it couldn't be helped. Excited that she might have found a clue to her daughter's whereabouts, she looked quickly around.

She saw a demon lying on the rocks far below. Its face was caved in, sporting two arch-shaped marks. Pegasus hooves, she concluded with a grim smile. Her heart raced with anticipation.

She looked up. One demon was coming out of a narrow crack in the rock. A young tree that had been torn out by the roots lay at its side. Again, she rushed forward.

As soon as she saw the hidden glade, she knew it was where Randia and Stefan had gone. The privacy of the little pool would have made it an ideal retreat for her aquaphilic daughter, and the perfect trysting place to bring her lover. Easily accessible only from the air, they would have needed Windheart to carry them up to it. The signs of a hastily abandoned picnic only confirmed her suspicions.

Several demons were searching the chamber. One of them, a large and powerful creature with an unusually strong aura of magic, turned in her direction. With a shock, the Queen saw it held Randia's lute in its hands. With another shock, she saw it was grinning at her.

"Much too good for a common wizard," it said thoughtfully. Its voice had a harsh, grating quality, like fingernails being scraped along a chalkboard. "Or one of those spineless priests. The Archmage himself, perhaps?"

It held up the lute and, with a wicked smile, crushed it in its massive claws.

"Or the Queen, searching for her brat? Yes, that must be it. Don't worry, elf-witch. We'll find her soon enough."

Fury clouded Elena's thoughts. Her power stabbed out, and the creature's head snapped back in an explosion of sudden agony.

Before the monster could recover and strike back, though, she was gone. The little pool faded around her, and she found herself back in the sky dome. The King and the prince turned to face her. Her eyes lost their faraway look as she met their gaze.

"I couldn't find Randia and Stefan," Elena said at last. "But I found where they went. A hidden glade in the southern cliffs. The demons are hunting them."

"There are caves and ravines that run all through that part of the bluffs," Danor said. "If Randia knows them, she might evade a search for some time."

A smile touched Gerard's lips. "A hidden cave complex?" he asked. "If I know my sister, she'll have explored every inch of it. That gives me hope that she might still escape. Is there a way into or out of the city from there?"

"Some of the caves lead to openings on the side of the cliff," Danor replied. "I suppose they might contrive to climb down into the Upper City, but it would be dangerous. They'd be better off hiding in the hills."

"They can't," Elena said. "Once the demons pick up their trail they'll be hunted down, no matter how well Randia knows those caves."

"Then we'll need to find her first," Gerard said. "Mother, do you think you could do that? Maybe make contact with her?"

The Queen shook her head. "I don't dare try. One of the demons spotted my scrying. They'll be on the lookout for it now. If I found her, I might give her away to them."

"Then we'll have to trust her to make her own way to safety," Gerard said decisively.

They lapsed into a foreboding silence. Danor finally broke it by turning back to the portal.

"They'll start moving out, soon," he said grimly. "They've already marshaled an overwhelming force around the amphitheater. Their general has us, and he knows it."

The prince started. "Do you think the city is lost, then?" he asked. His voice sounded shaken.

"I don't see how we can withstand them," Danor replied. "Not against this many. When their main force attacks, it'll overrun the entire valley."

He leaned in toward the viewing port, staring at it intently.

"Can you get us closer?" he asked suddenly. "I want a look at this general of theirs."

"You don't think it's Emil?" Elena asked.

Danor shook his head. "Zomoran may call himself a warlord now, but he's no military commander. Someone else is directing this attack." He paused, and then added: "Or some *thing*."

"I can try," Gerard said. The image in the viewing port shifted, flying down toward the hellgate.

"There," Danor said suddenly, pointing. "About halfway between the dome and the marketplace."

The image slowed to a stop. In its center, they saw a demon with a snake-like head perched atop a long, serpentine neck. Its skin was scaly and its body reptilian, with long, slender limbs. Although it looked small and weak for a demon, something in its bearing — and in the deference it received from the monsters around it — filled them with dread.

"So powerful," Elena whispered.

Danor glanced at her. She was staring at the creature, but with her eyes closed, as if looking at it with an inner sight.

"I've never sensed anything like it," she said. Her voice was trembling.

Nor will you again, Queen Elena, a voice said.

They started. They had heard the voice not with their ears, but in their minds. It spoke with a cold, commanding menace that raised the hairs on the back of their necks.

The King whirled back to the portal. The demon had turned to face it from the other side. Its single, great eye was looking right at them. A shiver ran down his spine as he realized it could see them just as well as they could see it.

"By the Light, Emil," Elena whispered, in a voice filled with horror. "What *have* you unleashed on our world?"

"Who are you?" Danor demanded aloud. "What do you want?"

I am Borr, the mental voice replied. *Demon Lord of the Horde. And what I want, Danor Killraven, is your kingdom. And your death.*

The transparent ward around them suddenly flared a bright red. Elena's eyes flew open, and she staggered. Gerard's viewing port exploded in a shower of incandescent sparks. The dome went black, as though night had fallen on the city. They found themselves standing in darkness.

"What happened?" Danor demanded anxiously. "Elena, are you all right?"

"I'm not hurt," she replied. She reached out tentatively to touch the now inky surface of the shield around them.

"The tower ward is holding," she explained with relief. "The demon's spell can't penetrate it." She turned to face them, eyes haunted. "But it's blocking the dome's scrying enchantment completely. We're blind."

On the Hunt

Gorath opened its eyes. The pain in its head was finally beginning to fade.

Shaking with fury, it searched the glade for the Queen's presence. It found nothing. She had gone.

"Are you all right, Captain?" one of the demons asked.

Gorath backhanded it almost absentmindedly. It spun through the air and landed in the pool with a loud splash.

"Send for more fliers," it ordered. "Have them search this entire section of the cliffs. Have any sign of them or where they could have gone brought to me immediately."

So, I am on the trail of your brat, it thought angrily. *That much is certain now, Elena Starlight, if it wasn't before. Lord Borr will have plans for you, so I won't have the opportunity to pay you back for that insult. But I can make her suffer for it instead. And if I return with the head of a royal that escaped our net, so much the better. Especially given how spectacularly the "Captain of the Horde" seems to have botched his job at the palace.*

It grinned evilly, fangs gleaming in the rays of the midday sun that shone into the chamber from above. *Yes, this turn of events might work out quite well for me ...*

A Memory of Death

Randia probed the hard surface of the wall. The dim light from the cave opening to the ravine faded quickly, until it was little more than a dark shadow in the field of darker shadow that grew behind them. Then the wall turned a corner to their left, and the light was lost.

They walked together in darkness. Randia seemed familiar enough with the way not to pause, and led them steadily onward. After a while, though, her steps faltered. Stefan felt her hand trembling in his. Then, softly at first, he heard her weeping.

"Randi, are you all right?" he asked.

"Blackness," she said.

Her voice was barely a whisper. There was nothing in it, now, of the confident princess he knew so well. Instead, he heard a frightened girl, alone in the dark.

"It's all right, Randi," he said. He moved closer to her and slipped an arm around her waist to hold her. Her entire body was shaking uncontrollably. Her breath came in panicked gasps as she clutched at him.

"Blackness!" she repeated, sobbing. "We fell into blackness, Stefan. The pain! They tore us apart!"

The flat, purposeful efficiency that had kept her going during their escape from the glade was cracking. He caught her as her legs buckled. All the emotions she had been holding back seemed to break loose at once, overwhelming her with grief and despair.

"I'm here," he said simply. "Let it out, darling."

He held her in his arms as her tears flowed in the darkness. He stroked her hair, trying to soothe her. She cried for a long time. Although he couldn't see it, he felt her raise her face toward his when her sobbing finally began to subside.

"Thank you, Stefan," she said.

"You're welcome," he said gently.

She slowly stepped away from him.

"Can you walk?"

"Yes."

Again they clasped hands. She reached for the wall, and they continued to make their way through the cave. They walked in silence for a while, until Randia finally broke it.

"I think I'm okay now," she said firmly.

"I'm glad," he answered. "I was worried about you. I've never seen you like that."

"I was an idiot," she said. Her voice was rueful, but matter-of-fact.

"For what?"

"For holding my bond to Windheart like that. I should have known better. I almost got us both killed."

"What happened?" he asked.

"I wanted to save her. I thought that if I stayed in her mind, I could convince her not to sacrifice herself, get her to try to escape."

"I didn't know that a pegasus bond could be held that strongly. Or that far away."

"It can't," she admitted. "I'm still not sure how I was able to do it. I do know that it depends on the strength of the rider's mind and magic. Grandfather Acheron could call *Starburst* from miles away."

"Perhaps you inherited some of his ability," Stefan offered.

"Perhaps. Mother certainly did. Anyway, it caught me by surprise. I tried so hard to hold on to the bond that I lost myself in it. I couldn't separate myself from her."

"That sounds dangerous," he said tentatively.

"It is. There are stories about what can happen to a rider that shares a mount's death. The trauma can be devastating. Some never fully recover from it, are never the same again. It's even been known to be fatal."

She paused.

"I think that's why I went ... numb for a while," she concluded. "I couldn't feel anything. It was like I was watching myself from the outside. All I could think of was what to do to survive."

"You seem to be recovering now, though," he observed. His tone was worried, but hopeful.

"Blind, dumb luck," she said dismissively. She gave his hand a squeeze. "With a little help from my quick-thinking lover, of course."

"There's no harm done, then." He sounded relieved.

"I suppose not. And I'm glad she didn't have to die alone. That I could be there with her at the end."

They turned another corner. Stefan saw light streaming softly into the cavern from an opening ahead.

"Where do we go now?" he asked.

"This cave opens into another ravine," she said. "We'll follow it east, and then take another cavern through the cliffs to the north. That one will leave us on the bluffs just above the south side of the Upper City. We'll be able to climb down from there."

He stopped. She turned to face him.

"I don't see the point of taking you into the middle of a massacre,"

Stefan protested. "Couldn't we stay here, hidden in these caves and ravines?"

Randia shook her head.

"The demons are clearly after my family," she said. "And when they find the remains of our picnic, they'll start searching the bluffs. Then they'll search the ravines. If we stay, we'll eventually be trapped and captured, or killed. Besides, I have another idea."

Stefan reluctantly resumed walking. "Which is?"

There was a long pause before Randia spoke again. Stefan watched her face anxiously in the slowly growing light.

"The city is lost," she said at last. Her words came in a rush, as though she had to fight with herself to get them out. "I know a path that will bring us out of the bluffs just above the High City. From there we can travel east, and then down a long stair, to the Silver Star Adventurer's Academy."

They squinted as they walked out again into the light. Soon they were making their way along another tree-lined ravine like the one they'd followed before.

"You mean to find your grandfather, then?" he asked. "The Archmage?"

"Grandfather Killraven," she confirmed. "If anyone would have a way to survive this attack, it's him."

Stefan frowned. "Won't he go to the defense of the palace?"

She shook her head.

"That's not the way Grandfather thinks. He *never* does anything except on his own terms. What you're suggesting is exactly what the demons would want him to do. Come out in the open, so they could destroy him. That's why I'm sure it's the one thing he *won't* do."

"Then what *will* he do?" Stefan asked.

"I'm not sure," she admitted. "But the Star is probably the best defended location in the city. More so even than the palace or the Cathedral. It's not just its physical and magical defenses. An entire community of the most highly skilled adventurers on the Eastern Continent lives there. It's the safest place to go, if we can reach it. And if we *do* end up having to flee the city — and I'm sure that in the end, we will — then no one is more likely to have an escape plan than Grandfather."

"Maybe," he said reluctantly. "But it still sounds risky."

"So is anything else we might try," Randia countered. "Including trying to hide here."

"And you think it's less dangerous than making for the palace?"

She nodded. "Windheart died flying over it. She tried to reach it for safety and failed. I saw what was going on there through the bond. It was overrun with demons, Stefan. The guards were scattered and the conference room was cut off."

"Do you think the rest of your family could have survived the attack?"

Randia was silent for a long time.

"I don't know," she said at last. "But even if they did, they would still be trapped at the palace. And if they somehow managed to escape it ... I'm hoping they'll do the same thing I'm planning. That they'll try to make their way to Grandfather at the Star. Either way, there's nothing we can do to help them."

Stefan nodded. "We'll make for the academy, then," he agreed.

Randia pointed toward a thick grove ahead of them.

"We'll need something to help us climb down that last bit of the cliff from the cave to the city," she said. "There are vines growing from the trees and along the ravine walls. We should collect some."

After an hour of walking — and after they had cut and wound some of the vines together into a makeshift rope — they reached another cave opening on their left. Randia turned to Stefan before they went in.

"This is the last leg of our trip," she said. "We'll exit from an opening on the side of the bluff. It's hidden by a crag and some trees growing into the cliff-side. It'll give us some cover, and from there we should be able to see what's happening in the city."

She took his hand again and looked up at his face. "Are you ready?"

Stefan hefted the improvised rope on one shoulder and lifted his club.

"As ready as I'm going to be," he answered. His voice was determined. "Let's go."

Chapter 7 - Quest of the Archmage

The Prince's Mission

Light grew around them as the blackness obscuring the magic ward began to fade. Soon it had disappeared completely. The early afternoon sun shone once again onto the top of the tower.

The King turned to the Queen and the prince, and sighed. "I suppose we'd better head back down into the palace," he said. "The others will be waiting for us to return with orders."

Gerard shook his head. "We can't go back without a plan, Father. We still need to figure out what to do!"

Danor laid a hand on his son's shoulder.

"There is little we *can* do," he said sadly. There was a haunted look in his eyes that Gerard had never seen before. "Except brace ourselves for the next attack, and face it as bravely as we can when it comes."

"We can't just give up!" the prince exclaimed.

"Of course we can't," Danor countered. A note of stiffness crept into his voice. "But we're short of options, son. Or do you have a recommendation?"

"Right now our forces are scattered," Gerard replied, without hesitation. "We need to unite them."

He pointed down at the church grounds where they lay in the High City, south and east of the palace. "The warrior priests at the Cathedral are our nearest allies. Fighting demons is supposed to be their holy mission. We should begin with them."

"You suggest a sortie?" the King asked. "Break the blockade to join forces with the Church?"

"As a start," Gerard agreed. "But we can't stop there. We'll need the wizards at the Grand Academy and in the craftmage's guild. The adventurers in residence and training at the Silver Star. The soldiers from the army base at the eastern gate. The guard stations scattered throughout the city. Every able-bodied Carlissan who can take up arms needs to be marshaled. We have to find a way to coordinate them in a united defense."

"Going on the offensive will be risky," Danor cautioned. "If it fails, they will finish us."

"In the face of armageddon, we must be prepared to risk all," Gerard countered.

"A fair point," Danor conceded. "But that won't be enough. Not against this force."

"No," Gerard agreed. "But it *could* buy us some time. And perhaps enough time, if we can also get word to Grandmother at the Elven Citadel. She could send fliers across Carlissa to rouse the countryside. To Mount Cassandra, to the mountains, even to Rayche. The pegasus warriors will ride to our aid as soon as they know what is happening. And in the face of a demon invasion, Grandfather Acheron might even convince the mountain giants and the sky dragons to join them."

"Perhaps," the King agreed. "But how can we do any of that, trapped here in the city?"

Gerard sagged. "I don't know," he conceded. "But one thought keeps running through my mind. *The Archmage could find a way.* We need his help, Father. But where is he?"

"Exercising common sense," Elena scolded him. "Your grandfather is no fool, Gerard. If I know Lenard — and I do — he's biding his time. Studying the enemy, devising a plan, marshaling his resources, and waiting for his best opportunity to act."

"Act?" Gerard asked. "To do what? Lannamon is already in danger of falling!"

She gestured toward the center of the city.

"To shut down that hellgate," she said. "It threatens more than just Carlissa. As long as that thing is open, the entire continent is at risk. Perhaps even the whole world. He's not going to move rashly when the stakes are this high. Not with that demon lord watching and waiting for him to make a mistake."

Gerard began pacing excitedly.

"If he's developing a plan, then we need to figure out what it is. Anticipate it, try to support it."

Danor's eyes perked up at his words, and he looked casually toward the Queen. She met his gaze and nodded. Gerard was too distracted to notice the furtive exchange.

"Grandfather is clearly waiting for something," Gerard went on. "Something he needs, or needs to know, or needs to happen, before he can make his move. But what?"

"I believe I know what it may be," the King said. His voice had a cautious note to it.

Gerard looked at him with sudden interest. "What, Father?"

"The ring," Danor explained. "It would be far more effective in his hands than it ever was in mine. And I was able to use it to fight an entire company of elite demons."

Gerard's eyes lit up. "Of course!" he cried. "You said that Grandfather was a master of its power, and that he didn't even need it to become Archmage. Imagine what he could do with it now! Would he not be like a demigod, were he to wield the full force of its might?"

"I have always thought so," the King mused. "And though he never said as much, I believe that is why he eschewed using it, and bequeathed it to me as soon as he could."

Gerard frowned. "I don't understand," he said.

"Your grandfather is the greatest wizard in all of Kalara, Gerard," Danor explained. "And heir to its greatest throne. But he has always disliked the very idea of wielding power over others. That is why he was always such a reluctant king. It's why he refused the crown until he had no choice — when his brother, King Victor, was killed, and he was the last of our line."

"What does that have to do with the ring?" Gerard asked.

"It has an effect on the wearer. More so over time, and the more it is used. It ... *encourages* the temperament to wield its power to rule. That, at least in part, is what it was made for. It takes wisdom and strength of will to keep that influence in check."

"I see," Gerard said. "Has it affected you, too, then, Father?"

"To an extent," the King replied slowly. "But I spent many years under your grandfather's tutelage, studying how to rule justly and wisely. And the unique bond I have with your mother has also helped to keep me grounded."

He glanced at Elena, and she smiled at him.

"So that's why he abdicated in your favor when you were old enough to take the throne," Gerard said.

"And why he gave the ring to me when he did," Danor added. "I can't think of anyone with less of a taste for the role of 'demigod' than your grandfather."

"Surely he would use that power now, though," Gerard said. "To save the world from an invasion of demons?"

"He would, if he could reach it," Elena agreed. "And without that demon lord, Borr, springing a trap to slay him the second he came out in the open to try."

"Would it give him enough power to defeat the demons and save the city?" he asked.

"I have no idea," the King said candidly. "I don't know my father's limits. I'm not sure that even he does. But if it is at all possible, then he would be the one who could do it."

"And even if he could not, it might still give us the edge we need," the Queen added.

"How?" Gerard asked.

She nodded toward the magical ward that surrounded them. "I cannot break the demon lord's spell that blinds the tower. But with the power of the ring, Lenard could do so easily. And if he could use it to augment the tower's enchantment ... even just to scry the Elven Citadel and send a message to my mother about our plight ..."

Gerard nodded. "That settles it, then," he said, with sudden conviction.

"Settles what?" Danor asked.

"Grandfather cannot come to the palace to retrieve the ring, or he would have done so already. That means we need to figure out how to bring it to him."

"That's easier said than done," Elena observed. "There are a lot of enemies between us and the Silver Star. If he's even still there."

"It can't be a matter of fighting our way through," Gerard said. "That's what the demons want us to try. Meet them on their terms, where they have the advantage."

Elena smiled. There was a thoughtful look on her face.

"Deceit or stealth might serve where brute force fails," she offered tentatively.

Danor shook his head. "Neither of those are my strong suits."

"What about me?" the prince asked suddenly.

"I could cast a spell to cloak my presence," he explained, when they turned to face him. "While I brought the ring to Grandfather at the academy."

"Against a city full of demons?" Elena demanded incredulously. "It would never work, Gerard. Their combined magic would shred your casting long before you could make the crossing."

"But if *I* used the ring?" he pursued. "To strengthen *my* magic?"

Elena looked at him, her face torn by indecision. Danor, however, was beaming with pride. He removed the ring and held it out to Gerard.

"Put it on," he commanded. "It is not easy to control, and you will need time to get used to it. Wielding it will fill you with an immense sense of power. You can easily lose yourself in it, so be careful."

The prince took the ring and placed it on his finger. "Thank you, Father," he said gratefully. "I won't fail you."

"We will provide you with a diversion," Danor continued. "Your sortie. We will try to reach the Cathedral, and time it to distract the demons when you set out."

"He can't just walk across the city, though," Elena protested. "Not through legions of demons, hoping desperately to hold a cloak long enough to make it all the way to the Star. It's too dangerous, even with the ring. And it would take too long."

The prince shrugged. "What other choice do we have?"

A small smile appeared on the Queen's face. "I may have an idea," she said.

"What?" Gerard asked.

"I read the reports of your confrontation with Lord Zomoran. I was particularly intrigued by that levitation spell you cast to ride down from the palace wall. It's the same one you came up with for the tower lift, isn't it?"

"Yes, it is, actually. Why?"

"Do you think you could do it again? Hold it and the cloak,

together, using the ring, long enough to make it to the Star?"

Gerard turned to look out over the city. His eyes were wide.

"Do you realize what you're suggesting?" he asked incredulously.

"Fully," she said. "You'll need to cast your levitation and cloaking spells, point yourself in the direction of the Silver Star, take a running leap from the top of the tower, and ride the winds across the firth to the south side of the Upper City. Do you think you could do it?"

Gerard struggled to control a queasy feeling that began fluttering in his stomach.

"It's a thousand feet to the ground," he protested weakly. "And in plain sight of the entire city. If *either* spell failed ..."

Danor smiled. "You were saying something a minute ago, about daring all in the face of armageddon?" he asked gently.

"I can conjure a wind to aid you," Elena said reassuringly. "And I can make it look like it's intended to hamper the movements of the flying demons, so it doesn't arouse suspicion. That should help you make the crossing more quickly."

Gerard nodded. "That extra push should at least give it a chance," he said, his voice firming.

Then he paused. "I don't think I should aim directly for the Star, though," he continued at last. "I'm afraid the time and the distance will be too great. My levitation spell is easy to cast and to maintain, so that won't be a problem. The hard part will be holding a cloaking spell in the full sight of thousands of demons."

"Most of them won't be looking up," Danor said with a smile.

"That'll help," Gerard agreed. "Perhaps it *could* work, if their attention were diverted by the sortie. But every second I spend exposed will be a risk. Even using the ring."

"Where do you want to head, then?" Elena asked.

"I'll try for a closer point in the Upper City. Someplace high up along the ridge. Once I land, I can find cover among the buildings, and approach the Star from behind and above."

Danor pointed down toward the demons that were approaching the academy from below. "It'll also help you avoid that strike force," he said.

"It's a good plan, Gerard," Elena agreed. "And it has another merit that you haven't mentioned."

The others turned to face her. They saw that her eyes were glistening.

"Yes," Danor said. "If Randia tries to climb down from the cliffs, she'll re-enter the city somewhere near where you land."

"That occurred to me as well," Gerard said quietly. "I'll keep watch for her, Mother, and bring her safely to Grandfather if I can find her."

Danor walked to the parapet and looked down into the city.

"The demons are preparing to move," he said grimly. "They're forming companies to fan out from the amphitheater."

Elena and Gerard came to his side, and the Queen nodded. "Yes," she agreed. "It's starting."

The King turned to Gerard. "If we attempt this plan, then we must be prepared to act now. Are you *sure* about this, son?"

"I am," the prince answered. "Let there be no delay."

Danor reached out and folded him into a powerful hug. Openly crying now, Elena threw her arms around him as well.

"Go with all our love, Gerard," she wept. "And our hopes."

The King broke his embrace and held the prince away from him by the shoulders. They shared a long look.

"I cannot begin to tell you how proud of you I am, my son," he said earnestly. "Save yourself, and save your sister." His glistening eyes hardened. "And make these monsters regret the day they ever decided to come to our land."

Gerard gripped his arms and nodded. "We will do that together," he promised.

He turned to Elena and kissed her cheek. "I love you both."

"Then let us make ready," the King said. Without another word, he turned and strode resolutely toward the stairs to the palace below.

The Charge

"Are you certain about this, my liege?" General Banderman asked. "I'm spoiling to take the fight to these monsters as well, but it will be dangerous to assault such a large force."

The two stood in the center of the palace courtyard. Soldiers and horses geared for battle were falling into formation around them. The

King's black warhorse, Storm, stood beside him, arrayed in barding of gleaming bluesteel. Danor nodded impatiently.

"The demons are finishing their muster," he replied. "We have little time left to break the siege before reinforcements arrive. If we don't act now, we will lose that opportunity."

"But will the warrior priests stand with us?" the general asked skeptically. "The high priest has repudiated the royal family. Even now he refuses to join the sortie, declaring that he must remain here to protect the High Council. Will the Church side with us, or with him?"

"With us," the King said. "The alternative is utter defeat at the hands of the demons. They know it."

He turned to face the door to the lower level of the palace, where the Lord Inquisitor had gone to protect his charges.

"I cannot understand what has gotten into Salmanor Hardin," he added in a low voice. "He's always been pompous, and a loose cannon that's never loved the Crown. But this is strange behavior even for him. And high priest though he may be, I cannot believe that he speaks for the whole of the Church. Many defied him over the incident with Lord Zomoran and the Inquisition."

"You think they will do so again?"

The King nodded. "With even greater vehemence than before."

"I hope you are right," the general agreed. "Cyrus looked ready to kill him after the battle, and Palanad like he'd offer to help. Despite the way he's trying to cozy up to the council, he made more enemies today than he did friends."

Danor waved a hand. "That's a matter for another time. Are your forces ready?"

"Everything has been prepared in accordance with your orders, my liege," the general confirmed. "Four fifths of those who can still fight will join us in the sortie. The elite guard and I will accompany you and the Queen in the van. We will be the point of the spear that strikes toward the Cathedral."

"And the others?"

"The rest of the soldiers will follow on foot," he continued. "They will form a wedge around the wizards, who will shield their flanks and attack any demons that harry them with magic. The rest will remain to defend the castle under the command of Lord Rugon and

Mage Lantar."

The King nodded. "Very good."

"What about the prince, Your Majesty?" the general pursued.

The King shook his head. "My son has another task," he said simply. "Working magic at the summit of the tower. Give orders that no one is to go up there, and that he is not to be disturbed."

Banderman saluted and stepped away to carry out his orders. The cavalry stood mounted at attention, surrounding the royal couple. Danor turned to the Queen.

This is it, my love, she spoke in his mind. *It may be that in moments, we ride together to our deaths.*

Can I not convince you to stay at the palace? he asked. *We need a wielder to remain here and defend it, and we cannot depend on the high priest. Palanad would gladly ride with the sortie instead.*

Elena smiled. She touched his face gently with her hand.

Of course you can't, she thought simply. *Just as you would not abandon me to the demons, I will not leave you to fight without me now. We are one, lion of my heart. We live or die together. That is how it has always been with us, and it will not change now.*

The King smiled as he felt his own words touch his mind. He took the Queen into his arms and kissed her.

The soldiers around them cheered when they broke their embrace. "For Danor and Elena!" they cried. "For the King and Queen of Carlissa!"

Elena grinned at them as the King blushed. Her voice rang clear and strong as she turned to the assembled warriors.

"With such valor on our side," she cried, "we cannot help but prevail! Forth now, men and women of Carlissa! Fight for your lives and your homes! Fight for your land, your loves, your children, and all that you hold dear! Fight for your King, and the promise of all our tomorrows!"

The magic of the Queen's voice unleashed was like a flame set to tinder. Hearts swelled with courage and determination. Weapons clashed against shields. Wild cheering erupted in the courtyard.

"Death to the demons!" they cried. "For Queen Elena! For King Danor the Defender!"

Danor vaulted into the saddle, and there was another burst of cheering as the Queen mounted at his side. Her steed, Lightshaft, bore no armor, only a coat that was as white as Storm's was black. The two horses reared and whinnied as one, calling a challenge to their enemies.

"To battle!" Danor cried. "Ride now!"

The guards in the gatehouse rushed to respond to his order. Arms sent wheels spinning, and the portcullis rose swiftly above the inner entrance. The bar on the outer gate was lifted and flung aside, and the great doors opened wide.

Down the hill and just out of bowshot from the walls waited the enemy. Battle demons had arrayed themselves in a long line across the tip of the valley. Winged creatures flew over it in endless patrols. The bulk of their force was concentrated on the main road, where a branch forked from it to the south. Behind it, the Divine Way ran into and through the vast estate of the Church in Lannamon.

The demons saw the opening of the gate and jeered. They waved their weapons, jumping and prancing with glee. Their harsh voices bellowed in anticipation of slaughter.

With the suddenness of the shuttering of a lantern, the light of the sun was cut off. A storm cloud formed overhead, a dark ceiling that hovered low over the ground below the palace. Bright flashes of lightning arced within it, lighting the darkening city with sudden stabs of illumination.

Horns were raised along the battlement. The sound of their challenge rang out in a harmony of different notes, echoing clear and strong along the walls of the valley. Thunder crashed, joining the horns with a rhythm like the beating of a gigantic drum. The cries and taunts of the enemy were drowned out as the City of Rainbows was filled with their relentless song.

And in the midst of that song, the storm at their shoulder and the Queen's lightning in their wake, the King's cavalry charged through the gate to descend upon the demons that had invaded their land.

Side by side, Danor and Elena led the charge. Straight down the palace road they raced, their sights set directly on the monsters that stood between them and the Cathedral. The creatures scrambled in alarm, trying to move quickly into formation to meet the attack. Winged demons swooped in, abandoning their patrols along the line to reinforce them.

Then the storm struck. Bolts of lightning exploded from the darkening sky, striking again and again into the midst of the marshaling forces. Monstrous bodies flew flaming, scattering like leaves as electric death rained into their ranks from above.

A powerful wind sprang up, blowing the winged demons along with it. Vortices of spinning air descended from the raging storm, their widening funnels emerging suddenly from the menacing cloud to stab down and envelop their foes. Flying monsters were caught and slammed into the ground. Others careened wildly through the air to smash against the rocky walls of the valley.

In the middle of the pandemonium, the cavalry struck. Bluesteel spears lanced through the milling demons. Guardian thrust into one of the staggering creatures, piercing straight through its body.

A dozen of the enormous creatures went down in the first strike — but the enemy's line did not break.

The demons possessed magic of their own, and they brought it against the charging Carlissans. A gout of dark fire burst from the mouth of one; a knight fell, immolated. Battle demons that had avoided the cascade of lightning banded together and drove forward. Another bolt lashed down at them; it split into a dozen smaller strikes that grounded all around them, doing little damage. Flying demons buffeted by the wind dove earthward, furling their wings and rushing to join the battle on foot. Others flanked the cavalry, trying to surround them and attack from their rear.

"Mage's Fire!" General Banderman ordered. "Forward and left! Now!"

Flasks flew from the beleaguered guards. A dozen explosions rocked the earth. Creatures were blown from their feet, and fighters on both sides staggered from the blasts. A sheet of blue flame shot up among the monsters, setting some of them alight. They ran, screaming, away from the line of battle.

Danor surged forward, calling to his men. He veered right as Guardian struck off the sword-hand of a demon that had leaped into his path.

"Forward!" he cried. "To Divine Way! We must win through to the Cathedral!"

The cavalry followed. Their flank protected for the moment by the conflagration of Mage's Fire, they hit the creatures before them with the full force of another charge. More whirlwinds descended from the storm to ride at their head, trying to sweep the creatures out of their way.

But still the line of demons held.

Monsters surged forward to replace their fallen and block the road to the Cathedral. A rider was impaled on a long horn that emerged from the snout of one. She was lifted into the air and flung aside with a shake of the creature's head. Another demon, gigantic and grotesquely muscled, tore a boulder from the ground and threw it into the midst of the cavalry. It took a rider out of his saddle and crushed the warhorse of another that rode behind him.

"It's no good, Danor!" Elena cried. "We can't break through!"

"The priests aren't coming," General Banderman shouted bitterly. "We have to fall back!"

"No!" Danor bellowed. "We must hold until they arrive! It's our only hope!"

Elena gritted her teeth. She was already taxing the limits of her magic, but she tried to draw more deeply on it. A maelstrom of wind and ice whirled out of the storm above, descending into the creatures that stood in their way. Some were driven back, blinded, staggering against the arctic blast.

But still the line of demons held.

Storm reared wildly as the King slashed with his sword. Guardian slapped a red-glowing weapon aside; it missed his head by inches. The great blade struck again and again, lacerating a demon's hide and scoring its dark armor.

The monster dropped to the ground and spun in a circle. A huge, spiked tail swung out, striking the King's mount squarely in the side. The bluesteel barding withstood the spikes, but the blow knocked the warhorse to the ground. Danor flew from the saddle and landed hard on the stone road.

The tail rose to deliver a killing strike, but it never fell. The rest of the demon's body followed it into the air, disappearing into the funneled maw of a descending whirlwind of sleet.

"Retreat!" Elena cried, galloping to his side. "Defend the King and fall back!"

"Belay that order!" Danor roared. He struggled to his feet. "Stand fast and drive on!"

Another demon surged toward him. The King ran forward to meet it. Guardian swept in a wide arc, and its blade opened the creature's midsection. It staggered back with a howl of pain.

My love, we must withdraw! the Queen pleaded in his thoughts. *If we don't, we will be killed!*

If we retreat, we will die anyway, his mind answered. *Gerard was right. They will storm the palace, or burn us in. If we stand alone, we will fall alone.*

A claw slashed at him. He pivoted out of its way, and Guardian severed the wounded demon's arm at the elbow. Shields of azure magic sputtered feebly around him, and then winked out.

"The demons are suppressing my magic!" she shouted. "And the priests are not coming!"

"Not yet. But our men are!"

Elena turned to look back. The mages and foot soldiers had finally caught up with them. A surge of men at arms with gleaming pikes swarmed around them, forming a ring encircling the Queen and the dismounted King. They impaled the wounded demon and then set their weapons into the ground, bracing for another charge.

"We can hold yet!" Danor called. "We have to give the priests more time!"

The enemy was also regrouping. The storm lessened as the demons' magic combined to counter the Queen's power. The wall of Mage's Fire had burned itself out. The line of monsters, at first spread out along the tip of the valley, was converging on the King's force.

Danor could see, though, that their movements were oddly disorganized. He frowned. They could be setting the jaws of a trap for his force, but they weren't.

"The enemy doesn't have a commander here," he said. "They're just charging in blindly, trying to force us back. There's little strategy to their attacks."

"I think you're right, my liege," General Banderman agreed. He had raced to defend the King when he saw him fall, and now stood at his side. "That may give us an opportunity, if we can seize it quickly. But can we?"

The enemy's numbers were swelling as more of them reached the road. "Not on our own," Elena replied.

"Attack, while we still have a chance!" Danor cried. "With me, men of Carlissa! Forward!"

Spells erupted from a group of tower wizards. The two forces clashed, blood and ichor spraying in a heated exchange. But still the line of demons held.

And then the bells of the Cathedral began to toll.

Again and again the bells rang. Their peals echoed, clear and strong, from the hills of the Upper City. The horns at the palace once again took up their notes in response, and the valley was suddenly filled with the sound of their music.

Danor looked up toward the Divine Way. A spurt of tears formed in his eyes at what he saw.

A wave of white magic was rushing toward them along the road. Even as the demons tried to turn to face this new threat, the wall of light struck them from behind. Panicked screams of rage and pain ran along their line, as they recoiled from the blinding surge of power that had suddenly arrived to envelop them.

The Queen laughed. "For the Light!" she cried.

Her voice was a musical sound of surprise and relief that tore through the desperate mood of the Carlissans. The demons' counter-spells shattered like crystal on stone. Her magic seized control of the storm once more, and bolts of lightning descended again from the maelstrom into the monsters' ranks.

"Strike now!" Danor ordered.

Hope swelling in their hearts at the pealing of the bells and at the call of their king and queen, the troops engaged the wavering demons. Caught between the hammer of their attack and the anvil of the priests' magic, the enemy's line finally broke. Blinded by the enchanted light and their skin burning from its touch, the demons scattered, running back down the palace road toward the center of the city.

The Carlissan warriors pursued them. Several of the creatures fell, struck from behind by pikes, arrows, or magic. But the King called them to a halt and ordered them to regroup. The wave of light seemed to obey him as well, stopping to form a wall between them and the fleeing enemy.

Danor looked back up the road to the Cathedral. A long line of soldiers and priests was racing to meet them, all girded for war.

Several hundred armored cavalry galloped at their head, and many more followed behind on foot.

A tall, determined looking man in gleaming bluesteel chain mail swiftly dismounted and strode forward. When he was before the King, he dropped to one knee and placed a fist over his heart in salute.

"The Cathedral answers your call, Your Majesty," he said proudly. "We have come to fulfill our ancient duty to defend the Children from the Dark. I, Augustus Darren, Captain General of the Order of Light, pledge our forces to your command. The Church of the Divine stands with the Crown of Carlissa."

The Leap

Gerard watched the charge from the top of the tower. He had cast his cloaking and levitation spells. Now he was waiting for an opening to make his move.

His eyes shifted toward his goal. The spire of the Silver Star Adventurer's Academy rose into the sky at the end of the southern arm of the cliffs that surrounded the city. The flying demons were giving it a wide berth. A few of them had made the mistake of approaching it too closely, and been blasted from the sky by bolts of magic from its fortified walls.

None of the attacks appeared to have come from the Archmage himself, who had yet to give any sign of entering the battle. Gerard wasn't surprised. There were other wizards at the Star capable of defending it, at least for the time being. His grandfather would be busy behind the scenes, preparing a more potent response to the horde's attack.

Levitating across the city from the top of the palace tower meant flying almost lengthwise along the line of the firth. Once he jumped, he would be driven by momentum and the Queen's wind, and would have little control over his movements. If he misjudged, he would crash into the cliff-walls at the southern end of the city.

The desperate plan had seemed daunting earlier. Now Gerard felt an almost reckless sense of confidence about it. It was unlike anything he had experienced before, and he knew it must be coming from the ring. He felt its magic flowing through him, filling him with almost unimaginable power. The feelings were every bit as intoxicating as his father had warned, but he was having some success in controlling them. He reminded himself sternly to keep his mind on guard.

He looked down. The battle demons advancing on the Star were climbing the terraces into the southern arm of the Upper City. If they moved too quickly, they could scuttle his plan. If he didn't make his jump soon, they might cut him off.

He looked up to gauge the position of the flying demons. He smiled when he saw what he had been waiting for. Most of them were moving to intercept the attack from the palace. For now, at least, his path across the center of the city was almost completely clear.

A stab of worry for his parents derailed his thoughts. The demons converging on the road to the Cathedral would overwhelm their charge. The power sang in his mind, and he suddenly found himself abandoning their entire plan. He would adjust his jump instead to come to their aid. He would drop from the sky into the midst of the enemy, using the ring to summon a rain of starfire to slaughter them …

Gerard shook his head. *That would be madness*, he told himself sternly. He might turn the battle for a time, but he couldn't save the city. He needed to get the ring to his grandfather. The Archmage could use it to bring down starfire a hundred times more powerful than anything he could manage.

Defying the raging emotions that flowed through him, he forced himself to remember his limits. *Stick to the plan*, he scolded himself ruthlessly. He turned once again toward the far side of the city and set his eyes on his goal.

Then he was sprinting toward the edge of the platform. He felt a brief tingling sensation as he passed through the ward at the top of the tower, and then he was soaring through the open air above the palace.

Chapter 8 - A Hope of Escape

Descent to the Upper City

Randia rappelled quickly down the surface of the cliff. The bundled and twisted vines slid wetly through her hands and left a slick coat of green slime on her palms and fingers. Her feet expertly pushed off from the bluff in a series of quick leaps and stops. In less than a minute, she had descended from the narrow ledge to the top of the tower below.

Stefan watched her with apprehension as she released their makeshift rope and jumped onto the building's roof. Its pitch was steep, and she had to lean forward and grab at the tiles to keep from falling. The vine-rope, one end tied to a boulder high above, dropped away from her to slap hard against the wall of the bluff. It had held the pair's weight better than she had expected.

The angled roof had a gabled window that faced the valley. Stefan was crouching next to it, holding on to the frame for support. Randia scrambled carefully to his side.

The tower rose along the cliff-wall from the highest level of the Upper City South. From its summit, they could see the whole of Lannamon in the valley below. Companies of battle demons were forming, preparing to move out from their base in the amphitheater. Randia pointed.

"The winged demons are moving," she whispered. "It looks like they're setting up to fly cover for those infantry squads. The sky is clear here, at least for now."

"Another stroke of luck," Stefan agreed softly. "Let's hope it holds up."

He turned to the gabled window and tested it. It was locked, but the shutters were open. Through it, they saw a man dressed in the livery of the city guard. He was standing a few paces back and staring at them. He looked frightened.

Stefan smiled at him and tapped the glass. "Hi," he said cheerily. "We're a bit lost. Do you think you could let us in, and give us directions to the nearest archmage?"

The man shook his head, eyes wide. Then he turned and bolted from the room.

"Wonderful," Randia groaned. "We'll have to try to get in ourselves. I don't want to break the glass if we can help it, but we can't stay out here."

"What do we do, then?" Stefan asked.

She grinned. "I did tell you I picked up a few spells over the years, didn't I? Performer's tricks, mostly. But I also have a bit of a sneaky side. If you haven't figured that out yet."

"I would never have imagined," he said in mock surprise. "Do you have something to open the lock?"

She didn't answer. Instead, she focused her eyes on the sash bar inside the window. Then she summoned the Magic, in the way that her brother Gerard had taught her. The bar began to move slowly, sliding up and away from its locking position. Before long the task was done, and Stefan was lifting the window open. They climbed quickly inside and shut it behind them.

They turned to look at the room. It was a large, circular chamber, and appeared to be a study of sorts. Books, tables, and chairs were set haphazardly around it. At the far side, a stairway climbed down through the floor along a curved wall.

Standing before that stairway were half a dozen of the city guard, weapons drawn and bows nocked. They were aimed directly at them. Randia lifted her hands slowly.

"Don't shoot," she said. "We're no threat. In fact, we need your help."

"Don't let them speak!" one of the men cried. His voice sounded panicked, and they recognized him as the guard who had fled the room earlier. Fortunately, he wasn't one of those holding a bow on them now. "They'll put a spell on us!"

Stefan glanced at Randia. "They think we're demons," he said cautiously. He raised his hands as well.

She nodded. "Of course. And small wonder. As far as they can tell, we just appeared out of nowhere on their roof!"

"Didn't you?" the nervous guard asked.

"No," she said. "We were hiking in the ravines behind the bluff. We climbed down from an opening in the cliff-wall."

"And right into a company of the city guard, it seems," Stefan added.

"This must be one of the towers on the south side," she agreed.

"Another stroke of luck," Stefan noted. "Assuming they don't shoot us."

One of the guards wore a lieutenant's insignia on her shoulder. Flaming red hair in a short cut framed a face with copper skin and alert brown eyes. She looked at them intently.

"I don't think they're demons, Will," she said, lowering her bow. "In fact, I think ... Princess Randia, is that you?"

Randia heaved a sigh of relief.

"Yes, it is," she said. She nodded toward Stefan, her hands still raised. "This is my fiancé, Prince Stefan. As I said, we need your help."

The lieutenant slid the arrow over her shoulder and back into her quiver. "Stand down," she ordered.

She took a step forward and dropped to one knee, laying her bow on the ground at her side. The others, surprised, quickly followed her lead.

"Lieutenant Clarissa Kay, Your Highness," she said formally. "Ranking officer of Guard Post Twenty-Three. My soldiers and I are at your command."

Escape Plan

"Would you like another, My Lady?" Jameson asked.

Diana shook her head. "No thank you, Master Rivers. One to calm my frazzled nerves was quite enough."

She smiled at Orion's look of relief. Her first round had brought on a bout of mortified stammering from the young scholar. It appeared that buying a drink in a bar for a teenage student he'd just met had sorely tested his sense of propriety. She'd insisted, finding herself unable to resist teasing him. She turned to look at him now, eyes still twinkling with mischief.

"It would be tempting to get very drunk today, but it might not be a good idea," she elaborated.

The innkeeper looked at Orion, who shook his head hastily.

"None for me, either," the young scholar said earnestly. "We should keep a clear head in case we need to act."

She turned to hide her grin as the innkeeper took her glass and wiped the bar. There seemed to be many sides to her companion. Lecturing to a class, or even reacting to an unexpected crisis, he was decisive and confident. She was certain from his surprising command of etiquette that he'd been trained at court. Yet despite that, he could revert unexpectedly to a shy and awkward scholar.

"You're waiting for something," she said pointedly.

Orion nodded.

"The Archmage. He won't let the city fall without a fight. When he acts, we'll need to be ready."

"What will he do?"

"I wish I knew. Whatever it is, though, it will be something that no one expects."

"It sounds like you know him well. Did you study with him long?"

He shook his head.

"Not well at all, actually," he admitted. "I was only there for one year. He made it a point to guest lecture at least once in all the first semester courses, though. To get to know the new students. He was always looking for sparks of talent. Everyone was on their best behavior when he came to class, trying to impress him." He chuckled. "Almost no one ever did."

Diana smiled. "But *you* did?"

"I wasn't trying to. I had no time for it."

He paused. The look on his face was thoughtful.

"He told me later that was what caught his attention," he said at last. "He said he could see that all the other students were trying to figure out what to say to score points with him. I was giving my full attention to just trying to understand him. I didn't raise my hand once during the whole class, and that certainly wasn't normal for me."

"You were his student, then?" the innkeeper asked. He had overheard their conversation and was standing near them behind the bar. His eyes were attentive.

Orion nodded. "When the class was over, many of them lined up to ask him questions. He waved them off, telling them he had no time for them. They were very disappointed."

Diana leaned forward, intrigued. "Then what happened?" she asked.

"I was walking toward the door when his voice suddenly called out: 'Hold a moment, Mr. Deneri. I'd like a word with you.'" He paused again. "It's hard to convey what that was like to anyone who's never heard him in full character."

"I have," she said. "Though only once. My father's been the Dorian ambassador for the last year, and I've spent much of that time at the Carlissan court. He made certain I met everyone there that he considered important."

"So you know what I mean," Orion said. "He could be very kindly at times, though I only discovered that later. But when he means business, he's more intimidating than anyone I've ever met. He made it clear that no one else was welcome to remain, so the rest of the class — my instructor included — scattered."

"He wasn't angry with you, though?" Jameson asked.

"Quite the opposite. Once we were alone, he started asking me questions. He seemed to know exactly what I'd been working through in my head during his lecture, because he started right at the beginning and took me through my entire chain of thinking. Some of his questions were new ones that I hadn't had time to consider, but I saw their implications at once and started following those threads as well."

"That sounds amazing," Diana said. Her eyes were shining with interest. "What were you talking about?"

"It was a technical topic about the nature of magic. I couldn't explain it now without a two-hour digression just to set the context. But I'd studied the philosophy of magic, and I knew enough to understand where his questions were leading."

"That must have been frightening," Jameson said. "How long did it last?"

Orion shook his head. "It wasn't frightening at all. We talked for nearly two hours. I spent the rest of the day and evening feverishly writing notes."

"So that's how you became his student?" she asked.

He shook his head. "That came later, when he was scheduled to teach an advanced class on magical theory. That was in the fall semester. He taught rarely, and whenever he did, registration was by invitation only. When I received mine —"

The braying of horns cut off his story. Orion turned from the bar and cocked his head, listening. The sound was distant, but it rang clearly, carrying along the walls of the valley. Heads perked up in the gloomy common room. Expressions of hope emerged cautiously on some of their faces.

"That sounds like it's coming from the palace," Jameson ventured. His voice sounded tentative.

A crash of thunder followed, rolling and echoing through the hills around the city. Then they heard pounding feet rushing down the stairs. Davin came stumbling into the common room, eyes wild with excitement.

Orion shot to his feet. "What's happening?" he demanded.

"The King!" Davin said. "At the head of an army of knights, charging from the gates of the palace! The Queen rides with them and calls lightning down on the enemy!"

A cheer exploded throughout the common room. The merchant woman began weeping softly.

Diana grinned. "About time," she said. "We should prepare. If a battle is about to start, we should be ready to do what we can."

She turned to the innkeeper. "Master Rivers, do you have a knife I can use?"

He nodded as he drew a sword belt from beneath the bar and began strapping it on. "Take whatever you can use from the kitchen. The rest of you, too. Anyone who wants to arm himself. This may be our chance to strike back at last!"

Orion looked around the room, and then turned to the innkeeper. There was a worried expression on his face.

"I agree we should arm ourselves," he said. "But I think we should be cautious. The King and the elite guard are valiant, but even with the Queen's magic, I don't believe they have the strength to repel an attack of this size. The most they're probably going to accomplish is to drive it back temporarily."

Diana frowned. "You're not giving up, are you?" she said.

"Of course not. But just running out to join the battle will only get us killed. We need a plan. A *realistic* one."

"What do you suggest, then?" Jameson asked.

Orion paused.

"A charge from the palace should draw away most of the flying demons," he said at last. "It'll give us an opening to make a break to the east."

"You want to flee?" Diana asked. Her eyes were narrowed and accusing.

"We can't accomplish anything here," Orion countered. "The demons will just slaughter small pockets of civilians like ours when they march into the city. We'll need to join up with a larger force to be effective."

Davin nodded in agreement. "That makes sense. Where do we go, then?"

"There's a military base near the outskirts of the city. If we can reach it, there should be protection for those of us who can't fight." He stole a glance at the elderly shop owner. "And for those of us who can, there will be weapons, and some strength in numbers. At least we could reinforce the garrison there. We can't do any good here."

The others fell silent, considering his words. Diana faced him, eyes smoldering with frustrated anger.

"I want to strike back, too," he told her gently. "But we can't. Not now, not from here. And I don't think King Danor would want us to throw our lives away in a futile gesture of support. He'd want us to live long enough to strike a blow that made a difference."

"That might even be part of the reason for the charge," Davin added. "To draw the demons toward the palace, and give people trapped in the city a chance to retreat and regroup."

Orion nodded. "That thought had occurred to me as well."

Diana let out a long breath. "I suppose you're right," she said at last. Her words came out slowly and with difficulty. "I'll go upstairs to tell Cooper the plan. I want to have a good look at the city myself. If we do get a chance to make a break for the army base, then I guess we should probably take it."

Diana sprang quickly up the stairs, taking them two at a time. Orion turned to the innkeeper.

"Let's see about those weapons, Jameson," he suggested.

The minutes passed swiftly as the group armed themselves with whatever they could find. Most of it turned out to be long knives from the kitchen. A quarterstaff, a few clubs and a pitchfork rounded out their makeshift arsenal.

When they were almost ready, Orion noticed that the old shopkeeper hadn't moved from her seat near the wall. She was still sobbing weakly. Her face was exhausted and drained of color. She looked up and saw him watching her.

"I'm not going with you," she said softly. Her voice was resigned. "I'm staying here."

"It won't be safe, ma'am," Davin said.

"I don't care. It's not safe out there either, whatever you say. I'm an old woman, and I don't have the strength to run halfway across the city."

"We'll help you," Davin offered.

"No," Henry cut in. He walked across the room and sat down at the woman's side. "Else is right. It's the Day of Judgment, and we won't scurry for our lives in desperation to escape our sin. When the demons come, I'll meet my end here, and I'll do it with dignity."

"There's nothing dignified about being torn apart by rampaging monsters," Orion said. "Is that really how you want your life to end?"

The old woman smiled and patted Henry's hand. "We will pray together for mercy from the gods. From Lady Tianth, and from Lord Akun, the all-seeing. That they may witness our faith and rescue us — or take our souls to join with the Divine."

"We can't force you —" Orion began.

The clanging peal of the Cathedral bells rang out suddenly. The horns from the palace joined them in a cacophony that echoed throughout the valley.

Diana flew down the stairs and into the common room at a run. "You were right!" she cried.

She raced up to Orion and threw her arms around him. Her eyes were alight, and a broad grin split her face. He caught her arms and tried to push her gently away from him, but the effort failed completely.

"Right about what?" he asked. His voice sounded awkward.

"Joining forces! Don't you hear the bells?"

Orion looked at her, his eyes still a question. After a moment, she seemed to realize what she was doing. She stepped back and let go of him, trying to compose herself.

"Oh, of course, you can't see it from here. The King's force won through to the Cathedral. The warrior priests are riding out to meet them. There's a wall of magic cresting at their head like a wave. It's sweeping the demons before them!"

Another cheer ran through the common room as Cooper came down the stairs, slinging a bow and quiver over his back. Davin stepped forward and clapped Orion on the shoulder.

"It's just as you told us," he said. "Divided we die, but together, we have a chance. The King will unite us, one group at a time — starting with the Church!"

Jameson turned to the pair at the table. "Do you still want to stay here?"

Henry looked at the old shopkeeper, and she nodded.

"The charge will fail," he replied. "The priests are at the head of the corruption, and the gods won't heed their call. We will wait here, and pray for redemption."

Diana's eyes narrowed.

"That's crazy," she said indignantly. "The worthy are those who fight for their lives. They don't sit and wait to die."

The others started, and the shopkeeper flinched at her words. Davin grinned in appreciation. Orion studied her, trying to understand her sudden outburst. Henry, however, only stared at her, unmoved.

Orion sighed. "We can't force them," he said. "And we don't have time to argue."

"He's right," Cooper said. "We need to go now."

"Where?" Jameson asked. "Toward the Upper City, to help the King?"

Diana turned her back on the pair at the table.

"We'd never make it," she said. Her voice was harsh. "The demons may be retreating from the priests right now, but there's still an entire army of them between us. Orion is right. We need to go down to the Lower City and east to the army base."

Cooper nodded. "From upstairs, we could see groups of people coming out of hiding to do the same. Most of them are running east along the firth. Even the guard stations are emptying."

"They're abandoning their posts?" Davin asked. He sounded surprised.

"I would," Orion said. "When the demons turn this way, an isolated company of guards isn't going to even slow them down. If they regroup with the main force, they'll at least have a chance of forming a line and holding it."

"Then we stick to the plan," Diana agreed. "Join the soldiers, and help when they're ready to drive against the enemy."

The others nodded. Orion cautiously opened the door a crack and peeked through.

"The streets and sky look clear for the moment." He hefted the club he'd made from a table leg and rested it on his shoulder. "Let's go — now!"

Prince in Flight

The first few seconds of Gerard's flight were a blur of spinning and panic. He struggled to bring both under control.

As he'd expected, his levitation spell was holding. As he'd also feared, the force of his sudden jump had upended him. The unpredictable gusts that blew along the slopes of Mount Cascade weren't helping.

He braced himself, waiting for his somersaulting to come under control. One of the first things he'd had to design into his spell was a stabilizing component. Without it, levitating objects would do just what he was doing now: tumble uncontrollably once they were suspended in the air. The dweomer was doing its work, but with maddening slowness. He waited through a seemingly interminable period of dizziness and disorientation, fighting to keep down a wave of nausea.

Finally, he stopped spinning. A steady wind at his back replaced the gusts near the mountainside as he moved out over the city. That was his mother's spell, driving him on toward his goal. He could see it ahead in the distance: a far line of cliffs that rose above the south side of the Upper City.

He looked down. A brief wave of vertigo gripped him at the sight of the earth far below, but it faded quickly. He was an experienced Pegasus rider and accustomed to flying high above the ground. His mother had insisted on that, bringing her entire family to her homeland in the Nurian Mountains to learn the ways of the Sky Elves and their winged partners.

He tried to get his bearings. The hills at the western end of the valley were already dropping away below him. He was easily a thousand feet above the valley now, and his altitude increased as he approached the lower ground around the firth. The speed he was moving at surprised him.

He turned to observe the battle behind him. A surge of pride ran through him as he watched his parents driving relentlessly forward, fighting against seemingly impossible odds. He saw the warrior priests' hasty muster at the Cathedral gate. He watched as they summoned their magic, and began their charge down the Divine Way as the bell-boys raced into the towers to grab the ropes and sound the toll.

He forced himself to look away. His parents would be all right. They had their mission, and he had his. The air before him was almost empty of demons. His way across the city was clear.

He looked down. He was passing almost directly over the hellgate, where the demons were marshaling around the tip of the firth. The ground below was thick with the massing army. What he saw made him queasy with despair.

He couldn't count the creatures, but there seemed to be many thousands of them. They had overrun the amphitheater and were spilling into the surrounding streets. And they were doing it with a ruthless efficiency that belied the stereotype of demons as rampaging and impulsive monsters.

He frowned. Their conduct bespoke a military training, and a discipline long lost to the demons of Kalara. He fell to studying them, hoping to bring some useful information about the horde when he reached the Archmage.

The Hellmen were smaller than the rest. They were roughly human sized, and easily recognizable by their characteristic red skin and red and black armor. There seemed to be thousands of them, collected into their own battalions, apart from the rest of the invaders.

The demons were a mixed lot. Even the smallest and weakest, he knew, would be a match for several skilled soldiers. The elite demons were the most powerful and least numerous. He saw hundreds of them, scattered throughout the host in what looked like positions of leadership.

Most imposing were the battle demons. Large, muscular, and physically powerful, these armored juggernauts could overwhelm and break nearly any opposition. Even one looked to be a match for a full squad of soldiers. His breath caught when he saw a company of them running toward the palace road.

He started to examine the forces around the tip of the firth, but thought better of it. He knew that some of the more powerful demons could sense being watched or scried, and he had already tempted fate more than he should have. His cloaking spell was still holding, but he could feel the never-ending pressure of the demons' magic threatening to penetrate it.

He heard the tolling of the Cathedral bells — and soon after, felt the rush of his mother's wind strengthening at his back. Smiling, he turned his gaze toward his goal, and settled himself for a long wait. Even with the wind's help, it would take a while to complete his journey.

To his surprise, he found himself rising. Updrafts had developed in the high airs from the ebb and surge as the Queen and the demons battled for control of the storm. He shrugged. He'd have to take care not to overshoot the southern bluffs, but he could compensate for it.

He looked to his right and frowned. He had expected to see the countryside to the south above the level of the cliffs. The foothills of the Eldar Mountains receded slowly into the distance there, dotted with small towns and villages. Their many vineyards made the region a well-respected producer of fine wines. The hills eventually faded out, giving way to the dense forests of northern Carlissa.

The day was clear. From this height, he should have been able to see as far as the border of the forestland. Instead, all he could make out was a wall of low-hanging clouds. They hovered over the hills, dark and menacing, obscuring his view of the countryside.

He glanced behind and saw that this couldn't have been from his mother's conjuring. She had summoned a single, large thunderhead that rose over the High City, around and above the palace. It billowed many thousands of feet into the sky, looking like great wads of cotton piled high on top of each other. Bolts of lightning lanced down from it at irregular intervals, followed by peals of booming thunder. But it was isolated, tucked for all its height and fury neatly into the shadow of Mount Cascade.

The clouds to the south, though, were hanging low to the ground. Perhaps if he were to rise a bit, he could make out more about them from above …

His frown deepened as he adjusted his levitation spell to carry him higher. He wasn't certain that was a good idea, but he found himself fighting a feeling of dread that he couldn't shake. He kept his eyes trained on the cloud bank as he rose, and saw that it wasn't just sitting over the foothills. It was moving, edging quickly around the bluffs. And he could see the trail it had taken. Wisps of mist were burning away in the shape of a long, dissipating tail that went its way along the southern arm of the Eldar Mountains.

He squinted, looking directly ahead. An arm of clouds had emerged from the bank. Its leading edge had already passed the city's eastern outskirts. It was turning slowly northward, working its way around the City of Rainbows.

Gerard's blood ran cold.

He looked left. Another bank of clouds was working its way around the city on the other side. Before long, the two arms would meet, surrounding Lannamon in a ring of fog.

With a sinking feeling, he finally recognized the clouds for what they were: a spell storm. They weren't as tall or as violent as the thunderhead his mother had called, but they were similar magic. Unlike hers, however, they weren't being used as a weapon. They were a cloak.

The cloud walls passed the end of the bluffs and came together in a dark mass. Gerard stared at it. It seemed to be tinged with a reddish haze, brightening and dimming, as though flames were erupting and subsiding in its heart. And he could just make out shadowy forms circling inside the brume, large and winged ...

At last, he understood.

The demons at the hellgate were not the only invasion force coming to Carlissa. The monster that he and Aron had faced on the day of Zomoran's rampage was not the only one of its kind among the magus' allies. The flame dragons and the fire giants, long ago banished to the blasted mountains of the north and west, were returning to their ancient war with the men and elves of the Eastern Continent.

Gerard closed his eyes, and his head sagged in defeat. With a surge of despair, he knew in his heart that Lannamon, City of Rainbows, was truly lost.

Chapter 9 - The Hammer Falls

The Trap is Sprung

A long line of warrior priests marched down the road from the Cathedral. The Knights of the Light had already reached the King and Queen and formed a hastily assembled guard around their position. They were the elite of their order, mounted warriors with great skill at arms and strength in the Divine Magic. The wall of white fire that routed the demons had been their conjuring, driving like a wave before them as they galloped in to attack.

"Your arrival could not have been more timely, Captain General," Danor said. He clasped Darren's arm. "The Crown welcomes your aid with all its heart."

"It is my duty and my honor, Your Majesty," he replied. "Together, perhaps we can finally strike a blow against these monsters!"

The Queen embraced him and kissed his cheek. "Thank you, Augustus," she said. Her voice was thick with emotion. "We were despairing of anyone coming to help."

"All except the King," General Banderman said. His voice rang with pride and admiration. "He kept driving us on, still believing when the rest of us had lost faith."

Augustus Darren bowed his head. The others saw with surprise that there was a look of shame on his face, but anger burned brightly in his eyes as well.

"I deeply regret the delay, Your Majesty," he said. "There was a …

disagreement among the leadership at the Cathedral about what action should be taken."

Elena frowned. "What happened?"

"The high priest left orders that the Church would no longer render support of any kind to the Crown," Darren explained. General Banderman suppressed an oath. "Some of the senior clergy insisted on obeying that order in the most dishonorable way possible."

Danor glanced at the Captain General's normally immaculate armor. It was stained with blood. "I take it that disagreement has been resolved?" he asked.

"It has. The cowards have been dealt with. As Captain General of the Order of Light, I have assumed leadership of the Church of the Divine in Carlissa. I now command its forces in the city. They *will* rally to your banner."

Banderman shook his head, and his face was livid. "When I get my hands on Salmanor Hardin —" he began.

Darren cut in before the general could finish. "You should know, Your Majesty, that it is my intention — if we survive this battle — to place the high priest under arrest for treason against the Covenant. He will face the judgment of his own inquisition."

Elena's eyes widened. "You suspect him of betraying us? Of being in league with the enemy?"

Darren nodded. "To leave such an order, right before a demon attack on the palace? It strains credulity to believe that a coincidence."

Danor shook his head. "Why did he prosecute Zomoran for heresy, then? That makes no sense."

"Zomoran?" Darren asked. "Is he involved in this as well?"

"He leads an army of Hellmen to take the Grand Academy," Elena said. "We also believe him responsible for the hellgate allowing the demons to enter the city."

"He has allied himself with a powerful demon lord named Borr," Danor continued. "Emil Zomoran is behind all of this. The Captain of the Horde even declared the invasion in his name."

Darren's eyes narrowed. His face was hard.

"So this attack is his doing," he said. "Another traitor to be brought to justice —"

"Your Holiness!" a voice cried.

Darren stopped, turning. A young courier in the livery of the Order of Light was forcing his way through the crowd. When he reached them, he fell to one knee.

Darren nodded to him. "Rise and report, Kal," he said briskly.

Kal rose swiftly to his feet. "Major Dennis sends word. His lookouts have spotted a large force of battle demons. They're headed this way. At least a hundred of them. He believes they intend to break the charge and repel it — back to the Cathedral, or to the palace. Or both."

"How long?"

"Ten minutes at most, sir."

Darren turned to the King. "We will need to array our forces, my liege. And quickly. Can your wizards flank the monsters on the north?"

General Banderman nodded. "The palace guard can cover them, as before. The warrior priests can take the south."

Elena was looking intently to the east. "Danor ..." she said tentatively.

Darren nodded to the general. "And the knights — yours and mine— can take the center. We'll surround their force and crush it!"

Danor frowned. "This is a tactical blunder on their part. And coming from this demon lord, it surprises me. A hundred battle demons are a formidable force, but it's not enough to break our charge. He's sending them right into the jaws of an easily set trap."

"Danor," Elena said again. Her voice was louder this time, and more insistent.

He turned swiftly to face her. "What is it, my love?"

They all looked as she pointed. In the distance, they saw two masses of roiling clouds moving in across the firth. Like enormous doors of dark grey, they seemed to be sliding slowly closed, shutting out the rest of the world. Red lightning flashed within them, lighting the sky with a glow of hellish light.

"It may not be such a miscalculation," she said slowly. "Those clouds have been surrounding the city while we fought."

"Why?" Banderman asked.

"To conceal a second attack force."

Darren nodded. "I think the Queen is right," he said tightly.

"Why?" Banderman asked again. "What makes you so sure?"

Darren's lips drew into a thin, grim line. "Have you ever fought a dragon, General?" he asked.

Banderman shook his head. His face had gone suddenly pale.

Darren pointed. "That glow in the clouds … it's dragon fire, if I've ever seen it. And I have."

"By the Light," the general whispered.

"This isn't just an invasion of demons," Elena said. "Zomoran's gathered the remnants of the Dark to lead against us as well. He's trying to undo the Taming."

The Guards of Company Twenty-Three

Randia watched as Lieutenant Kay opened the door to the guard tower and peered out. She heard the clash of battle in the distance, but there didn't seem to be any fighting nearby. The ringing of the Cathedral bells carried through the city, along with the sounding of the palace horns.

Kay turned to look over her shoulder. "I think the warrior priests have joined the battle," she said. "That'll draw even more of the creatures away from here. We should be clear, at least for now."

Randia nodded. A tear ran down her face as she listened to the sounds from the city.

"That'll be my father at their head," she said. "No one else would have the courage to lead a charge against an army of demons."

"You think your family survived the attack on the palace, then?" Stefan asked tentatively. His tone was hopeful.

She nodded again. "Mother, for certain. She has Grandmother's command of the elements. Those thunderclaps are hers, calling a storm down on the enemy."

"And the horns from the palace sound the King's Call," Kay agreed. "With help from the Cathedral, he might drive through the blockade."

Stefan pointed.

"He might, if he's swift. See? Most of the demons are still mustering around the amphitheater. They're only moving out now, to take and control positions within the city."

"That gives us a window of opportunity," Kay agreed. "But we'll have to move quickly. What is our mission, Your Highness?"

"We need to reach the Silver Star Adventurer's Academy," Randia replied. "And the protection of the Archmage."

"That may not be safe," one of the soldiers said cautiously. "There's a large force of demons moving through the city below us. We could see them from the tower. They look like they're headed for the Star as well."

Randia and Stefan exchanged glances.

"Do they think they can take the academy?" he asked. He sounded skeptical.

Randia shook her head. "If they have the power to do that, then we're all doomed."

"It doesn't matter much either way," Stefan said. "If they're cutting us off from reaching him."

"I don't think so," Kay said. "The demons are climbing up from the Lower City. We can cut along the terrace behind us, and then down the stairs at the eastern end of the bluff. That'll let us reach the Star from above."

"Shouldn't we strike west, though?" Will asked. "If the King and Queen and the priests are all driving toward us, shouldn't we try to bring the princess to them?"

"It's too risky to take her into a battle zone," Stefan said flatly. "Her plan's the right one: get her to the protection of the Archmage."

Kay's eyes hardened as she looked at the young soldier. "And that's leaving aside the fact that those aren't our orders," she told him. "The princess is in charge here. You don't speculate on what's best for her. She decides, and you carry out her commands." She raised her eyebrows. "Clear?"

Will's face turned white. He saluted hastily. "Yes, Lieutenant," he said.

"All right then," Kay said. Her voice rose as she called out orders. "Kenn and Jean scout ahead, right and left flanks. Go."

Two soldiers ran out the door and disappeared onto the road outside.

"The rest of you: escort formation," she continued. "The prince and princess in the center. Nothing gets near them that hasn't gone through you first." She pointed to two men with bows. "Archers with me at their side. We go to work if the ring is broken. We give the scouts a ten count, and then hoof it."

The seconds ran by quickly as she counted them down. Then she glanced at Randia. The princess nodded.

"Okay — Guards of Company Twenty-Three! Move out!"

One after another, the soldiers ran through the door into the street. Randia and Stefan went next, followed by Kay and her archers. The group fell quickly into formation and ran along the road to the right.

As they expected, the sky and surrounding roads were clear. Randia couldn't see the force that was moving on the Star, but knew it was at least two terrace levels below them. For the moment, it was no threat.

The scouts led them expertly through the Upper City to the east, picking a route to keep them out of the open as much as possible. They cut through a row of hedges, across the yard of an estate, and under the boughs of a small copse of woods. They dashed through a small park, fording a stream that ran through it. Randia glanced down and saw that it fed just below them into an artery of the city's vast system of aqueducts.

They finally stopped in a small glade surrounded by a wall of trellises. Flowering vines ran along and through them, providing a cover of foliage that gave the little garden a feeling of privacy. Some trellises arched over the north end of the clearing, forming a kind of inflorescent pavilion.

An opening in the trellis wall gave a view of the city below. A spur extending from the cliff wall to their right bordered the path next to the glade. It turned to block the way ahead, breached only by a tunnel that led through it to the east.

"Three minute rest," Kay said firmly. "Under the pavilion. Get your wind, everyone. There's little cover from here on until we reach the stairs down to the Star."

Stefan sank onto the grass of the glade, panting. Randia sat beside him and kissed his shoulder.

"How do you feel?" she asked.

"Exhausted," he said. His voice sounded cheerful despite his heavy breathing.

"What about you, Your Highness?" Kay asked.

Randia waved a hand at her. "Don't worry about me. I'll be fine for another sprint when you're ready."

Stefan grinned at the lieutenant. "She doesn't wind easily," he said, with a conspiratorial wink.

Two scouts ran toward them from the opening in the path ahead. Kay turned as they came to attention before her. "Report, Jean," she said.

One soldier saluted. "There's something odd going on in the sky up ahead," she said tentatively.

Kay stiffened. "Go on."

"It's a bank of clouds. Out past the end of the city, surrounding it. It rolled in from the north and south in the last few minutes. It doesn't look natural."

Randia got up and walked to the opening at the north end of the trellis wall. She looked out, craning her head to the side.

"Your Highness, please!" Kay said, aghast.

Stefan gasped. "Pull your head back before someone sees you!"

Randia ignored them. She studied the sky and then turned back to the others.

"It's another spell storm," she said. "The pattern is the same as the fog over the amphitheater before. I can even feel some of the magic, this time. It's a large and powerful conjuring."

"Why?" Kay asked. "Can you tell what it's for?"

Randia took a deep breath. When she spoke, her voice was grim.

"The last time the enemy did this, it was to conceal an attack force. If I'm right, our path to the Silver Star is about to get even more difficult than it was."

Warlord of the Academy

Lieutenant Kieran Caldor was thrown to his knees on the marble floor. A cry welled up in his throat, a mixture of pain and despair. He managed to keep it to a short, gasping sob. He kept his head bowed.

His wrists and ankles were bound behind him. His arm was bleeding, and the pain in his shoulder was intense. *Dislocated*, he thought numbly. Nothing that couldn't be healed when he had a chance to get medical attention. *If* he had a chance to get medical attention.

He tried to recall what had happened. The academy staff had hastily barricaded the doors to the Dean's Library after they had arrived. He'd sent the students to shelter with the others in the auditorium at the center of the building, beneath the great dome. Then he and his men had joined the defense, standing with the guards and the professors of magic.

They'd had little time to prepare. Orion and Diana had quickly been proven right when the lookouts on the rotunda spotted a large force of Hellmen approaching. In minutes, they had been surrounded, with no hope of escape.

The attack had been brutal. Hellman casters had bombarded the building with fire, shattering its walls and makeshift fortifications. And Lord Zomoran was at their head. The magus took down many of the defenders himself, sundering their magical barriers with almost contemptuous ease.

Kieran frowned. How had his arm been injured? It must have happened when the doors exploded, and a tornado had swept through the room. He remembered being picked up by the whirlwind, but nothing after that.

He slowly risked lifting his head a little. He was kneeling on the marble floor of a circular auditorium. Others were lined in rows beside and around him. Some were guards, like himself, while others wore the robes of academy professors. Many were hurt, their faces bruised and their clothes splattered with blood. All of them were bound as he was.

He looked cautiously around, and saw that more prisoners were bound behind him. They took up half the hall, all kneeling in rows like himself, head down. The rows were far enough apart for Hellman guards to stroll among the captives. They watched them, whips in hand.

He searched for his charges from the palace. It didn't take long to spot them, kneeling together several rows behind. Their fine clothes stood out dangerously from the other students. He found himself caught between feelings of relief and dread at the sight: relief that they had survived the carnage, and dread for what was to come.

One thing was certain: he had failed in his duty to keep them safe.

He saw bodies strewn around the circumference of the room. None were moving, and he saw no sign of his men. Many of the dead lay face up with their throats cut. Wasn't that what Hellmen did after a battle? Separate out those who had value as captives, and summarily execute the rest? And *he* was still alive. Did that mean —

A lash struck his shoulder. He flinched, biting back a cry. A Hellwoman soldier with a whip stood to his side, her expression lit with what he could only interpret as delight. Her eyes met his with a look of predatory hunger.

"Head down," she ordered, smiling. She spoke in Carlissan, but her accent seemed strangely unsuited to the words. It was thick and alien. He wondered how much of his language she actually spoke, or if she were simply using a memorized phrase.

He dropped his gaze immediately to the floor. He held himself rigid, not daring to move. She walked by behind him, slowly, laughing. Her leather-clad legs brushed his back, and she tousled the hair of his bowed head playfully as she passed. He shuddered at her touch.

He remained motionless, keeping his head down. His arm ached, and stabs of pain lanced through his shoulder. His knees hurt as they pressed against the hard marble floor. He lost track of time as he waited, kneeling.

Finally he heard a cold voice call out, clearly and in excellent Carlissan. It bore barely a trace of the accent he'd heard from the guard earlier.

"Captives of the Hellman Collective," it said loudly. "You will remain kneeling and obedient. Any defiance will be met with swift and brutal reprisal. You will now raise your heads to be addressed by your liege, Zomoran, Warlord of Carlissa."

Kieran looked up. The speaker was a Hellman officer in black armor. He stood at the head of an entourage of red and black clad soldiers, and his helmet was off. The vermilion complexion of his face seemed almost to glow with a volcanic red light.

The officer stood aside and dropped to one knee. The surrounding soldiers followed suit, parting to open a path between them. Through that path walked the magus himself. He reached the officer's side, and then rested a hand on his shoulder.

"Rise, Colonel Y'Thra," he ordered. His voice resonated not only with power and authority, but a hint of impatience. "You and your soldiers have done well here today."

Y'Thra stood to attention at Zomoran's side. The magus raised his staff and gestured with it at the kneeling prisoners.

"Today dawns a new day in the history of Carlissa," he declared. "And an end to the long oppression of those you call the 'People of the Dark.'

"Since the Taming, they were driven underground, or forced to live in the harsh territories far to the north and west. They were denied the equal access they deserve to the rich lands of Kalara by you, the so-called 'Children of the Light.' All of that will now change."

The assembled Hellmen burst into applause. Zomoran waited patiently for their cheering to subside.

"It is fitting that this new age should begin here, in Carlissa, in the halls of the Grand Academy. For it is here that a new order of learning will be created to replace the old. The decadent Church of the Divine is at the heart of that old order, but its days — and its lies — are numbered."

He began to pace. His manner dropped abruptly into what seemed more suitable to a lecture.

"They gave a name to those lies. 'The Covenant,' they called them, and cast them in terms of a battle between 'Light' and 'Dark.' As if all those who followed the Way of the Will were creatures of the night — or that all creatures of the night are evil, to be feared and killed. You can see the foolishness of that even now, as our forces take your city from you under the light of the midday sun.

"Now you will finally learn the truth: that your 'Covenant' is a tissue of falsehoods. It is a doctrine forced upon you, thousands of years ago, by a pantheon of emasculated gods. Their aim was to use it to keep you weak. To frighten and control you. To rob you of your heart, your strength, your courage, your dignity, your self-assertion. Those same gods have long since retreated before our power to the far reaches of the cosmos. Their pathetic magic can no longer save you."

Quiet cries and sobs rose from the kneeling prisoners. Zomoran paused to look sternly at them, glowering in disapproval. Y'Thra gestured with one hand, and the whips of the Hellman guards went to work among the crowd. When the crying had finally subsided, the magus continued.

"That is why I have come. To bring knowledge to you of the *Way of the Will*, which, in your ignorance, you call the 'Dark.' Under my tutelage, you will learn the truth that your masters in the Church have kept from you all these centuries. You will learn that the *true* path to the Divine — and to spiritual glory — lies not through weakness and humility, but through strength and audacity. Through the *will* of the strong, and the honest submission to them of the weak. To prepare them for the afterlife, where those with the strength of *will* shall impose it on the very Divine itself."

He cast his gaze around, and his face adopted a kinder expression.

"Many of you cannot be blamed for your weakness and broken spirits. What else could be expected of you, raised under millennia of indoctrination? Even your Covenant, amid its lies, admits the truth: that by its own emasculating doctrines, you are but *Children*. Under my teaching, you will finally grow up — and learn to become *men*."

He looked down at the regents, and at the professors in the front ranks, and his face hardened. His staff swept toward them in a menacing gesture.

"But for those of you who should have known better, there can be no redemption. You chose the life of seekers and teachers of knowledge and truth. But you have betrayed that calling.

"When my fellow academics came among you, we sought nothing more than to call your attention to the existence of other ways. And for that, you condemned us to the fire. You cast us out, giving us over to your inquisition. To be murdered for daring to speak the truth. But unlike you, we are not weak, and we are no longer children. We refused to surrender to your treachery. And today is your day of reckoning for that betrayal.

"Some of you may yet be redeemed, if you can unlearn the weakness and evil of your 'Covenant.' But that is a right you will have to earn. The rest of you will serve the Will, as is your destiny. And your children will learn the lessons that you could not. Their generation will remake your nation, and lead it into the embrace of history."

"Emil, please!" a voice cried.

It was one of the regents. He was shaking his head violently, and tears were running down his cheeks.

"Listen to reason! Perhaps we were harsh with you, and for that we are truly repentant. The Crown itself took the Inquisition to task, and chastised it for your prosecution. But to lead demons into the heart of Carlissa — you cannot believe this is a just response! We —"

The Warlord glanced at Y'Thra. The colonel nodded and made another hand gesture. A Hellman guard near the speaker dropped his whip, drew his sword, and beheaded the man in mid-sentence.

Cries and gasps filled the auditorium, and the whips went to work again to silence them. When the room had finally quieted once more, Zomoran continued.

"This marks the first day of my rule over your nation. Today, we have conquered your capital, and the rest will fall swiftly to our demon army. Henceforth, you shall know me as Warlord Zomoran, Black Magus of Carlissa." His voice hardened implacably. "You will know me as both liege and teacher, and you *will* learn your lessons well."

He turned his back on the crowd and faced Y'Thra. "Are your troops ready, Colonel?" he asked.

Y'Thra nodded. "Everything is prepared, Your Excellency."

Zomoran nodded. "Then let it begin. Take slaves among the prisoners as you please. My only command is that the professors and regents be forced to witness The Taking. Spare them from death long enough to do so. They are yours to dispose of afterward."

Y'Thra frowned. "Are they to be spared from the Taking itself, then?" he asked.

Zomoran smiled. "Not at all. That will be your choice. If they 'witness' it from firsthand experience, then all the better."

Y'Thra smiled. He saluted, fist to heart. "It will be as you command, my liege," he said.

He turned to face the auditorium as Zomoran strode from the room. He extended his right arm with his hand open. Then he closed it into a fist with a slow, grasping gesture.

A whoop of excitement went through the assembled Hellman troops. Some of them broke off to assume positions around the room, weapons at the ready. The rest — led by Y'Thra himself — gathered into groups that began picking their way among the rows of prisoners. Some of them were made to stand, to turn clumsily with their bound ankles, examined by both hand and eye.

So this is how the Hellmen take slaves, Kieran thought numbly. Would they take him, too? Or would he be killed? He thought he should be terrified, but he found that all he could think of were the students from the palace. He turned to watch them, and saw with horror — and as he'd feared — that Y'Thra and his lieutenants were making straight for them.

He tried to twist against his bonds, to break free, to go to their aid. His reward was a stab of pain from his injured shoulder. He was powerless to stop what was about to happen. He had failed in his charge. They would pay the price for that failure, and dearly.

He saw Y'Thra force the girls to stand for examination, one at a time. Some of them wept openly, begging for mercy. The Hellman laughed, ignoring their pleas.

As he watched, he thought suddenly of Orion and Diana. They had chosen to disobey his order and run off. He felt empty of his earlier anger now, even grateful for their defiance. Had they survived? Would they manage to escape? Or had they already been killed — or worse — by the horrors that were descending on the city?

He saw that Y'Thra was smiling. He had settled on Lady Candace. Kieran wasn't surprised; she was a notorious beauty among the young nobles. He was holding her bound wrists behind her with one powerful hand; the other was tearing away her dress with frightening ease. He saw her sobbing and wailing, her body exposed, as he touched her.

As if their leader's choice were a cue, the others began taking captives as well. Kieran didn't understand the ritual, but it was plain that the bonds-grasping was their gesture of laying claim to a prize. He noted numbly that there seemed to be an unspoken order to the choices. Each Hellman was watching one of his fellows, waiting for him to choose before taking his turn.

He lowered his head and closed his eyes. He tried to shut out the sound of Lady Candace's screaming, but he couldn't. Her every shriek was like a stab to his heart — shredding his pride, his honor, his sense of manhood. He had failed her. He had failed them all.

A hot, slender, powerful hand grasped his bonds from behind. Startled, he looked up.

The Hellwoman guard who had lashed him earlier was staring into his eyes. She was smiling. Though it didn't seem possible, her expression had become even hungrier and more predatory than before.

"*Ahk vind kalth dormo khul*," she said. Her voice was husky with undisguised lust.

She still held her whip in her free hand. Gently, almost tenderly, she stroked his face with it.

Kieran closed his eyes, and she laughed. His unmaking was complete. He was no longer an officer of the palace guard. He was a prisoner of the Dark, utterly defeated.

Chapter 10 - The Diaspora

The Demon Lord's Command

Borr's serpentine lips curled upward in a rictus of satisfaction. The clouds surrounding the city had become a great wall that shut out any view of the outside world. Its last spell had reached completion, and it was ready to move the final pieces for its endgame.

It turned to its left. The winged demon lieutenant Usnaroth stood there, its bat's head watching its master with disciplined anticipation. Next to it knelt the enormous figure of Incanus Thad, head pressed to the ground. Black ichor still dripped from the wounds that Aron's sword had dealt it.

"It is time," Borr said. Its voice was soft, but thick with menace.

Usnaroth raised a great paw to its shoulder in salute. "What are your orders, My Lord?"

"Give the signal," it replied. "With the arrival of our allies, we need wait and prepare no longer. Keep only a single brigade here to defend me and the gate. Have the rest march out to take the city."

Usnaroth nodded. "What of our air forces? They have suffered many casualties in the battle with the palace guard."

"You may withdraw the winged demons from the battle by the Cathedral. They have done their part well in preventing the King's charge from breaking out of the High City, but we no longer need them there. I will send some of the dragons to take over that responsibility."

Borr's snakelike neck twisted around in an almost languid motion. Its head looked west along the palace road.

"Send another regiment of battle demons to reinforce them as well," it added absently. "Just in case. I doubt we will need them, but I intend to risk no further surprises today."

"Who shall I assign to command the charge, My Lord?"

Borr let out a hiss of displeasure. "There is still no sign of Captain Gorath?"

"No, My Lord. It is not on the battlefield. Pack leader Nagoth claims the captain ordered it to establish a barrier formation, and then left to conduct some kind of investigation."

Borr whipped its snakelike head around in agitation. "Nagoth is little more than a grunt. No wonder the line collapsed."

"Yes, My Lord. It said that Gorath mounted a wyvern and took off toward the southern bluffs. It hasn't been seen since."

"Take command of the attack yourself," Borr said. "See to it personally, Usnaroth. Do not fail, and do not leave your post."

"Shall I start a search for Captain Gorath?"

"No. It is no longer important. Do order it to report to me immediately if it reappears. Gorath has never been a fool, and there may be an acceptable reason for its absence." The thin smile returned to its lizard-like lips. "I will give it a chance to explain itself before I rip out its brain."

It turned back to the hulking demon. "That is all, Lieutenant. You are dismissed."

"As you will, My Lord," Usnaroth replied. It saluted, and, wings beating furiously, took once again to the air.

Borr lowered its gaze to Incanus Thad. The Captain of the Horde knelt, axe on the ground before it, awaiting his master's judgment.

"You have greatly disappointed me, Incanus," Borr said softly.

"Thanks to your failure, we have not yet taken the palace. Many of our strongest demons were maimed or killed. Most of the royal family survived what was supposed to be a decapitation strike. Even now they lead a force against us, trying to unite with the warrior priests of the Church. Have you anything to say for yourself?"

"Only that we encountered far stronger resistance than we had been led to expect, My Lord Borr," Incanus Thad said. His booming voice had lost its former power and resonance. His body shuddered, and his head flinched as if from a painful memory. "But that is no excuse. I submit myself to your will for judgment."

"Ordinarily, I would dismiss such a defense as the bravado of a weakling," Borr said thoughtfully. "But fortunately for you, I have looked into your mind and seen your memories. The minds of others who survived the strike corroborate your story."

Incanus Thad continued to kneel at his master's feet. He said nothing.

"The King called upon an unknown magic, unexpected and extremely powerful. Had I known that you would face such a threat, I would have ensured that your team was better prepared. Our ally and our spy are also to blame for this, for their faulty intelligence."

"Yes, My Lord," Incanus Thad said quietly. "As you judge and will it."

"There is also the matter of Aron Killraven to speak for you. Despite the threat from the King's magic, you struck a major blow against the royals by slaying the elder prince. And by making yourself the target of her wrath, you took the Queen out of the battle as well. Had it not been for the untimely arrival of the mages and their guards, that sacrifice would have turned it in our favor."

Borr's great eye suddenly narrowed dangerously.

"But there is no room in my horde for a damaged battle captain," it hissed. "The elf-bitch's attack has shaken you, Incanus. You must gather your will to recover from it, or you will be of no further use to me."

Borr signaled for the demon to rise. Incanus Thad struggled to his feet.

"Go forth and re-join the fight — *now*. Master yourself, and re-claim your strength. Distinguish yourself in the battle, and you may yet be redeemed."

It bared its teeth menacingly, and the threat in its expression was unmistakable. "Quail, and I will feed you to the dragons myself."

Incanus Thad looked into the demon lord's great eye. A hard expression took hold of his face. He nodded slowly, and then saluted, fist to shoulder.

"It shall be as you command, My Lord Borr," he said.

The Horde Captain's wings spread out, beating the air. With a roar, he launched himself into the sky. He flew toward Mount Cascade and was quickly lost to sight.

Nowhere to Run

"The Lord of the Horde is springing its trap," Elena said. Her eyes had once again taken on their faraway look. Her face was ashen.

"Don't risk it, my love," Danor said anxiously. "If that demon lord senses you scrying and attacks, without the ward to protect you …"

Her eyes slowly returned to normal. "Your warning is well taken," she said. Danor noted with a sudden stab of concern that she was trembling.

"What did you see, Your Majesty?" Darren asked anxiously.

"The arrival of the dragons is what Borr was waiting for," she said. "Its forces are finally moving out to take the city. And there are more battle demons headed our way."

"And the dragons?" Danor pursued.

The Queen turned to look at him. She was crying.

"Flights and flights of them," she whispered. "Fire giants ride them. They are girded for war, carrying great swords and spears."

She buried her face in her husband's shoulder. His arms went protectively around her as she clutched the flanges of his armor.

"We're beaten, Danor," she wept. "They've emptied the strongholds of the Dark. And still their demons come through the gate."

She raised her eyes to his.

"There's no way to win against a force like this. There's nowhere to run, and no way to escape. The entire world will be taken. This is the beginning of the end for the Children of the Covenant."

"What do we do, then?" General Banderman asked. His voice sounded shaky. "Do we surrender?"

"No," Darren said firmly. "We fight to the end, until we are sent into the Light of the Divine."

Danor kissed his wife's hair. Then, slowly, he held her weeping form away from him.

"We're not beaten until the last man has fallen," he said. He was smiling. "And I will need your help now more than ever. Will you still stand with me?"

Elena nodded.

"No matter the battle. Again and again, you've held us together against impossible odds. I won't give up now, no matter how hopeless it looks. And if we are truly to meet our end today, then I'm glad it will be with you at my side."

Banderman nodded. "We fight, then. What are your orders, Your Majesty?"

Hiding from Dragons

A flight of winged shapes emerged from the eastern clouds. Enormous reptilian forms with scales of glistening red sailed toward the city. Jets of flame shot from their nostrils, licking the air before them with darting tongues of fire.

Randia's eyes widened. "Dragons!" she cried.

Stefan grabbed her around the waist and pulled her to the ground. "Everyone, down!"

"Do as he says!" Kay rapped. "Under the pavilion. Keep out of sight. We don't want to be spotted."

In seconds, the rest of the company had followed her order. Randia and Stefan crawled toward them.

"We can't make it to the Star by hiding here," she whispered. "Shouldn't we run for it?"

Stefan shook his head firmly.

"Those dragons are coming this way," he said. "And the winged demons are resuming their patrols, too. If we break cover now, they'll see us. All we can do is wait."

"For how long?" she whispered.

"Until the sky is clear again," Kay said. "The prince is right. We'd be in their line of sight, and there's no cover in the streets ahead."

Randia closed her eyes. There was a long pause before she spoke again.

"Lieutenant, can your scouts keep an eye on the dragons?" she asked quietly. "And the demons? Don't ask them to risk themselves. Have them stay out of sight, but let us know what they see."

"I'm already doing that, Your Highness," another voice replied. She looked up to see a tall, thin scout named Gerrold crouching next to the pavilion opening. He was peeking around its edge.

"What can you make out?" Stefan asked. "How many of them are there?"

"You saw only the first group," Gerrold answered quickly. "They're coming in waves, one after another. About five dragons in each flight. I see three flights so far, and they're still coming. And it's not just dragons. There are giants using them as mounts. Big, with flaming red skin. They're like enormous Hellmen riding them into war."

Randia's voice fell. "Fire giants," she whispered. The others turned to look at her.

"They've been nearly unheard of on the eastern continent for over a thousand years," she explained quietly. "But they still have strongholds far to the north and west, mainly in the Walls of the World. The Dorians have had border skirmishes with them over the centuries."

"If that's where they're from, then they've traveled clear across the world for this fight," Kay said. "Why attack Carlissa, and not another land that's closer? Dorian, or Thressa?"

"Zomoran," Stefan said. "He's the reason. He must have architected this invasion, and cast the magic that opened that hellgate."

Kay nodded. "That would explain why they came here."

Randia sighed. "If all we can do is wait, then we'll wait," she said resignedly.

She slipped a hand into Stefan's and looked into his eyes. He reached out with his other hand to gently touch a single tear that ran down her cheek.

Flight to the Lower City

The group ran down Tribute Street to the east. Orion had tried to keep them on the first terrace of the Upper City North for as long as he could. Staying on the higher ground had given them a good view of the Lower City, and he'd wanted to maintain that advantage for as long as possible.

They were not alone. Hundreds were running along the road with them. A steady wail of screams flowed in their wake as they streamed away from the center of Lannamon.

Orion brought them out of the flow of refugees and came to a halt. A sheer wall towered ominously above them, blocking their way forward. It was a rocky ridge that descended from the dwindling cliffs above and hooked down into the valley. The towers of the Silver Star Adventurer's Academy glinted on the shoulder of a twin spur across the firth to their south. The spurs marked the eastern ends of the Upper City.

"This is as far as we can go," Orion said. "There's no way forward along the terraces. We'll have to descend to the Lower City here."

The others gathered around him. Several of them fell to the grass beside the road, panting with exhaustion.

"Finally, a rest," Davin said. There was a grateful note to his voice as he gasped out the words.

Cooper slapped him on the shoulder as he settled next to him. "A little hard exercise will do you good, scholar-boy," he said.

Diana came to Orion's side. She shielded her eyes against the sun with her hand as she followed his gaze. The only road around the cliff spur wound into a long curve that ended in a wide, flat area along the northern shore of the firth. Unlike the relatively pastoral manors of the Upper City, it was dense with buildings and an extensive network of streets.

"There's no avoiding it any longer," she agreed. "But we're in a good position. The flying demons must still be gathered over the battle in the High City. There aren't many of them out here."

Jameson came to stand next to them. He pointed back to the west.

"That won't last," he said.

The other two looked, and then nodded.

"We don't have much time," Diana said.

Orion turned to the others. "I'm afraid we can't rest yet," he said loudly. "We need to keep moving. Right away."

"Oh, come on," Davin said, still breathing heavily. "We can't run all the way to the east gate in one go!"

"The demons are preparing to march into the streets," Orion said. "It looks like they're finally ready to take the city. Our window of opportunity to escape is going to close, and soon."

"How long do we have?" Cooper asked.

Orion paused briefly before answering. "I'd say that if we don't get most of the way to the eastern barracks in the next half hour, it'll be too late."

Jameson nodded. "Let's go, then. Lead the way."

Orion turned and started jogging down the road to the Lower City. Diana fell in at his side, and the others followed in their wake. Despite the many homes and buildings of the Lower City, its broad avenues provided more room for the thronging refugees to spread out than the narrow streets of the terraces. The crowd thinned around them as they descended into the land around the firth.

"There!" Orion said, pointing.

In the distance, they saw a large, low complex of buildings and fortifications. They were built in a line reaching from the water to the remnants of the northern cliff wall. They were still two miles away and it was hard to make out details, but none of them could mistake the sight.

A sea of soldiers was mobilizing for battle. Their weapons and armor glittered brilliantly in the midday sun. Two thousand strong were already marching toward them in waves of disciplined ranks, and several warships had set into the firth to sail alongside them. More were mustering behind.

Jameson let out a loud whistle, and the others cheered.

"At last!" Davin said. There were tears in his eyes.

"Took them long enough!" Cooper said, grinning.

"That was to be expected, though," Jameson said.

"Why?" Davin asked.

"The city had no warning of the attack," Orion replied. "Only a small part of the brigade would have been ready for immediate deployment. Sending it out alone would have been suicide."

Jameson nodded. "Marshal Gray's been doing what everyone else has, even the enemy itself. Organizing a force large and well prepared enough to be effective."

"He's got that now, though," Orion said. "How long do you think before we meet up with them?"

Diana squinted. "The leading edge looks to be about a mile and a half away. Fifteen minutes with luck, if we keep our pace."

They kept running. The sun was beginning its afternoon descent toward the slopes of Mount Cascade, but its bright rays were veiled as it fell behind the Queen's storm clouds over the palace. The light dimmed ominously around them as they went.

Diana lifted her head to look at the sky to the east, and frowned. Another bank of clouds had formed around the outskirts of the city, behind the fortifications of the army and navy bases. Red light flickered amid the pall like flashes of scarlet lightning.

She turned. Clouds had settled around the rest of the valley as well. They hung menacingly over the bluffs and the shoulders of Mount Cascade. She could still see patches of blue directly overhead, but the city seemed to be surrounded by an ominous wall of dark grey.

Five dragons emerged suddenly from the cloud ahead. One flew over the firth, and the others flew over the north and south banks of the city. Huge, red-skinned giants rode them as mounts, waving enormous flaming swords and spears.

Another wave of dragons emerged from the cloud, and then another. With a chorus of deafening roars, they swept into the City of Rainbows from the east.

"Lord of Light!" Jameson swore.

The group came to a skidding halt. The dragons were headed right toward them.

"Trapped!" Davin cried. His voice was panicked. "What do we do now?"

Orion turned to look over his shoulder. The leading edge of the force from the amphitheater was closing quickly as it fanned out into the city.

"We can't stop," he said. "Or the demons will overtake us. We have to keep going!"

"Into a dragon's jaws?" Davin yelled in disbelief. "Are you mad?"

"They'll fire the city," Jameson said grimly. "We'll be running into an inferno."

Diana's head snapped to their right. "Cut across toward the firth," she said.

Jameson shook his head. "The docks will burn, too."

"Better to be closer to the water than not," she countered.

"I can't swim!" Davin cried.

"But you can burn, scholar-boy," Cooper snapped.

Diana looked around. The streets were emptying. A few people were turning to flee back toward the approaching demons, but most were running into the buildings nearby, searching frantically for cover.

She looked back to the west. The demons were fanning out into the streets behind them. They were breaking into smaller and smaller groups as they went. The tendrils of their advance were slowly saturating every alley of the Lower City.

"There may be dragons ahead, but at least so are our soldiers," Diana said. Her voice was frantic. "There's nothing behind us but demons!"

Orion pointed to a street that angled away to the southeast.

"Darby Lane cuts across toward the firth," he said. "Let's go!"

More flights of dragons sailed into view as they ran. The first wave kept a straight course without slowing or stopping. Those that followed, though, descended to attack.

Diana sobbed as she stole glances at the unfolding battle. The soldiers weren't expecting an attack from their rear, and had focused all of their attention on the city side of the walls. They barely had time to realize the danger before the dragons struck.

Horns and alarms began a frantic braying as the second flight fell upon the barracks. Great gouts of fire burst from the dragons' jaws as they strafed the defenders. A few panicked volleys of arrows flew up to meet them, but had little effect. A company of marshaling soldiers died horribly, enveloped in the inferno, and part of the fortification erupted into flame.

The first flight of dragons passed over the group from the Smiling Nymph. The monsters' great wings beat furiously as they sped toward Mount Cascade.

"They're heading for the palace," Orion said. "To join the battle in the High City."

"The King and the priests must have hit them pretty hard," Jameson noted. "The enemy is trying to bring in reinforcements to put them down."

"And the dragons keep coming," Diana said, her voice numb. "I can see at least four flights coming in behind them. No, wait — there's a fifth one, now."

Orion looked up and nodded. The following monsters descended to attack the city as they came. They flew low and slowly, destroying whatever they found in their path.

"They've staggered their formations to cover the spaces between them," he said. "They'll rake through the city like strokes from a flaming comb. Nowhere will be safe."

"That first group will be here any minute," Diana said. "We need to find somewhere to hide!"

The Order is Given

"Archers, loose!" General Banderman cried.

A hail of arrows flew into the air. They arced gracefully toward the regiment of battle demons that surged toward them. The King and his forces still held the high ground along the palace road, forcing the enemy to lumber uphill.

The first group of demons had waited for reinforcements. That had given the Carlissans a chance to prepare their line, but it had given the first flight of dragons time to reach them as well. Now both were closing to attack. The dragons dropped into a long, flat descent, jaws brimming with fire.

"Priests, ready!" Darren cried. "And ... now!"

Once again, the great wall of white magic shimmered before the defenders. Five blasts of fire blossomed out from the strafing monsters, striking into it. The flames dissipated in a red glow as they tried to penetrate the barrier, and failed.

"Riposte!" Darren cried.

The wall of white shot upward, enveloping the attackers in its incandescent glow. A prismatic volley of spells erupted from the line of mages to follow it. The dragons howled at the barrier's touch, and veered away as the bursts of magic struck them. The wall faded as the creatures broke off.

"That was encouraging," Banderman offered. He was grinning.

Danor shook his head. "That was a feint to test our strength. And to give us false confidence."

Elena pointed down the road. "Those demon reinforcements are almost on us. The dragons will hit us again when they engage our front line."

Darren grimaced. "The Wall of Light is not easy to conjure. We can't keep using it to drive them back. They will break through eventually."

"Then we'll be ready with swords," the general said.

Darren turned to look directly at the King. "We'll need to fall back," he said.

Banderman started to object, but the Captain General raised a hand to cut him off. "We can bloody their first strikes, but we can't withstand repeated attacks. Not from a force like this, and not out in the open. And not with those dragons coming. We will need to retreat to the palace, or to the Cathedral. You must choose which."

The King returned his gaze steadily. "We can't split up again," he said. "And if we fall back to one, the enemy will take the other — and likely destroy it." He looked steadily into the Captain General's eyes. "Are you prepared to let that be the Cathedral?"

Darren nodded. "If that is your order. And you must decide quickly. We have little time to prepare."

Danor sighed. "Let it be the palace, then. It's designed as a fortress. Despite the damage from the earlier attack, it is more defensible than the Cathedral."

Banderman nodded. "I'm forced to agree, Your Majesty."

Elena turned suddenly to face Darren. Her voice took on a hard, almost ruthless tone.

"We will fight on, as our King commands. But we must now take thought for the likelihood of defeat as well."

"What do you propose, Your Majesty?" Darren asked.

"If we fall, there must be those who will survive. To carry the fight, and the word of the Light, into the future. The legacy of the Covenant in Carlissa must be preserved, Augustus. Do you understand me?"

He nodded reluctantly, and then signaled with one hand. His attaché stepped forward, a look of surprise and confusion on his face.

"I do. The order is ancient, and has not been given in the memory of the Church since the end of the Grim Times. But we have maintained the tradition despite its age and seeming irrelevance. The roster still exists. Those on it know what must be done."

Elena nodded. "Good. We will draw their forces after us. Our retreat to the palace will give them time and cover to carry it out."

The attaché's face paled. "The Diaspora?" he gasped.

Darren turned back to the King. His face was tortured.

"I head the roster," he said slowly. "If the order is given, then I must withdraw from the field to join my brethren. I cannot do so unless you release me from my service to the Crown."

The King looked at his wife. "Are you sure of this, my love?" he asked.

"You know it must be done, Danor. We've already set it in motion ourselves."

He glanced toward the far end of the city, and the tower of the Silver Star Adventurer's Academy. He nodded.

"Augustus Darren," he said loudly. The heads of the nearby officers turned abruptly at the sound of his voice.

Darren straightened to attention. "Yes, my liege?"

"You are ordered to execute the Diaspora of the Children in the Kingdom of Carlissa." An uproar of gasps met his declaration, but the King's powerful voice rose easily above it. "You will begin immediately. Do you understand and accept this obligation?"

Darren nodded. "I do."

"Who is senior commander after you?"

A tall, powerfully built woman in silver armor with a winged helm stepped forward.

"I am, Your Majesty. General Vala Orleans."

Darren looked at her. She knelt before him, laying her sword at his feet. His voice was stone when he spoke.

"Rise, Vala Orleans, Captain General of the Order of Light."

She did. Their eyes shared a long, silent moment. Then Darren turned and, without another word, strode to his horse. Several dozen of his knights fell in behind him. In moments, they were galloping back toward the Cathedral, away from the field of battle.

"We will miss his aid in what is to come," Danor said.

Elena smiled. "We will. But I also cannot imagine a better man in whom to entrust the future of the Children."

Vala turned to face the King. "What are your orders, Your Majesty?"

Danor sighed in resignation. "We retreat to the palace," he said. "We will make our stand there."

Chapter 11 - Treason in the Palace

The Ward

Palanad Lantar stood on a high balcony of the Wizard's Tower. To his right, a group of mages struggled to load a large red crystal into a rotating mount affixed to a hastily erected stand.

He pointed to the east. "There!" he said. "Do you see it, Cyrus?"

Lord Cyrus Rugon squinted. Clouds and driving rain hung low in the sky and obscured their view from the tower. There was a sudden flash of lightning. The councilor blinked, trying to clear the afterimage from his eyes.

"It's hard to make out anything through Elena's storm," he said tentatively. "And my vision isn't what it used to be. What am I looking for, Palanad?"

The court mage was quiet for a long time.

"The Queen's isn't the only weather magic at play here," he said at last. "A bank of clouds is surrounding the city. Outside the line of the bluffs. It's nearly complete now."

Lord Rugon turned to face him. "Is it a danger?"

"I don't know. The casting is very skilled. It's so subtle that I didn't sense it until now."

The councilor frowned. "What could it be for? Does Zomoran plan to strike at us with a storm of his own?"

Palanad shook his head. "Emil is no match for the Queen's command of the elements. He knows it."

Lord Rugon turned to look back out over the valley. "Perhaps this demon lord the King told us of is responsible."

A flash of red erupted in the sky to the east. They saw it clearly despite the driving rain. The crimson glow lit the clouds surrounding the city and reflected brightly from the surface of the firth at the end of the valley.

Lord Rugon started. "What was that?"

Palanad was already running from the balcony. He went down a short corridor and entered a wide laboratory on the top floor of the Wizard's Tower. A handful of mages still worked there, conjuring feverishly at enchanting tables, struggling to prepare magical devices for the battle.

"Dragons incoming!" he cried. "Across the firth!"

Exclamations and oaths rang out as Lord Rugon ran up behind him. The old councilor's face had gone white.

"How many?" one of the wizards called out.

"Not sure," Palanad responded. "But it's a lot. You can see the glow from their flame breath through the clouds all the way from here. It must be at least two dozen."

He spun to another of the mages. "Lester!" he barked. "Get out there and help with that crystal cannon. If it's not set up to fire in ten minutes, it'll be too late."

"If they attack the tower, can we defend against them?" Lord Rugon asked, as Lester raced out the door to the balcony.

"Perhaps," the court mage said.

He turned to a young woman in a grey apprentice's robe. "Aria! Get to the library and bring back Bouthan's *Dracono Incana*. It's a big book with animated flames on the cover. There should be a spell in it to set up a ward against dragons. The rest of you drop what you're doing and help prepare a circle to cast it."

Lord Rugon nodded. "I'll go down the tower to warn the soldiers. And I'll need to tell the council what's happening as well."

Palanad fell into step beside the old councilor.

"I'll come with you," he said. "Much as I hate to admit it, I'll need Hardin's help to spell the tower."

Lord Rugon's face distorted in anger and disgust.

"Couldn't the prince help you?" he asked. "And shouldn't we warn him, anyway? About the dragons?"

Palanad shook his head firmly.

"My orders from the King are explicit," he replied. "No one ascends to the Sky Chamber or tries to disturb the prince. Not for any reason, on pain of death. The stairs have been locked and spelled against entry."

"What kind of magic could he be working?"

"I don't know. I can't sense anything at all from up there."

They reached the enchanted elevator. Palanad touched the controls, and the platform descended toward the great hall.

Lord Rugon grimaced. "I suppose Danor must have a good reason for this secrecy," he said. "Whatever the prince is doing, it must be important."

"No doubt. Besides, I can't imagine that he doesn't know about the dragons already. With the tower ward, he should be able to see the threat better than any of us."

They rode the rest of the way in silence. When the platform stopped, they got off and walked quickly through a heavily guarded door behind the tower stairs. They entered a long, narrow stone passageway.

"Will Salmanor help?" Lord Rugon asked at last. "With casting your anti-dragon ward?"

Palanad shrugged. "I don't know. Refusing to help the King against a demon attack, and this peculiar fixation with defending the council to the exclusion of his other responsibilities ... I can't understand what's happened to him."

"Do you think he can be trusted?"

"Not the way he's behaving. But we have little choice. This spell is extremely difficult. As far as I know, no one's even tried it for hundreds of years. My wizards are all skilled, but none of them commands the raw power that it needs. I *might* manage it on my own, but if I failed ..."

"You think it's too risky to try without him, then." It was a statement rather than a question.

Palanad took a deep breath and nodded.

"Unless the Queen returns or the prince comes down from the tower. But he has to help, Cyrus. He's the high priest. It's his duty to the Covenant. He must see that."

They came to the end of the passageway. Another group of guards stood there on either side of a heavily barred door. Portal and frame alike were set deeply into the surrounding rock and reinforced with bluesteel plating. An intricate rune at its center glowed with a soft white light.

The court mage touched his staff to the rune. There was a sound of heavy metal bars moving, and then the door swung slowly open. He and Lord Rugon stepped quickly through the opening.

They found themselves in a large chamber surrounded by walls of solid granite. Cots and chairs were scattered around it. Most of the High Council — except for a few like Lord Rugon, who had insisted on joining the defense — sat or lay nervously on the haphazardly placed settings, whispering together in small groups. Much of the palace's civilian staff was gathered there as well.

The councilors rose swiftly and came forward as the pair entered. Baronet Kuhl, head of the Carlissan Trade Guild, pushed himself to the front of their line. His face was red with anger, and his voice sputtered with frustration and outrage.

"What is happening?" he demanded. "Why are we being kept here, in the dark?" His face turned toward Palanad. "The council demands to know what is being done to defend the city from these demons, Mage Lantar."

Palanad returned Kuhl's hostile gaze with a look of cool patience. "I answer to the King, not to the council," he said.

"And the King left *me* in command of the palace," Lord Rugon added. His voice was less cool and less patient. "*And* I am senior member of the council here. You would do well to remember that, *Baronet*, and to temper your peremptory tone. The city is under attack. We cannot afford the time for political posturing."

"It is as I told you," another voice said. The councilors parted to reveal Salmanor Hardin standing at the back of the group. The serving maid from before still clutched his arm, staring at him with a mixture of terror and adoration.

"They keep you here, holed away in a stone prison," he continued, "hiding their failure from us, and their treason to the Light." He nodded to the councilors around him. "You, who *truly* serve the people, and not the petty interests of a dynasty that has failed them."

"No one is 'holing you in here,'" Lord Rugon replied, heat rising.

"The King ordered that you be given sanctuary from the attack. But I won't deny anyone who asks the right to stand with the rest of us on the battlements."

Hardin shook his head. "Empty lies, and treason to the Light," he said airily. "The Killravens have led you to this disaster, and you must all now pay the price."

"If you want to speak of treason —" Lord Rugon began hotly.

"We came to ask for your help, Salmanor," Palanad cut in, speaking over the councilor's angry retort. "Zomoran has brought dragons against the city. We need your aid to ward the palace. There's no one else left strong enough to help."

Lady Rayne started, her eyes going wide. "The Queen? The prince?"

"The Queen is at the King's side, leading a charge against the demons in the High City," he replied. "And the prince is sealed in the Sky Dome performing an important task for the King. They can't help."

He turned to the Lord Inquisitor, eyes pleading.

"We only have minutes until they arrive, Salmanor. You know the spell we need to cast. Without it, they will reduce the palace to blackened rubble."

The high priest shook his head. His eyes were hard.

"It will be a proper end to this corrupt regime," he said flatly. "And life under the Dark a fitting penance for those who served it."

The court mage's eyes went wide, and the councilors surrounding him turned to stare at him in shock. Lord Rugon's mouth worked uselessly as he tried to form words and failed.

"You can't mean that, Your Grace!" one of the councilors cried.

Kuhl's eyes narrowed as he looked at the inquisitor, but there was a hint of shrewdness in his gaze. "You counsel surrender?" he asked cautiously. "Making accommodation with the Dark?"

Hardin waved a hand. "Those who remain loyal to the Light will be saved. The rest will be conquered and enslaved. It is what they deserve."

The serving girl looked up at him, eyes adoring. "You will save the rest of us, Your Holiness," she said simply. Her voice was filled with faith and conviction.

The high priest looked down at her. He patted her hand, which still rested on his arm, and nodded. There was a dreamy, faraway expression on his face as he responded.

"I will," he said.

There was a long silence. Palanad and Lord Rugon exchanged astonished glances. Some of the councilors did the same, moving slowly and furtively away from the high priest.

Palanad studied him carefully. The fevered look in the inquisitor's eyes clashed with the strange calmness of his mien. When the court mage finally spoke, there was a tone of dawning comprehension in his voice.

"His mind is broken," he said firmly.

Lord Rugon turned to him, eyes wide with astonishment. "What?"

"His sanity is gone," Palanad said. "It's like he's caught in a dream or fantasy of personal omnipotence. He's convinced that all this is happening to others, but not to himself."

The high priest laughed. There was a distant, almost disconnected quality to the sound.

"The Light will preserve me, and those who follow me. For the rest of you, it is already too late."

Infiltrator

Palanad frowned. Something was wrong. For a man like Salmanor Hardin to snap so suddenly, and with so few warning signs, didn't make sense. If he weren't the high priest, whose magic was among the strongest in the Church, he'd suspect that he'd been enchanted ...

As a full magus, Palanad was extremely sensitive to the flow of magic around him. He could feel only traces of it now: resonances from his own earlier conjuring, the casting of his colleagues in the tower, and the more distant spells from the battle in the city, coming slowly closer. To veil a dweomer strong enough to break the inquisitor's mind from senses as keen as his would require incredible strength and skill ...

Icy realization seized him, and he reached for the Magic. There was little time for subtlety if what he suspected were true — and fortunately, he didn't require it. Such a powerful enchantment would surely betray itself under an active divination ...

He sensed it immediately. To his spelled sight, it appeared as restraints binding Hardin's body: manacles on his wrists and ankles, a band around his waist, a spiked collar on his neck. Heavy black chains were attached to them, their lines all running off to his side.

He heard a constant murmur of whispers as the apparition took shape. He couldn't quite make out the words, but they seemed to be part of the vision his divination was showing him. It was almost as though they were pulsing along the chains and into the high priest's shackled form. They had a soft, seductive sound, reassuring but insistent, and unrelenting.

His eyes followed the line of chains to where they joined. They met in what appeared to be an iron haft, so that the high priest's body seemed almost to be ensnared on the hooks of some hideous cat-o'-nine-tails. It was held with a loose, casual arrogance in the hand of a figure that stood at Hardin's side.

Palanad's gaze flashed from the hand up to the holder's eyes. It was the serving girl.

Her other hand rested on the inquisitor's arm, as though leaning on him for support. To his diviner's sight the fingers appeared as if tipped with long, black claws, digging cruelly into the flesh of his blood-soaked arm.

He knew at once what he was facing when he met her gaze. Her eyes stared into his, glowing with an evil red light. And they knew he had seen them.

Succubus.

Palanad reached for the Magic again, this time in desperate panic. What a fool he had been! Thinking the palace secure, at least for the moment, he had erected none of his magical defenses. The demon stood only a few feet from him, and he was completely exposed to her veiled power.

Even as he realized his vulnerability, he saw the tendril of a new chain lash out from the cat's handle. It wrapped itself around his throat with the sound of a snapping whip. He tried to open his mouth, to cry out a warning to the others, but nothing happened. He found himself unable to speak or move, and the Magic began to slip from his grasp. *I can only stand here, paralyzed and helpless, at the demon's mercy,* he thought. *I am beaten.*

No, he told himself harshly. Those weren't his own thoughts. They were whispers from his enemy. His mind raced, searching for an escape.

He could see that the chain around his neck was thinner than any of the others emanating from the succubus' grasp. Her hold on him was weaker than the enchantments binding the inquisitor. Her disguise had given her a long time to cast those, and with a slow subtlety that ensured the high priest did not know what was happening to him. That disguise had been perfectly chosen to take him off his guard, exploiting his well-known weakness for piously innocent maids.

But *he* was a different matter. *He* was aware of her presence, and he was fighting her. Was she really strong enough to dominate him while holding her spell on Hardin, and cloaking all of that to keep even the Queen from sensing it?

Bracing himself, he once again seized the Magic, and lashed out at the succubus. Her eyes narrowed in anger and surprise. Time seemed to slow for them as they struggled for control of his mind and body.

You cannot defeat me, mortal, the demon thought to him.

Palanad's lips twitched into a small smile of defiance. Slowly, painstakingly, he began to erect a mental shield that would shatter his binding chain and protect him from her spell.

I don't need to defeat you, his mind stabbed back. *All I need is to expose you. I will strip your disguise, so that the others will see you for what you are.*

I will kill you before you have the chance. And you do not have to die. Your city is lost, and there is nothing to be gained by resisting. Yield, and I will spare you.

Palanad's heart raced with anticipation. He had detected strain in the demon's mental voice. That was a good sign, and doubtless unintended on her part. His divination spell was doing its job, piercing her veil and giving him information that she would rather have kept hidden.

You cannot kill me without revealing yourself, he thought back. *And you cannot subdue me while keeping up both your veil and your hold on the high priest. You're strong, but you're not that strong.*

You are wrong, wizard, her mind hissed. The hiss gave the lie to her words. *I will feed upon your soul if you defy me.*

Her thoughts suddenly took on a more seductive tone. *Do not make that necessary*, they said soothingly. *If you surrender, I will reward you. And the rewards I can bestow are beyond your imagining.*

Your bargaining betrays your weakness, demon, Palanad thought back grimly. He felt the beginnings of his mental barrier snap into place. A few more seconds and he would have his voice back and could warn the others. *Flee now, and release your hold on the inquisitor. It is the only way to save yourself.*

The succubus' red eyes blazed. *Not the only way, wizard*, she thought, her mental voice savage with fury.

And then she was gone from his mind. The chain lashing him evaporated. Without her resistance, his mental defenses slammed into place like the dropping of an iron gate. He blinked in surprise, momentarily disoriented.

Save us, My Holy Lord! He means to destroy us all!

He drew in a frantic breath to shout a warning, but it was too late. With a snarl of hatred, Salmanor Hardin drew a dagger from his belt and lunged at him. Before anyone realized what was happening or could try to stop it, the inquisitor had plunged the blade into his heart.

Blood erupted from Palanad's mouth, and his warning cry was drowned in a spray of crimson. It stained the high priest's robes with wild splashes as Hardin raised the knife and struck again and again, stabbing at him with maniacal abandon.

"Traitor to the Light!" he shrieked. "Wielder of unholy magics! You have brought this on us! You and the corrupt dynasty you serve —"

Lord Rugon leapt forward and caught his dagger arm as it tried to descend for another stroke.

"Salmanor, are you mad?" he cried. "Stop it! You're killing him!"

Murder

Screams echoed through the stone chamber as Lord Rugon and Salmanor Hardin wrestled for the dagger. Palanad Lantar fell to the stone floor, blood streaming from half a dozen wounds in his chest and neck. His dead eyes were already glazing over as they stared at the ceiling with an expression of shock and horror.

Hardin brought his other hand around and tried to slam it into

Lord Rugon's face. The councilor blocked the blow, and then countered with a fist to the inquisitor's jaw. Hardin rocked back, stunned. Lord Rugon twisted his grip on the high priest's knife-hand, trying to pry the weapon from his grasp.

Lord Desmond jumped into the struggle, grappling Hardin from behind. Together, they forced the inquisitor to drop the dagger. It fell clattering to the floor, still covered with Palanad's blood.

Then the guards were rushing in beside them. They grabbed Hardin's arms and pinned them behind his back. He struggled wildly, eyes wide with madness.

"You have betrayed yourselves!" he cried. "And now you must live as slaves to the Dark as penance!"

His head turned to the side, and he looked at the serving girl. "But I will not allow you to drag the pious down with you! The faithful will yet be saved by the Light!"

A nimbus of red formed around Hardin's body. With cries of pain, the guards fell back from its touch, their armored gloves suddenly glowing as though heated over a forge. He started toward the serving girl, but then stopped. She was backing away from him, hand held in front of her face, screaming.

The sound of a sword being drawn from its sheath rang through the milling panic. Lord Rugon stepped toward the high priest, his blade flashing in a swift and decisive thrust. Salmanor Hardin reeled back, the sword buried in his chest. Blood gushed onto the inquisitor's already gore-stained robe as he sank slowly to the ground. When he finally came to rest, his eyes, too, now stared at the ceiling.

Lord Rugon bent over the body of Palanad Lantar, searching it for signs of life. When he found none, he bowed his head.

"Shall we call for a healer, My Lord?" one of the guards asked tentatively.

Lord Rugon raised and shook his head. "No. Mage Lantar is beyond help."

"And the high priest?"

He rose and stepped over to the fallen inquisitor's body. He grasped the pommel of his sword, and, with a violent wrench of his arm, yanked it free. Hardin spasmed weakly, blood fountaining from the gaping hole in his chest. Then he was still.

"I have to get back to the tower," the councilor said thickly. "The others need to know what has happened. Especially the wizards. I don't know what they can do now to stop what is coming, but they have to be told."

His gaze swept around the room. "These two men were the last chance we had to ward the tower against the dragons that are coming," he said loudly. "I think we have another few minutes before they begin to destroy the palace. Take them to make peace with the Gods. They will probably be our last."

With an abrupt turn, he spun on his heel and strode toward the door. The serving girl, unseen by the others as they stared in dread at Lord Rugon's back, allowed herself a brief smile.

Payment

Salmanor Hardin's consciousness floated in a haze of white. He could no longer feel his body. The pain of his wounds was gone. The harsh reality of the world had finally faded from his awareness.

A form appeared at his side. It was the serving girl, looking up at him with adoring eyes.

Ah! he thought. *There you are, little one. You are safe with me then, too, here in the Light.*

She laughed.

Clueless to the end, Salmanor Hardin. So easy to delude, to manipulate. So desperate to vindicate a faith that you never truly felt.

He looked at her in confusion. The light around him suddenly changed, taking on a menacing black and red color.

What? he asked.

The girl waved an ethereal hand in dismissal. *It is of no consequence. Our dance is done, and I no longer need to cloud your thoughts with madness. You should find them clearing shortly. All that remains of this part of my mission is to deliver my message.*

A stab of fright ran through his mind. That he could still experience such emotions in his now ephemeral state filled him with sudden dread.

The serving girl laughed again. *Is the afterlife not living up to your expectations, Your Grace? I'm afraid that you will have to get used to that.*

Hardin's mind roiled in panic. *What is happening to me?*

The girl gestured with one hand toward her bosom. The bodice of her dress unlaced itself and parted, revealing her bared breasts. Her skin was flushed and red. A blood-red gem on a chain rested against it, hanging from her neck.

I do find taking a soul to be incredibly arousing, you know, she continued breathlessly. *And you did so anticipate pleasuring me while we've talked these many months. It's only fair that I share that with you while I show you your new home.*

My new ... home?

Why, yes, Your Grace. Your body is dead now, courtesy of Lord Rugon's considerable skill with a blade. She paused, a look of mock thoughtfulness on her face. *I think he may have objected to you murdering Mage Lantar. Carlissans can be so funny about that sort of thing.*

Slowly, painfully, the madness began to unravel from Hardin's mind. *Lantar ... murdered? And I'm ... dead?*

She nodded, lustrous black hair flouncing with mock eagerness.

Extremely. But don't worry. I've taken precautions to ensure that your spirit isn't wasted just yet. You have so much to experience before moving on to the Divine.

Memory flooded back into Hardin's awareness, along with a full understanding of all he had done. His mind screamed in horror.

My mission didn't quite go according to plan, she continued absently, as his scream dissolved into a cacophony of helpless mental sobs. *The King's magic ring was quite a surprise, I must admit. And then there was that meddling court mage ... Still, I think I handled those unexpected developments rather well. Yes, all things considered, I believe that my master will be pleased with how it turned out.*

Where are we? Hardin demanded. *And who — what — are you?*

The girl's eyes began to shine with a menacing red light. The tips of her fingers grew into black claws, and there was a flash of fangs as she smiled at him. He recoiled from her in panic.

My name is Liana Desire, she said. *I am a succubus in the service of his magnificence, the Demon Lord, Borr. My message for you is from our ally, Zomoran, the Black Magus, now Warlord of Carlissa. He says that he hopes you enjoy his payment for what you and your inquisition did to him and his colleagues this Yule.*

She waved a clawed hand around them, and then at herself. *As for where you are? This is all just a vision I am giving you, of course. To help you understand what has happened to you.*

Her eyes flashed again as she touched the gem that hung at her bosom. *This is your new home, inquisitor. I do hope that you like it, because you are going to be here for a very long time.*

Liana laughed as Hardin's mind screamed again. This time, it did not stop.

Ah, yes, she said. Her eyes closed, and her lips parted in ecstasy. *I do so enjoy this part ...*

Chapter 12 - The Massacre of Lannamon

The Herd

Orion watched Diana peer around the corner of the burning shop. A dragon had passed almost directly overhead, leaving a blazing line of flame in its wake. Fire was spreading around them. The scant protection of the alley they'd huddled into for cover was quickly becoming a furnace that would roast them alive.

The first few minutes of their flight had dashed any hope of finding shelter. The dragons had strafed the city, leaving great swathes of ruin in their path. Wherever they struck, no one survived, whether hidden indoors or running in the open.

Realizing that not being in the creatures' path was their only hope of survival, Orion had led the group on a series of desperate sprints through the Lower City. They'd dashed madly in one direction to avoid the monsters in one flight, only to be forced to run in a different direction to avoid the next. Long lines of flame had roared into life behind them as they'd dodged, frantically trying to avoid the burning buildings around them.

He tried — and failed — to guess how long it had been since the dragons had first appeared. Their panicked flight had become an unbroken blur of destruction and terror, and he'd long since lost track of time. The roar of the monsters and the relentless and terrified screams of the dying had escorted them the whole way.

They'd already lost two of their number. The first had stopped to help a woman injured by falling debris; the rest of the building had collapsed on top of them. The second had simply left the group without warning, stumbling with a look of exhausted terror into an abandoned home to hide. Orion had seen a dragon hit that block a few minutes later, leaving a blazing inferno in its wake.

They'd covered about half the distance to the docks. It was an extraordinary accomplishment under the circumstances, but their attempt to reach the meager protection of the water had clearly failed. The last dragon had turned the city to their south — in the direction they had been running, toward the firth — into one long flaming wall. Fire stretched across their path as far as they could see, making further progress impossible. And the flames were spreading in their direction.

The leading fingers of the demon advance were reaching into the surrounding streets. They'd seen one monster kill a fleeing family, gleefully slaughtering parents and children alike with long, curved claws. Another walked boldly along a broad avenue, roaring and preening as it went. Several people were impaled on the long, bony spines covering its enormous body. One of them was still screaming.

Orion noted — now that he had a rare moment to think — that the demon attacks were less aggressive than they should have been. They did not hesitate to kill, but they seemed more intent on terrorizing people into fleeing from their advance. There might be a key to their strategy in that — if indeed there were one, beyond spreading horror and death.

He didn't know what it was, and he had no time to figure it out. What he did know was that the turn of each corner now carried the risk of running into the monsters. It was only a matter of time before the demon force swept through the entire area on its march toward the soldiers at the eastern end of the Lower City.

Their alley opened onto a lane that ran at an angle to the northeast. Diana pulled back from the corner and turned to the others.

"It's clear to the right," she said. "But that won't last. People are running onto the lane from the left, trying to escape the block that dragon just fired. A mob is going to come by here at any moment."

As if cued by her warning, a chorus of new and louder screams arose from around the corner. Orion nodded toward the sound.

"If we don't leave now, we'll be trapped between that crowd and the fire. Go!"

Diana was already sprinting before he'd finished his sentence. The others managed to get ahead of the crush of refugees and headed along the lane. A few of them could still run, and the rest stumbled along as best they could.

The group stretched out despite their efforts to stay together. Some fell behind, and a few of the faster refugees overtook and passed them. The wall of fire continued in a long line to their right, completely blocking the way south.

The ground rose slowly beneath them as they went. *That probably means we're heading into Cherry Hill*, Orion thought. He smiled. The elevation would give them a better view, and a chance to see what was happening around them.

The lane came to an intersection. A street that curved in from the south merged with it, and the two widened into a broad avenue that headed directly toward the eastern end of the city. A park ran along the north side of it as it rose into a small hill. The height and the open ground gave them their first unobstructed view of the army base since the dragon attack had begun.

The fortifications were in flames. Pockets of soldiers and a handful of battle mages still manned the walls, trying desperately to bring spells and the remaining ballistae to bear on the circling dragons. Huge bolts and stabs of conjured power lanced up at the monsters as they passed overhead or stooped to attack. The defense hadn't been in vain; several of the beasts lay dead on the ground, or crashed and impaled upon the spiked battlements.

Some dragons had continued on toward the palace, but the rest had circled back to land near the dwindling wall of bluffs to the north. They had dropped off their riders and risen again to continue their assault from the sky. The fire giants, girded in heavy black armor and wielding enormous weapons, were wading through the burning city to strike at the defenders' northern flank. The spreading flames had no effect on them, giving a terrible advantage to their attack.

Flying demons were returning to the eastern end of the city. They circled the divided army, harrying their ranks and searching for weaknesses to exploit. Descending without warning, they would swarm like locusts to attack small groups of soldiers that had become separated from the regiment's main body. They struck hard with weapons and magic, slaughtering them without mercy. Then they scattered back into the sky, circling, waiting for another opening to pounce on the overwhelmed Carlissan soldiers.

Orion's lips tightened grimly as he took stock of what he saw. The dragons had concentrated on breaking the army formations. Earlier, a disciplined regiment had been marching resolutely toward the heart of the city. Now it was fractured into separate groups, each fighting the spreading flames around them while desperately trying to hold against the monsters' attacks.

It wasn't until he saw the line of fires ahead of them, though, that Orion finally realized what was happening. His face white, he spun to look behind. What he saw confirmed his fears.

Slowly, pass by pass, the dragons had sliced the north end of the Lower City into strips. Between each strip, a long wall of burning streets and buildings ran toward the approaching demons. The lines continued ahead, cutting the army into separate groups, walling them off from each other by flame.

"*Damn*," Orion said harshly. "I should have seen that earlier."

Diana looked at him, startled. "What?" she asked.

Instead of answering, he turned abruptly and started running to the north. "This way!" he called.

He ducked into a narrow alley. It was blind and appeared to be deserted. When he neared its end, he stopped, waiting for the others to catch up.

He was relieved when he saw they'd all followed. Davin cursed as the group collected again. He'd tripped on a missing cobblestone and barely kept from falling.

Diana came to Orion's side and looked at him. "What?" she asked again.

"The demons' plan," he said. His voice gasped as he tried to catch his breath. "I didn't see it before."

The crowd of refugees on the lane outside the alley began to pass them by. They had seen the soldiers ahead and were running toward them with cries of hope.

Diana arched her eyebrows pointedly. "What?" she repeated, this time with emphasis. There was a hint of impatience in her voice.

"We need to keep away from the fires and soldiers," he said. "And get under cover. Fast."

Davin sputtered, but all that came out was a wheezing cough.

"That's crazy," Jameson said. The harsh bark of his voice betrayed his frayed nerves. "The soldiers are our only protection in this chaos!"

Orion shook his head.

"Our forces are being cut into groups and separated by fire. That's why the dragons strafed the city the way they did. They left long strips of flame leading back to the enemy's ground forces."

"So?" Davin demanded.

"I couldn't see it until we reached the higher ground, but there's a road in the center of each of those lines."

"So they're cutting channels of fire to march along?" Diana offered.

Jameson's expression sobered abruptly. "Are demons resistant to fire?" he asked.

"Some of the stronger ones could certainly use them," Orion said. "But that's not their plan. I didn't understand *that* until I saw the giants moving through the flames to flank the soldiers from the north."

Diana's eyes went wide. "Hellmen," she breathed. "They're all but immune to normal fires, aren't they? Like the giants?"

Orion nodded. "They're probably passing us in force through the channels right now. The enemy has control of the air, so our commanders may not even see them coming."

"What will they do?" Cooper asked.

"If I were their general?" Orion replied. "Surround the soldiers. Hellmen and giants attacking from the burning lines to the north and south. Dragons hitting them from the east and demons attacking from the west."

Diana gasped. "That's why you led us off the road," she said. "That entire area ahead of us is about to become a killing zone."

Orion nodded as another piece of the puzzle fell into place in his mind.

"Did any of you notice that the demons were more intent on terrorizing the people into fleeing than on killing them?" he asked. "That's why. They're deliberately driving civilians into that area."

Cooper looked confused. "What for?"

"To compromise the soldiers' defense," Jameson said. A look of comprehension was dawning on his face as well.

Orion nodded. "To divide their attention," he added. "To force them to defend not only themselves, but a stampede of unarmed citizens. To blunt the army's attacks and firepower by using the people as human shields. To make our forces afraid to use their full strength out of fear of civilian casualties. To give themselves a tactical advantage by sowing chaos among the defense."

Diana took a long breath. "And we nearly ran right into it."

"All right," Jameson said. "So what do we do?"

"We hide," Orion replied. "Keep out of sight and let the Hellmen and the demons pass us on their way to engage the soldiers."

Jameson frowned. "I thought we were going to help," he said.

Diana shook her head. There was a note of ruthless calm in her voice when she spoke.

"It's too late for that," she said quietly. "It was too late when the dragons arrived. This isn't about trying to win anymore. It's about not being counted among the dead."

"There may still be a chance later," Orion added. "If the battle takes a turn toward our side — if reinforcements arrive from the palace, or when the Archmage makes his move. Then we can come out of hiding to help. But for now, there's nothing we can do."

Diana pointed back toward the road outside the alley. Fleeing and screaming civilians were still running along it.

"There *is* something we can do," she said. "We can warn those people that they're running into a trap. Now that you've figured out their plan, that would help foil it. And it would save lives."

Orion's eyebrows shot up, and he smiled. "We could at that," he said.

A look of fiery determination returned to Diana's bright green eyes. "Who's with us?" she asked fiercely.

"An excellent plan," a voice agreed from above. "Sadly, it has an important flaw."

They looked up at the unexpected sound. The voice had an ugly, hard-edged timbre. It was not deep, but had a disturbing reverberation to it that set the listener's teeth shaking.

A demon sat on the edge of a roof to one side of the alley. It wasn't one of the larger monsters — it looked to be barely seven feet in height, if that — with mottled blue skin and stunted bat-like wings.

"You may call me Nalef, humans," it continued. Its tone was conversational and amused, but its yellow cat-eyes shone with undisguised menace. "And you have my compliments. The witless wonders commanding your defenses don't have a clue what is coming, and here you've figured it all out on your own! It's a pity I'll have to reward such cleverness by killing the lot of you."

Several of the group backed away toward the street, eyes widening in terror.

"No, don't try to run," Nalef warned. "If you do, I'll make sure your death is very, very painful." It chuckled. "Can't have you spoiling the slaughter by spooking the herd now, can we?"

Diana's eyes fixed on the demon. They had lost none of their fire from the moments before.

"Can we take it?" she asked softly.

Orion slowly raised his club as his knees bent into a defensive stance. "Do we have a choice?"

Jameson's sword rang as he drew and pointed it at the monster. "None whatsoever," he said.

The demon looked down at them. It smiled a grin filled with wicked, curved teeth.

"I was hoping you'd decide to make this interesting," it said. "The invasion's been rather dull and much too easy, so far!"

It leaped from the corner of the roof, and there was chaos.

Closing In

The demon Ashrach stood before the door of the guard tower. It stared impatiently at the scout. "Well?" it demanded.

The scout demon crouched close to the ground. It was a small, thin monster covered in red fur. It had a canine snout that was conspicuously large for its size, and it was snuffling noisily.

It rose slowly to its feet and turned to its commander. "We have their trail," it said confidently. "Human scents, a lot of them. And a hint of elf. Maybe a half-elf."

"How long?"

"An hour ago. Maybe less."

Another creature looked up along the line of bluffs and nodded. It had a bird-like head with enormous eyes.

"Yes, I see it now," it said. "A vine rope near the roof of the tower. They climbed down from the cliffs above. Probably entered a window."

"Just as the captain suspected," Ashrach said. "He thought they might try to re-enter the city near here. Good work, both of you."

The little dog-like demon made a pleased whimpering sound. The other inclined its bird-like head, but said nothing. Ashrach turned to face it.

"You will report to the captain," it said. "We will leave a trail for it to follow." It raised a clawed hand in a gesture of caution. "Fly swiftly, Keeah. Gorath will not be pleased at any delay."

The bird-like head bobbed in acknowledgement. A pair of white and gold wings unfurled from its back. They beat hard as it rose into the sky and flew off along the cliffs to the west.

Ashrach turned back to the dog-faced scout. "Lead us to them," it ordered. "As quick as you can. The rest of you, with me. We have a royal to hunt!"

Fight Together

Nalef landed in the center of the group. Diana leaped wildly as it struck. Its claws raked empty air where she had stood only moments before. It roared in anger and frustration as its first kill slipped from its grasp.

Orion spun. He swung his club with all his strength and hit the monster squarely in the temple. Pain shot up his arms as his weapon splintered, but the demon seemed unfazed by the blow. It flexed its wings with a contemptuous growl, spreading them around itself like a pair of leathery shields. One of them hit him in the shoulder and sent him sprawling.

Nalef stooped to finish him, but the others were already moving to attack. Jameson charged it from behind, swinging his sword with both hands. It struck the creature in the back and rang from the impact. Cooper loosed an arrow that ricocheted crazily from its chest, narrowly missing Davin. Several others charged, wielding makeshift clubs and butcher's knives.

The attacks left only shallow lacerations in the demon's scaled hide. But they were enough to distract it as Orion crawled frantically away. Enraged, it beat its wings again, spinning and slashing at the humans around it. One went down, screaming in agony, chest torn open by its claws.

That proved to be too much for some of the group. Most of them were plain townsfolk who had no experience with or temperament for fighting. Now they were being forced to battle a demon in close quarters. Several of them dropped their weapons and ran.

Orion saw them as he struggled back to his feet. In horror, he noticed the shape of a dimly glowing red glyph on the ground, between them and the main road. It lay directly in their path, and they were speeding heedlessly toward it.

"Don't try to run!" he yelled. "It's a trap —"

His warning came too late. The glyph flared brightly as they stepped past it, and then exploded. A storm of flame bloomed around them and formed a barrier that blocked any escape from the alley. Shrieks of pain and terror were suddenly cut off as the fleeing refugees' burning bodies disappeared into the wall of fire.

Nalef barked a guttural laugh. It slashed at another of the townsfolk with its enormous claws. A woman fell, gurgling helplessly, blood gushing from her ruined throat.

"Fight together!" Orion yelled. What little cohesion their group had was about to break. If it did, they would be dead; the demon would finish them, one at a time. "It's our only chance!"

"Fight together!" Diana cried in response. She stepped in, slashing with the butcher's knife she'd taken from the kitchen of the Smiling Nymph. It scored a long, shallow gash on the demon's right wing. It beat at her, trying to knock her down, but she was already leaping out of its reach. Nalef roared in frustration as she once again avoided its attack.

"Together!" Cooper's voice rang. There was a whistle as another arrow struck the demon in the side of the head. It bounced off, leaving a gash in its bony temple.

Most of the others echoed the call and rallied. Kitchen knives and makeshift clubs lashed at the monster, and rocks flew. Jameson stepped forward with a thrust of his sword and was rewarded with a hit on Nalef's shoulder.

Not everyone was willing to join the fight. There were doors and windows in the surrounding buildings, and several of the group ran toward them. Davin stumbled toward a tall fence at the back of the alley. His shoulders shook in terror as he looked for a handhold to scale it.

Orion's gaze swept around. As he feared, he saw more of the dimly glowing glyphs set to cut off any escape. The demon had been thorough in casting the spells of its trap.

"Don't run!" Orion cried again. "There are traps set all around us!"

Davin glared at him. His eyes were wide with panic.

"Damn!" Cooper blurted. "Scholar-boy is gonna crack!"

"Shut up, Cooper!" Diana yelled. "You're not helping!"

She dodged a blow from the demon's tail and stepped back as two others waded in to attack. "Davin, don't!" she called. "We need you! Fight with us!"

"I don't believe you!" Davin screamed. "We can't fight that thing! You're just going to get us killed!"

He spun and jumped, grabbing at the slats, and tried to scale the fence. One of the other refugees reached a window at the same time and tried to smash it with a club. Orion turned away, sickened, as another roar of fire took their lives.

"Ri!" Diana called. She'd stooped to pick up a dropped pitchfork and was holding it in her left hand. She tossed it to him with a quick flick of her arm. He caught the weapon and spun it, testing its weight. Then he stepped forward with the others to face the demon.

He saw with surprise that it was facing him as well. Its wings beat and its arms slashed at its attackers as though it were trying to ward off a cloud of annoying insects. Half of the refugees lay dead around it, the cobblestones stained with their blood. But it was looking at him, and there was anger in its demonic visage.

Those traps were supposed to take most of us out, he realized suddenly. *It must have spent most of its magic setting them. That's why it's not using spells to fight us now.*

"You're the ringleader," Nalef barked. "You and that girl of yours. I'm going to kill you now."

Orion's eyes widened. He lowered the pitchfork and braced

himself.

That's why it's so angry with me, he thought. *I rallied the others not to run. It didn't expect so many of us to fight, and now it's worried it overextended itself. And it thinks I'm the principal threat.* He nearly laughed aloud, but he kept his mind on the approaching monster. *Now, how can I use that …*

He spun abruptly and ran. The demon's nostrils flared angrily as it leaped after him. It was fast and powerful, and at a full sprint, it needed only seconds to overtake him. Orion felt its breath on his back as it raised a clawed hand to strike.

He had been making for the missing cobblestone in the alley that Davin had tripped over a few minutes earlier. As he ran over it, he whipped the pitchfork around in his hands, planted the weapon's butt firmly into the opening, levered the head up to point directly behind him, and slid under the swipe of the monster's claws.

The demon's hide could have turned an ordinary stab from the weapon. One delivered with the full force of its own charge behind it was another matter. The wooden shaft splintered as Nalef impaled itself on the fork, and the tines sank to their full length into its gut.

Orion desperately tried to duck under the demon as it stumbled, howling in pain and anger. Monstrous legs struck him with the force of a hammer as they tripped over him, throwing him to the ground.

His head hit the cobblestones as he fell. Diana's eyes widened when she saw that he did not get up.

To Find the Courage

Lieutenant Kay raised her head to look at Gerrold. "I haven't seen any dragons in a while," she said. "Have they all passed?"

Gerrold pulled back from the corner of the pavilion opening to face her. He wore a troubled expression.

"I think so," he said. "Some have gone on to the palace. The rest are attacking the army fortifications at the eastern end of the city."

"How is the battle going there?" Stefan asked.

"Not well. They hit their defenses from behind. The barracks are aflame, and the dragons are setting fire to the city."

"We can't just keep waiting here," Randia said. Her voice was thick with frustration.

Gerrold shook his head. "There's a patrol nearby. They'll spot us if we try to move."

Kay crawled slowly to Gerrold's side. She looked out carefully.

"To our north, near the edge of the terrace," she agreed. "They're not a normal patrol, though. They're moving too slowly. And it looks like they're splitting up ..."

Her head snapped back from the opening.

"They're in a search formation. They're looking for something."

Randia and Stefan exchanged glances. "Us?" Stefan asked.

"It doesn't matter," Kay said. "Whether they're looking for us or not, they're going to find us."

"What do we do?" Randia asked. There was a hint of panic in her voice.

"You need to run, Your Highness," Kay replied. "You and the prince. When I give the signal. Down the path to the east. We'll scatter and create a diversion. If we're lucky, they'll miss you in the confusion."

Randia's eyes widened. "You can't," she gasped. "You'll be killed!"

Kay smiled grimly as she unlimbered her bow. Crouching, she scuttled across the glade to Randia's side.

"That goes with the job, Your Highness," she said gently. "We fight to defend Carlissa — if necessary, to the death. For King, and for country."

Slowly, she raised her fist to her heart in salute. "And for our princess," she added.

Tears spurted from Randia's eyes. She reached out and grabbed Kay's hand.

"No," she sobbed. "I don't want anyone else to die for me!"

Kay smiled at her. When she spoke, her voice was thick with emotion.

"I never had the chance to tell you how much I admired you, Your Highness," she said softly. "For so many things. For your independence, in choosing your own path in life. For becoming a bard, against all the expectations of the nobility. It helped give me the courage to make my own choices as well. That's why I'm wearing this, today." She gestured at her uniform with her free hand.

"Then there was the way you would walk through the streets of the city, playing and singing for the people. Talking with them, listening to them. Always kind, always encouraging, always caring what they thought and felt. We called you 'The Princess Bard.'"

Randia sobbed again. She threw her arms around Kay and held her tightly.

"I came to every one of your performances," Kay continued. "And not just for your skill with music, or your amazing voice. It was for the *joy* that I heard in your songs. For the enthusiasm they cried. For life, and for everything good that we could make of ourselves. For the inspiration they gave me, and so many others, that all those things were truly possible."

She slowly pulled back from Randia's embrace. She was crying too, now. Her brown eyes stared deeply into the princess' blue ones, holding them.

"Your people love you. And that is why you *must* survive the horrible thing that is happening today. It is why you *must* find the courage to let us die for you. I know that will be hard, and that it will hurt you terribly. But you can do it. Honor us by keeping our spirit alive. By fighting for life, and never giving up."

A hard glint of determination formed amid the tears in Randia's eyes.

"I will," she said firmly. "In your honor, and in your name. And I will never forget you!"

Stefan nodded. There were tears on his face as well.

"When you give the signal," he said. "We'll break for the tunnel. We'll run, and we won't look back."

Kay looked at the other soldiers. Their faces were grim. The archers had readied their bows, and the rest had drawn their swords. They knew what was coming, and they faced it with determination.

"Gerrold, Jean," she said. "You and Richard make your way back along the path we took here. *Quietly.* When you hear my whistle, start making a lot of noise. Make it loud. Then run back toward the guard tower. Try to get any demons that see you to follow."

She turned to Richard. "If they break off or seem reluctant to pursue, use your bow. Pepper them with arrows until they adjust their thinking on the matter."

"And the rest of us?" Kenn asked hesitantly.

Gerrold, Jean, and Richard ran quietly out of the glade. Kay turned to the others.

"Same drill, from here. Ten count after my whistle for them to start their diversion. Then the prince and princess run. Another ten count and we start ours. By the time the demons reach us, they should be into the tunnel and on the road to the Star. We make a lot of noise and draw the monsters' attention away from them. Pelt any demon that so much as looks to the east with arrows and rocks."

The others nodded. Kay waited, looking as though she were counting down time in her mind. After a minute, she raised her fingers to her lips.

Her whistle never sounded. It was cut off by a blood-curdling shriek from the way the three guards had gone.

Kenn's head snapped around. "That's Gerrold!" he hissed.

"Too late!" Kay barked. "They're already closing in!"

She turned to the princess. "Go!"

Stefan and Randia leaped to their feet and sprinted toward the eastern exit.

Kay nocked an arrow and, rising to a crouch, aimed it at the path to the west. She could hear harsh cries now, and the sound of heavy feet on the stone of the walkway.

Another shriek pierced the air. This one was from Richard, she knew, from the deep timbre of his voice. It ended abruptly with a horrible burbling sound.

A dog-faced demon ran into view, crouching low to the ground. It raised its head, snuffling loudly. When it saw the fleeing princess, it let out a loud howl.

Kay put her arrow through its eye. It fell backward into a flowerbed with a strangled whine.

She drew again, her hands a blur of confident, expert motion. She loosed as a second demon ran into view. The arrow struck a bony ridge on its forehead, leaving an ugly gash in its wake. Another shot took it in the neck. Black ichor spurted through its fingers as its clawed hands clutched frantically at the wound.

Another figure emerged from the archway to the east. It was bull-headed and heavily muscled, and a chain hauberk of dark metal covered its body. It straightened to its full height and leveled a massive sword in front of it.

Randia's eyes widened as the demon loomed before her, blocking their escape. She grabbed Stefan's arm and tried frantically to stop. They skidded on the stone walkway, feet sliding out from beneath them. They landed on the ground, hard, and found themselves sitting directly under the point of the enormous weapon.

Kay spun toward the monster and loosed again. The demon's gaze swept toward her, and it raised its hand in a warding gesture. The arrow ricocheted in mid-air with a loud *spang*. She fired a second time, and then a third, and the demon deflected each arrow with a contemptuous flick of its clawed hand.

Randia and Stefan back-crawled wildly away from the massive blade as it hung only a few feet above their heads. When they were clear, they scrambled to their feet and ran back under the pavilion. The guards quickly formed a circle around them.

The bull-demon's face twisted into an expression that might have been a grin or a snarl. It stepped forward as more demons poured into the glade from the western entrance.

"Trapped at last," Ashrach said. Its demonic voice sounded amused, and very satisfied. "You led my captain on quite a chase, little princess. But there is no escape now."

It turned to Kay. She stood, arrow nocked and drawn, aimed at the monster's face.

"You are outmatched," it said. "Surrender and disarm. If you resist, you will all die."

Kay's eyes arched in surprise.

"A demon, offering quarter?" she said. Her voice was thick with mockery and contempt. "Isn't that a bit out of character?"

"Quite," Ashrach agreed. "Let's say that your soldiers have stumbled onto a bit of good fortune. My captain's orders are to take the royal alive, if possible. He wants to be the one to deliver her, intact, to the Master of the Horde."

Kay stared acidly at the creature as more demons filed into the glade. She could see that it was right. Their company wouldn't last a minute against the force that was surrounding them.

"But you humans are so fragile," Ashrach continued. "If you put up a fight, she might end up being damaged with the rest of you. So to avoid that, it suits me to offer you an opportunity to surrender."

Its monstrous gaze hardened. "*One* opportunity. A very *brief* one."

Kay looked over her shoulder. Randia had drawn her knife. The princess' eyes were narrowed, and her face grim. Kay smiled at her and turned to the creature again.

"You'll have to earn this victory, demon," she shouted. "Guards of Company Twenty-Three! *Attack!*"

Chapter 13 - Hero's Refrain

Prince's Descent

Gerard breathed a sigh of relief. Crossing the firth had taken longer than he planned, but he was finally approaching the cliff-wall above the southern terraces. His dangerous and unpredictable flight across the city was almost over.

The coming of the dragons had nearly exposed him. Several of the great monsters had flown around him on their way to attack the palace. Their piercing eyes had sorely tested his cloaking spell, and he feared several times that it would falter. The power of the ring, though, had never wavered.

Unfortunately, the wind had. The tide of battle had turned on the slopes of the High City, and the Queen's storm had dissipated. The gusts that carried him so quickly at first had faded to an ordinary breeze. As a result, the last half of his journey had progressed with agonizing slowness.

He looked around. The clouds had dispersed, and the sun was descending toward the summit of Mount Cascade. The tower of the Silver Star Adventurer's Academy still gleamed in its light. He noted grimly that it was a good distance away to his left, and that it was under siege. Its closest entrance was a full level below him.

His eyes darted around, searching for the quickest way to reach it. He saw a walkway ahead of him that emerged from a copse of trees and enclosed gardens. It ran lengthwise along the city's highest terrace, and then through a tunnel in a rocky spur that jutted toward the firth. The path then turned north and west to follow the spur's far edge, until it descended in a winding stair to the academy's rear gate.

Gerard frowned. That last part of the way paralleled a sheer precipice that marked the east end of the Upper City South. There were no gardens or orchards along that rocky path. It was cut into the stone of the spur and alarmingly exposed.

Movement caught his eye. He saw a large demon climbing down a stony crag above the tunnel's far exit. He drew a deep breath and held it. Was it making for the stair as well? He watched cautiously as the creature dropped from the crag, landed on the path, and then turned and entered the tunnel.

He sighed with relief. The monster was moving away from the academy, not toward it. He could avoid it by waiting to land until he reached the far side of the spur. He smiled and prepared to adjust his descent.

A piercing scream stopped him.

A bolt of fear shot down his spine as he turned toward the sound. A pack of demons was rushing along the path from the west. One of them held aloft a soldier in the livery of the city guard. The man dangled by one arm; the other had been torn off.

He heard curses and the ring of steel. A cacophony of demonic battle roars followed, harsh and triumphant. He couldn't see below the canopy the monsters were approaching, but he knew what was happening. A group of guards had been ambushed in the gardens and were about to be slaughtered.

Without thinking, he prepared to come to their aid. Then he stopped.

He could see that the demons were a formidable force. He *might* defeat them using the power of the ring. But was it strong enough to let him *cloak* that battle as well? If he failed, then any hope of reaching the Archmage in stealth would be lost. Did he dare take that risk?

His eyes closed in pain. Every emotion in him cried out to help the guards, and that to turn his back on them would be an unforgivable act of cowardice. Would he ever be able to live with such a choice? To look at himself in a mirror, after abandoning them to their fate?

The ring sang to him with a promise of power. It reassured him that it would, indeed, grant him the ability to defeat the monsters. The guards were innocent people who would be butchered if he did nothing. He could save them. He *should* save them.

Slowly, he shook his head. He had to think of the survival, not just of a group of soldiers, but of the kingdom — and, perhaps, the very world itself. His mission was that important. If he jeopardized it to save them, then that choice could consign millions to slavery and death.

He was heir to the throne of Carlissa, now. He had to think, not just like a man or even a wizard, but like a king. The feeling tasted bitter in his mind and in his heart, but he knew what he had to do. He would honor the unnamed guards who gave their lives to keep his mission safe — as indeed he knew they would have, had they known what was at stake. But he had to move on.

"Stefan!" a vibrant, female voice cried. "Look out!"

A bolt of horror shot through Gerard's heart.

He knew that voice. He knew it from playing together as children. He knew it from endless talks as they walked the city, confiding in each other with their secret thoughts and dreams. He knew it from songs that had never failed to move him to laughter or tears. And he knew it from a thousand other treasured moments running across the span of his young life.

"Princess, get behind us!" another voice called.

There was no doubt. The guards — the very ones he'd been about to leave to their fate — were defending his sister. If he didn't act, the demons would kill her.

Resolve burned in Gerard's heart. He didn't even think about what he did next.

He reached into the ring. He drew on its magic with all the strength that he could find within himself. He kept drawing on that power until he felt he was about to explode with its force. Then, when he thought he could hold no more, he drew more still.

The ring's energy flooded through him like a raging inferno. At a flicker of thought, an aura of silver magic bloomed into being around him. It was stronger than any shield he had conjured before, or even *imagined* possible.

He fixed his eyes on the pavilion and drew his wand.

He had promised his parents — and himself — that he would save his sister if he could. A stroke of luck beyond all hope had brought him to her in the nick of time, armed with the power to do so. He would rescue her, or he would die trying.

And if he risked the world on that choice, then so be it.

With a cry of defiance, eyes blazing with argent fire, Gerard Killraven dropped like a falling star toward the battle.

Buying Time

Diana's eyes widened as she watched Orion fall. Before Nalef could finish him, though, she saw Jameson leap onto the demon's back. He gripped his sword with both hands and pointed it down as the monster sprawled on the cobblestones.

"It's hurt!" he cried. "Now's our chance!"

There was an area of relatively bare flesh around the creature's wing joints that its scales didn't fully protect. It was a necessary feature to allow the wings to beat freely, and Jameson didn't miss it. He stabbed, driving his sword's point directly into the spot. It was a quality weapon — an heirloom from service in the army as a younger man, Diana guessed — and it bit hard into the monster's hide. The blade sank into its back, and black ichor fountained from the wound.

Nalef let out a roar of pain and fury as Diana and several others rushed forward. The demon beat its wings wildly, trying to knock Jameson off its back. The wing with the wounded pinion flopped awkwardly, but the other had lost none of its strength. It swatted the innkeeper as though he were a fly. He flew through the air to land a dozen feet away, skidding and rolling on the cobblestones. He shook his head and tried to rise, but then stumbled and fell, his left leg twisting at an awkward angle.

Clubs and knives descended on Nalef as it surged to its feet. Jameson's sword still protruded awkwardly from its back as it lashed out with its arms in a wild frenzy. One of its attackers fell screaming, disemboweled by the creature's talons.

Diana smiled grimly as she ducked under a blow. She noted with satisfaction that Orion's pitchfork had done nearly as much damage to the monster's front as Jameson's sword had to its back. The tool's head protruded from its midsection, just below the sternum. The tines had sunk deeply into its flesh, and shards of splintering wood had left deep gashes in its leathery hide.

They attacked again. The survivors were the most determined of the group, and they knew that their only chance was a fight to the death. The demon was weakening, but the price was high. They battled on, dying, one by one.

Diana slashed at Nalef's good wing with her knife. It roared as the blade struck, and then spun to face her, eyes wide. Its talons raked the air, but missed her again as she jumped quickly out of their way.

Its tail lashed out as well. The bony protrusions hit another refugee in the side of the head. The woman flew backward, her face crushed and her neck broken.

Nalef stalked toward Diana. She backed slowly away from it, looking around for support. She saw Cooper standing near the end of the alley to her right. Her eyes widened as she realized that all the others had fallen.

Cooper's bow sang again. An arrow hit Nalef in the chest, joining several other shafts that stuck from the creature's body. Along with the sword and pitchfork, they made the monster look like an enormous pincushion.

Murderous fury filled the demon's eyes as it turned away from Diana to face the archer.

"Shit!" Cooper cursed.

The mid-joint on the demon's bat-like wings sported a pair of prehensile claws. The ones on its good wing curled around the hilt of the sword protruding from its back. Slowly, with a grunt of pain, it pulled the blade from its flesh. Its mouth curled into something resembling a grin as it took the weapon in its hand.

Cooper drew and loosed, again and again, as Nalef lumbered toward him. His shots grew wilder and more desperate as the monster closed.

Diana saw a slight movement among the bodies on the corpse-strewn ground. She had forgotten Jameson. One of his legs appeared to be broken, and he must have passed out from the pain when he tried to stand on it. But now he was crawling, slowly, as the demon stalked past him. He looked like he was trying to reach a hatchet that one of the others had dropped ...

The effort twisted his hip and elicited a fatal gasp of pain. The demon spun and stabbed downward. The innkeeper's broken body collapsed to the cobblestones, his own sword sticking from the back of his head.

Cooper loosed his last arrow, and it hit Nalef in the face. The shaft glanced off the bone and ricocheted, leaving an ugly gash across its cheek. The monster roared angrily, and, leaving the sword in Jameson's body, moved again toward the archer.

Diana looked around in desperation. The flames blocking the alley's exit still burned hotly, cutting off any escape. She searched for other survivors, but all the eyes she saw were lifeless …

All except two.

A stab of relief ran through her when she saw Orion. He was blinking and shaking his head, and trying to clear a stream of blood that ran into his eyes from a cut in his scalp. Nalef must have knocked him out when it stumbled over him. Now he was slowly trying to get back to his feet.

Diana heard Cooper scream once, in a voice that was suddenly choked off. She turned in time to see the archer die, the demon's fangs tearing into his throat.

Her mind raced. She could see that the battle had taken its toll on Nalef. Black blood streamed from wounds all across its body, and it was visibly slowed and weakened. She was unhurt, and aside from his cut, Orion didn't appear to be injured either. Together, they *might* still beat the thing. He just needed a minute to clear his head, and then he would be back in the fight …

A spike of fear ran through her as she remembered Jameson. Orion wasn't going to get that minute. The demon would kill him before he could recover. Then she would be facing it alone, and it would finish her.

She needed to buy Orion time to get back on his feet. And she had to do it *now*, before the demon made *him* its next target. But how?

And then she had it. It was so simple that she smiled.

"Hey, demon-breath!" she yelled. "Don't tell me that's the best you've got?"

Nalef turned to face her. It glared as she danced in a little circle, waving her arms.

"Some warrior demon you are!" she laughed. "Cut up like a roast by a few human civilians!"

Nalef ran toward her with a roar. *Good,* she thought. *That's it. You just so want to wring my neck, don't you …*

Despite its injuries, the demon closed the distance with surprising speed. Diana stood, waiting for it, free hand on one hip. Her stance displayed a contemptuous disrespect for the monster that only seemed to enrage it further.

A claw lashed at her neck. The blow should have taken her head from her shoulders, but she was ready for it. She ducked at the last moment and threw herself into a forward roll past the demon's right side. The crippled right wing tried to move awkwardly to block her, but failed. She slashed at the creature's leg with her knife as she slipped under its grasp. Then she was up again, making a show of dancing away from it and laughing.

"Oh, what prowess!" she cried. Her voice was thick with mockery. "What's the matter, demon? Did you get separated from the pack that was protecting you?"

Nalef bellowed as it spun to face her. She saw with satisfaction that its face was even redder than before.

"Girl!" it screamed. "I will rip out your beating heart with my claws and eat it!"

Diana forced herself to smile as the monster surged toward her. She tried to project an air of satisfied contempt, and to control the fear that churned in the pit of her stomach. She was beginning to understand the risk she'd taken by goading the demon into such a rage. If her gambit failed, it wouldn't just kill her. Her death would be long, and the fiend would make certain that she suffered.

Diana backed slowly away from the monster. She held her knife carefully before her. Her muscles tensed, preparing for another wild dodge.

Get up, Orion! she thought desperately. *I can't do this without you!*

Princess Beset

The guards of Company Twenty-Three attacked.

Stefan drew the sword he'd taken from the post's armory. To Randia's horror, and before she could stop him, he leaped forward to charge with the others. Arrows whistled over their heads as the group hit the monsters, screaming in desperate defiance.

The reckless advance caught the pack by surprise and forced back its front rank. A wolf-like beast with long fangs fell, hit by the thrust of half a dozen swords. The guards cheered.

"Formation!" Ashrach yelled angrily. It strode forward, holding its enormous blade before it in one hand.

"Stefan!" Randia cried. She raced ahead, brandishing her knife. "Look out!"

The demon waved a clawed hand. The head of a guard next to the young prince snapped backward. The guard collapsed as though he'd been struck by a hammer, blood fountaining from his shattered face.

"Form a line and hold it!" Ashrach bellowed. "No one gets through!"

A horned demon reached for Stefan. He brought his blade around desperately to defend himself. Spittle sprayed on his cheeks as the monster roared into his face.

Kay drew and loosed in one swift, smooth motion. The head of her arrow glinted with blue fire as it flew, taking the demon in the throat. It fell back, dark ichor burbling from its mouth and pierced neck.

"Princess, get behind us!" Kay cried.

A second creature grabbed at Stefan. He struck with his sword at its outstretched claws. The blade bounced off a scaled arm, leaving only a shallow laceration in its wake.

Randia reached his side, and her knife flashed. The demon leaped back in pain and surprise. Blood splashed from a deep gash in its chest.

A line of guards forced themselves in front of the pair. Randia grabbed Stefan around the waist with one arm. His eyes opened wide as she yanked him from his feet and carried him swiftly away from the fighting. Kay stepped in front of them as Randia set Stefan down behind the front line.

The princess' eyes were lit with anger. "Are you trying to get yourself killed?" she yelled.

Kay drew and loosed again. "Stay behind us!"

"How many more of those bluesteel arrows do you have?" Randia asked.

"Only one," Kay said. She stole a glance over her shoulder at

Stefan. "And with respect, Your Highness, I don't want to waste it on
—"

She broke off suddenly. "Down!" she cried.

Randia dropped and turned. A wraith-like demon had floated
through the pavilion opening. It was gliding toward them,
soundlessly, its bony hands outstretched.

Kay drew and fired again, right over the heads of the startled
prince and princess. The arrow passed through the ghostly figure
with no effect.

"Randi!" Stefan rapped. "Your knife!"

Randia slapped the hilt into his outstretched palm as he ducked
under a swipe of the spectral claws. He flipped the blade expertly in
his hand and threw, and the knife hit the wraith squarely in the chest.
It screamed once, and then vanished in a cloud of exploding vapor.

Kay lowered the bluesteel-tipped arrow she'd been ready to fire.
"An enchanted blade?" she asked.

Stefan nodded as he helped Randia to her feet.

"A gift from her grandfather," he explained. "And we had
something of a knife-throwing act for a while." He winked. "I got quite
good at it."

Kay spun toward the line of demons again, seeking another target.
The fight had progressed with grim predictability. Half of the guards
lay dead, their blood staining the stone walkway. The rest were falling
back, trying futilely to parry the monsters' attacks. One fell as she
watched, its head scythed from its shoulders by a demonic blade.

"This is it," she said. "They'll be on us in seconds."

She took careful aim and loosed her bluesteel arrow at Ashrach's
left eye. It seemed to shudder in mid-flight, bending slightly from its
path. It struck the demon's face instead, leaving a long, ugly, gore-
gushing gash.

Stefan turned abruptly to look at Randia. Her eyes had suddenly
gone wide with surprise. "What is it?" he demanded.

"I don't know," she said. Her voice had a preoccupied quality, as
though she were listening to something. "A touch of magic. Something
... familiar, and yet nothing I've ever felt before ..."

Ashrach howled. It raised its hand again and gestured toward
Kay. She stared at it as the remaining guards fell in around her,

preparing for one, last, desperate stand. She looked into the monster's small, bovine eyes, and smiled defiantly.

"For the Princess Bard!" she cried.

A bolt of silver fire stabbed down from above. Guards and demons alike blinked and covered their eyes against the flash.

When Randia recovered her sight, she saw the great bull-demon stumbling unsteadily. The weight of its great sword seemed suddenly to be pulling it off balance.

It took her a moment to realize why. The monster's left arm had been pointed toward them, about to kill Kay with a burst of demonic power. Now it was gone. All that remained was a smoldering scar cauterized at the creature's shoulder.

She looked up. A figure sheathed in silver fire was descending toward the glade with impossible speed. It gestured as it fell, and a spray of magic streaked toward the demons.

"Guards! Fall back!" it cried in a thunderous voice.

The monsters barely had time to realize what was happening. A chorus of panicked shrieks rose from their ranks as they leaped wildly to evade the attack. Many were cut off as the fusillade struck, its targets consumed in bursts of blinding white flame. Randia looked on in wonder as a dozen of the demons simply died, burned to ash where they stood.

"*Starfire*," she breathed.

There was a rush of wind as the figure landed. His boots struck the ground with a loud report, and the stone cracked at the force of their impact. His brown cloak billowed around him like a cape in a gale.

When the figure straightened, she saw it was a man. A living armor of silver fire sheathed his body, and his right hand held a familiar wand. In his left, Flamebane shone with a cold, white light.

"It's the prince!" Kay cried. "Rally to Prince Gerard!"

Randia stared, wide-eyed, at her brother's right hand. It wore a golden ring with a blue stone on the third finger. She could sense its power. It burned with an impossibly intense magic, unlike — and far stronger — than any she'd experienced before.

She was shocked to realize that she couldn't just *feel* the ring's magic. She could *hear* it as well. It was as though it were singing to her in her mind. There were no words, only song and music — like a coloratura voice backed by a full orchestra, ringing through a triumphant crescendo.

She shook her head, vision blurring with tears. The beauty of the song was overwhelming. Her heart reeled with love and relief — at seeing her brother, alive and safe and there to rescue them, arriving in the very nick of time ...

That's what the song is about, she realized. *It's the triumphant refrain of the beloved hero, arriving to save the day. How am I hearing that?*

Gerard faced the demons. With cries of "To the prince!" the remaining guards rushed toward him. Hope returned to their eyes as they fell in at his side, weapons raised.

"Disperse, servants of evil," his voice boomed. Randia had never heard her brother speak with such confidence and authority. For a moment, she thought she was listening to her father. "Flee, and you may live."

The point of Ashrach's great sword pressed into the ground. It leaned on the weapon to steady itself, and then, slowly, regained its balance. It turned its bull head to look at its left side, where its arm had been only moments before. Then it faced Gerard.

"The Horde of Borr does not fear death, princeling," it said. "And it does not flee its prey. You may be powerful, but you cannot defeat us all. The horde will take you."

It yanked the point of its sword free from the stone and leveled it at him.

"We have two royals in our grasp, now," it roared. "Glory awaits, and Gorath will have the soul of any Deman who balks at this fight. Take them!"

Chapter 14 - A Fight for Their Lives

Duel to the Death

Orion struggled unsteadily to his feet. His head ached, and a loud ringing sounded in his ears. Blood dripped into his eyes from a cut in his forehead, and he drew a sleeve across his brow to wipe it away. He shook his head to clear it, but that only made the ache worse.

Thumping feet and heavy breathing penetrated his tinnitus. He thought he could make out screams and battle in the distance.

We were fighting a demon, he remembered. *What's happened? Where are* —

He heard a young woman's voice. It was light and mocking, thick with sass and derision. It cut through the ringing in Orion's ears and helped him to recover his senses.

"Hey, monster breath!" Diana taunted. "Over here!"

He staggered to his feet and looked around. Bodies and gore littered the alley where they had made their stand. A wave of nausea hit him as he realized that their entire group from The Smiling Nymph had been slaughtered. Only he and Diana were still alive.

He blinked, not fully believing what he saw. She was dancing around suggestively and laughing, waving a butcher's knife in the air over her head. She looked almost as though she were doing a bizarre ritual dance.

She was goading the demon to attack her. Was she *insane*?

Nalef pursued her. The head of the pitchfork still protruded from its chest. Black demon blood ran freely from it and a score of wounds that slashed and pierced its body. Arrows studded it like a pincushion.

He smiled grimly. His companions had not gone down without a fight.

Nalef tried to rush her, but it was visibly slowed from its injuries. Its clawed arms swung wildly, but it couldn't touch her. She ducked easily beneath one swipe and backed away from the next. Then she taunted it again.

Orion tried to make sense of what he was seeing. For all her bravado, he knew she couldn't keep this up for long. Even with its wounds, it was only a matter of time before the demon wore her down and caught her. When it did, would it just kill her? If she made it angry enough, it might do far worse.

Diana retreated, and he noticed that she was moving directly away from where he stood. Their eyes met for just an instant before she disappeared from his view behind the monster's body. It turned to follow her, its back to him.

Then Orion understood. Her taunts were drawing it away from him, buying him time to recover. *And it had worked.*

With a shock, he realized that he already owed Diana his life. The demon should have slain him at the first sign that he was getting back on his feet again. If not for the young girl's desperate courage, he would be dead now.

His eyes narrowed. Even together and with the creature's injuries, he didn't know if they could kill it. She had wagered torture or worse against an easy death for a chance to save both their lives.

He saw that Diana was being backed into a corner of the alley with nowhere to run. He had only seconds to act on the chance she had bought them.

His eyes darted frantically around for a weapon and found Jameson's sword. It was still protruding from the back of the man's ruined head. The handle stood at hand-height, in almost a direct line from where he stood to the monster's back. It was practically calling to him.

He smiled as he ran. He reached the innkeeper's body, grasped the pommel, and pulled with all of his strength. His heart leaped as the blade came free. He raced on, hoping desperately to reach Diana in time.

He saw he was going to be too late. The demon roared, rearing up to its full height, fists clenched — not to kill, but to strike her unconscious. Whatever end it had planned for her, it would be slow.

A year at the Silver Star had taught him how to use a blade. He saw the huge, ugly wound in the monster's back where Jameson had stabbed it before, and knew what to do. He grasped the pommel with both hands and raised the sword to strike.

Diana ducked suddenly as Nalef fell on her. To Orion's shock, she scooted right between its enormous legs. Its full weight behind a blow that never landed, the monster lost its balance and fell. Its fists struck empty air as it stumbled to the cobblestones. Orion rushed past Diana to leap on its exposed back.

He stabbed. The sword pierced the unprotected flesh around the base of the demon's wing, sinking deep.

Nalef roared. It tried to slash its wings at Orion to knock him off, but both were now useless. It tried to stand, but the ground beneath it was slick with its own ichor. It slipped and stumbled as Orion levered the blade back and forth, trying to widen the wound.

The monster gripped the wall next to it with its claws. It heaved itself slowly back to its feet. Orion yanked the sword from its back and jumped away.

Nalef crouched in the alley and turned to face them. Black blood smeared its body and flowed freely from its wounds. A wild, desperate fury burned in its eyes, replacing its arrogant confidence from before. With a sudden chill, Orion realized they had literally backed the monster into a corner.

When it sprang, though, he was ready for it. He pivoted left as the demon's claws tore at him, and brought his sword up to slash at its belly. He drew the blade across its hide, hard, as his instructors at the Star had taught him. The weapon opened a long gash that spurted more of the creature's dark ichor.

His elation was short-lived. Nalef was also pivoting, and he had forgotten the monster's tail. It slammed into his chest, knocking him to the ground. It spun and pounced, fangs gleaming, ready to tear out the young scholar's throat.

Diana lunged over his body and slammed her butcher's knife into the demon's eye. Its own momentum drove the weapon deep into its head and wrenched it from her grasp. Fangs and claws slashed the pair as the monster howled, trying to twist away from the unexpected attack. Diana cried out and stumbled backward.

Orion crawled desperately away from the creature. His arm and back burned where Nalef's claws had raked them, and his chest ached. He scrambled back to his feet and faced the demon, sword in hand.

Nalef was weaving unsteadily, but it was still standing. It reached up with one claw and yanked the knife from its face. Then it turned its remaining eye on the two humans, and let out a long, low, menacing hiss.

Diana circled away from it to one side. Her eyes were wide.

"Light!" she cursed. "Won't anything *kill* this damned monster?"

Orion grimaced. A red stain was growing on Diana's blouse to match the one on his arm. From the ache in his chest, he was fairly certain the demon had cracked one of his ribs. Despite the pain, he could still swing his sword, though, and Diana was already stooping to pick up a new knife.

Their eyes met, and she nodded. Once again, they closed to attack.

Orion found later that he couldn't remember the rest of the battle, or how long it lasted. When he tried, all he seemed to recall was a nearly endless series of exchanges with the wounded demon. Nalef would lunge for him, and Diana would distract it with jeers or a thrown rock. It would turn to her, and he would use the opening to step in and hit it. He would leap back to escape its claws, and she would attack or distract it. Again and again, blow after blow, with the demon weakening and slowing, bit by bit, but never dying. Never dying, blast it!

And then he was on top of the monster, hitting it again and again ...

"Die, damn you!" he cried in frustration. "Die already! Die! Die!"

A pair of slim hands grabbed his shoulders from behind. He looked up, startled. It was Diana.

"Orion, that's enough!" she said. Her voice was raspy with exhaustion.

He looked down at the demon's body. He had been hacking at it with Jameson's sword. It wasn't moving.

He looked past her toward the exit from the alley. The way back to the street was clear. The wall of fire trapping them was gone.

"Did we finally kill it?" he asked softly.

She nodded.

"We've got to get out of here," she said. "And find somewhere to hide."

He listened. It was difficult to hear anything above the rasping of his own haggard breathing. He thought he recognized harsh voices, and the tramp of boots. The sounds were coming closer.

"Can you make that out?" he asked.

"Yes," she said. "It's the same chant the Hellmen sang when they marched on the Grand Academy. We can't go back to the street, and it's too late now to warn anyone about the trap. We're already cut off."

Orion pointed toward the back of the alley. The glowing glyphs drawn on the stone were gone.

"It should be safe to scale that wall now," he said.

She nodded. "Where will it lead us?"

He shrugged. "Somewhere that's not here. That's the best we've got, right now. Come on."

Prince's Stand

Drawing on the ring had helped Gerard understand, at least a little, the artifact's powers and limits. It magnified his magic many times over. Its well of power was enormous. But it was not infinite — and cloaking his flight across the city had already spent much of its reserve.

Now he had not only to *maintain* that cloak, but to *extend* it to cover the entire glade. If *any* of the thousands of other demons in the city pierced it, to see an epic battle taking place on the terraces of the Upper City, they would be lost. The alarm would spread and reinforcements would surround them in minutes. His sister would be taken and murdered, and his mission to bring the ring to the Archmage would fail.

He grimaced. Summoning a rain of starfire had forced him to draw heavily on his magic. It was the most powerful spell he knew, and few wizards could cast it. He'd hoped it would panic the demons into flight — but clearly, that wasn't going to happen. Emboldened or cowed by Ashrach's goading, they were rushing him.

He was going to have to fight.

He swept his wand in an arc before him. White fire bloomed from it into the front line of monsters. The ring's power surged through his spell, slicing through their defenses. Several of the weaker ones fell, cut in half by the line of flame. The rest reeled back, howling in pain, some set aflame.

The second rank didn't even slow down. They leaped over their burning allies or shoved them aside and charged.

The guards moved to meet them. At Gerard's command, curved shields of silver bloomed in the air before them as they threw themselves between him and the monsters. There was a savage exchange of blows, and a chorus of loud howls and cries. Several men and demons fell. But the shields — and the line of soldiers they were protecting — held.

Kay's bow sang. Her arrows glinted with a soft, argent glow as they flew. That glow ran across the blades of the guards and the plates of their armor as well. They fought fiercely, emboldened by the prince's magic, their weapons now striking with devastating effect.

Gerard lifted his arms and cast his levitation spell. Once again, he rose into the air. Ashrach's company had only a few flying demons, and they were circling, looking for an opening to attack. They were the greatest threat, since they might fly off in search of reinforcements. He had to take them out, and quickly.

The ring blazed with silver light. Gerard's wand pulsed, and another fusillade of starfire erupted from it. The blinding white bolts arced toward their targets with deadly precision. The winged monsters died, their ashes falling like snow onto the heads of demon and defender alike.

The move exposed him. Fire and lightning struck him as he hovered in the air. A hail of spears, rocks, and arrows followed. The fire dissipated harmlessly, snuffed out by Flamebane's magic. The rest bounced off or were absorbed by his fiery armor.

He gestured with his wand. Spells of all kinds erupted from its tip and sped toward the demons, one after another. Fire, ice, and lightning blew through their ranks, and the ring cut through their defenses like a knife through paper. He concentrated his attacks on the center of their forces, hoping to undermine their press on the guards.

He struck, again and again, never daring to pause or let up, killing demon after demon after demon. He could *not* let Randia be taken by these monsters. He had to force himself to keep going.

A chain whipped up at him. He tried to rise away from it, but he hadn't seen the danger in time. It wrapped around his legs and held. Powerful arms dragged him toward the ground.

He brought Flamebane around to slash at the links. They parted, but it was too late. Three more chains lashed toward him. One wrapped around his sword arm, pinning it to his side and twisting Flamebane from his grasp. Another curled around his waist, and the third around his neck. He was pulled to the ground and disappeared beneath the mob of demons.

Randia screamed. "Gerard! *No!*"

She stooped to grab her fallen knife and sprinted forward. Stefan ran beside her, brandishing his sword.

Kay was already running ahead of them. "Break their line!" she cried. "Whatever the cost! He'll be dead in seconds if we don't!"

Gerard's mind raced for a way to free himself. The ring's fiery armor was holding, but he knew it wouldn't last long under the vicious assault. He had to do something right away, or he would be overwhelmed.

The ring's armor magic was new to him, but he was a quick study at such things. He could tell that it was designed to work not only as a defensive power, but *offensively* as well. Perhaps all he had to do was "turn up the heat" a bit ...

His armor flared brilliantly as the ring responded to his command. Tongues of silver flame licked greedily at the demons. There was a loud hissing and popping sound, like fat thrown onto a roaring fire. The magic seared their skin and hides like the press of a branding iron. They threw themselves backward, howling in agony.

Gerard hauled himself to his feet and spun. He looked around, brandishing his wand. Several of the demons had fallen to the ground and were writhing in pain, their bodies disfigured by huge, sizzling burns. The argent fire had ignited one completely; it ran, immolated and screaming, toward the archway to the east.

"Randi, stay back!" he yelled. "I'm all right!"

He wasn't out of danger yet. At least ten of the creatures still stood against him, and they appeared to be the most powerful of the group. They circled, looking for an opening to attack. Some of them brandished long weapons that glowed eerily with demonic magic. Now that they had seen the hazard of touching his flaming armor, they were taking care not to get too close to it again.

With loud cries and ringing steel, the guards fell on the monsters from behind. Gerard smiled as he once again extended his silver shields to protect them, and to enchant their weapons. One demon went down under their onslaught, impaled by a dozen sword blows.

Kay bent down to one of the fallen creatures. It was the one she'd shot to save Stefan, and it still had a bluesteel arrow embedded in its throat. She tore the missile free, inspected it, and smiled. Then she sprang up onto a stone bench, nocked it, and drew, searching for a target.

"Don't let the burning one get away!" Gerard called. "It'll raise the alarm!"

Kay nodded, aimed, and fired. The arrow took the fleeing demon in the back. It collapsed, its spine severed, flaming like a dropped torch.

Ashrach barked orders in its fiendish tongue. Some of the remaining demons followed it to charge the guards. The rest turned on Gerard.

The prince staggered as they struck him again. The battle was using up more and more of the ring's reserve. His fiery armor was growing dull, and his counter-attacks weaker and more limited.

Dizzy with exhaustion, he lost track of time. All he knew was that demons kept attacking him, and that he kept striking back — killing them, one at a time, with maddening slowness. Block, blast, stagger, riposte, again and again, draining the ring of every drop of power it could give him ...

Then he blinked. He looked around, searching for the next foe to strike. There wasn't one. The creatures he'd been fighting were all dead.

He turned. Only four of the guards remained. Kay still stood on her stone bench, arrow nocked, looking for a clear shot. The other three stood in pitched melee with the two remaining demons. One was Ashrach, swinging its enormous sword wildly with its remaining arm. The other was a huge gorilla-like beast. The feathered shaft of one of Kay's arrows stuck from the side of an elephantine head.

Ashrach's great sword flared with red magic, and then slashed down. The remnants of Gerard's weakening shield around the guards shattered, and one of them fell, headless. The other two were knocked to the ground.

Then the demon ran straight for Randia. Stefan cried out and leaped in front of her, brandishing his sword.

Gerard cursed. His wand snapped desperately to cast another spell. Kay's last arrow hit the demon in the back and bounced off, unable to pierce its dark armor.

Ashrach raised its sword. Stefan braced himself, but the gesture was futile. The great blade would kill them both with a single blow.

A large, disembodied silver hand appeared before the demon and stiff-armed it in the face. The monster's head snapped backward with a loud crack, and it dropped its sword. The hand wrapped itself around the creature's throat and lifted it from the ground. It surged forward, carrying Ashrach through the air and away from the princess. Then it slammed its head, hard, into the stone of the walkway.

Kay dropped her bow as she leaped from her stone bench. She needed another weapon. Her eyes swept the corpse-choked battlefield, searching frantically ...

The other demon tore the throat from a guard and dropped her lifeless body to the ground. It turned to face the last soldier, who was still struggling back to his feet. It charged.

Panicked, the man grasped at a long, metal spear that lay beside him. It was a demon weapon, and its shaft glowed with a dull, red light. He planted the butt into the ground and aimed its point at the charging monster, but it didn't even slow down. It lowered its head and gored the man as the spear struck into its chest. With a trumpeting roar, it lifted him from his feet, impaled on its tusks.

The demon grabbed the spear with a gorilla-like hand, yanked it from its torso, and threw it away. Then it shook its elephantine head. The wound in its chest sprayed black ichor as the man flew through the air to land a dozen feet away, unmoving.

The monster looked around. It saw Stefan and Randia, standing alone and unprotected. It lowered its head and stumbled toward them, tusks extended.

Gerard's eyes went wide as he saw the demon charge his sister. Frantically, desperately, he groped for the power to cast another spell …

Stefan's wrist flicked. Randia's knife flew from his hand and embedded itself in the monster's face. Its head reared back, and it staggered, black blood fountaining from where its left eye had been.

"Your Highness!" Kay cried. "Look out!"

She stooped to pick up a sword. Then she raced toward the prince with every bit of speed she could muster. She *had* to reach him in time …

Gerard summoned a bolt of magic and sent it streaking toward the demon. The blast took it in the temple. Fragments of its elephant-like head exploded into the air in a puff of red-black smoke. It skidded sideways and then crashed to the ground.

Randia turned toward her brother with a smile of relief. Then she screamed.

"Gerard! Behind you!"

Gerard turned to see the point of a spear. It was the one the other demon had torn from its chest, and its shaft glowed with evil runes. Behind it stood Ashrach, the bull-demon's face lost in a smear of gore. It stabbed at the prince with all the strength left in its remaining arm.

"*Karach!*" it cried.

Dark magic ran along the weapon as it struck. Gerard's armor flared brilliantly, but its strength had been spent. He felt the spell shatter as the weapon plunged into his chest …

Ashrach yanked the spear free and prepared to strike again. It saw the look of horror on Randia's face and grinned in triumph. Without the prince to defend them, the others would be easy to kill or capture. And then it would take all the glory for itself …

Kay leaped on the monster from behind. Her left hand grabbed one of its bull horns and pulled back its head. Her right arm reached around, weapon in hand. With a snarl, she drew the blade across its throat.

Flamebane flashed as it sliced through the demon's hide. Ichor fountained from the massive wound as the enchanted blade opened its neck to the bone. She jumped aside as Ashrach fell onto its ruined face — and then, with a series of swift, brutal strokes, hacked the monster's head from its body.

When she was done, she turned to the others. Gerard had staggered beneath what remained of the pavilion and collapsed. Randia knelt beside him, and Stefan was at her shoulder. She was cradling her brother's head in her lap, crying uncontrollably.

Hideout

Orion stepped carefully through the ruined entrance to the house. Splinters of what remained of the door lay scattered around the foyer. It was eerily quiet inside.

"The demons hit this place earlier," he declared grimly. "Probably as part of that sweep to herd people toward the battle."

Diana nodded. She looked at the path and the garden around the entrance. It had been trampled by large feet, many with claws or hooves. The destruction continued through the home in a line of gouged walls and broken furniture, finally exiting out the back door.

The house was built into the side of Cherry Hill. It seemed to have avoided the fires. Despite the damage, it was still in surprisingly good condition.

"They smashed the door," she offered. "Then they drove whoever was hiding inside out the back and along the streets with the rest."

She turned to look at him. "We should search for survivors."

Orion frowned. "I doubt anyone could have hidden from a demon pack," he said. "But someone might have taken refuge here afterward. Let's look around."

They did. It took only a couple of minutes to confirm that the house was deserted.

Their search ended when they descended a set of stone steps into a basement larder. It was cool, and seemed to have been built into a small recess in the southern side of the hill. The outer wall was of brick, and it had a single, elaborately curtained window. Orion walked up to it, drew the valence aside a few inches, and peered cautiously out. After a minute, he stepped away and looked thoughtfully at Diana.

"I think this is a good place for us to hide," he said at last. "We're near the edge of the hill, and the window has an excellent view of the city. We'll be able to see what's going on outside. There's food and drink, and we should be able to get some rest."

Diana looked toward the window. "Can we get out that way?" she asked nervously. "I'm not keen on being trapped here if something comes down the stairs."

Orion nodded. "It's large enough for both of us to climb through if we have to. But I doubt anything will come looking for us. The demons have already been through here and done ... what they planned."

"Drive the people toward their staged massacre," Diana said. Her throat ached with dryness, and her voice came out raspy and harsh.

She swayed suddenly with exhaustion at the thought of finally being able to rest. Orion caught her as she sagged and helped her to sit on a box of vegetables. He looked anxiously at the red stain that had spread across the left side of her blouse.

"Easy," he said. "The demon hit you pretty hard. You're losing a lot of blood."

She nodded, putting her head in her hands. "I feel dizzy all of a sudden," she said weakly.

He straightened. "Stay here," he said. "We both have wounds that need tending, but I don't think mine are as bad as yours. There should be some bandages upstairs, and maybe some salves. I'll fetch them, and some cushions for us to rest on."

She grabbed at his arm as he moved away. "No!" she cried.

He turned back to her, surprised. She looked at him sheepishly.

"We shouldn't separate," she said finally.

"It's all right. I won't be long, and I won't be far."

"Of course. You're right. I'm sorry. I don't know what came over me."

He gave her a small smile.

"Shock," he said. There was just a hint of a conspiratorial glint in his eye. "From the blood loss, no doubt."

She managed to grin at him despite a wave of nausea. "No doubt," she agreed.

Diana put her head in her hands again as Orion climbed swiftly up the stairs. *What is wrong with me?* she thought. Wounds or no wounds, a fear of being left alone wasn't like her.

She thought about Orion as he searched the house for bandages and medicines. They'd been partners since their meeting on the wall at the Grand Academy, and he'd been a steadying presence throughout the day's chaos. She had friends among the other young nobles at the palace — but with her blunt tongue and independent streak, she'd never been much of a "team player." Their impromptu partnership had formed so naturally that she hadn't realized until now how unusual that was for her.

Still, it was no excuse to let herself go soft. What would her father say?

She heard footsteps and looked up. Orion was struggling down the stone stairs. He'd thrown several blankets over his shoulder and was carrying a large, bulging bag. He set them down and grinned.

"We're in luck," he said. "The owners had a variety of medicines, as well as clean bandages."

Diana looked into the bag with interest. She picked up a tin of ointment, unscrewed the top, and sniffed. Her eyes lit up.

"Tranzalin," she said approvingly. "One of the best healing salves there is."

He gave her a look of surprise. "It sounds like you know your medicines. I was afraid I was going to have to guess at how to use some of these."

She shook her head. She lifted one of the bottles, and then another.

"Tincture of deathsbane," she said. "And if I'm not mistaken, this is a vial of regenera. You're right that we're in luck. These will do the trick."

He smiled. "Where did you learn so much about medicinal alchemy?" he asked.

She put down the bottles and stood. She began to undo her blouse.

"My mother taught me. Here, help me get this thing off so we can clean the cut on my chest. We'll need to start with a wet cloth."

She was halfway through the laces before she realized he hadn't moved. She looked at him curiously, an inquisitive glint growing in her green eyes.

His face colored visibly, and he tried to look away. "I, um —"

She laughed.

"You're so funny, Orion. You can battle demons to the death, and then you blush at a girl taking off her shirt. Everything we've braved together today, and this is what you blanch at!"

He gave her a sheepish smile. She went back to unlacing her blouse.

"I'll need you to clean and dress the wound," she said, matter-of-factly. "Or it'll become infected. Nalef raked me from my back all the way across my chest. I'm not sure how deep it is, but it burns like hell."

She finished with the laces and slid her torn blouse gingerly from her shoulders. She wore a white camisole below it, which was slashed as well. The fabric around the slashes was soaked with blood.

"You got that saving my life," he said softly.

She turned to look at him. She tried to focus on his face, but her eyes were suddenly blinking with tears. Without warning, she found her head buried in his shoulder, her chest heaving with sobs.

Orion folded his arms around her gently and squeezed his eyes shut. They held each other, shuddering and crying together, the tension of their shared nightmare finally releasing itself in a flood of uncontrolled tears.

Chapter 15 - Last Hope

Fall's Vigil

Elena Starlight stepped unsteadily through the door to the wizards' lab. Danor ran to her side and caught her as she sagged into his arms. He carried her to a chair and set her down in it.

"Are you all right, my love?" he asked. His voice was raw with worry and exhaustion.

"It is done," she said. "The apprentices and I have completed the ward. It will keep the dragons from approaching the palace."

As if on cue, a series of loud *thudding* noises sounded outside the tower. They were followed by the roar of the monsters echoing along the slopes of the mountain, screaming in pain and rage.

Lord Rugon knelt at the Queen's other side. "Thank the Light," he said.

The King took her hand and held it. "Are you all right?" he asked again, insistently.

"No, but it doesn't matter. The spell took everything I had, Danor. My power is all but spent."

"But you'll recover, Your Majesty?" Lord Rugon asked. "Won't you?"

She looked at him and shook her head. "We won't live long enough for that," she said simply.

Then her eyes hardened.

"How did this happen, Cyrus?" she asked fiercely. "We left Palanad and Salmanor both to defend the palace. *They* should have cast this ward. And now they're dead? And Hardin by your own hand?"

Lord Rugon closed his eyes.

"I don't understand it," he said. "The high priest was mad. He murdered Mage Lantar, right before our eyes. He raved about surrender and becoming slaves to the demons, and then turned his magic against us. If I hadn't —"

His voice choked off, and he bowed his head. The King laid a supportive hand on his shoulder.

"It wasn't your fault, Cyrus," he said. "We heard it from Augustus Darren himself. The high priest left orders that we were to be abandoned by the Church. There's no doubt about what happened. He was corrupted by the Dark."

Elena shook her head. "It still doesn't make sense," she said softly. "Why did he prosecute Zomoran, if he was in league with the demons?"

Danor squeezed her hand.

"I fear we have no time left to solve that puzzle, my love," he said. "Our part in all this is quickly drawing to a close."

They saw General Banderman coming toward them across the room. Vala Orleans strode at his side, her silver armor gleaming in the afternoon sunlight.

"The Queen's magic is working," she said, saluting. "The dragons have withdrawn from the palace."

"I'm afraid it will earn us only a brief respite," Banderman added. "Another regiment of battle demons is moving into the High City to replace them."

"The Horde Master is already rearranging its forces," Elena said. "It was prepared for this."

Danor nodded. "The dragons could have brought the palace down around us. Now it will have to storm it with demons instead."

"Can we stop them?" Vala asked.

"No. But without the dragons, it will take them longer, and they will suffer greater casualties." His face hardened. "If we are to die today, then we will make them pay dearly for our lives."

The Queen struggled to her feet, slowly and painfully. Danor put an arm around her waist to steady and support her.

There is nothing else now that we can do, Elena said in his mind. *Except to keep the demon lord's attention focused on us. To distract it. To give Gerard time to complete his quest.*

I am afraid you are right, my love, he thought to her. *If there's any hope now, it lies with our son, and with my father. And with Randia, if they can find her.*

Danor held her close and kissed her. Then he turned to face the others and took a deep breath.

"The demons are going to breach and take the palace," he said. "We have one last hope, a slim one, of which I can tell you nothing. I am truly sorry for that, especially because of what I must now ask. For you to trust me without explanation, knowing it almost certain that none of us will live to see that hope."

Lord Rugon dropped to one knee and saluted. The others followed his example. "Command us, my liege," he said firmly.

"We must hold the enemy for as long as possible," the King said. "The Queen and I will lay down our lives for that last hope. We ask you to stand with us."

General Banderman rose. "For King and Carlissa!" he cried. "To the last man!"

Vala Orleans came to her feet beside him. "The knights of the Church stand with the King of Carlissa!" she echoed. "For the Covenant! Against the Dark, until we are taken into the Light!"

Danor nodded. "Thank you all. Listen carefully, then. Here are my orders."

The Passing of the Torch

Randia stared, wide-eyed, at the hole in her brother's chest. Somehow she made herself speak, but her voice was strained with panic.

"We need to stop that bleeding!" she cried.

She was dimly aware of Kay kneeling at Gerard's other side, and then of Stefan taking off his cloak and handing it to her. The lieutenant's eyes widened as she examined the wound. It was pulsing streams of blood that had already drenched the prince's shirt.

She pressed the bundle of cloth over it, and then looked at Randia. She shook her head.

"No!" Randia sobbed. "He's still alive!"

Kay shook her head again. "I'm sorry, Your Highness. The spear pierced his heart. He should be dead already!"

Randia tried to blink away her tears. "There must be something we can do!"

"There is," a voice said softly.

It was weak and strained, and Randia was shocked to realize that it was Gerard's. She looked down at his face. He was gazing up at her and smiling.

"Don't talk," she pleaded. She placed her hand gently against his cheek. "We'll find help. Just hold on!"

Gerard shook his head.

"The lieutenant is right," he said. There was a wheezing burble to his voice that sent a shiver of fright up her spine. He reached up to take her hand and held it.

She started again to try to quiet him, but stopped. His eyes were locked on hers. His expression was desperate, entreating.

"There *is* something you can do, but not for me," he said firmly. "Only the ring's magic sustains me now, and that won't last long. *You must listen to me*, while we still have time."

Randia had sensed the ring during the battle. Now, with it touching her skin, awareness of its power flooded her mind. She found herself nodding, unable to deny him.

"What is it?" she asked. "I've never felt anything like it."

"My mission," he replied softly.

He smiled at her look of puzzlement.

"It's an artifact, a secret heirloom of our house," he continued. "I didn't know about it until today. Father used it to defend against the attack. Without it, the demons would have taken the palace."

"How did you get here?" Stefan asked. "Weren't you at the palace, too?"

"I used it to levitate, cloaked, across the city, from the mage's tower to here." He waved his other hand at the corpse-strewn glade. "And to slay these demons."

Randia only looked at Gerard, her eyes serious and attentive. Stefan and Kay exchanged astonished glances.

"You said you were on a mission, Gerard," Randia asked gently.

"Was it to save me?"

"No," he replied. "Though I promised to, if I could find you. I was to bring the ring to Grandfather."

He looked into her eyes, and his gaze became searching and hard.

"That mission *must* succeed, Randi, or the world is lost. You can sense why, can't you? What you can feel when it's near you, when you touch it?"

"The song," she said softly. Her face had a faraway look. "So majestic, so powerful ..."

Gerard smiled. "Of course. Father said it would affect each of us in our own way."

"I don't feel anything," Stefan said tentatively.

Gerard shook his head. "You can't. Only a Killraven can wield it."

"And in the hands of the Archmage ..." Randia began. Gerard nodded weakly.

"Father said it would make him like a demigod. Bringing it to him is the only hope we have left of stopping the invasion."

"We were trying to reach him, too," she said. "To make it to the Silver Star. Is he still there?"

"I don't know, but I hope so — or at least that you can pick up his trail. Grandfather went into hiding the moment the invasion began. The demon lord who leads it is hunting him. He must have cloaked himself, as I did to travel here."

"Stefan and I will go," Randia said firmly. "Lieutenant Kay will guard you. We'll find Grandfather and bring him to you. If this ring is so powerful, then perhaps he'll be able to use it to heal you."

Kay and Gerard exchanged knowing glances. He turned back to his sister and slowly shook his head.

"You still don't understand," he said. "Although I believe the lieutenant does. *I'm already dead*, Randi. The ring's magic will let me delay that for another few minutes, but that is all. When I'm gone, it will be up to you to bring the ring to Grandfather. *You* will have to complete my quest."

Randia stared at her brother, eyes wide. She found herself unable to speak.

"You say that you were cloaked?" Kay asked. "Is that why there were no enemy reinforcements? Because you were using magic to keep the rest of the demons from seeing our fight?"

Gerard turned to her. "You're very perceptive, Lieutenant," he said appreciatively. "Do you understand what that means?"

Kay nodded. "It means that spell is either spent, or is about to be. It means that at any moment, the demons in the rest of the city could notice a battlefield littered with the bodies of an entire company of their soldiers, and come to investigate."

She looked at Randia. "It means we need to go, Your Highness. *Right now.*"

Gerard beamed at her. "Bright, as well as valiant. I'm glad that my sister will have someone like you to help protect her."

The young officer's cheeks colored. "Thank you, my prince," she said softly. Randia saw that her eyes were glistening.

A fit of coughing wracked Gerard's body. Blood sprayed from his lips as he fought to bring it under control. His grip tightened on Randia's hand until the knuckles turned white.

"The magic is fading," he said weakly. "There is more that you need to know, and little time left."

She nodded numbly. Tears were running down her cheeks.

Gerard turned to Stefan. His wand glowed dimly with silver magic as he handed it to the young bard.

"Take this," he said. "Use what power it has left to protect her."

Stefan nodded. He, too, seemed unable to speak.

Gerard turned to Kay. She knelt at his side, one hand pressed to his chest to try to stem his bleeding. She still held Flamebane in the other. He took it from her and extended the hilt to his sister.

"Aron is dead, Randi," he said solemnly. "You are now heir to the throne of Carlissa."

A whimper of horror escaped Randia's lips. Gerard continued without pause.

"Mother and Father were still alive the last time I saw them, but their counterstrike has failed. They've been driven back to the palace, and the demons and dragons are massing for an attack. They have no chance of withstanding it. *You* will have to be prepared to lead our people."

Randia's eyes widened as the full implications of what he was saying finally hit home.

"No!" she cried. "Not me! I can't!"

Gerard shook his head weakly. "I'm so sorry to have to lay this burden on you," he said. "I know it's not what you wanted."

"Grandfather —"

"— is old," Gerard interrupted. "He will help you, but he cannot lead this fight. I think we both know that. Carlissa will need him to be its archmage, but it will need you to be its queen."

She shook her head violently.

"*I'm a performer*, Gerard! I sing, I dance! I write ballads and act in comedies! I'm no wizard, no warrior! I can't lead people to fight demons!"

Gerard reached up to touch her face. His eyes were determined. For some reason she couldn't explain, the confidence she saw in them frightened her deeply.

"You will be everything you need to be, Randi," he said. "I've known you all your life, and nothing has ever stopped you once you put your mind to it. Mage, warrior, commander, adventurer — you will be all these things, and more. You are truly the Princess Bard, and one day, they will call you the Bard Queen."

Gerard coughed again. He turned to look at Stefan, then at Kay. Randia's throat caught when she saw his eyes glazing over.

"Protect her," he whispered. "You *must* bring her and the ring to the Archmage. Every hope we have left depends on it. And help her with what comes after. She will need you."

"I will," Stefan said simply. He looked at Randia and nodded. "To the end of my days."

"With my life, Your Highness," Kay said fiercely. "I swear it!"

Randia saw that he was slipping away. With an effort of will beyond anything she had mustered before, she forced the confusion and grief from her mind. Her brother was dying, and she had to be strong for him. She would not fail him in his final moments.

"I will do what must be done," she said. Her voice rang with a confidence she did not feel, but she knew this was not the time to show it.

Gerard smiled at her. "I know you will," he whispered. "And one day *you* will know it, too."

The muscles of his face slackened. Randia bent down to kiss his cheek.

"I love you, Gerard," she said. "Go now into the embrace of the Divine."

"I love you too, Randia," he whispered.

Then, slowly, the light faded from his eyes. Gerard Killraven, Wizard Prince of Carlissa, was gone.

Randia wept at her brother's side. She felt Stefan's hand on her shoulder, but no comfort could reach her through her grief.

Grim Wait

Diana drew herself slowly out of Orion's arms. Her face was still wet. Her green eyes were wide and vulnerable as she looked into his.

"And you saved *my* life," she said simply. "There's no sense keeping score."

He shrugged. "I suppose not."

"I'm just glad you came after me, back at the academy. I would never have made it this far without you."

He shook his head. "Nor I without you."

She smiled. "We make a pretty good team, don't we?"

He nodded. "We do. And we'll get through this thing together."

She chuckled.

"I like your optimism. The way you never give up, even when facing hopeless facts with brutal honesty. I can't imagine what it would have been like, going through all of this, without an ally like you at my side."

Diana stood slowly. She turned away from him and pulled the camisole over her head. Like her legs, the muscles of her arms and torso were toned and athletic. Orion winced when he saw her back.

She looked over her shoulder at him. "What do you see?" she asked.

"Two long slashes," he replied. He tried to keep the worry out of his voice.

"I know that. What else?"

"They're about two inches apart. Both run from a pair of ugly wounds that begin just below your left shoulder blade. That's probably where Nalef's claws first hit you. They run around your back under your arm to your chest."

"How bad are they?"

"One's shallow, and looks like it's already clotting. The other's pretty deep."

She looked relieved. "That's about what I expected."

Orion pulled a ceramic jug from his bag and poured some water onto a small cloth. "I'll start cleaning them," he said. "I know how to do a basic field dressing from my training at the Star."

She shook her head. "We can't bandage them yet. We'll need to treat them for closure first."

His eyebrows arched. "With what?"

"With a mixture of tranzalin and regenera. In the right proportions, they'll combine to form a paste that we can spread into the wound."

She rummaged in Orion's bag, selected a few additional items, and set them on top of a short stack of boxes. She removed the cover from the tranzalin and looked into it, as if trying to judge how much was left. Then she unstoppered the bottle of regenera and slowly poured some of the blue liquid into the jar, stirring the mixture constantly with a small spoon.

"We'll need to treat the wounds in three steps. Wash them with water, and then apply the deathsbane to prevent infection. Finally, we'll treat them with the mixture I'm preparing. We'll need to get the medicines deeply into the wounds, even where they've started closing. Don't be afraid to pull them open again if they have."

"That's going to hurt," he warned. "The deathsbane, especially."

"You bet it will. But it's necessary. We can't be too careful with strikes from a demon's claws."

"I suppose not. But why the paste? I thought you were supposed to drink regenera. I've never heard of applying it directly into a wound."

She nodded. "Regenera only activates when it's absorbed into the bloodstream. Normally, that's best done by drinking it. Pouring or swabbing it into a wound is usually a waste, because only a little of it ends up being absorbed."

She took the spoon out of the jar and set it down. "That's where the tranzalin comes in. Mixed and applied properly, it'll leach the regenera into the bloodstream right at the site to speed-heal the wound."

Orion looked at her skeptically. "I've never heard of such a thing. Are you sure you know what you're doing?"

"Of course I do. I'll start by treating the slashes in my chest and side. Then I'll do your wounds, and you can treat my back. Watch carefully so you can see how I do it. It's not hard."

She extended the jar to him. "Here, hold this. And give me that cloth."

She went to work on her wounds, and he was impressed at the speed and confidence of her movements. She quickly re-opened and cleaned the cuts with water and cloth. Then she applied some of the deathsbane to a small ball of cotton and, hissing in pain, swabbed them with it. Finally, she dipped her fingers into the ointment and began smearing it into them. When she was done, she nodded at his torn jacket and shirt.

"Your turn," she said.

Orion stripped off his ragged shirt, and Diana nodded appreciatively as she examined him. His build was slim, except for a cut of lean muscle that hinted at recent and rigorous training. A long gash ran across his arm and back, similar to hers, but not as deep. The left side of his ribcage sported a large, purpling bruise. He winced as she touched it.

"Looks like you may have cracked a rib or two there," she said. "Nothing much I can do except wrap it. The regenera we have left over should help."

"Where did your mother learn so much about medicines?" he asked.

"At the temple of Nalendra. Before my father took her as his wife."

Orion's eyes widened. He nearly dropped the ointment.

"Your mother was a priestess consort?" he asked. "Doesn't that involve some kind of mortal contest?"

She nodded absently and started cleaning his wounds.

"The challenge is rare. Even in Dorian, where the ancient traditions still have the force of law. It's even rarer for a challenger to survive it, much less win. But my father is extremely capable, and he's always been very ambitious. Winning my mother's hand was a coup that solidified his rising star within our government."

"Is that how he won his assignment as the Carlissan Ambassador?"

"It helped set his career on that path. His ambassadorships followed a long series of progressive assignments that included advising and later serving as a provincial governor."

"He sounds like an impressive man," Orion offered.

"He is," Diana said. The note of respect and affection in her voice was unmistakable.

"And he has equally high standards for his family," she went on. "I have half a dozen different instructors, you know. Our class would have made you my seventh."

Orion whistled.

"I would have loved to have that many teachers when I was growing up. What are you studying?"

"Pretty much everything. Medicine and religion with my mother. Natural philosophy, literature, art. Engineering. *Rigorous* athletics. And I have a personal tutor who came with us from Mandor, to make sure I'm well versed in our national history and statecraft." She wrinkled her nose. "That's the boring stuff."

"I suspect you're a good student."

"Of course I am. My father expects me to excel at everything I do. And he's not a man you want to disappoint."

"Your Carlissan is excellent," he said, as she began bandaging his wounds. "And you have barely any accent at all. How long have you been studying it?"

"The language? About a year and a half. I started when we learned my father would be taking his position here. We only came to Lannamon last summer. Before that, he served as Ambassador to Rayche."

She paused for a while. There was a wistful look in her eyes.

"I spent my early teens growing up in Highpeak," she said finally. "The mountains there are even more beautiful than in Lannamon."

"It sounds like you have fond memories of it."

Diana tied off the last bandage. "I do," she said.

She picked up his shirt and handed it to him, and he started to put it on. "All done. Now I'll need you to do the wounds on my back."

She reached around for her hair as he finished buttoning his shirt. Her long chestnut tresses were badly disheveled, and she had trouble pulling them around the nape of her neck and over her shoulder.

"You're clear on what to do?" she asked.

He nodded as he picked up the cloth and wet it again. "I watched you carefully. It seems pretty straightforward."

He set to work cleaning the wounds on her back. He saw her muscles tighten as she braced herself against the pain and tried to make his ministrations gentler. She shook her head.

"Don't do that. You need to clean them thoroughly. My wounds are deep, and it's going to have to hurt. Don't try to spare me."

"All right," he said. "There's one thing I don't understand, though. Shouldn't we be stitching these? Especially the gashes in your back?"

"No," she said. "There's no need."

"Why not? Won't they leave terrible scars otherwise?"

"That's the beauty of the paste I prepared. Tranzalin is a medical astringent. It'll pull the wounds closed so that the regenera can heal them."

"That's remarkable," he said. "And now that you mention it, I think I can actually feel mine tightening. Like you said."

She nodded. "We were lucky you found some. It's not very common."

"I suppose we were due for a break. You'd better brace yourself. I'm about to apply the deathsbane."

"I will. So where was I? Oh, right. I was talking about growing up in Highpeak —"

Diana's back arched abruptly, and she gasped.

"I told you to brace yourself," Orion said.

She looked over her shoulder at him, eyes flashing. "I did," she said, through gritted teeth.

"You warned me not to be gentle. Do you need a minute?"

She looked away, and he could see her balling her hands into fists. "Of course not. I'll get through it."

She gasped again as he resumed swabbing her wounds. "But maybe you should talk for a while," she added, her lips tight.

"All right. What should I talk about?"

"I don't know. Tell me about yourself, your family."

Orion was quiet for a while as he worked on her back. When he finally spoke, there was a note of reluctance in his voice.

"There's not much to tell. I'm from a merchant family. They operate the Deneri Trade and Import Company. They have extensive contacts at court, and in the Merchant's Guild."

"Ah," she said. "That explains some of it."

He frowned. "Some of what?"

"Your dual personality. The philosopher who can fight demons. The shy boy with a mastery of court etiquette." She chuckled. "You took the other girls completely by surprise with that performance back in class, you know."

He shook his head. "I was trained from a young age to be 'presentable' to the lesser nobility. But I've never felt myself defined by that, or by my family."

"And yet you wear both roles well."

He shrugged. "Perhaps."

"Is that why you became a scholar? Because you didn't like the life your parents were pushing you toward?"

"No. I did that because I love learning. I always have."

"And your training as an adventurer?"

"That's ... a different story."

She nodded eagerly. "Tell me about it."

He did. By the time he related his conversation with Dean Lander before the class, he was done bandaging her wounds. They finished by sharing draughts from what remained of the regenera. Diana looked thoughtfully at him as she re-laced her blouse.

"I admire your determination to set the course of your own life," she said at last. "I've always had a streak of independence, but I've never even thought of resisting my family's expectations of me."

"That sort of thing isn't exactly encouraged in Dorian society," he offered.

"No, it's not. But you've had remarkable support for it here. From professors at the academy, even the Archmage himself. I guess that's what's always fascinated me about Carlissa. Even the princess, allowed to become a *bard*. That would be unheard of in my homeland."

Without warning, she walked to the window and pulled aside the valence. Orion came to stand by her side, an inquisitive expression on his face. They looked out on the city together.

The Carlissan resistance was broken. Fires raged everywhere, and columns of smoke rose like orange pillars into the reddening sky. The walls and towers of the army base had been shattered and were being consumed in a raging inferno. The only soldiers they could see lay dead. Hellmen, demons, giants, and dragons roamed or flew over the streets, destroying, killing, and taking prisoners at will.

They turned to the west. An enormous force of battle demons was surging against the palace. The outer gates lay in ruins. Explosions and reports of magic echoed through the valley as the defenders fought a losing battle to hold the fortifications. Shadows were reaching across the city as the sun moved down toward the shoulder of Mount Cascade.

"All that is gone now," she said bitterly. "Even if the people survive, and the demons don't just slaughter us all. That budding spirit of independence will end."

She turned to look at Orion, face haunted. "It's going to be lost forever, isn't it?"

He shook his head. Diana was surprised to see that defiance still burned in his eyes.

"There's one last hope," he said quietly.

"What?"

Orion pointed across the firth to the Silver Star Adventurer's Academy. Another brigade of battle demons swarmed around it, but its tower still stood, gleaming proudly against the afternoon sky.

"The Archmage," he said. "He would never surrender the city without a fight. I don't know what he's waiting for, or what his plan is. *But he has one.*" His eyes hardened. "And this battle won't be over until he's played his hand."

Diana rested her head on his shoulder. She didn't try to hide the tears that welled again in her eyes.

"Your faith in him is ..." Her voice trailed off.

He smiled at her. "You don't share it," he said simply.

"No, but it inspires me. So I'll believe with you, Orion Deneri. I'll join you in your last hope."

She looked out again at the burning city. "We have nothing else to believe in left."

He sighed. He glanced back at the boxes of food, and the pile of blankets.

"We don't know how long we'll have to hide in here," he said. "We should eat something, and try to get some rest."

Chapter 16 - The End of the Beginning

Heartbreak

Kay laid a hand on Randia's shoulder. "We must go, Your Highness," she said urgently.

Randia slowly lifted her head. Her hands and hair were stained with blood from cradling her brother as he died. She was still crying, but her tear-stained eyes were alert. She looked around the glade and nodded.

"You're right," she said.

She gently took the prince's hand and slipped the Ring of the Killravens from his finger. Then she bent one last time to kiss his forehead.

"Goodbye, Gerard," she said.

Then she stood, braced herself, and put on the ring.

She hadn't known what to expect. She had supposed the artifact would flood her mind with power, and hoped it would give her strength to fight their way through to the Silver Star. It surprised her to find that wearing it felt very different. She could sense its magic, but had no inkling that she could wield it in combat or to cast spells.

She heard the song again, now clearly in her mind, a coloratura voice backed by the sound of a full orchestra. Its notes rose in triumph and grandeur, more beautiful, and more poignant, than anything she had imagined before. She gasped at the sound, feeling overwhelmed and helpless at the emotions that it stirred in her.

Stefan was immediately at her side, holding her arm. "Randi, are you all right?" he asked.

Of course. Father said it would affect each of us in our own way.

She heard her brother's words again in her mind, and understood. The King was a warrior at heart, and the ring had given him the power of an epic hero. Gerard was a wizard, and it had given him the power of an archmage. Her grandfather was the Archmage, and it would give him the power of a demigod — power enough, they hoped, to stop the end of the world.

And she? Hers was the heart of a musician. She could feel the ring augmenting that ability, just as it had those of her father and brother. She could hold a dozen complex melodies in her mind as clearly as if played, without flaw, by as many orchestras. And she could weave those melodies together into a tapestry that would transcend anything heard before.

She wept new tears from her already brimming eyes. The music she could compose with this artifact would remake her art. It would bring audiences to a crescendo of emotion, to a rebirth and renewal of the spirit.

But it was not a battle power. It offered her nothing to stop a horde of demons.

She felt the metal change as the ring resized itself to fit snugly on her smaller hand. Slowly, she turned to face Stefan. She nodded.

"I'm all right," she said. "It just ... took a moment to adjust to."

"Can you use its magic?" Kay asked hopefully.

Randia shook her head. "Not unless I want to try and sing the demons to death."

"What?"

She shook her head again. "Never mind."

Kay bent down to the prince's body. Gently, almost reverently, she unbuckled and removed his sword belt. She slid Flamebane into its scabbard and extended it to Randia.

"You can use that better than I can," the princess said.

Stefan shook his head. "Gerard was right. This is more than just a weapon. It's a symbol. You need to carry it."

Slowly, reluctantly, Randia nodded. She took the belt from Kay and buckled it around her waist.

Stefan flipped Randia's knife in his hand. "This has worked pretty well for me. I'll hold on to it, if you don't mind."

Randia unfastened the sheath and handed it to him. "Not at all. You were always the better throw in our act, anyway."

"Just let me fetch my bow, and Richard's quiver," Kay said. "He had some bluesteel arrows, but I don't think he got the chance to use them. He shouldn't be far."

Randia nodded. "Be quick. While you're at it, check to see if there are any more demons that way. The trees block our view from here, and we need to know if we'll have any pursuit."

Kay sprinted toward the entrance to the glade as Stefan looked at his other hand. It held the prince's wand, still glowing softly.

"Gerard bound the last of his magic into this when he died," he said. "I can feel it. The fading remains of his cloaking spell, and ... a burst of power." He looked up at her. "Like one last arrow in a magical quiver."

Randia followed his gaze. She could see the two auras playing over the surface of the wand. One, grey, looked to be in danger of flickering out. The other, bright silver, thrummed as though impatient for release.

She nodded. "You keep it. It may come in —"

She never finished. The wand's flickering grey aura suddenly winked out in a shower of red and black sparks.

Her eyes widened in terror. "Oh, no —" she began.

The sound of scuffling boots and thudding feet reached them from the path to the west. Kay's cry shattered the still air with a single word.

"Run!"

The pair sprinted toward the eastern end of the glade, and the tunnel that led to the Silver Star Adventurer's Academy.

The sound of a powerful blow rang through the air behind them. Randia turned in time to see Kay fly through the entrance to the garden. She slammed against the stone wall at its southern end and slid down it, leaving a red smear along its rocky surface. She crumpled to the ground and did not move.

A massive demon strode into the glade behind her. It saw Randia and Stefan, and smiled. When it spoke, the sound grated on their ears, like nails being scraped against a chalkboard.

"I am Gorath," it said. "And at last I've found you, little princess."

Stefan grabbed her arm. "Run!" he cried.

Tearing her eyes away from Kay's body and blinking back new tears, Randia turned to follow him.

Gorath shook its head violently. It raised one arm and drew its hand down in a sweeping gesture before its face.

"Goh nul zah na ta," it chanted.

A sheet of flame appeared before the tunnel opening. Randia and Stefan barely skidded to a stop before running into it. They were trapped.

They turned again to face the demon as it strode into the garden. They watched as it looked around, surveying the battlefield, littered with the bodies of guards and monsters alike. Its gaze rested briefly on Ashrach's headless form, and then finally on the body of the prince.

"Impressive," it said. "A full company of my demons. All dead, by a handful of guards and one wizard. From the signs, a royal who fought like the Archmage himself." It chuckled. "That's the second time today."

It turned to Randia. She glared at the creature in helpless fury.

"And it won't be the last, monster," Stefan said boldly. "One scion of the royal house of Carlissa still lives. Flee, or you'll share their fate."

Gorath laughed, slapping its thighs with its enormous clawed hands. "Well played, princeling!" it roared.

It gestured at the slain demons. "Unfortunately for you, I'm not as simple as my underlings. You're bluffing, of course."

"Don't be so sure —" Stefan began. Gorath cut him off with another burst of laughter.

"The puzzle wasn't difficult to solve," it continued, almost conversationally. "Surely the same power was at work here that the King used to repel our first attack on the palace." He gestured to Gerard's body. "A power that he gave to his son, who used it to escape and to come to this place. A power that he gave to his sister when he died, and which she now wears on her left hand."

A shiver of panic ran down Randia's spine. *The monster knew about the ring.*

"But it's a power she does not know how to use," the demon continued. "That is easy enough to tell from the hatred in her eyes. If she could, she would already have burned me to a cinder. If she could wield this mysterious artifact, I would already be dead."

Stefan was silent, and Gorath smiled again.

"It is over, princess," it said. "I would prefer to deliver you alive to my master, Lord Borr. But I do not *need* to." It gestured to Stefan. "I will give you a chance to surrender. If you do, I will spare him. If you do not, he will die slowly."

The fingers of Stefan's hand whitened as he gripped Gerard's wand. "You will not take her while I live, demon," he said acidly.

Randia's eyes darted around, looking for a way out. She saw none. The tunnel entrance was the only one they could reach, and the demon's flaming barrier blocked it completely ...

Flaming barrier.

She didn't stop to think about what she did next. She closed one hand around the hilt of her brother's sword. Her other hand grabbed Stefan's, and she looked into his eyes.

"Trust me!" she cried.

He barely had time to nod in surprise. Randia spun and drew Flamebane from its sheath. The two turned, and, hand in hand, ran toward the entrance to the tunnel.

Randia felt the sword's icy magic rush through her as they entered the blaze. She saw a cold white light flare along the blade, which seemed to react with an almost palpable anger at the fiery magic's touch. The white glow formed a frosty aura around them, driving back the flames.

Seconds later, it was over. They were past the fire and running madly through the tunnel.

Gorath roared in surprise and anger. The pounding footfalls of its pursuit echoed through the granite passageway behind them.

Randia tried desperately to think of a way to escape the monster. She and Stefan were fast, and the demon was large. They might outrun it for a while, but they would never lose it. It would keep after them, tirelessly, until it had them, or it was dead. That meant a race to the Star, trying to reach her grandfather before they were caught. They had to keep running.

The passage turned, and she saw light at the end of the tunnel. Once they were out, they would be on a curving road that led to the shoulder of the bluffs above the academy. If they could get close enough, then perhaps the mages in the tower would see their plight, and could do something to help ...

A loud report sounded behind them. Randia saw the bright blue flash of a lightning bolt illuminate the granite walls of the tunnel. Sparks and stone chips rained down in the passage behind them. Cold fear stabbed through her as she realized how close they had just come to death.

"Come on, Stefan!" she gasped. "Run! With all you've got!"

That was when she sensed that something was terribly wrong.

Stefan had fallen behind. She could no longer hear his breathing, or his footsteps. In panic she slowed, looking over her shoulder.

He was standing in the center of the passage. His posture was resolute and determined. He was looking at her with a mixture of love and resignation, and he was crying.

She skidded to a halt. She heard Gorath lumbering toward them. In seconds, it would turn the corner behind them.

"Stefan, come on!" she screamed.

He shook his head. His bard's voice resonated powerfully as he called to her.

"We both know what I have to do," he said. "Run, Randi — and always remember that I love you."

Gerard's wand flared to brilliant life in his left hand, and he drew her knife with his right. Armed with the enchanted blade and the last magic of a dead wizard, he turned and braced himself for the demon's charge.

Perhaps it was part of the power of the ring she now wore, but time seemed to stop for her as she stared at the unfolding scene. Stefan knew that Gerard's wand lacked the power to kill the demon. The most he could do was slow it — and when the magic was spent, he would die. He was sacrificing himself to buy her time to escape.

She started to run to him, to stand with him. Then she stopped.

The consequences of that choice unfolded in her mind with ruthless clarity. If she joined him, they would both die. They would die together, but they would die — and Gorath would take the ring. Her mission to bring it to the Archmage would fail, and their last and only chance to stop the demons would be lost. The city would fall.

And with the hellgate to endlessly replenish their numbers, the world would inevitably follow it into slavery to the Dark.

She remembered the tale of Calindra. Wielding the Shield of the Defender, she had stood against the horde, defeated its captain, and destroyed its hellgate. Now the Age of Legends was playing itself out again. Only this time, there were no gods to protect them. The Archmage was their only defender. Without the ring, he would fail.

She loved Stefan with a passion beyond anything she had ever known. How could she go on without him? His bright smile, his quirky humor, his handsome roguishness, his bold audacity? Her heart ached to scream that *no, she couldn't* — and to run to him, and die at his side.

But if she did, then his sacrifice would be in vain. What he was doing was an offering of love, not only to her, but to the world itself. If she stayed, then she would be surrendering to the very evil that he had chosen with his last act to defy.

And if she ran, then even if by some miracle she survived, she would never be free of the pain of abandoning him. Her heartbreak would be endless.

Stefan's fate was sealed. She could die with him, or she could honor his last stand by trying to complete her quest. Those were the only choices she had, and she had no time to choose.

All of those thoughts flashed through her mind in a fraction of a second. When they were done, she knew what she had to do. Her voice choked with grief as she called out to him for the last time.

"I love you, Stefan!"

Then she ran.

She didn't look back, couldn't look back. The tunnel opening seemed to rush toward her, its light broken and scattered through the tears that flooded her eyes. Her breath came in gasping sobs, and her chest felt like it was being constricted by a metal band.

The concussion of another lightning strike cracked through the passage. But the bolt never reached her. Stefan had blocked it with her brother's wand. He had saved her.

Behind, she heard Gorath's roar of anger, and Stefan's challenge.

"For the Princess Bard!" he cried.

And then she was out of the tunnel. The sky was clear, and the light was bright despite its fading with the westering sun. She blinked, trying to adjust her eyes and to clear away her tears.

She was on the far side of the spur, now. The path from the tunnel merged onto a road that ran to her left. The view ahead was blocked by a line of trees and homes, but she knew that the bluff dropped away sharply just on the other side of them. She kept running.

Behind her, she could hear Stefan's confrontation with the demon — the monster's roars, his cries of defiance, the concussions of magic. The opening of the tunnel seemed to amplify the sounds like a megaphone. She would hear every moment of his end as though she were right at his side. She braced herself as she ran, knowing what was to come.

When it did, she thought she would be prepared for it. She was wrong.

Gorath's roar rose in a note of triumph. Stefan's voice met it in a cry of defiance, suddenly cut off. There was the sound of an impact, and then a long pause.

And then she heard him scream.

It was a shriek of agony. She knew it was involuntary, and the pain needed to force such a cry from him. The demon had him in its claws, and it was tearing him apart.

The shrieks continued for what seemed like an eternity. She heard the monster's laugh as the cries rose higher and higher in pitch, all dignity now gone from the young bard's voice.

She found herself screaming with him as she ran. But she did not stop.

A horrible *wet* sound mixed in with Stefan's shrieks. They faded quickly and were gone. The screeching of Gorath's voice broke the silence that followed.

"Your consort is dead, princess!" it cried. "Surrender, and I will spare you his fate!"

Randia stumbled and fell against a tree at the side of the road. She still carried Flamebane in one hand, and the sword's edge bit into the bole and stuck fast. For a few moments she could do nothing but lean there, mind and spirit numb. She felt her world collapsing around her, all of her dreams turning to ash.

Then she shook her head and forced herself to straighten. The worst was over. All that was left now was the race.

She grasped Flamebane's hilt and ripped the sword from the tree. Running with it in her hand was keeping her off balance, slowing her down. She slipped the blade into its sheath and snapped the buckle back into place. Then she moved again.

The next minutes were a blur. To her relief she once again felt a peculiar sense of detachment, as she had earlier in the day. It helped her focus on what she needed to do to survive. On running, and making it to the stair that led down to the next terrace of the city.

Behind her, she could hear the lumbering of Gorath's pursuit. It was closing on her, slowly and relentlessly. Stefan had bought her time, and she could only pray that it would be enough.

The road ahead took a sudden, sharp turn. Randia sprinted around the rocky corner and found herself at the edge of a cliff. To her right, she saw the winding stair that led down toward the Silver Star. And beyond the stair and several hundred feet below, she could finally see the eastern end of Lannamon.

The scene that met her gaze seemed taken from a nightmare. Fires raged, uncontrolled, throughout the city. Bands of demons, dragons, and Hellmen were everywhere, pillaging and killing at will. The Carlissan fleet had been burned or sunk, and the army base on the north shore of the firth was little more than a ruin.

She barely noticed it all. She stared instead, wide eyed, at the Silver Star Adventurer's Academy. It stood just ahead of her, at the bottom of the stair and the base of the cliff.

It was burning.

The main gates had been shattered and great gaping holes had been torn in its walls. Demons surged in and around them, invading the grounds. Loud reports of magic boomed as blasts of fire and lightning tore through the few defenders who remained. The adamant and bluesteel spire of the great tower, once the pride of the academy and her grandfather's home, was a solid column of flame.

The Star had fallen.

She stumbled forward to stand at the brink of the cliff and stared at the vista of destruction. Her one hope had been to reach the academy, to bring the ring to her grandfather. That hope was now gone.

I should have died with Stefan, she thought numbly. *I've failed them. I've failed them all. I'm too late, and now the world will pay the price.*

Her eyes wandered across the burning city. Bitter despair churned in her soul like bile.

It's all my fault. All because my brother stopped to save me. If he had let me die, then perhaps he could have gotten here in time to stop this.

She heard Gorath roaring behind her. The demon's voice was very loud now, and very close. It would be on her in seconds. There was nowhere left to run, and nothing left to run for.

She looked down from the brink. A dozen waterfalls cascaded from the southeastern cliffs to her right, and fell, misting, into a network of pools and reservoirs. Aqueduct channels ran along the cliff-face below, branching out to feed the lower terraces as they extended toward the center of the city.

Heart numb with the loss of everything she loved, the demon crashing through the trees only moments behind her, she leaped from the precipice and into space.

The Fall of House Killraven

"The demons are taking the palace?" Kuhl demanded angrily. "And the King has abandoned us? To hide at the top of his tower?"

Lord Rugon sighed. The other councilors and what remained of the palace staff stood in a semicircle before him. Their faces wore a mixture of anxiety, fear, and entreaty.

"With the Queen and the prince," he said. "To make a last stand. To kill as many of the enemy as they can before they die."

Gasps ran through the safe room. Several people began to weep softly. One backed away, shaking his head and repeating the word "No," with a slow, rhythmic cadence.

"What happened?" Lady Rayne demanded. "How did it come to this?"

"We fought the demons at the gate," Lord Rugon said. He closed his eyes, and a shudder ran through his body. "But there were thousands of them. We held them as long as we could, until we were driven back into the main hall."

"And our forces?" Kuhl pursued.

"Most of the guard and the warrior priests are dead. What

remained of the Knights of the Light withdrew into the tower to make their stand with the King."

One of the serving girls rushed forward. She took his arm.

"Is this the end, My Lord?" she asked. Her voice was terrified, and her innocent, doe eyes ran with tears. "Are we all to die here today?"

He patted her hand gently. He met her gaze with a look that was kindly and protective.

"I do not know, my child," he said. "My orders were to withdraw here with what remained of the guard, and to protect the council." His eyes hardened with a sudden bitterness. "And to surrender when the demons finally broke through to take us."

Kuhl's eyes widened. "The King wants the council to give up?"

Lord Rugon shrugged. "He said that our deaths would serve no purpose. He believes they may spare us."

The serving girl lowered her head. "Is there no hope, My Lord?" she asked meekly.

He closed his eyes, remembering his last conversation with Danor and Elena.

"I wish I could tell you, child," he said. The candor in his voice surprised him. "The King spoke of a last hope, but said that he could not reveal it."

She looked up at him, eyelashes fluttering shyly. "But surely he gave you some idea of what this hope might be?"

Lord Rugon looked at her and shook his head sadly. *God, but the girl is beautiful,* he thought. *So innocent, so vulnerable. I wish there was something I could do to protect her. She deserves to know the truth ...*

"He said he could tell us nothing," he said. "And asked us to trust him. All I know is that whatever this hope is, he does not believe that he and the Queen will live to see it."

Kuhl had turned to the others. He was arguing that they should do as the King commanded and surrender to the enemy. No one saw the girl move a slim hand to touch Lord Rugon's arm. Her dark eyes peered searchingly into his.

"You are hurt, My Lord," she whispered. "And bitter, that your King ordered you to stand with the council. That he would not let you make that last stand with him and die at his side."

A sob escaped Lord Rugon's lips. He nodded, feeling suddenly grateful for her empathy and understanding.

"Yes," he said. "But he believes Zomoran will spare the council. That he will try to co-opt and corrupt it. That someone whose heart can be trusted must remain with it, to work on for the good of the Carlissan people."

The girl sighed. Raising herself on tiptoe, she gently kissed Lord Rugon's cheek.

"Thank you, My Lord," she said. "For all you've done for us. And the King is right. You will need to find a way to work with the new rulers of Carlissa. To bring the people together under their rule, for the good of all. It is a grave responsibility. But I know the King chose wisely in selecting you for it."

He smiled. His eyes looked slightly unfocused as he patted her hand again. "You are quite welcome, my dear," he said absently.

A guard stepped toward him. "My Lord?" he asked tentatively.

Lord Rugon shook his head as if to clear it, and then faced him. "Yes?"

"The demons are coming down the passage," the guard said. "All of my men have fallen back to the entrance to the safe room. Do you have any further orders?"

The serving girl stepped quietly away from them. A shimmering grey mist seemed to form around her as she walked briskly toward the exit. No one noticed it, or her. She strode through the doorway and made her way up the long corridor to the great hall.

She heard loud sounds ahead. When she turned a corner, she saw a line of battle demons coming toward her. The passage was barely wide enough to accommodate their great size.

They saw her as she saw them. The lead demon growled. With a wicked smile, it charged.

Her eyes flashed with magic, and a blood-red gem appeared on a chain around her neck. The demon staggered, clutching its head. The others looked at her with sudden fear as she waited for the creature to recover.

"Report," she said at last. Her voice was no longer meek, but filled with power and menace. "And do it on your knees."

The monster stumbled forward and fell groveling before her.

"Forgive me, Lady Desire," it said. "I did not recognize you. I thought you were —"

The girl's eyes flashed again, and the demon gasped. "Report," she repeated. Her voice was impatient.

"The palace has fallen," it choked. "All except the sky dome and whatever is down this corridor."

She placed a hand on the demon's head and stroked it, as though petting an animal. The creature shuddered, its eyes rolling up in a look of ecstasy.

"Good boy," she said. "So the royals are making their stand at the summit of the tower?"

The creature nodded. "Yes, Mistress. Incanus Thad prepares the assault to breach it."

The girl's eyebrows arched. "So the Horde Captain has mastered himself," she mused. "Good. I will join him."

The demon bowed its head subserviently. "Yes, Mistress," it said.

"Take your troops to the end of this passage," she continued. "You will find a heavily fortified safe room. The last of the guard are there, protecting civilians and the council. You will parley, and offer to accept their surrender." Her eyes hardened. "You will *not* kill them, and they are *not* to be given to the Hellmen. Is that clear?"

The demon looked up in surprise. "But why —"

It looked down again when it saw her suddenly dangerous expression. "Yes, Mistress," it said hastily.

The girl smiled. "You may injure a few of them in the process if you wish. But not too badly. They are witnesses to a particular event, and I want word of it to spread."

She fingered the gem that hung at her throat. "Widely," she added. "Do you understand my orders?"

"Yes, Mistress," the demon replied.

"Good. Now clear a way for me to pass."

It scrambled to its feet and pressed itself against the wall of the passage. The creatures behind it quickly did the same. The girl walked past them, barely acknowledging their presence.

When she reached the great hall, she saw it was filled with demons. They backed away hastily as she walked by them. She made her way to the base of the palace tower and looked up.

Feathered objects sprouted from her back in a blur of dark magic. They grew quickly into a pair of black wings that unfurled as she sprang into the air. They beat powerfully, carrying her straight up the shaft of Gerard's magical elevator. The levitating disk had been smashed, and the rubble of its remains lay strewn on the ground below.

She hovered as she came level with the top of the stairs. A great, jagged hole gaped where the fortified door to the wizards' laboratories had been. She floated through it, and, dainty feet touching the tiles once more, made her way toward the center of the complex.

She observed the devastation with satisfaction. The labs were piled with the bodies of wizards, priests and demons, all torn apart by claw, sword, or magic. Rubble from walls obliterated by blasts of fire and lightning choked the way.

She stopped when she found a group of battle demons clustered around a short ascending staircase. It ended at a gleaming metal door reinforced with bluesteel. Runes and wards glowed brightly along its surface. Before the door, axe in hand, stood the massive figure of Incanus Thad.

The Horde Captain turned to her as she approached. A broad grin appeared on his demonic face.

"Lady Desire," he said. His voice boomed loudly in the enclosed space. "Is your infiltration finally complete?"

The demon was over twice her height, and could barely stand erect even in the high stairwell. She stroked a hand absently along his massive thigh as she came to his side.

"It is," she said. "The only secret left appears to lie with the royals themselves."

Incanus Thad growled. "Do you mean to capture them, then?" he said. His voice was heavy with disapproval. "To interrogate them?"

She shook her head reluctantly.

"No," she said. "It's probably just a lie told to bolster the defense. And the Killravens are too dangerous to risk it. They need to be killed, as swiftly and as brutally as possible." She looked into the demon captain's eyes. "I'm here to lend a hand with that."

"Good," Incanus Thad said. His thundering voice sounded relieved. "Your help would be timely." He waved his axe, Destruction, at the enchanted doorway. "We need to shatter these wards."

The girl studied them and nodded.

"We will need to draw power from your battle demons. But this entrance is narrow, Incanus — and there will be three royals waiting for us, with whatever remains of the knights and the wizards."

The great creature shrugged.

"There are over a thousand of us in the palace now," he said. "Usnaroth circles the tower with two squadrons of our elite sky demons, and Lord Borr itself prepares to throw the full strength of its magic against the tower ward. They wait only for my signal."

The girl nodded. She turned to face the demons behind them.

"Prepare yourselves," she said.

They closed their eyes and began to chant softly in their infernal tongue. Liana's gem responded with a glow of red light. The Horde Captain lowered his axe, and the massive blade came to rest against the girl's throat. For a moment, it looked as though it were going to take her head. Then Destruction touched the gem, and the magic spread like wildfire into the weapon's edge.

The axe blazed like a crimson sun as Incanus Thad turned, faced the portal, and braced himself to strike. Then the giant demon swung it with all of his strength.

"Karach!" he cried.

Destruction struck the door with a blinding shower of sparks. The wards flared brilliantly, but held. The demon whipped the weapon around and struck again.

"Karach!"

Again the wards flared, but this time a red glow mixed in with their white-blue radiance. A deafening screech reverberated through the tower, as though the door itself were screaming in agony. When the sparks cleared, there was a long, red-glowing gash in its surface.

The axe came around again. This time, all the demons cried out in unison.

"Karach!"

The door exploded in a burst of fiery magic. The two halves flew from their hinges to land on the stairway above. Incanus Thad leaped through the opening, which was suddenly bright with the light of the westering sun.

"Troops forward!" he cried. "And give the signal!"

The girl stood back as the demons rushed through the doorway and up the stairs. Almost immediately, she heard the sounds of battle engaged. Cries of "For the Light!" and "For King and Carlissa!" mixed with the roar of the monsters, and with concussions of magic. She waited until all of the demonic soldiers had gone through the opening, and then followed unhurriedly behind.

An icy wind whipped around her as she stepped onto the summit of the tower. The sun was settling low over the slopes of Mount Cascade. The spires of Lannamon and the waters of the firth glinted below in its fiery light. Smoke lit with an ominous red-orange hue rose in columns around the city.

She saw with a stab of disappointment that the battle was already over. Around her lay the bodies of a small force of wizards and knights, and a handful of demons. Only a few of the Carlissans had retreated to the top of the tower, and they were already dead.

Or most of them were. The battle demons were gathered in a semicircle around the east end of the sky dome. Before them stood Incanus Thad, his thunderous voice booming in the high airs.

"We meet again, Queen Elena," he said. "Are you ready to finish what we began this morning?"

Elena's voice rang with defiance.

"If you mean, are we ready to die, monster," she said, "then we are. You may kill us, but you have not won the true battle. *That* remains yet to be waged."

The demons made way for the girl as she came forward. When the last of them had parted, she found herself face to face with the King and Queen.

Elena Starlight's long blonde hair blew freely in the wind atop the palace tower. Azure fire blazed in her hand. At her left stood Vala Orleans, and at her right, King Danor Killraven. His sword, Guardian, shone with a warm, golden radiance as he held it above his head, ready to strike.

The girl smiled at them as her black, feathered wings unfurled once again behind her. Elena's eyes widened in sudden understanding.

"You!" she cried.

The girl curtsied. "Liana Desire," she said. "Succubus in the service of His Holy Magnificence, the Demon Lord Borr. Farewell, Your Majesties. As we tried to inform you earlier, your reign is at an end."

Destruction whistled above Incanus Thad's head, and Liana's gem blazed with red magic. Their wings beat in unison as they rose into the air and, backed by a legion of battle demons, leaped to attack.

Chapter 17 - Heart of Steel

The Flume

Air whistled by Randia's head as she fell. She twisted her hips and grabbed her scabbard to keep it from flailing. She had one desperate chance. If she missed — or the sword snagged on *anything* — it would be over.

Her legs and backside slammed into a hard, stone surface as she plunged into rushing water. It was smooth and narrow, curving around her, angling downward. She held the scabbard hard along her leg and pointed her toes, trying to keep herself from bouncing off into space.

For a few heart-pounding seconds, she felt her back riding up out of the current and along the side of the aqueduct. Her right leg rose out of it completely, threatening to toss her into the air again. Then her body slid back down into the channel. She tried to hold her breath as the water rushed over her, submerging her in its icy embrace.

The aqueduct was built into the eastern side of the cliff-spur where the southern tier of the Upper City ended. Randia rode the channel feet-first as it dropped steeply away from the ledge she had stood on only moments before. Freezing mountain water flowed around her in a loud rush as her body slammed against the inside of the stone conduit. She thought she could hear the muffled sound of Gorath's enraged cursing above, but it quickly faded into the distance.

She tried to flatten herself into the narrow channel. The stone around her was smooth and worn, and she slid easily along its surface. She knew that would allow her to pick up tremendous speed, which she hoped would quickly carry her far away from the pursuing demon. But that speed was a double-edged sword. One mistake would smash her body on the rocks or toss it out over the cliff. She tensed, ready to lean to either side to steer her way.

She raced through the flume. The light dimmed or vanished abruptly as the aqueduct ran under overhangs or through tunnels in the cliff-face, and she was slammed around without warning by its sudden turns. She was nearly split in half when it separated into two different runways, but managed to veer into one of them at the last moment.

She felt herself rising along the right side of the canal as it banked to the left. The light around her brightened, and she risked lifting her head for a few gulps of air. The cliff was curving to face north and merging into one of the terraces of the Upper City South.

The channel pulled away from it in a long, flattening bridge that dipped, and then abruptly ended. Water gushed over its edge. It glinted in the light of the westering sun as it dropped into a reservoir below.

Randia knew it would be only seconds before she hit the cascade, and there was little she could do to prepare. Her heart thudded as she braced herself, holding her free hand above her head. If her timing was off, the drop too far, or the pool too shallow ...

Then she was over the lip and riding the waterfall into space. For a long moment she hung there, suspended in air. Then she arched her back and, with a skill that came from years of practice, transitioned gracefully into a flawless reverse pike. Her body arrowed into the reservoir and disappeared beneath the surface of the water.

Tricked

Liana searched frantically among the bodies at the summit of the tower. Usnaroth landed nearby with a dozen elite demons at its side. Incanus Thad strode to meet them.

"It is done," the giant demon said. "The royals are slain. Take their heads for the palace gate."

Usnaroth's bat-like features looked pleased, and it gestured to two of its companions. "That should break what's left of the city's resistance," it said.

"Is there any word on the princess?"

"Yes, finally. One of the demons under Gorath's command just reported in. She was hiking in the bluffs to the south when the attack began. The captain is tracking her as we speak."

"Ah," Incanus Thad said. He sounded disappointed. "So that's why Gorath went missing. We should go and help with the hunt —"

Liana straightened abruptly. Her black wings flared and beat the air as her eyes flashed in rage and frustration.

"So *that* was their secret hope," she said softly, as though to herself.

Incanus Thad looked at her in surprise. "What are you talking about?"

"We have been tricked, Incanus. Prince Gerard's body is not here."

Incanus Thad's face darkened. "I thought you said he had been left at the top of the tower. To perform some kind of conjuring."

She shook her head. "That's what the royals told everyone. The Queen must have sensed my magic and staged a deception. Their stand was a distraction, to give him time to flee ..."

She whirled suddenly on the Horde Captain.

"That ring, Incanus," she said. "The one the King wielded against you earlier. He's not wearing it now." She turned to Usnaroth. "And he didn't use it in his charge either, did he?"

Usnaroth shook its head. "I saw no sign of a magic ring."

"He gave it to the prince, then," she said, her eyes narrowing. "That's how he escaped the palace undetected. We have a second royal on the loose — and he's armed with a powerful artifact."

Heart of Ash

Randia swam along the stone bottom of the reservoir. She had only just avoided slamming into it, face first, at the nadir of her dive. Flattening that dive had taken all of her strength and skill as a swimmer — but she had managed it.

She couldn't stay underwater for long. She'd had to hold her breath through much of her flume ride through the aqueduct, and her lungs were burning. She sighted on the shimmering light from the surface above and moved toward it with powerful strokes.

She found that Flamebane was hindering her movements. It was a light sword, made by elven smiths from some of the finest bluesteel ever forged, but it was still a sword. It weighed her down in the water and slapped about awkwardly as she kicked her legs. Despite the difficulty, she didn't think for a moment of letting it go. It was all she had left from her brothers, and she knew she would need it.

Spots were appearing in her vision when she finally broke the surface. A short swim took her to a set of stone steps that rose from the water and onto a narrow ledge. She rested for a minute when she reached them, helplessly heaving in huge gulps of air.

When she had finally stopped gasping, she looked around. The reservoir was a large pool carved from granite. To her dismay, she discovered that she'd lost both of her shoes during her ride through the flume. Drenched and barefoot, she climbed the stairs and vaulted over a short metal fence at the top.

She found herself on a tiled plaza. It was another of the many walking paths that laced the Upper City. It ended to the north in an ornately carved balustrade that looked out over the edge of the second terrace.

Shock ran through her as she realized where she was. She had traveled over a mile down toward the firth in a matter of minutes.

She saw with relief that there were no demons near her. A handful wandered her level of the Upper City, but most were concentrated around Lannamon's crumbling centers of defense: the palace, the Cathedral, the Silver Star. She reached the balustrade and leaned heavily on it, bracing herself for what she knew she would see.

The City of Rainbows had been conquered. Every bastion of resistance had fallen, its walls lying in ruin or flame. Even the palace was crawling with monsters. The sky chamber at the summit of the Wizard's Tower was thick with the flitting shapes of winged demons.

She started along the walkway to the east. The path skirted the creatures razing the Silver Star, and she watched them warily as she followed it. Had they slain her grandfather as well? Was his own head soon to appear on the gate before his tower, heralding the final defeat of the Children of the Covenant?

She watched the shadows lengthen across the city as the sun

touched the shoulder of Mount Cascade. The long twilight was coming to Lannamon, but it would be another hour before the sun fell behind the horizon. Until then, the lingering dusk of mountainset would cover the valley, an ambient golden light reflecting into it from the sky and clouds above.

She thought of everyone who had died to save her. Windheart. Gerard. Kay, and the guards of Company Twenty-Three. And Stefan, the love of her life, who had been torn to shreds by the creature that now pursued her.

She looked numbly at the city as she walked. Aron was gone, and her parents were certainly dead by now as well. Everyone she loved was being taken from her, and everything good in the world was being destroyed.

She shook her head, and tears splashed across her face. She had failed. She would never find her grandfather. The city was lost, the world would end, it was her fault — *and there was nothing she could do about it.*

No, there *was* one thing she could do. She could at least put an end to her torment. All she needed was her brother's sword.

The Crucible

She was reaching for Flamebane before she realized it. She drew the blade and held it in the air before her.

She felt the leather and bluesteel as her fingers curled, white-knuckled, around its hilt. She stared at the sword as if seeing it for the first time.

This was made for them, she thought suddenly. *For the monsters that had taken her family, her future, and her love from her life.*

It was made to kill them.

She felt the smooth texture of the ring on her other hand. She could still hear its song calling to her, but it was faint now, as though coming from an impossibly great distance.

She looked at the burning city. She saw the life fading from Gerard's eyes. She felt Windheart's belly being torn open. Stefan's dying shrieks echoed in her mind.

The demons had done this.

Her desperate flight had given her no time to think or to feel. Now her emotions were finally forcing themselves through her numb grief. She felt a cold, hard anger — and with it, sprouted a seed of burning hatred.

Those feelings washed through her, like lights in the dark. Her despair scattered before them, like ash in a wind. Her soul clung to them desperately, like a lifeline to one hanging over an abyss.

The ring's song changed. Its theme shifted into a variation, tense and ominous, beginning a slow progression toward the crescendo it had always promised. It became subtly louder, as though not quite coming from such a great distance as before.

She closed her eyes and rested the flat of the blade against her forehead. She let the rage burn through her, free and unrestrained. It was an alien feeling to her kindly soul, but it comforted her. It left her with an odd sense of confidence and determination — and of clarity.

She thought about her promise to Gerard, that she would do what must be done. She had said the words. She knew now that they had been empty.

Her people would need guidance, leadership, and inspiration. A frightened victim could not give that to them. And that was what she had been.

All she had done that day was to *react*. To run, desperate and afraid, to keep one step ahead of the monsters that pursued her. To shed a tear for each protector that died to buy her a few more precious seconds of life.

But Gerard had believed in her — and with a quiet confidence that had terrified her. Why had it terrified her?

She knew the answer now. It wasn't demons, death, and slavery to the Dark that truly frightened her. It was the woman she would have to become to fight them.

She had to let go of that fear.

Again, the theme shifted. It was building quickly now. A rush of exultation ran through her as her heart leaped with it toward its crescendo.

She could no longer be the "Princess Bard." That person — kind, fun-loving, and innocent — could not cope with the world that now faced her. The blood of everyone who had died for her that day had already proven it.

She had to commit herself to the battle that was ahead. To find a way to bring the war to her enemies. To *stop* being a victim.

She forced herself to remember Gorath's face, and Stefan's screams. Her body shuddered with hatred for the creature that had murdered him. Her soul seized on that hatred like a weapon. It *was* a weapon. She would *make it* a weapon.

A blast of horns rang out in her mind, powerful and defiant. Her thoughts — and the song — surged ruthlessly toward their climax.

The anger, and the hatred ... they would give her the strength she needed. To become something else. Something stronger. Something ... harder.

They would be the crucible to forge a heart of steel.

The crescendo struck her like a physical blow. It filled her with a promise of justice, of redemption, and of revenge. That she would never, *ever*, feel powerless again.

New tears flowed from her tear-stained eyes. But this time, they were not tears of grief. They were tears of hope. She cried with love for her world and for her people, and with determination to be their defender. And with anger, and hatred, for everything that threatened them.

The song washed over her, through her, and filled her. And as it did, the Ring of the Killravens began to burn with awakened magic.

Warrior Princess

Randia stood there for a long time, eyes closed, sword held before her. She let the song flow through her mind and soul, waiting for the sound of heavy footsteps. When she finally heard them, she was ready.

"A fine chase, little princess," Gorath's grating voice said. She thought she could actually detect a note of respect in it. "Especially the aqueduct ride. It was inspired."

She didn't move, didn't open her eyes. "I'm glad you approve," she said coldly.

"I do. But as you can see, you cannot lose me. And there is nowhere left to run."

"No," she agreed. "There isn't."

Gorath's heavy tread resumed. "Then it is time for you to surrender."

She shook her head. A small smile appeared on her lips.

"You haven't won yet. Not while the last Killraven still lives."

Gorath chuckled. It continued toward her, massive feet thudding on the tiled walkway.

"Come, now, princess. Accept your fate. Your city is lost, and no one is coming to save you."

She turned. Flamebane swept around in a graceful arc as she leveled it at the monster. Locks of wet hair clung to her face as she opened her eyes.

"The question is not who is going to save *me*, demon," she said steadily. "It's who is going to save *you*."

Gorath stopped. It looked at her, suddenly wary.

A stiff wind swirled around her body. An aura of azure light shimmered for just an instant as it blew through her hair and clothes. When it was gone, the water drenching them had vanished. All that remained were a few puddles on the tiled walkway at her feet.

"This is pointless," Gorath said. "You cannot defeat me with simple magic tricks."

Her body moved into a fencer's stance — blade forward, left hand extended behind her. Her hair, now dry, framed a face that was set with a hard, cold hatred.

"You sent the demons that killed my brother," she said. "And murdered the love of my life. Now I'm going to kill *you*, Gorath. You're going to be my first payment to your masters for what they've done here today."

The demon began to move again. It circled slowly toward her, claws extended.

Randia waited, trying not to show her trepidation. She *had* begun to grasp the ring's battle power, but her hold on it was tenuous. It was the song that had finally connected her with it, once she had fully committed herself to the fight. But how much control would it actually give her? She was untrained in spellcraft, and any magic she tried to wield with it would be raw and clumsy at best.

"A pity," Gorath said at last. "It would have been a coup to bring you in, alive and undamaged. I suppose I'll just have to settle for …

alive."

The demon's arm lashed out, and an aura of dark green magic leaped from its outstretched claws. It formed into a massive hand that streaked toward her, fingers outstretched.

Randia braced herself. The song thundered in her mind as her sword arm swept back, and then struck. Flamebane's blade glinted with blue fire as it severed the groping digits in flight, and then impaled the palm with a quick riposte. There was a deafening *shrieking* noise, and the hand exploded in a shower of sapphire sparks.

Gorath's eyes widened. It gestured with its other hand. Crimson electricity snapped and played around its claws, and then sprang toward her in a bolt of red lightning.

Randia raised her left hand, palm outward. The Ring of the Killravens blazed with blue flame as the lightning struck. She screamed as the blast scorched her arm, but she held firm, pressing against it with all of her strength.

For a long moment, the electricity surged back and forth between their outstretched hands, crackling and dancing around them like a living thing. Then the song leaped in her mind. Gorath's arm jerked back, and it emitted a grating snarl of pain. There was a smell of burned flesh as the lightning backfired on the monster with a flash and a loud report.

Randia wavered for a moment, and then caught her balance. She lowered Flamebane before her, holding it at the ready, her left hand balled into a fist at her side. The ring was shining brightly now, with a pure, blue magic that matched the color of her eyes — eyes that glared at the demon with hatred and defiance.

Gorath stepped back, breathing heavily. It stared at the ring on her hand, and a shadow of uncertainty passed over its demonic features. Then it circled toward her again, approaching with even greater caution.

"Simple magic tricks," she said scornfully. "Shall I show you another?"

The demon stared at her, eyes burning with anger and frustration. She tried to brace herself for what would come next.

Gorath roared. Its battle cry echoed loudly along the walls of the bluff. Then it was bearing down on her, claws outstretched.

Randia had only seconds to react. Gorath sprang high into the air, clearly giving up on any plan to take her alive. It meant to crush and rend her with all of its brutal strength.

The song sounded fast and true in her mind as the demon struck. She felt the ring's magic flowing through her, investing her with strength and speed beyond anything she'd felt before. Gorath seemed to slip into slow motion as she surged forward, ducking under its leap. Flamebane slashed as the monster's claws whistled through empty air above her, and she felt the blade bite hard into its flesh. Then she tucked into a roll and came up behind the creature, spinning to strike at it again from behind.

The demon screeched in pain as the sword cut deeply into its arm. Its great feet cracked the tiles of the walkway as though from the force of twin hammers. Then it, too, was ducking aside and whirling to face her. The hand of its injured arm arced toward her in a spray of black ichor, fingers clenched.

Randia lunged, stabbing, but the demon wasn't where she expected it to be. She tried to shift back into a defensive stance, but the move had put her dangerously off-balance. She saw the fist coming at her face, and, in panic, struck out with her left hand to block it.

Gorath was nearly twice her height and many times her weight. The impact *should* have shattered her arm. But the ring flared with sapphire brilliance, forming a shield of blue energy that desperately tried to deflect the strike.

It was almost enough to save her.

Their fists came together in a bone-crushing concussion. Gorath screamed as the shield around her hand collapsed in an explosion of azure magic. She heard the song falter as a dissonant chord suddenly appeared in its proudly defiant theme. A stinging shock shot up her arm, and the blow threw her backward. It spun her like a top, hurling her around and down to sprawl face-first on the ground.

Randia lay on the tiled walkway. A desperate part of her yelled that she had to get back to her feet, to continue the fight, but her stunned mind and body wouldn't respond. She tried to crawl away from the demon, but found that she couldn't use her left arm. She started dragging herself along the ground with her right, and realized with a sudden shock that she'd lost her sword. Panicked, she lifted her head to search for it ...

An enormous clawed hand closed around her throat. She choked, suddenly unable to breathe, as it lifted her into the air. She clutched it with her good arm, trying to ease the pressure on her neck. She struggled desperately to break free, but it was no use. The demon thrust its face into hers as she dangled in its grasp, feet kicking helplessly above the ground.

She found herself staring into Gorath's eyes. Its labored growls of pain were so close, and so loud, that she could feel them resonating in her chest. Its breath was like a hot, stinking wind on her cheeks. It snarled at her and bared its fangs.

Randia's eyes darted around. She saw that the demon was standing with its back to the stone balustrade bordering the edge of the terrace. Its other arm hung limply at its side, a ruined mass of gore, burnt flesh, and swollen, broken knuckles. Behind it lay a fifty-foot drop to the lowest level of the Upper City.

Gorath's eyes narrowed, and it squeezed its hand.

Randia heard the song spiral out of control. She reached for it as it built toward a defeated crash, and tried to steer it back to a theme of hope. The effort was futile. She grasped desperately again for the ring's magic, but all she could touch were a few last glimmers of its power. She focused them against the demon's hand, trying to keep it from crushing her throat, from tearing into her with its claws ...

Gorath chuckled cruelly. It watched her with a demonic grin, clearly enjoying the sight, and the feel, of her helpless struggle.

"Perhaps," it growled. "If you'd had more time. To learn to use your power. But your time is up, little princess."

Her head swam, and her vision blurred. She felt blood run down her neck as the monster's taloned fingers cut her skin. Her struggles slowed, weakening. She was seconds from unconsciousness and death.

With the last of her strength and glaring with unrepentant hate, she spat in the demon's face.

Gorath growled in anger. It drew back its head, fangs flashing.

Then its eyes shifted, looking over her shoulder. Randia saw with surprise that they were focused on something behind her. They widened — and for the first time, she saw terror on the demon's face.

The pressure on her throat vanished as Gorath dropped her. Her bare feet stung as they hit the tiled path, and her legs crumpled beneath her. She stared up at the monster as it towered over her.

Gorath was waving its good arm in a desperate incantation. A shield of crimson magic took shape before it — and then was struck by a blinding flash of white. Randia blinked, momentarily blinded.

When her vision returned, she saw Gorath slowly sinking to the ground. Its knees buckled, and its body twisted sideways. Its face came into view, staring sightlessly down at her.

Through it, she saw the light of the setting sun.

Where the creature's forehead had been, there was now a hole penetrating the length of its massive skull. Behind and above it, a puff of black smoke rose into the fiery orange sky. Then it collapsed, falling backward without a sound to disappear over the rail onto the terrace below.

She blinked again, trying to clear her eyes. She struggled to her hands and knees and looked up.

An old man was striding toward her. He was tall and gaunt, and wore a white cloak above the buckles and leather of a dark green adventurer's tunic. His face was clean shaven, and his hair a shock of neatly trimmed white that framed his elderly features. In his hands, he carried a tall staff of shining blue metal tipped with an orb of clear crystal.

She sobbed in deliverance. It was her grandfather. It was Lenard the Archmage.

Chapter 18 - The Terrible Truth

A Brush With Armageddon

Randia struggled to clear her head. The world still spun as she tried to rise. She failed, falling again to the tiled walkway.

She felt her grandfather kneel at her side, and a steadying grip on her shoulder.

"Quickly," he said. His voice was gentle, but insistent. "The ring."

She tried to focus on his face, and it seemed to help quell her dizziness. His kindly grey eyes were filled with relief, but also with desperate urgency.

"What?" she asked.

"The ring," he repeated, extending his hand. "We have only moments, and our lives depend on it!"

She was shocked to hear a hint of panic in his voice. It sobered her immediately. She removed the ring and, taking his hand, slipped it onto his finger.

He rose swiftly to his feet. He turned to face the railing over the heart of the city and raised both hands. One held his staff, and the other now wore the ring. Both shone with a sudden white fire as she felt him summon their magic.

She was a Killraven. Her very blood was attuned to the ring's power, and to that of its wearer. She had felt that power before, and heard its song, when her brother Gerard had wielded it. She had touched it herself, however briefly and weakly, in her battle with Gorath.

What she sensed from her grandfather now went so far beyond either that she could only gasp in amazement. She had always *known* that he was the Archmage, but she had never truly understood what that meant.

She understood it now.

The ring's magic connected them. Through it, she sensed the dire threat they faced. A malevolent presence was scrying for them. She could see it in her mind, like an evil, disembodied eye, sweeping back and forth across the southern part of the Upper City.

She felt her grandfather's cloaking spell. She could almost see it, like a grey mist shimmering in the air around them. And she knew it would not be strong enough to hide them. The immense power of the eye would cut it to shreds if its gaze fell upon the spot where they now stood — and it was only seconds from doing so. They would be caught, unless …

Her heart leapt as the song trumpeted in her mind. It rang with the sound of a hundred horns, announcing the start of a new theme — one that swept away the defeat and despair she had struggled with only moments before.

Lenard held up his hand, eyes closed in concentration. She felt his magic surge through the ring to reinforce the spell …

The eye fell on them. Randia held her breath as she felt its stare. She sensed its strength pressing against the cloak, trying to pierce it. She was naked to its gaze, her soul exposed to its malice, without hope of escape …

Again the horns sounded their heroic note, and her fear vanished. The eye moved on, sliding over the rail and down toward the terrace below them.

Randia climbed slowly to her feet. She came to stand by her grandfather's side and laid a gentle hand on his arm. She wanted desperately to embrace him, but something told her that now was not the time.

The old wizard took a long, deep breath, and then slowly let it out. He was shaking.

"I hope the world never knows how close it came to its end in that moment," he said finally.

"Are we safe for now?" she asked.

He shook his head. He walked to where Flamebane had fallen to the tiled walkway and picked it up. He extended the blade to her, hilt-first, and she took it.

"No," he said. "The demons are moving to search this part of the city. We need to get away at once. Can you walk?"

She nodded, sliding the weapon back into its scabbard. "Where to?"

"I'll lead the way. Stay close so I can keep the cloak tight around us."

Randia slipped her arm into his. Without another word, they turned and strode from the edge of the terrace.

Silent tears ran down her cheeks as they walked back toward the cliff spur that rose above them to the Upper City South. There was hope yet. At least one person she loved had *not* been taken from her this day.

The Sanctum

Randia looked up along the sheer face of the cliff. She could see the channel of the aqueduct she had ridden high above her. Its runners were carved into the stone of the bluff itself.

"Which way now?" she asked. It was the first time she had spoken since they had started their walk.

Lenard looked down at her and smiled. "Up, of course," he said.

He slid an arm around her waist, and she did the same. Air rushed suddenly past them as they flew up along the rocky surface.

They had set out none too soon. She could see the enemy's forces moving to cut off the surrounding area, trying to prevent any escape. A cloud of monsters was circling the gardens on the highest level of the terraces above them.

She closed her eyes, trying to shut the pain out of her heart. They had found the carnage of their earlier battle. The demons. The guards of Company Twenty-Three. Her brother's body — and Stefan's.

"Is that where Gerard died?" Lenard asked quietly.

She looked at him in surprise. Her blue eyes met his steel grey ones.

"How did you know?"

Lenard sighed. "It's true, then. I feared as much when I felt you use the ring after him."

"You felt the ring's magic? When Gerard fought the demons to save me?"

"Ah. So that's what happened. Yes, I knew it had to be him. The power I sensed was unmistakable. He was the only other Killraven who could wield it with such skill."

She rested her head on his shoulder, suddenly understanding.

"But you couldn't find us," she said softly. "Because of his cloaking spell."

Lenard nodded. She could see tears running suddenly down his cheeks.

"I tried, Randia. I scried for him, with all the strength I *dared* bring to bear. I knew that you needed me, and that you were with him. I felt your imprint on the ring too, like a heroic song accompanying his battle. But I couldn't come to you."

"You can hear the song?" she asked, astonished.

"Of course. When *you* began to wield its power, uncloaked, it was like a beacon to anyone with our family's blood. It's what finally drew me to you at the end — just in time."

He shook his head, struggling to hold back his tears.

"But I couldn't save Gerard. I nearly exposed myself to the demon lord trying, but it was no use. Not with my grandson's strength and skill, and with the ring's power behind it."

Randia was silent for a time. Her grandfather was the Archmage. To everyone — and perhaps especially, to her — he had always been a paragon of confident knowledge and power. She had never seen him look as he did now: like a vulnerable old man, helpless to stop the deaths of almost everyone he loved.

She was surprised to find that it didn't unnerve or frighten her. An intense empathy for him welled inside her, and she tightened her grip around him. She knew how he felt.

"He was magnificent," she said finally. "He held that cloak, levitating all the way across the city from the palace. And over an entire company of demons as he defeated them." Her face clouded as she remembered Ashrach, and the spear. "Almost all of them."

She'd lost track of their movements as they talked. When she looked around now, she saw that they had risen high along the cliff wall. They slipped into a slim crevice in its face and her feet touched the floor of a narrow cave.

"Where are we?" she asked.

"An antechamber of sorts."

"To what?"

He smiled. "Come on. I'll show you."

He stepped into the narrow opening. It was barely wide enough for one of them to pass; she had to step behind him to follow. She rested her hand on his back, unwilling to let him out of her reach.

The crevice met up with a series of cracks just like it, all leading in different directions. Lenard's staff shone with a soft light as he confidently picked a twisting path through them. He led them deep into the stone of the cliff. It took only a minute for her to become completely lost, but she followed him without hesitation. He was her grandfather, and she trusted him completely.

After a few minutes, he came to an abrupt halt. The place where he stopped seemed unremarkable, just another spot partway down the length of one crack that laced the interior of the cliff. He turned to face the wall on his right and tapped it with the tip of his staff. The crystal head rested against it for just a moment. Then it slid into the stone, disappearing into the rock as though it weren't there.

Randia's eyes arched. "An ethereal lock," she said in wonder. "I've heard of them, but I've never actually seen one."

"I have something of a fondness for them," he said. "They can be quite useful. Quickly now. Right behind me, and don't stop until you reach the other side."

He stepped into the wall and vanished.

She cautiously placed her hand against the stone, and it, too, disappeared into the wall. The sensation was odd, as though she could feel the rock inside her body, in her very bone and muscle, as she passed through it. Unnerved but determined, she took a deep breath and pushed herself forward.

She was dismayed to discover that the best speed she could manage was relatively slow. It was like trying to walk through water, only thicker and more viscous. She slogged on, holding her breath.

She stumbled when she finally emerged. After she'd caught her feet, she looked around — and gasped.

She was at one end of an enormous hexagonal room. Enchanted apparatus were everywhere: mounted to the walls and ceilings, and scattered around the floor in a haphazard arrangement. Magic played around them, snapping and buzzing with immense power. Along one side of the hexagon, she saw an active scrying panel showing a view of the city from above. On the opposite wall gleamed a dark black surface, shimmers of silver and gold playing around its edges and along its face. The wall opposite her had a door in the center that opened into a long corridor, leading into darkness.

In the center of the room stood a large, circular table. Metal plates inscribed with runes were set into it in rows around its circumference. Many of them glowed or flashed with multicolored magic. Lenard stood next to it, turned partly away from her, facing the scrying panel. His hands danced over the plates, touching them in a rapid and bewilderingly complex sequence.

Randia stared at the chamber with wide eyes. It was every magician's wildest fantasy of what a wizard's laboratory could look like. It made the one at the summit of the palace tower look like a child's playroom. She tried to find her voice and nearly failed.

"What is this place?" she breathed in wonder.

Lenard chuckled, but his eyes didn't waver from what he was doing at the mysterious table.

"Welcome to the Sanctum of the Archmage, my dear," he said simply.

She walked slowly toward him, unable to tear her gaze away from what she was seeing.

"The Sanctum!" she exclaimed. "But that's just a myth! A legend of the Archmage Aldran, first of the Killraven kings of Carlissa." She tore her eyes away from the room to look at him. "Isn't it?"

"Obviously not," he replied drily.

She stood by quietly, unable to find words.

He continued his work with the glowing symbols. There seemed to be a pattern to his movements, but she couldn't understand it. He was clearly using the rune-plates to prepare some kind of magic — but whatever it was, it was beyond her comprehension.

She saw and heard changes in the magical apparatus around her.

One by one, the devices came to life. Intense magical energy played in and around them, humming with a promise of immense power. Panels of bluesteel runes set into the walls burst into incandescence, flashing in dizzying, incomprehensible sequences.

Minutes passed in silence as the Archmage worked. When at last he seemed to have finished, he turned to face her.

She knew that the moment had come. Whatever urgent magic he felt the need to cast had at last been made ready. Without words, they stepped into each other's arms. They stood holding each other, crying and sharing their grief, for a long time.

City's Fall

Diana woke with a start. The glowing red eyes faded away. She looked around frantically, trying to remember where she was.

Orion left the window to come to her side. She lay on the floor, wrapped in the blankets he'd found earlier. He put a hand on her shoulder to steady her.

"Easy," he said. "It's just a dream. We're safe for now."

She stared at him for a moment, as though she didn't know who he was. Then memory flooded back, and she nodded.

"What time is it?" she asked.

"About half past mountainset. The light will be fading soon."

"And the city?"

He closed his eyes. "It's fallen. The palace, the Cathedral, even the Star. They're all in flames."

She pushed unsteadily to her feet. "I need to see it," she said.

"You should get some more rest. You're exhausted —"

She shook her head. "I need to see it," she repeated.

Her voice was calm but insistent, and he nodded reluctantly. They stepped quietly to the window together. For a time they looked out, saying nothing.

"Look at what they've done to the City of Rainbows," she said finally. Her voice choked, but there was a hard edge of anger in it as well. "The death and destruction they've wreaked, and on the best people I've ever known."

She turned to Orion. "It can't be allowed to stand, can it?" she asked.

He shook his head. "No. And it won't."

She smiled. "You're still waiting for the Archmage?"

He nodded.

"He's not coming, Orion. He's either dead, or he's fled. And I wouldn't blame him for it." She waved a hand at the burning city. "Not in the face of this."

"Perhaps," he said quietly. "But I'm not giving up. Not yet."

Aldran's Legacy

Lenard stepped back. The old man's face was stained with tears, but the vulnerability in it was gone. His expression was determined.

"Everything is ready," he said firmly. "We'll both need to prepare."

Randia nodded. "What will you do? Gerard said you would use the power of the ring to defeat the demons."

Lenard smiled sadly. "Is that what he told you?"

Randia felt a knot of dread take shape in the pit of her stomach. She suddenly understood.

"It's not true, is it?" she asked.

Lenard shook his head. "No," he said quietly.

She let out a long, slow breath. "Why would Gerard lie to me?"

"I wouldn't blame him. It's likely what your parents told him as well, to motivate him on his quest."

She looked at him bitterly. She felt the one hope she'd been holding onto slipping away.

"Then you can do nothing?" she demanded. She immediately regretted her harsh tone, but found that she couldn't stop herself. "All that conjuring you just did — what was it for, if not to strike back at the enemy? If not to —" Her voice choked, but she forced herself to continue with gritted teeth. "To make them *pay* for what they've done?"

Lenard's steel-grey eyes were hard. He looked at her for a long, silent moment.

"I said I couldn't *defeat* the demons. I didn't say I could do *nothing*."

She drew a deep breath to calm herself as he gestured to the scrying panel. It showed a high aerial view of the city, teeming with monsters.

"There are over thirty thousand of those creatures in Lannamon now," he said sternly. "That's nearly a match already for the combined armies of the Eastern Continent. More of them come through that gate every minute. And the leader of this horde — a demon lord named Borr — is powerful, and has powerful servants. I'm extremely flattered at your confidence, but the notion that even *I* could defeat such a force is —"

He broke off, and she could see him biting back his words. "I'm sorry," he said, after a long pause.

She shook her head.

"I'm the one who should apologize, Grandfather. The girl who wanted to sing and dance, instead of learning magic and combat. To help prepare for a day like this. I have no right to ask so much of you."

She took his hand and held it.

"But then, what *can* we do? Stefan and I were headed for the Star because we thought you might have a way to escape."

Lenard looked at her, suddenly grave. "He was with you, then? Is he ..."

"Dead," she said. The word was like tearing off a bandage, but it ended the pain quickly. "Buying me time to reach you."

He lowered his head. "I'm sorry, Randia."

"Is that what this was always about, then?" she asked. Her voice was thick with bitterness. "This quest with the ring? Gerard finding me, and the three of us using its power to flee the city?"

He nodded.

"I suspect that was your parents' true goal when they sent Gerard on his quest in the first place. And we will do that, once the plan I've prepared here is set in motion. But flight would only delay our deaths. That horde will conquer the world if it is not stopped. It *has* to be stopped."

Randia walked to the scrying panel and looked at it. Her eyes were drawn to the image of the dome of purple magic that shimmered in the fading light. She touched it with a slender hand.

"That's what you mean to do," she said finally, turning to him.

"To destroy the hellgate."

He nodded again.

"I honestly don't know if I have the power," he said candidly. "World gates leading to the demon realms are outside even my experience. But I have to try. If I don't — or if I fail — then all of Kalara will be lost."

He gestured at the room around them.

"Aldran did not share all of the secrets he found in the ruins of Janthala. This 'Sanctum of the Archmage' is filled with artifacts that he thought too powerful — and too dangerous — to fall into anyone else's hands. It has been the charge of our line, handed down for the last two centuries, to guard this legacy."

"You mean to use their power to destroy the gate," she said.

"Yes. I began the preparations as soon as I realized what was happening. The castings required to channel their magic were complex to say the least, and they took a great deal of time. Even with the sanctum's cloaking ward it had to be done with great care, to avoid drawing the demon lord's attention."

"Is it that powerful?"

"It is formidable, and it has artifacts of its own at its command. I've been playing a game of magical cat and mouse with it all day — one that I almost lost several times."

"As I saw. What would have happened if it had found you?"

"If it had fixed its sight on me?" he asked. "It would have been over. Cloaking spells have their limits, even in my hands. Once it had pierced mine, it would have known where I was, and sent its full power — and its strongest minions — against me."

He walked to where the Silver Star Adventurer's Academy showed on the scrying panel. The tower was a still burning column of flame.

"It brought one creature in particular — a fire demon assassin of immense strength — that is almost a match for me by itself. That 'Crimson Slayer' is what finally breached the defenses at the Star."

A note of intense pride crept into his voice.

"The adventurers who stayed put up an incredible fight," he continued. "They cast the dragon ward, as your mother did at the palace, and forced the battle demons to storm the grounds. They slaughtered hundreds before they were finally overwhelmed. They kept the enemy's focus on them, helping to distract it from searching for me."

He smiled. "And for you, and for your brother. Your parents' charge, and their last stand at the palace, did much the same. We would never have made it this far without their sacrifices. They gave us the one slim chance we have to stem the tide of the dark."

"Then we still have one?" she asked hopefully.

"A chance? Yes. But we have to face the terrible truth about what that chance really is. It is not a chance to save the city. It is already lost. It is not a chance to save Carlissa. The demons will sweep across our land and conquer it. Nothing can stop that now."

Randia closed her eyes. Her heart sank as she thought of her people at the mercy of the demon horde.

"It may not even be a chance to save the world," he continued. "Even if we fix their numbers by destroying the gate, even if we kill many of them in a last, desperate stand, they still may be strong enough to take Kalara. But we have to try."

He held up the hand on which he now wore the ring. It was shining with white magic.

"And this was the key," he said. "I had to labor in desperate hope that your parents would find a way to send it to me. I could not complete the spells I needed without it. Thanks to you and your brother, they are now ready."

"Just tell me what to do," she said firmly. "I'll do anything I can to help."

He walked to her and put his hands on her shoulders.

"We have to be ruthlessly honest about what stands before us, Randia. The best-case scenario — the *best* case — is that we will succeed in destroying the gate, flee Carlissa, and spend the rest of our lives fighting an apocalyptic war to contain the evil that has already entered our world. Are you prepared for that?"

The rage — and the hate — burned brightly in her heart as she answered. "I am."

He kissed her forehead. "Then let us begin."

He turned and gestured to the darkened doorway. "It's time for you to come forth," he said.

A figure stepped through the opening, and Randia gasped. It was her grandfather.

The new archmage smiled at her. "Don't be alarmed," he said. "I'm here to help."

Another person stepped through the opening. She stopped beside him and took his arm.

"As am I," she said.

Randia stared at the second figure, mouth hanging open. It was *her*.

"Simulacra," Lenard said. "Their creation is an incredibly arcane process, and one that I've mastered through ... recent study. With their help, we will not have to give our own lives here today."

Randia's simulacrum stepped forward and took her hand. "We will do that for you. So that *you* can live on, and carry on the fight."

Randia frowned, confused. "But *why*?"

"So that Zomoran and his demon lord will think you both perished in the stand we're preparing to take," Lenard's simulacrum explained.

"And that the royal family is destroyed," her twin added. "If they are not convinced of that, they will hunt you without relent."

The Archmage smiled. "And I *do* plan to convince them of that," he said.

Randia nodded in understanding.

"You mean for us to fight on in secret, then. In disguise. Behind the scenes, and in the shadows."

"Yes. A few will have to know the truth, of course. Your grandparents, and your uncle Nimrod. Augustus Darren, who on your father's orders has initiated the Diaspora. I sent many from the Star to join him. They will be our first allies. We will unite them into a resistance against Zomoran and his demons."

Randia reached up to touch her simulacrum's face. "They seem so real," she said. "Can we ..."

"You needn't grieve for us," her twin said. "We are merely copies, programmed with a simulation of your own thoughts and memories. But that is all. We have no consciousness as you understand it. We're not actually ... real."

Randia turned to look carefully at her grandfather. "And us?"

Lenard gestured to the black panel on the wall behind them. Its surface shimmered and then resolved itself into the image of a small wizard's laboratory. The walls and ceiling were finished in a rich walnut, giving it an incongruously cozy look.

"Blackwing Lodge," Randia said. "In your hidden valley. You brought me there once, years ago."

"Yes. The panel is a portal. One of the sanctum's many artifacts. The 'escape route' you surmised I would have."

She gave him an astonished look. "That valley is in the Nurian Mountains. It's hundreds of miles south of here."

He nodded. "I will need you to watch over me there during what is to come."

She shook her head. "I don't understand."

"I will be taking our last stand personally," he said. He nodded at his doppelgänger. "Through him."

"He will possess me," Lenard's double explained. "His consciousness — and the full power of his magic, including the ring — will be invested in my form. We will destroy the gate, if we can, and kill as many of the enemy as his remaining power allows."

"And I will stand openly at his side," her twin added. "To bring the song against them as well. Channeling your own potential through the ring and adding it to his, if you are willing."

"And when we fall," Lenard's double concluded, "everyone will believe that the last of the Killravens are no more."

Randia's eyes narrowed. She looked at her grandfather suspiciously.

"But won't you die, then, too?" she asked, nodding at his simulacrum. "When he is destroyed?"

Lenard sighed. "I won't lie to you that it's not a risk," he said. "If something goes wrong. If it doesn't, then my consciousness *should* return to my body afterward. That's why I will need you to watch over me, Randia. Until it does, I will be in a coma, and completely vulnerable."

His eyes went wide as she dropped to one knee. Her hand clasped the hilt of her sword as she knelt before him.

"I am yours, Archmage," she said. "Take my power. Take my life if you need it. Make it into a weapon to bloody the monsters that have done this to us — and to our world."

Her twin knelt by her side. Lenard laid a hand on each of their heads. Randia felt the ring's magic once again rushing through her, the song ringing triumphantly in her soul …

Her double started. She turned to Randia, and they shared a long, slow look of understanding.

"For the Princess Bard!" her twin said, grinning.

Lenard released them and turned to his double. "It is time."

Both Randias rose as Lenard lifted his staff. His simulacrum stepped forward and grasped the shaft. The crystal blazed with sudden fire, and then subsided.

Lenard's eyes rolled up in his head, and he sank toward the floor. Randia caught him and lifted him into her arms.

The Archmage's double stepped next to her. Gently, he removed the ring from Lenard's hand and put it on his own. Then he looked at her.

"I am here, now," he said. "Take my body and go through the portal. I will destroy it behind you."

Randia nodded. "Good luck, Grandfather," she said. "To you — and to all of us."

She walked to the opening. Then she paused on the threshold and looked back at the image of the burning city. When she spoke, her voice was cold and hard.

"This is not done between us, Emil Zomoran. I vow by all that is holy that I will not rest until you have met vengeance for this unspeakable evil. By my soul, I swear it. I will hunt you, and fight you, without respite, for the rest of my life. Until the day when I see my blade in your heart, and the light fading from your eyes at my hand."

Then she turned and stepped through the portal. There was a brief shimmering in its surface, and they were on the other side.

Lenard watched his granddaughter go with a troubled expression. Then he waved his staff. There was a flash of white, and the doorway exploded into a thousand fragments.

Chapter 19 - The Last Stand

The Challenge

Lord Rugon knelt before the gates of the royal palace. The survivors of its taking were arrayed around him on the wide plaza above the road to the High City. They, too, were on their knees, heads bowed, hands bound behind them. The rest of the council knelt in a long line to either side of him.

Hellman soldiers had been waiting for them when they were led out of the palace. Now the fire elves marched among the captives, weapons at the ready, watching for any sign of defiance. Their volcanic red skin contrasted starkly with the gleaming black of their armor.

"You have been brought here to bear witness to your defeat," a voice said. It was cold and hard, without a trace of mercy or feeling. Lord Rugon tried to brace himself against his helpless anger. He knew that voice. It was Emil Zomoran, Lord of Westreach.

The magus stood before him. A Hellman officer was at his side. With his head bowed, Lord Rugon could only see the soldier's powerful legs, encased in plated armor of black steel. The thong of a whip dangled from a hand that rested beside them.

"Your capital has fallen," the voice continued. "Look now to see what is left of the once royal family of Carlissa."

He closed his eyes. He knew what he would see if he lifted his head and opened them. The sight would bring an end to his long life of service to king and country.

Wails erupted around him, confirming his fears. Then he heard a whip whistle and crack. He gasped as the lash struck him.

"You were told to look," a second voice said. It was clear and masculine, with a cold, hard timbre. "All of you. If you disobey, you will be flogged."

Slowly, reluctantly, Lord Rugon lifted his head and opened his eyes. A sob escaped his lips at the sight before him.

The demons had raised a long row of pikes before the gate. Atop each was mounted a severed head. His gaze ran numbly across the line, recalling the names he'd known well. In his mind, he said a prayer for each of their souls.

Palanad Lantar. General Banderman. Vala Orleans. Elena Starlight. Aron and Danor Killraven. Go now into the embrace of the Divine, my dear friends.

He saw a winged demon circling the gruesome scene. It landed and handed a round object to one of its fellows. *Another head for the pikes,* he thought. *Soon they will all be here.*

He watched the fading of the light. Mountainset had passed, and the sun was falling below the horizon. *As the sun sets on the world, so does the dark come to claim us all,* he thought suddenly.

Except the light *wasn't* fading. He could see it, now, growing around them. He didn't dare look behind him for fear of the whip, but he was sure that the Blood Moon was rising over the southern ridges of the Upper City. It was another omen.

The new head was quickly staked beside the others. It was Prince Gerard's.

"Where's the princess?" a voice suddenly called out. "And the Archmage?"

The speaker was a woman in the livery of the palace guard. Her cheeks were wet, but her eyes were alive with defiance. The Hellman officer spun on her, his face a mask of outrage.

"You don't have them, do you?" she cried savagely. "They've escaped! You haven't won yet!"

The Hellman stalked toward her. He stood before the woman for a long moment, staring into her tear-stained eyes. Then the whip rose and struck. She screamed and fell to the ground, a red welt blooming across her cheek. Lord Rugon turned away, unable to watch.

The illumination continued to grow around them. It wasn't just the red light of the Blood Moon, he realized suddenly. It wasn't even coming from anywhere in particular. It was ... an ambient glow, emanating from the very air around them.

His head snapped up as he realized that it could not be natural. He saw that some of the others had noticed it, too. Even Zomoran was looking at the sky with an uneasy expression. He slowly raised his staff, as if testing the glowing air with his magic.

The Hellman officer, however, his attention fixed on the young guard — Daria, he thought her name was — still seemed unaware of it. "Their heads will join the others soon enough," he said icily. "And *you* need a lesson in obedience. One that I —"

A deafening peal of horns rang out over the valley. Like the light, it didn't come from any one place. It was just around them — powerful, majestic, and inescapable.

The Hellmen screamed, covering their ears. But the hearts of the Carlissans leaped with renewed hope. They knew the notes for what they were: a cry of challenge, and a call to battle.

Answered Faith

Orion surged to his feet. The horns resounded all around him, setting his heart aflame with a sudden, desperate hope.

He saw Diana standing by the window. She'd been unwilling to tear her eyes away from the sight of the burning city, and he'd known that she needed to be alone with her thoughts. He'd reluctantly left her to keep watch and lain down for a few minutes of fitful rest.

He rushed to her side and put a hand on her shoulder. She was trembling.

"What is it?" he asked.

She turned to him and shook her head. Her green eyes were wide and gleaming in the growing light. She quickly made room for him to stand next to her.

The horns faded, their last notes echoing along the walls of the valley. In their wake, and to the pair's astonishment, followed the music of an overture. The sound surrounded them, seeming to come from everywhere at once. It was like standing in the center of a symphony orchestra as it began its performance.

The theme was understated, but pregnant with power and promise. It didn't progress in any particular direction. Instead, it began a series of variations. It seemed almost to be exploring and learning about itself, slowly developing the characteristic passages of its movement.

Orion looked out at the city. He had expected to see the glooming grey of dusk descending over Lannamon, punctuated by the flaming red of unquenched fires. To his surprise, he saw the city coming to life with iridescent light. Like the song, it seemed to be everywhere at once, as though the air itself were glowing with magical illumination. Silver, gold, white, and blue hues shone throughout the valley, brightening with each passing moment.

A wash of red shot across the firth as the Blood Moon, now fully risen above the shoulder of the southern cliffs, blazed with crimson radiance. He gasped at the sight. Kalara's moons could shine brightly at times, especially at rise and set, but *this* ...

"What's happening?" Diana whispered. Her voice was uncharacteristically small and awed. "I've never seen the moon like this. Either of them."

It was true. The Blood Moon seemed to be growing rather than shrinking as it rose into the night sky. And like the ambient glow over the city, its light, too, was slowly increasing in intensity.

"I don't know," he said. "But whatever it is, it's not natural. There's powerful magic behind it."

They watched the moonrise and the growing light with bated breath. Enraged demon screams rose throughout the city, accompanied by the relentless progression of the theme in its variations.

"It's the Light!" Orion cried suddenly. His eyes were wide with astonishment.

Diana looked at him. "It's what?"

"The Light. It's a spell, used by the knights of the Order of Light. Usually, it's conjured as a wave or wall of white magic. You saw it earlier when the warrior priests rode out to meet the King. It causes fear and pain in demons, and suppresses their powers."

"Is that why they're screaming, then?" she asked. Her voice had suddenly taken on a note of savage satisfaction. "Because this light is hurting them?"

"I think so. But this isn't just a battle spell, Diana. It's covering the entire city!"

The music began to change. Hints of a new theme emerged in its notes, a theme whose triumphal promise had been present in all that had come before.

"Look!" Diana said suddenly. "Something's happening!"

The moon had grown to dominate the southern sky. Now its disc was beginning to distort and shimmer. A face was taking shape in its scarlet contours. A face with steel-grey eyes, framed by a shock of white hair.

The face was known and beloved throughout the Kingdom of Carlissa. Cheers went up across the city as the people recognized it. Diana threw her arms around Orion with a peal of exultant laughter.

"You were right!" she cried. "Oh, Orion, you were right! He hasn't abandoned us!"

Orion stood by the window as she held him. Tears ran down his face as he listened to the song, building inexorably toward a powerful crescendo.

"Now we'll see," he said softly. "Now you monsters will know justice."

Diana nodded and squeezed him more tightly.

The face, now fully formed, turned its gaze down to the ravaged city. They both grinned when they saw it. It was very, very angry.

"Zomoran of Westreach," a voice boomed over the valley. "You who call yourself 'Warlord' of Carlissa, and have brought the scourge of a demon horde to the lands of Kalara. You have murdered my people and my kin. Now prepare yourself — to face the wrath of Lenard the Archmage!"

Ready to Strike

Liana looked up from the massacre site in the gardens of the Upper City South. She had already sent Gerard's head on to the palace. Now she was searching for a survivor to interrogate about the fate of the princess.

As she stared at the enraged face looming over the city, though, she finally understood what had happened. Randia had escaped and brought the ring to the Archmage. Now they were wielding it together — against the horde.

She stepped away from the body of the flame-haired guard she'd been about to examine. A chill of fear ran through her, and she chided herself. It was ridiculous, of course. It was just a manifestation of this strange spell that had settled over them. Lannamon teemed with over a thousand score of her kind, led by the godlike power of her master, Borr. Artifact or no, they would swat this troublesome mage like a fly.

She turned to Incanus Thad. The giant demon stood nearby, also staring up at the Blood Moon.

"The Archmage has the ring, Incanus," she said. "And the princess."

"It is of no consequence," he replied. He hefted his axe. "We will crush this last stand, and put an end to this battle once and for all."

A shadow passed over them as a flight of dragons arrived. Fire brimmed from their jaws as they roared their defiance at the face of the old wizard.

"We need to find them first," she said. "That image in the moon is just an illusion."

Incanus Thad shrugged his massive shoulders. "Lord Borr will show us where to strike."

The succubus opened her mouth to reply, but never got out the words. The Archmage's voice once again boomed over the city.

"Let the battle begin," it thundered.

The song's movement reached its peak, and its new theme rang out with a sudden, clear call. It spoke of hope, and of redemption — of bitter sadness and soaring triumph, bought at a terrible price ...

Lenard's eyes blazed. Starfire erupted from them, lighting the valley as though twin suns had appeared suddenly in the darkening sky. Hundreds of bolts of the deadly magic sprayed toward the city in a wide arc.

The first salvo struck the dragon wing overhead. Each burst hit its target with uncanny precision, and white fire blossomed as the monsters were consumed. Their bodies turned into clouds of ash that fell on the city like snow, or slammed like bursting sacks of flour into the face of the bluffs.

Another rain of blasts dropped on the demons in the glade.

Several of them exploded in columns of white flame.

Liana looked around as the flash subsided. Incanus Thad still stood at her left, staring past her, his enormous red eyes blinking in shock. The battle demon to her right was gone. All that was left in its place was a smoldering grey pile.

She gasped as she whirled to look out over the city. The blinding storm of magic was falling on it in a rain of ivory fire. She saw individual streaks of the fusillade suddenly burst in mid-air as they struck flying demons or dragons. The sky over Lannamon exploded in a display that lit the night as though it were day.

She turned to Incanus Thad. "We must find that wizard!" she hissed.

"Lord Borr will trace him," he growled.

"We must be ready. You know what to do?"

He nodded. "I will bring the others," he said.

The demon unfurled his great wings and launched himself into the air. Liana watched him go, and then turned to the others.

"Follow me," she ordered. "And be ready when our master gives the sign."

As they left, they failed to hear a groan from the fallen soldiers behind them, or see the movement of a guard with short, flame-red hair.

Wrath of the Archmage

Borr touched the amulet that hung around its long, sinuous neck. Its lips stretched into the serpentine equivalent of a smile.

This Archmage had surprised it with his power and resourcefulness, but he'd finally made a fatal mistake. Even now, the Horde Master's magic was tracing his spells back to their source. The attacks were impressive, but not nearly enough to stop the invasion. And they were no match for the demon lord's own power.

It considered the spells as it probed them. The Light and the song were too diffuse to do the Horde any serious harm. At most, they would boost the morale of the wizard's people, and dampen that of its own forces. And the hail of starfire might kill a small part of its army, which it could easily spare.

All that would accomplish would be to give the Carlissans a few minutes of false hope — a hope that the demon lord would dash in one brutal stroke.

Its sight settled on a ridge of bluffs high in the Upper City South. A battle had taken place there, one that had somehow gone unnoticed until now. Ashrach's entire pack had been slaughtered, along with a company of guards and the wizard prince himself. The work of the Archmage, no doubt, using his clearly formidable cloaking skills to conceal it.

Its lizardlike smile faded. Something was blocking its scrying, something unexpectedly powerful. It could sense it now, like the ward over the palace tower, only much stronger. The trail of spells led to it and vanished, right into the rock of the bluff itself ...

Its smile returned. *I have you now*, it thought.

It raised a reptilian claw. A red spotlight stabbed from the sky and illuminated the face of the cliff. Everyone in the city could see it — and could hear the words that followed.

"I have spotted you, Archmage," its voice boomed. "And your granddaughter. In your hidden sanctum, on the southern cliffs. I, Borr, Master of the Horde, will now strip you of its protection and destroy you. I will put an end to your line, once and for all."

A strongbox bound in black metal rested behind the demon lord. Its snakelike prehensile tail slithered out and flipped it open. It withdrew a wand that glowed with a blinding yellow light and deposited it into the creature's hands.

Harsh roars and whoops rose through the city as the demons, emboldened by their master's words, took up a chant. It quickly drowned out the cheers of the Carlissans at the sight of the Archmage's face.

"Borr! Borr! Borr!" they chanted.

The demon lord held the incandescent wand above its snakelike head and began an incantation. It was in a forgotten tongue, ancient beyond the knowledge of even its most powerful servants. No one but demigods and the lords of the demon realms still understood the kind of power it could command.

It felt its own immense magic flowing into the wand, unlocking and augmenting its destructive energies. When the spell was ready, it pointed the rod toward the cliff, and at the sanctum buried within it.

It will all be over in moments, it thought with satisfaction. *This Archmage will be obliterated by forces he cannot begin to comprehend.*

"**Karach!**" it cried.

A beam of yellow fire shot from the artifact. It struck the bluff with a blinding flash, and an immense explosion lit the sky. The shock wave traveled across the city in moments, shaking the very bones of the valley. Men and demons alike rocked as the ground lurched beneath their feet. For a few brief seconds, wails of shock and despair from the horrified Carlissans mixed with jeers of triumph from the demons. Then both were gone, overwhelmed by a deafening concussion that drowned out every other sound in the city.

Thousands of tons of rubble flew into the air above the cliffs, and then crashed back down to earth. The upper terraces were pummeled mercilessly by the falling rock. Streets, homes, people, and demons disappeared beneath the sudden avalanche.

A long minute passed. A column of fire and smoke rose over the blast in a mushroom shaped cloud that loomed ominously over the city.

When the air finally cleared, the Carlissans saw in horror that the entire cliff-face below the cloud was gone. It had been sheared off as though from the blow of a titanic pick-axe.

Borr's gaze swept the site with satisfaction. The show of power had sorely taxed its reserves, but it had been worth it. It would utterly break the spirit of the people of Lannamon, and finally rid it of the vexing royal house of Carlissa ...

Its first hint that something had gone wrong was the song. The theme had been lost in the deafening concussion that had rolled over the city. It *should* have faded away afterward, with the princess' death.

It hadn't.

It was back, now, building again toward a new climax. And the strange light had not faded, either. It still shone in the air over the city, a relentless touch of pain and fear that weakened the horde and sapped its will.

When Borr finally saw the reason, its great eye widened in disbelief. And for one of the few times in its ancient life, it knew fear.

Amid the rubble of the cliffs stood the Archmage and his granddaughter. They were surrounded by a ring of blazing artifacts — and a shield of white magic.

The old wizard's face shone in the circle of the Blood Moon. He opened his mouth and laughed as the song once again reached its heroic crescendo. The sounds echoed across the valley, striking terror into the demon horde.

Lenard raised his staff. The sanctum around him was gone, obliterated by Borr's strike. But his desperate gamble had paid off. He'd feigned just enough vulnerability to goad the Horde Master into underestimating him.

He looked around and breathed a sigh of relief. Several of the artifacts had been burned out or destroyed, but the rest still blazed with power, ready at his command. His counter-spell, hastily cast and framed in the same ancient language used by his enemy, had protected them from the blast.

Parry and riposte. As he had hoped, the demon lord had overextended itself with its show of force. He had to strike now, before it could recover its strength, or bring more of its arsenal of servants or artifacts to bear.

The moment of truth was at hand. If he'd miscalculated the nature of the gate, or the distinctive resonances of its magic, then the world was lost. But if the spell he had prepared were true ...

"A fine display of fireworks, Lord Borr," the Archmage's voice boomed. "One that has, indeed, opened the door to my home. Now it is my turn — to close the door to yours!"

The ring blazed as he drew upon it with all of the strength and skill developed from a lifetime of magical study. Then he focused them, and the full power of the Sanctum of the Archmage, into a single, terrible attack.

"He's alive!" Diana sobbed. "And he's attacking the gate!"

She watched with Orion as a beam of coruscating prismatic energy stabbed down from the ruined cliff. It hummed with a deafening sound, like the ring of a gigantic tuning fork. The very air shook around it as it lanced through the sky over the broken city — and slammed into the shimmering dome of the hellgate from above.

The impact hit the valley like a hammer blow. The ground rocked as though from an earthquake. The beam held to its target and did not relent.

Borr stared in disbelief. It knew in bitter rage that it had been tricked.

But it was impossible. Only the most elite of the elder lords — gods and demons alike — understood the jealously guarded secrets of the ancient magic. This wizard, this human conjurer from a backwater world, could not possibly have the knowledge to counter a sunflare rod, much less destabilize a worldgate ...

And yet, clearly, he did.

A cold chill ran down the Horde Master's reptilian spine. It had seen the artifacts surrounding the Archmage. It could sense the potency of their magic. And it understood what its enemy was trying to do to the hellgate.

It quickly began a counterspell, but the attack had been too well prepared. It's response would take too long, especially after it had depleted its strength with the rod. By the time it was ready, it could be too late ...

Lenard strained against the magic of the hellgate. He could sense the complex pattern of its energies, the resonances of its enchantment. He tuned his beam to match them, to drive them past their limits. To tear the gate apart with its own immense power.

It fought back. Active dampeners had been designed into its dweomer to prevent the kind of runaway surge he was trying to create. He drove at it relentlessly with ringing pulses of magic. He wove complex harmonics to destabilize the gateway's enchantment and to counter its defenses.

For a long minute, those defenses held firm.

Then, slowly, the surface of the dome began to change. A spray of colors — red, yellow, green, and white — spread in a sudden webwork of luminous cracks from the beam's point of impact. Lenard's heart leapt as he pressed on, trying to widen them ...

Borr knew that it had only seconds to act. Its counterspell would not be ready in time. If it hesitated — and the gate fractured — then it would lose its only chance to return to its homeworld, and the seat of its own power. If that happened, its realm would fall to a usurper long before it could find another way back to reclaim it.

That was a risk it dared not take. Its voice thundered above the city, sounding a last, desperate call to arms.

"Demons!" it cried. "Dragons! Servants of the Dark! Slay the Archmage! At all costs!"

And then, Borr the Magnificent, Demon Lord of the Horde, turned — and ran.

It had never strayed far from the gate during the course of the invasion. At full sprint, its speed was astonishing. In seconds, it had fled through the shimmering dome and was gone from the world of Kalara.

Lenard watched the demon lord's flight with grim satisfaction. He redoubled his assault on the gate. He almost had it …

An explosion of magical fire detonated over his head. His shield absorbed the attack, but the shock nearly made him lose control of the beam. The cracks stopped growing, and it took all of his concentration to keep them from shrinking and healing instead.

The enemy was closing in. His shield was holding, but with nearly all his strength directed at the gate, he knew it wouldn't last long. He was running out of time.

Diana wept, resting her head against Orion's shoulder. She could see the demons swarming the Archmage's position. Thousands of them descended from the air or climbed like ants across the broken face of the cliffs. A flight of dragons was approaching from the east and would be on him in moments.

"I think I understand what he's trying to do to the gate," Orion whispered. "It's brilliant, but I don't think he's going to make it. He needs more time!"

Lenard screamed. He had drawn again on the ring's magic, straining his psyche, and his simulacrum's body, to the very edge of breaking.

One of the artifacts exploded in a storm of emerald lightning. He knew the others wouldn't be far behind. The power he channeled against the gate — power that would long since have burned any other wizard to ashes — was tearing them apart.

But he was not any other wizard. He was the Archmage. The

weight of the world lay on his shoulders, and he would not — could not — relent.

The shield around him was almost gone, but he dared not spare the strength to reinforce it. He had to focus on prying open the cracks he'd made in the hellgate. He just needed a little more time ...

He felt the fingers of Randia's double entwine with his. They touched the ring.

"The song is not enough," she said quietly. "You must use *all* of my power. You will need it to destroy the gate."

Lenard shook his head. "It's too dangerous. It could kill you!"

"The world hangs in the balance. And you heard my words before. I offered my life willingly."

"I can't!" he cried. His voice cracked in desperate denial. "I cannot lose *you*, too!"

He looked down to meet her eyes, to plead with her to understand. He saw her smile at him.

"You knew what I would say, Grandfather. That you must find the courage to let me die for you."

Finally, reluctantly, he nodded. Tears flowed down his cheeks as he gripped her hand. Then, through the simulacrum's bond, he drew deeply upon his granddaughter's magic. It was raw, unfocused, untrained, but it could be enough to tip the scales ...

The theme had progressed into a movement of pure tension. It had become difficult to hear over the whine of the beam, but it was still there. It spoke of equal forces, opposing each other, balanced, each waiting for the other to break ...

The Blood Moon shimmered. The face of the Archmage shifted, and another appeared at its side. They hung there, suspended like an enormous locket in the violently lit sky.

"It's the princess!" Diana cried. "She's fighting with him!"

Lenard's eyes widened. His granddaughter was almost completely untrained, but her potential ... it surpassed anything he had ever sensed before. *Even his own.*

His magic surged. His shields firmed, holding the demon attacks at bay. The prismatic beam pulsed with renewed energy. The dome of the hellgate fractured, blinding white cracks spreading across its surface ...

The explosion tore through the center of the city. The amphitheater and everything around it vanished in a suddenly expanding storm of white fire.

And then — just as suddenly — the firestorm *imploded*. The shattering surface of the hellgate shrank, drawing the bloom of devastation with it. Within seconds it had been reduced to a pinpoint of impossibly bright light — and was gone.

Everything around the dome went with it. In the blink of an eye, nothing remained except a crater a quarter of a mile across.

A deafening boom echoed through the valley. Air rushed to fill the sudden void where the imploding fireball had been. Gales and whirlwinds blew toward it, uprooting trees and smashing buildings. The waters at the tip of the firth, just within the radius of destruction, began to rush in like a waterfall to fill the newly created chasm.

Nearly four thousand battle demons had been stationed around the gate. They died in the space of a heartbeat, vanishing with the headquarters of Borr's invasion force.

"You've done it, Grandfather," Randia's twin said weakly. She sagged into the old Archmage's arms. Her face was pale and her breathing ragged. Her eyes fluttered.

"I must dissolve the link now," he said gently.

She nodded.

"We did it, didn't we?" she said softly. "We saved the world, you and I."

He shook his head. "Not yet. But thanks to you, it has a chance."

She smiled. Then, slowly, her eyes closed. The song faltered as she slipped from his grasp and crumpled to the ground. Her face faded from the circle of the moon, and was gone.

Lenard stared at her body for a long moment. Then a dangerous fire lit in his eyes as he looked up at the approaching demons.

"It is almost done," he said. "Your gate is gone, and your master fled. Now it's just you — and me."

Liana glided over the shattered ridge. Borr's attack had cut a deep crevasse into it, leading down to where Lenard stood over his granddaughter's body.

She saw the enormous form of Incanus Thad swooping in her direction. Beside him, a pair of man-sized figures rode the air in a chariot of fire. She turned and flew to meet them.

"The Archmage stands in the cleft below," she called. "We must combine our strength to destroy him!"

Warlord Zomoran, the Black Magus, gripped the reins of the flaming chariot. When he spoke, his voice was a stream of acid fury.

"Destroying the gate took nearly all his power. We have to strike now, while he is vulnerable — and without mercy!"

The Crimson Slayer made a slashing gesture with his flame hand.

"This Archmage is too full of surprises," he said. "We must be certain he is helpless before we move to finish him."

Liana smiled as she gestured toward the dragons and demons that swarmed around and below them.

"We have plenty of fodder for that," she said coldly.

The enchanted light had begun to fade, but the bursts of magic around the embattled wizard bathed the southern bluffs with a ceaseless illumination. Battle demons dropped on him from the ridge above, or climbed up from below. Winged demons and dragons strafed the open wound in the cliff where he stood, conjuring or vomiting jets of fire and lightning. The Black Magus and his escort called down bolts of arcane power — from a safe distance.

The Blood Moon, however, remained bright. And in the images on its face, the survivors of Lannamon witnessed the last stand of Lenard the Archmage. They saw the old wizard as he stood over the fallen body of his granddaughter, staff in one hand, ring blazing on the other, surrounded by the now-dead artifacts of an ancient ruin. They saw him battle defiantly, blasting monsters from the rocks or out of the sky, as they swarmed in to overwhelm him. They saw the endless sea of enemies that broke on the cliffs like waves, again and again, closing slowly and inexorably, amid the fading of his spells and the dimming of his shield.

They watched, waiting for the end they knew would come —

some in tears, others stoic and stony-faced, and still others raging with helpless anger. And when it finally came, they saw the bright flash of the detonation that gouged yet another hole in the southern cliffs of the City of Rainbows. They saw it vaporize all that remained of the Sanctum of the Archmage — and of Lenard and Randia Killraven.

Chapter 20 - The New Order

The Oath

Orion turned away from the window. The lights from the battle had faded and the Blood Moon had returned to its normal size. It rose into the night sky as darkness settled over the valley, punctuated by the red glow of the scattered fires that burned throughout the city.

"It's finally over," he said softly.

His legs folded beneath him, and he sat on their pile of blankets. Diana fell on her knees to face him. Her cheeks were streaked with dried tears, and she no longer seemed able to cry.

"What happens now?" she asked.

"The demons will take the city," he said. "They won't be getting reinforcements without the gate, but they're still a vast horde. Tens of thousands, I think."

"Enough to conquer Carlissa?"

He nodded.

"By tomorrow, Zomoran will send strike forces to seize control of the lands around the firth. He'll use the element of surprise while he has it, before the country can mobilize against him."

She took a long, slow breath. "That's how it usually begins," she agreed.

He looked at her curiously.

"I'm the daughter of the Dorian ambassador," she explained. "And my father made sure I was well educated in our history. My country was the last to be freed by the Taming, you know. We've had border skirmishes over the centuries with the enemy's few remaining strongholds. There are lands that have gone back and forth between their rule and ours, especially on the western shores of the Galerian Sea. My people know something of what it is like to live under the Dark."

He nodded. "Of course. I'd forgotten. So what will they do?"

Her face hardened into a controlled, emotionless mask. She was silent for a long time.

"They'll begin with the children," she said finally. "They'll remove them from their parents and take control of their education. They'll raise them to worship the demon lords and reject the Covenant. In a generation, the Carlissan people won't know their own progeny."

He sat for a long time, staring at the floor. She watched him, anxiously searching his face.

"Are you all right?" she asked at last. "That must have been hard for you to watch. I know how much you respected him."

He lifted and shook his head. He smiled.

"It was the greatest thing I've ever seen," he said. "And the most profound inspiration. It showed me something very important. Something that I think will keep me going, and give me the strength to do what must be done."

Her eyes opened wide in a question. She didn't have to ask it.

"It showed me how knowledge, valor, and wisdom can stand against evil," he said. "No matter how ruthless and powerful it may be. We may not have the strength to defeat it outright, but we can win battles against it. One at a time, through relentless and uncompromising opposition. Until one day, when we win enough of them to turn the tide."

She looked at him, face eager. "Yes. But how?"

"I don't know. But he bought us time to find a way. And he showed us the path to finding it. Search for their weaknesses, and learn how to exploit them. And never, ever give up fighting, no matter how hopeless things look or become."

Diana nodded. Her eyes were sparkling once again.

She still had her knife from their battle with Nalef. She picked it up and held it between them. Then she raised her other hand and turned it to face him.

"Diana, what —"

She pricked the skin of her palm with its point, and a bead of blood welled from it. It glinted a deep red in the crimson moonlight. She extended the blade to him as she held out her bleeding hand.

"Swear it with me, Orion," she breathed.

He looked at her, eyes wide. "A blood oath?"

She nodded.

"That we will dedicate our lives to avenging this day," she said solemnly. "That we will not rest until Zomoran is dead, and his demons are defeated and banished from this world. And that we will forever be allies in that battle, against all that is to come."

Slowly, resolutely, he took the knife from her. He looked directly into her eyes as he pricked his palm and placed it against hers. Their fingers intertwined as their blood mingled, running down their hands to their wrists.

"I swear it," he said. "Mind and heart."

"Heart and mind," she agreed. "I swear it with you."

They held hands silently for a long time, as the Blood Moon rose high into the night sky over the broken City of Rainbows.

The Warlord of Carlissa

Emil Zomoran stood before the gates of the royal palace. A few of his captives had managed to escape in the confusion surrounding the Archmage's attack, but none of the High Council were among them. Lord Rugon and the others now knelt again before him.

At the magus' side stood the succubus, Liana Desire. She had discarded her wings and the face of the servant girl from the palace and adopted the form of a Hellwoman soldier in tight-fitting black leather. At his other side stood the Hellman Colonel Y'Thra, whip dangling idly in his hand.

Zomoran walked along the line of prisoners, examining them one at a time. Finally, he spoke.

"Now it is truly over," he said stonily. "No resistance remains in the city. The Archmage has fallen, and with him passes the last of the Killravens. I, Warlord Zomoran, the Black Magus, now rule in Carlissa."

He paused as the bound men and women looked around uneasily. A thin, cold smile emerged on his lips.

"No doubt some of you are thinking, 'How is that possible? You have only taken Lannamon, Emil, and the rest of the kingdom will stand against you.' That is where your calculation goes wrong, my friends. For you are my friends, with whom I have worked for many long years. I would like to offer you the chance to do so once again."

Zomoran gestured with his staff. A scrying disk formed in the air before him, showing an image of the valley from high above. The Blue Moon had crested the line of the southern cliffs, and it was rising swiftly behind the Blood Moon into the night sky. In their shared light, they saw what had happened to the city.

Lannamon was devastated. At its heart was an enormous crater where the crossroads, the amphitheater, the marketplace, and the western end of the docks had once been. They saw the cascade of water from the firth as it rushed in to fill it, and heard its roar in the distance. Fires blazed, everywhere, many of them out of control.

Through it all crawled an endless sea of demons. Lines of them marched like long columns of ants along both shores of the firth. Dragons and winged demons soared over the southern bluffs, winging their way toward the river plains that lay at the western end of the kingdom.

"The horde that has come to Kalara is vast beyond count," the Black Magus intoned solemnly. "And its speed and power cannot be matched. It will sweep across Carlissa and conquer it. Your kingdom will fall within weeks."

He resumed walking as the councilors stared in horror at the scene before them.

"You now have a choice," he said. "To stand with me, and serve as my lieutenants — and to help restore order to the City of Rainbows. No one knows it, and its people, as you do. The old order is gone, but you can become part of the new order in Carlissa."

"What must we do?" a voice asked. Lord Rugon forced himself to choke off a snort of contempt as he heard Baronet Kuhl's voice.

Zomoran gestured to Liana with one hand, and she stepped forward. She placed the thong of her whip under the councilor's chin and looked into his eyes.

"Here are the words you will say, supplicant," she ordered. "'I,

Baronet Aloister Kuhl, do swear my oath of eternal fealty to the Dark, and as vassal to Warlord Zomoran, ruler of Carlissa.' Say it three times, slowly and clearly, with your head bowed."

Kuhl did as he was told, making no attempt to hide his eagerness. When he was done, Zomoran gestured for him to rise and clasped his hand.

"Welcome, Aloister," he said. The other councilors started. For the first time that day, they had heard a note of warmth in the magus' voice.

"Now the rest," Liana suggested. "Volunteers first. They will get extra points."

Lord Rugon closed his eyes tightly as others took the oath. *This can't be happening*, he thought numbly. *My liege and all his house dead, and now to swear loyalty to the Dark ...*

He remembered the King's words to him. *You must be strong, Cyrus, and prepared to do what must be done. To serve even the demons, so that you can protect our people. If you do not, then baser men than you will be chosen for the task — men who will not have their best interests at heart.*

"I will not take your oath, traitor," a voice said proudly beside him. Lord Rugon recognized it as Earl Jace of Carrolon. "The people of Carlissa will resist you with every drop of their blood, and all Kalara will rise up to defeat you. You —"

He did not finish. At a nod from Zomoran, Colonel Y'Thra drew his sword and struck. The body of the Earl of Carrolon fell dead on the tiles of the plaza.

"Take his head," the magus ordered coldly. "And stake it before the gate with the others."

I can't do it, Lord Rugon thought desperately, as a second councilor declared his defiance and was beheaded. *I cannot take that oath — not when others have had the courage to die with their honor unstained. Please, My King, do not make me do this ...*

The minutes stretched on interminably. He finally felt the touch of leather under his chin.

"You are the last, Lord Rugon," Liana said to him softly. "It is time to choose."

He braced himself for the words he would have to say. For the end.

No, he found himself thinking suddenly. *I must find a way to make accommodation with the new rulers of Carlissa. To bring the people together under their rule, for the good of all. It is the only way I have left to show loyalty to my King.*

Slowly, reluctantly, his heart sick with self-contempt, he spoke the words of fealty to the Dark.

The Truce

Let it be known that Warlord Zomoran, Black Magus and ruler of Carlissa, does now declare an end to the battle of Lannamon. In his grace and beneficence, he extends his mercy to you, the people of this city. But to enjoy that mercy, you must come out of hiding and give your oath of loyalty to the new order. Come forth, submit to his wise and just rule, and pledge your aid in the reconstruction of this war-torn nation.

All who do this will receive the Warlord's personal guarantee of protection as subjects of the Dark. Those who refuse will be hunted down, and a public example shall be made of them.

You have until sundown to comply, and to receive your mark of registration. Clerks will be stationed throughout the city to facilitate the process. They may be recognized by a standard bearing crossed golden feathers on a red background ...

Orion stepped away from the window. The morning sun shone through it onto his shoulders, framing his dark brown hair in its light. He usually kept it neatly combed, but now it was a disheveled mess.

Diana looked up at him from her makeshift cot. They'd tried at first to set and keep watches, but had finally succumbed to exhaustion. They'd slept until the criers had woken them with the rising of the sun.

"That's the third one," she said. Her long chestnut hair was even more disheveled than his, but she seemed not to notice it. "What do you think? Is it a trap? Or do they mean it?"

He sat on one of the boxes and looked at her. There was a thoughtful expression on his face.

"I saw one of their 'registrars' down the hill," he said at last. "A few people came out and approached him. They looked really scared. But they weren't killed, and they weren't taken."

"What happened to them?"

"The registrar wrote some information in a ledger. Then he gave them some kind of yellow pin to wear and sent them on their way."

"Then you think the truce is sincere?"

"I do. Or as sincere as bureaucrats of the Dark can be expected to be, at any rate."

He paused to look thoughtfully out the window again.

"And it makes sense," he went on. "Thanks to the Archmage, they need us now. If for nothing else, to replace the demons that would have come through the gate."

She nodded. "Conscripts for the army. Slaves to re-build the city, and to do its work."

"Yes. They can't afford to kill us any longer, but they will try to turn us. To intimidate or seduce us into accepting evil and making it a part of our lives."

Diana got to her feet. She looked at the stairs that led out of their hiding place.

"We need to decide what to do," she said.

"We can't stay here. They're sure to search this house when they start their hunt. They'll find us."

"We could hide in the city," she offered. "Move from place to place to avoid being caught, and make our way east. Then north into Elde, to seek the Elf-Queen's protection."

He shook his head.

"We won't be able to go out during the day without being spotted. And if we wait until night, we'll be hunted as we try to escape. Neither of us knows the streets well enough to hide from an army of demons." He sighed. "I'm not sure anyone does."

"Then we'll have to give up," she said. Her voice was resigned and matter-of-fact. "Come out of hiding, put on their registration pin, and lie our way through whatever loyalty oath they ask us to take."

"I don't see an alternative. And then?"

She turned to face him. Green fire blazed in her eyes.

"Then we fight them. In secret, however we can. We work to undermine the warlord's reign from the inside."

"How?"

"My father will help. My people know what it is to oppose the

Dark, and they'll never accept a Carlissa overrun by demons. I'll work with him. We'll start or join a resistance."

Orion sat for a long time, thinking. Finally, he nodded.

"Without reinforcements from the gate, Zomoran will have to think twice about antagonizing his neighbors," he said. "At least, not the ones he isn't prepared to invade and conquer outright. He'll make peace overtures to some, to head off the formation of an alliance. That should protect your father's diplomatic status for now."

He looked levelly into her eyes. "And yours," he added. "As long as you're not caught."

She smiled. "I'll be careful."

He stood up, his expression determined.

"We need to get you back to your family," he said decisively. "They can keep you safe, and they must be sick with worry for you."

She nodded. To his surprise, she reached out and laid a hand on his arm.

"Come with me, Orion," she said. Her voice was earnest. "You'll be safer with us. Father will reward you for protecting me, and for bringing me home to him."

"Protecting you?" he said, chuckling. "Half the time it seemed the other way around."

She frowned. "Don't joke. I'm being serious."

He shook his head slowly.

"I'll escort you there," he said. "It's a long walk to the High City, especially now that there's a lake where the crossroads used to be. But I need to head home as well. To see my own family, to make sure they're all right. We may not be close, but I owe them that much."

"Are you sure?"

"I'm sure. They're on the first level of the Upper City South, so bringing you home is almost on the way."

When they climbed the stairs and left the house, they saw activity finally growing again on the streets of Lannamon. More and more people were cautiously coming out, as they saw that others who did so were not harmed. Many of them shook and sobbed with fear — but they *did* come out.

Faces grimly determined, Orion and Diana descended Cherry Hill and set out on the road to the west.

AFTERMATH

Prologue

The Warning

Prince Nimrod raced down the stairs. He struggled to hear over the sounds, and to see despite the images, that flooded his mind.

He stopped when he reached the hallway, and exerted his mental discipline. His eyes slowly focused on his surroundings. An archway led into the great hall before him. The Peregrine King was striding through it, his face a thundercloud of surprise and anger. He didn't speak, but his telepathic voice boomed forcefully across the summit of Mount Cassandra.

Clear the peak! Tarnas ordered. *All except my son, and the Lead Pegasus. No one is to remain there when I ascend the steps. Move! Now!*

Nimrod grinned. The force of his father's personality was known throughout the Eastern Continent. On an ordinary day, or in an ordinary temper, his voice could cow or charm all but the strongest of wills. This wasn't an ordinary day, and the Peregrine King wasn't in an ordinary temper.

Nimrod sensed the chaos of panicked thoughts around them as elves and pegasi raced to carry out the order. He waited until Tarnas had reached him, and then fell in at his side.

"You heard it, too?" he asked.

The King nodded. "With me, my son," he said. "Quickly."

They stepped through the great doors and set out along the wide path that led from the rear of the palace. They crossed quickly through the garden of Mount Cassandra, its flowers blooming in fierce colors in the light of the setting sun. The trees at the garden's periphery towered around them, cutting off their view of all but the deepening sky above — and ahead, the peak of the great mountain that rose before them.

A steady stream of elves raced in their direction. They leaped aside as the pair approached, flowing around them like a river around a rock set firmly in its center. The prince saw that his father paid them no heed. His eyes were fixed firmly on the great stone stairs that rose along the face of the mountain past the garden's exit.

Pegasi and mounted warriors flew past them on either side as they ascended the steps. Nimrod knew that they had leaped from the mountain's peak, plunging fiercely away from it in response to the King's order. His father didn't run, but his long legs took the stairs three at a time. The prince struggled to keep up.

By the time they reached the wide, flat summit of Mount Cassandra, it was nearly deserted. Only one pegasus waited for them in the center of the great landing field: a tall, proud stallion with a white mane and wing feathers tipped with a fiery orange. His glittering black eyes regarded them with piercing intelligence as they approached, and his telepathic voice was cool and steady.

The calling is powerful, Starburst thought to them. *Far stronger than anything I've felt before.*

Nimrod saw a ghostly figure form on the peak beside them. In seconds, it had resolved into the transparent form of a woman in shining golden armor. It was Talina, Elf-Queen of the realm of Elde.

Mother, Nimrod thought to her. *You are receiving this as well, then?*

The elf-queen looked at him, and then at the King. Her deep blue eyes were narrowed, and they glinted with anger.

Tarnas, she said tightly. *I was certain this was your doing.*

The King shook his head. *Whatever this is, it is beyond even my power.*

There was a shimmer of light, and another ghostly figure took shape on the peak. A tall man in a wizard's robe of deep red regarded them coolly for a moment. Then his mustachioed lips curled slowly into a sardonic grin.

We appear to have been called to a meeting, he said.

Starburst whinnied and shook his mane. *Yes, Nicodemus. But by whom?*

Another figure appeared. A tall man with a sunburned complexion in armor of rough leather looked slowly around the group. His eyes stopped when he saw the Peregrine King.

Tarnas, he said. His mental voice was tight. *What is the meaning of this?*

Alladan, the King responded evenly. *We wait to learn that ourselves.*

Good, a new voice said. *You are all here. Then it is time.*

Nimrod started, and he turned. Another ephemeral figure had appeared at his side. The newcomer was tall and gaunt, wore a dark green adventurer's tunic, and carried a shining metal staff. A familiar face framed by a shock of white hair held eyes that blazed with an impossibly intense magic.

The Peregrine King's lips split in a thin line. *Of course,* he said.

Alladan's tanned features twisted in cold anger. *You dare much to bring me here, Lenard Killraven.*

I do, the Archmage said grimly. *Please listen carefully. We have little time.*

The mountains around them vanished, and the land seemed to blur. For a moment, Nimrod had the sensation of rushing hundreds of miles across the surface of the earth. Then the ground below them stilled. The face of Mount Cascade loomed behind them, and he found himself looking down into the valley of Lannamon.

His eyes widened at what he saw. The city was overrun. Demons, Hellmen and fire giants crawled through the streets. The shapes of winged demons and dragons circled in the air below them.

A sick horror knotted his stomach. From the gasps around him, he knew that the others were seeing it as well.

Emil Zomoran has opened a hellgate in the capital of Carlissa, the Archmage said. *Tens of thousands of the creatures have already entered our world. They are still coming.*

Nimrod glanced around. The others stood at his side, but they were all ghostly, ephemeral shapes, now — even himself. They were watching the horrific scene from a cliff along the face of Mount Cascade.

This is a telepathic scrying, the prince said. *An astral projection. You've brought our minds together, here, to see what is happening. To warn us, and to spread the alarm.*

Yes, Lenard replied. *The six of you wield the most powerful magic in the Eastern Continent. In the elven realms, in Rayche, and in the Northern Plains. You need to know the threat we now face — and be prepared to act.*

Talina's eyes widened as she looked down at the creatures swarming the palace. *Elena…* she began.

Danor and Elena are dead, Lenard said stonily. *As are Aron and Gerard. Randia still lives. She is with me, and will help me with what is to come.*

What is that? Alladan asked.

I have prepared a plan to stop this invasion and to destroy Zomoran's hellgate. It is desperate, and I do not know if it will succeed. However it turns out, Randia and I will likely not survive it.

No! Tarnas roared. *You must not! We will fly to your aid at once, Lenard. Just hold on!*

The Archmage looked at him sadly. He shook his head.

None of you can help with this, he said. *And there is no time. If this gate is not closed in the next few hours, the horde will attain numbers that even the combined armies of the world could not defeat. Randia and I are prepared to do what must be done. And it must be done now.*

Is there no other way? Starburst asked.

Lenard shook his head.

The scrying spell will dissipate once our last stand has ended. If we succeed, then you must be ready to take up the battle after us. Good fortune to you — and to us all.

The Archmage's figure faded, and was gone. Nimrod watched him disappear through a sudden sparkle of tears.

Good luck, Lenard, he whispered.

And then a deafening peal of horns rang out over the valley.

They watched, helplessly, as the battle unfolded. They heard Randia's song as it defied the demons with its heroic theme. They saw the Light as it covered the city. They laughed when Lenard's visage appeared in the face of the moon, and cried in triumph as his rain of starfire descended upon the enemy. They fell silent as the demon lord cried its challenge, and gasped as its magic blasted the cliffs. And they laughed again when they saw that the Archmage had survived, and cheered when he summoned his magic against the gate.

Talina stepped forward. Her eyes were wide.

There, she said. *Do you see? Randia stands at his side!*

The Peregrine King nodded. *I do*, he said. His mental voice was tight with pride.

They are bonded, Nicodemus said thoughtfully. *He draws on her magic to strengthen his own.*

Starburst shook his mane. He whinnied in alarm.

That is necromancy! he thought. *It is desperate, and it is dangerous!*

Alladan nodded. *It is*, he said. His ghostly features were lit with grudging admiration.

They watched the contest build to a stalemate. They saw the demons and dragons closing on the Archmage, and that he was running out of time.

And then they heard the voices. They knew they were coming from across the city, but they heard them clearly, as though right at their side.

The song is not enough. You must use all of my power. You will need it to destroy the gate.

It's too dangerous. It could kill you!

You knew what I would say, Grandfather. That you must find the courage to let me die for you.

They saw Randia's face join Lenard's in the moon. Then they saw his spell tear through the hellgate's defenses, and the explosion that obliterated it — along with the center of the city.

We saved the world, you and I.

Not yet. But thanks to you, it has a chance.

Granddaughter, Talina whispered. Her eyes were wide with grief. *No.*

Tarnas turned to the others. His face was a barely contained mask of rage.

We've seen what we needed to, his mental voice growled. *The Archmage will battle the demons until he is destroyed. But he and my granddaughter have bought us the chance we need. Now we must be ready for war!*

Chapter 1 - The Black Magus

Whom Do You Serve?

Emil Zomoran sat on the throne of Carlissa. The room around him was strewn with detritus and the floor still stained with blood, but the bodies from the battle had been cleared away. The doors were shut as the Warlord met with the remaining leaders of the horde.

Liana Desire had returned to her natural form: a voluptuous woman with black hair and red eyes. Wings of black feathers extended from her back to furl around her otherwise naked body. Incanus Thad stooped slightly to keep his head from brushing a ceiling that wasn't quite high enough for it.

Colonel Y'Thra stood with alert attention, his hand resting idly on the hilt of his sword. The Crimson Slayer slouched in a chair, a cup of wine disappearing into the shadow beneath the brim of his ostentatious hat. His face was as invisible as ever, but his body language spoke of restless boredom.

Usnaroth strode toward the throne and clapped a fist to its bearlike chest. "Word is coming in from our pack leaders," it said.

Zomoran nodded. "Report."

"The city is subdued. The people are all hiding indoors. Other than our forces, the streets are deserted."

"Good," Y'Thra said. There was a lazy drawl to his voice. It spoke of arrogant relaxation, but with a readiness for action at a moment's notice.

"So the outbursts of resistance that accompanied Lenard's attack have been quelled?" he asked.

Usnaroth nodded its bat-like head. "They collapsed with the Archmage's death."

"Then we have the city," Incanus Thad boomed.

The Crimson Slayer stood and turned toward them. "And a demon horde," he said acerbically, "with no master."

There was an uncomfortable silence. The Warlord finally broke it.

"Losing the gate is a great setback," he said slowly. "It cuts us off from the reinforcements we expected, and from the power and leadership of Lord Borr. It will force us to adapt, and to change our tactics."

"What it will force us to do," the Crimson Slayer said, with equal slowness, "is to decide who will rule here in its stead."

"I am Horde Captain," Incanus Thad said brusquely. "I will command the host in Lord Borr's absence."

"As you should, Incanus," Liana said. "And as you did for our lord when he was here. I think the Slayer's question, though, is about who should command *you*."

"I answer only to Lord Borr itself," Incanus Thad said hotly.

"That is not true," Zomoran replied.

He rose from the throne and faced the towering demon. His voice was stern and hard.

"It was I who discovered and opened the gate," he continued, "and made the invasion possible. You all know the price I set for my cooperation. *You* announced the arrival of the horde in my name. Have you already forgotten why?"

"Bah!" the Crimson Slayer said. He spat on the floor, and the fiery spittle started to burn its way through the tile like acid. "The deal cannot stand as made. Not with the gate destroyed, and in the absence of the horde's true master."

"Agreed," Incanus Thad boomed. "It must be adjusted."

Liana chuckled. "Careful, boys," she warned. "You might be overplaying your hand."

Zomoran's eyes narrowed dangerously. "The succubus speaks with wisdom," he said. "And she *is* the one among you who best knows the fire with which you dare to play."

He turned to watch as the Slayer drew his sword. Black lightning ran down the ebon blade and over its fiery runes. Incanus Thad slowly raised his axe.

"Still, it is to be expected," Zomoran continued. His tone was unworried, almost conversational. "You are demons, after all. You would not be devotees of the Way of the Will, were you not prepared to overthrow me."

Without warning, he lifted his staff. Dark energy ran along the shaft as he shouted a single word.

"Karach!"

Incanus Thad collapsed like a gigantic puppet whose strings had suddenly been cut. He crashed to the floor, spasming uncontrollably, as though suffering a seizure. Destruction flew from his hand to clatter uselessly to the tiles, followed moments later by the Slayer's blade. The fire demon stood rigid, head thrown back, and emitted a single, high-pitched shriek.

"My price," the magus said acidly, "since you seem to have forgotten it, was a contract with your master — one bound and enforced by its own magic. That we would be partners in bringing Kalara under its dominion, and that *I* would order and rule this world in its name. You are bound by geas of obedience to your master's will — and through that contract, by obedience to *mine*."

He strode to Incanus Thad. The Giant Demon lay on the tiles before him, writhing in agony. He growled as the warlord placed a boot on his throat.

"Whom do you serve?" the magus demanded menacingly.

"I serve — AARGH!"

"Again, demon. Whom do you serve?"

"I serve my master, Lord Borr!"

"And in its absence?" Zomoran pressed. "Whom do you serve in Kalara, in executing the mission of this horde?"

Incanus Thad's back arched. "You!" he cried. "I serve Warlord Zomoran, the Black Magus!"

Zomoran removed his boot from the demon's throat. The Horde Captain gasped in sudden relief as the magus turned to the Crimson Slayer.

"Whom do you serve?" Zomoran demanded.

"I will burn you to ash, wizard," the Slayer hissed. "After I take your soul with my blade!"

He flew through the air to slam against the far wall of the throne room. He began to shriek again. This time, he did not stop.

"Wrong answer, demon. Again. Whom do you serve?"

The Slayer screamed for nearly half a minute before he finally gave in. When the magus turned to Usnaroth, the winged demon repeated the declaration of fealty without being asked.

Liana laughed. "I told you you were overplaying your hand," she said. "A geas is nothing to —"

Zomoran spun toward her, again raising his staff. The succubus' words were cut off in mid-sentence. Her wings unfurled as her body arched — and she, too, shrieked in pain.

The magus allowed her to scream as he walked slowly toward her. His eyes narrowed cruelly as he idly ran the tip of his staff along the lines of her naked form.

"You are the most dangerous of them all," he told her icily. "Surely you did not think I would neglect to enforce my spell on you as well? While you scheme to work your magic to slowly seduce me to your will?"

"No!" she wailed. "No, no!"

His lips quirked into a smile. "I thought not. Now, whom do you serve?"

"I serve you!" she shrieked. "I serve Warlord Zomoran, the Black Magus!"

"I do not trust you, succubus," he said. "Say it again. Whom do you serve?"

He forced her to repeat the pledge, screaming it over and over, until she had been reduced to sobbing. When he finally released her, she crumpled to the floor in a quivering heap.

Zomoran walked slowly to the throne and sat down again. He looked at the assembled demons, one at a time.

"I trust that is now settled," he said at last. "Are there any questions?"

Incanus Thad had recovered his composure, and his axe. He gestured to the Hellman officer. "What about him?" he demanded.

"*Lord General* Y'Thra and his Hellmen are of *this* world," he explained. "They are not part of your horde and owe no geas to Lord

Borr. I have ... other means of securing their allegiance."

Y'Thra drew his sword and dropped to one knee before him. "As you command, My Lord," he said.

Zomoran nodded in a gesture of acceptance. Then he turned back to the others.

"Now, as I was saying," he continued, "we will have to adjust our tactics. Without the might of the full horde, we cannot simply sweep across the world as we had intended. Until we can find and open another gate to Lord Borr's realm, our plan to conquer Kalara will need to proceed with more caution."

Liana struggled to her feet, still shaking. She tried to furl her wings about her again, but seemed to have trouble controlling her movements.

"What do you command, My Lord?" she asked. Her voice was meek.

Zomoran smiled. "We will take Carlissa by lightning war," he replied. "I have already assigned objectives and am preparing written orders for the companies. You will oversee their execution, Incanus. I want them on the march by dawn."

"What about the Elf-Queen?" Y'Thra asked. "Her citadel is dangerously close to Lannamon. What if she strikes at us here?"

"We will keep a force in the city," Zomoran replied. "One large enough for that contingency. It will become our new capital and base of operations." He smiled again. "But Talina will not attack us. I am confident of that."

The others exchanged glances, but said nothing.

"Once we have Carlissa, we will be in a better position to search for a new worldgate artifact," he continued. "I know of ancient clues that should help with that. They suggest another one may even be in or near the kingdom. We will find it, and we *will* re-establish a link to our master, Lord Borr. That I pledge to you."

The demons seemed to relax at his words. Liana finally managed to furl her wings around herself once again.

"And after Carlissa?" she asked.

Zomoran sighed. "Then we will be forced to pause and take stock of our options," he said. "Lieutenant — excuse me, *Captain* — Usnaroth, what is your report on our troop and casualty counts?"

"Troop counts were lost with the command post," the demon replied. "We have our sergeants repeating them now. I estimate that about thirty-five thousand came through to this world. About a fifth of that — perhaps seven thousand — fell in battle with the Carlissans or in the destruction of the gate."

There was a long silence. Zomoran began to drum his fingers along the arm of the throne.

"Almost thirty thousand," he said. "Plus eight thousand Hellmen, a few dozen dragons, several hundred giants, and a scattering of other allies across the Eastern Continent. More than enough to take Carlissa, and likely Elde and Rayche as well. But we must be wary of overextending ourselves."

"And if all Kalara unites against us?" Y'Thra asked. "What then?"

Zomoran turned to look at Liana. The succubus flinched almost imperceptibly under his steady gaze.

"That will be our task," he said. "I have a plan. She and I will work on it together."

"And the city?" Y'Thra asked. "Shall we —"

Zomoran shook his head.

"Your Hellmen may have the night," he said. "To sate yourselves and to take slaves — as long as it is done in accordance with tradition and with the ritual. But there must be no more destruction, and the Taking must end at first light. Order must be restored, and the people brought in line and set to work. Putting out fires, making repairs, tending the wounded, restoring commerce." His eyes hardened. "Your captives as well, Y'Thra. They are now chattel of the Dark and not *only* for your pleasure."

The Hellman general nodded. His face was stoic, but a light of anticipation burned in his black eyes.

"That will be difficult," Liana said. "The people are terrified and in hiding. They will have to be flushed — or coaxed — out."

Zomoran nodded. "I have written a proclamation," he said. "Declaring an end to the hostilities, and offering a promise of safety for all who submit to my rule. Lannamon has been conquered, and its people need to learn that its new masters can be merciful — to those who obey them."

He looked around the room, and then waved a hand in dismissal.

"You all have work to do. Begin preparations for the lightning war and return to me in two hours. I will have written orders ready for you then."

The Secret

Liana made her way along the corridor toward the ruins of the Great Hall. Incanus Thad shuffled alongside her. His enormous form stooped to keep from brushing the ceiling. For the moment, they were alone.

"The magus is more dangerous than we anticipated," he said. His booming voice was surprisingly quiet.

Liana shook her head. "No," she said softly. "Lord Borr understood the danger. But it expected to be here to counter it. Without its protection, we are gravely vulnerable."

"Could he have orchestrated this?" Incanus Thad whispered. "To trap us here without our master, and under his power?"

She shook her head again.

"If he had, then he would not have been able to dominate us," she replied. "That is how the magic of the geas works. The contract binds *him* as well. He can enforce it on us only if he, too, pursues it in good faith."

She pursed her full, red lips in thought.

"And I think that was part of his demonstration," she added. "To show us who is master, surely — and he is, at least for the time being. But also to reassure us he really does intend to hold up his end of the bargain. To open a new gate to the homeworld, and to bring Lord Borr back to Kalara."

There was a long silence as the pair walked through the Great Hall and what remained of the palace gate. A group of demon lieutenants stood on the High Road, waiting for their arrival. Incanus Thad stopped before approaching them.

"So what do we do?" he asked.

"We bide our time," she replied. "None of us possess the power to free ourselves from the magus' domination, and we still have a mission to fulfill. To aid him in subduing this world for our master, and to prepare for its inevitable return."

Incanus Thad nodded. Then, suddenly, he lowered his great head next to hers. His eyes rested briefly on the blood red pendant that peeked out from the spray of black wing feathers that folded over her breasts.

Does he know?

Her eyes searched his, their gaze betraying just a hint of worry. *No.*

Can we hide it from him?

I believe so. We keep the secret in loyalty to our master, so the geas will protect it. But we must be careful, Incanus. We must not make the mistake of underestimating this Black Magus of Kalara.

The Horde Captain nodded, and straightened to his full height.

"Then let us get to work," he said aloud, as he resumed walking toward the waiting officers. "We have much to do, and the kingdom will not conquer itself for us."

Liana's eyes sparkled. Her feet left the flagstones as she floated into the air to keep pace with the great demon. "You might be surprised, Incanus," she replied cryptically. "You might be surprised."

Checkpoint

Orion and Diana encountered a line of Hellman soldiers barring their way. They were waving pedestrians to the side of the road where a large tent had been set up. Diana took in a sharp breath as one of them approached.

"No one passes without a registration badge," he said. His tone was firm, but he sounded bored.

"How do we get one?" Orion asked.

The soldier nodded toward the tent. "Queue forms to the right."

They started to comply, but he raised a hand to stop them. He pointed to the sword belted at Orion's hip.

"All weapons are to be confiscated," he said.

Orion unbuckled Jameson's sword and handed it to him. They got in line, and waited silently for most of an hour. When their turn came, they had seen and heard enough from the people before them to be prepared.

"Names?"

The clerk was an elderly Hellman with an officious manner. He wore a long green robe and a thick pair of spectacles, and spoke Carlissan with a heavy accent. Orion saw alert black eyes that belied the monotonous tone of his voice, and was immediately on guard.

"Orion Deneri," he replied carefully.

"Place of residence?"

"I have a small apartment on the north side of the Lower City. Kennel Avenue, number 12."

"Occupation?"

Orion took a deep breath. "Instructor at the Grand Academy."

The clerk looked up at him, eyebrows arching into his bald red pate. "Is that where you're going now?"

He shook his head. "No. I'm escorting my charge back to her home in the High City."

The Hellman looked at Diana. "Name?" he asked.

Diana fought to keep the loathing from her eyes. She managed, but just barely.

"Diana Dal Meara," she said stiffly. "I live with my family on Brightstar Street. Number five."

The Hellman relaxed and leaned back in his seat. A faint smile touched his lips.

"That's near the palace. Diplomatic estates, if I'm not mistaken. And Dal Meara ... the name's Dorian, isn't it?"

Diana swallowed, and then nodded reluctantly. "My father is the ambassador," she confirmed.

He nodded to Orion. "And Mr. Deneri?"

"My tutor. We were ... out when the fighting began, and took shelter together."

The old Hellman took a slip of paper from his desk and began to write. "Orange for both of them," he said.

Diana's eyes widened as an assistant produced the requested badges. "What does that mean?" she demanded. "Most people are getting yellow ones."

The clerk stopped writing and looked up at her. Then his eyes shifted to Orion. He chuckled.

"Real spitfire you've got there, Deneri," he said. "And a beauty, too." He sighed. "Shame she escaped the Taking. Slave like *that* would make me feel a century younger."

Orion fought to keep his face calm and his hands from clenching into fists. Diana lost the battle to keep the anger out of her eyes, but somehow stayed silent.

"Warlord Zomoran's decree is law, though," the clerk went on regretfully. "The truce began at dawn, so she's free to return to her family. With orders, of course. Same for you."

He handed the badge to Diana.

"Orange means you've been conscripted," he explained. "Lady Dal Meara, you will return home to let the ambassador know you are safe. In the evening, you will report to the Cathedral Hospital to help with the wounded. I expect your mother has already received the same orders from my counterpart in the High City."

Diana let out a long, slow breath. "Of course," she said carefully. "And my companion?"

The clerk returned to his writing.

"I can't spare an escort for every case like yours," he continued. "So I'm temporarily conscripting Mr. Deneri into the militia with orders to see you home safely." He looked up at Orion. "I assume you have no objection?"

Orion shook his head. "No, of course not. As I said, I was planning to do so already."

"Yes, I heard you. On the off chance that you need 'extra' motivation, these orders mean you are now responsible for her safety. If anything happens to her, or if she is not delivered safely to her father, then you will be hunted down and executed. Do you understand?"

"Yes," Orion said cautiously. "The soldiers confiscated my sword, though. I'll be hard pressed to protect her if anything ... 'happens.'"

The clerk chuckled again and returned to his writing.

"Show your orders to my men. They'll return your blade for the duration of your assignment. Keep in mind that authorization to carry a weapon makes you an acting member of the guard, and subject to the same discipline. Clear?"

Orion nodded. "Clear," he said.

"After that, you're to report to the academy. An instructional meeting is being held there this evening. You'll receive your new orders and learn about your new responsibilities then."

Orion took a breath. He fought to keep his face and tone neutral despite a growing feeling of rebellion at the clerk's words. Whatever new "instructional" responsibilities the demons had in mind for him, he was quite certain that he was *not* going to like them.

"May I visit my family first?" he asked cautiously. "They live on the first level of the Upper City South. I'd like to make sure they're all right."

The Hellman shrugged indifferently and continued to write. "If you have time between delivering Lady Dal Meara to her father and reporting to the academy at mountainset," he said, "then yes."

He paused for a moment to peer at Orion over the rim of his spectacles. "Just make sure you're not late," he added.

Chapter 2 - Homecomings

The Ambassador

Orion and Diana turned the corner onto Brightstar Street. The long walk across the city had taken them until midday, with only a couple of short breaks to rest.

Small estates sat recessed at intervals along the road. One of the nearer ones appeared to have been ransacked. Aside from that, they saw relatively little damage from the events of the previous day.

"That's it," Diana said, pointing. "The third gate on the right. It's just a few minutes' walk."

Orion nodded and started to move. She stepped in front of him and placed a hand on his chest.

"Not so fast," she said.

"Don't you want to get home?"

"Of course I do. But we need to talk first — privately. You know that once I'm seen, we won't have the chance."

He nodded.

"Of course. With these orders of ours, we may not be able to meet again for a long while."

"It sounds like you got the short end of them. At least they'll be putting me to work as a healer. They sucked you into the military right off the street."

He shook his head dismissively.

"I'm not worried about that. The clerk said it was temporary. So do those orders he wrote. He was using whatever resources he had at hand to get his job done. I just happened to be one of them."

She nodded wryly. "Hellman bureaucracy. Right up there on the list of their most famous talents — after rape and murder."

He chuckled. Then he quickly became serious again.

"I'm more concerned about reporting to the academy. It sounds like that's going to be my permanent 'assignment.' I wish I knew what to expect from it."

"We'll take things one day at a time. We'll get through it."

He smiled at her. "We?"

She punched him in the arm.

"Yes, 'we.' You haven't forgotten our oath already, have you? And everything we've been through together? We're partners, Orion Deneri." She looked into his face, her eyes suddenly searching. "Aren't we?"

He nodded. "We are," he said quietly.

"Then we need to make a plan. Introducing you to father as the man who saved me will give you an excuse to visit. You'll do that, won't you? So that we can share notes on finding or building a resistance? And so I can know you're all right?"

He nodded again.

"I will. Or at least send word, if I can. Just be prepared if I can't do it right away." He fingered the badge that was pinned to the remains of his shirt. "We may not have the freedom to make many choices for ourselves from now on."

They walked in silence down the length of the street. When they reached the gate, they found it locked. A heavily armed guard glared at them from behind it.

"No admittance, vagabonds," he said harshly. "Back up the street with you. You can find shelter in the Lower City."

Diana's nostrils flared in indignation. "Why, of all the impertinence —" she began.

Orion laid a hand on her shoulder, and she turned to face him. Her expression was surprised.

"I don't think he recognizes you," he said. "We are something of a mess, you know."

Diana looked down at her dress. It was torn nearly to shreds and stained with blood.

"Oh," she said sheepishly.

The guard stepped closer to the gate. "Lady Diana?" he gasped.

"Yes, Karl, it's me. And by the Light, please show a little more compassion to strangers! People have suffered terribly in the rest of the city."

"I am so sorry, Mistress!" Karl said. His tone was mortified. "I didn't —"

"I know," she interrupted impatiently. "I probably wouldn't have recognized me, either. And I'll forget it, too, and not tell Father, if you unlock the gate and let us in right away."

He was already fumbling for his keys. "Of course, My Lady," he stammered. "Of course!"

They heard a commotion ahead as soon as they were on the path to the manor. The door flew open when they were part way up the walk. A tall man in red leather armor with a short sword belted at his hip strode through the opening.

A sob escaped Diana's lips when she saw him. "Father!" she cried.

There was a rush of steps, and then the two were embracing fiercely. The man said nothing, but only held her tightly, eyes closed. Orion watched them in silence, feeling suddenly awkward and out of place.

When they finally parted, the man turned to him, and he had his first look at Damien Dal Meara's face. In the past, he was sure he would have found the harsh, proud lines and piercing eyes that openly weighed him unsettling, even intimidating. He was surprised to realize that today, he didn't.

"Father, this is Orion Deneri," Diana said. "The instructor for our class at the academy. We fled into the city when the attack began. He saved my life and protected me until he could return me home to you."

Orion executed a court bow — flawlessly, but omitting the flourishes. Something in this man's manner told him that unnecessary flamboyance would not make a good impression.

"Your Excellency," he said.

Slowly and deliberately, the ambassador extended his hand. Orion took it.

"I owe you a great debt, Instructor Deneri," he said. His voice resonated with power and authority. "We heard that the academy had been taken by Hellmen. We feared the worst."

"We only narrowly escaped that fate ourselves, sir," Orion replied.

"Kieran insisted on staying there for safety," Diana elaborated. The contempt in her voice was undisguised. "Orion and I were the only two with the sense to run. Did any of the others ..."

The ambassador shook his head.

"We've heard nothing of their fate so far. But we believe they were all caught in the Taking."

They stood in silence as he gave his daughter's ragged form a long, careful look. He took in the blood in her hair and on her torn dress, the bandages showing through the tears in her clothes, and the dirt and scratches that covered much of her body. He glanced briefly at Orion.

"You were attacked," he said finally.

Diana nodded. Her manner suddenly became oddly formal, as though she were delivering a report.

"We were."

"A demon?"

She nodded again. "Yes."

"How did you escape?"

"We killed it," she said. "At some cost. We weren't alone."

"You were the only survivors?"

"Yes."

"How badly were you hurt?"

"Mostly lacerations from the demon's claws. They will heal quickly. I performed or supervised the dressing of our wounds myself."

The ambassador turned. A few servants had gathered in the doorway to watch the scene. One was a young boy with a pouch slung over his shoulder.

"Bran," he called. "Run as fast as you can to the Cathedral Hospital. Tell my lady wife that our daughter is home. Tell her she is injured, and taking rest and refreshment after her ordeal."

"Yes, sir," the boy squeaked. He was sprinting toward the gate before he'd finished the second word. The ambassador turned back to Diana.

"You will have to tell me the full story later. For now, I will have the servants bring you something to eat, and then run a bath for you."

Diana bowed her head. "Thank you, Father," she said.

She looked at Orion. The ambassador followed her eyes and turned to face him.

Then, without warning, he clapped Orion on the shoulder. The scholar was certain the gesture had been intended as friendly, but he still staggered under the force of it.

"I won't have them run a bath for you, young man," Diana's father said with a slight smile. "But I think we can manage a washbasin and something to eat."

"Thank you, Your Excellency," Orion replied. "I can remain only briefly, though. I must return to my own family to see that they are well."

The ambassador nodded. "Of course. As I would expect."

He turned to lead the way back to the estate. Diana fell into step beside Orion, and they exchanged a brief glance.

"I think he likes you," she mouthed soundlessly.

Orion rubbed his shoulder. "I'm glad to hear it," he whispered drily.

The Final Break

Orion climbed the hill into the Upper City South. His family's complex — the grounds that included their home and warehouses — was on the first level of the terrace. It was near a main avenue that ran from the city's great crossroads. The location had been professionally chosen, since easy access to Lannamon's highways was an advantage for the headquarters of a trading company. It was prime and expensive real estate, and the Deneri clan had taken great pains to turn that investment into a source of status.

He had kept his stay at the Dal Meara estate as brief as courtesy allowed. He and Diana had washed the worst of the grime from their faces and hands, and had sat down to a light meal with her father. Orion had admired her mother's beautifully flowering garden as they ate and drank, and made small talk as the servants fussed over them. The ambassador had asked him about his life, his family, his studies, and his new post at the academy.

The questions had been polite, and precisely what Orion had been raised to expect from an afternoon calling. He couldn't shake the feeling, though, that beneath his casual manner Diana's father had been sizing him up intently.

She had insisted on re-dressing his wounds before he left. To his surprise and some discomfort her father had agreed, and remained to observe the process. Her manner became oddly formal and precise again as she removed his shirt and stripped off his bandages, directing the servants to bring new wrappings and a very specific collection of potent medicines and salves. He saw her father nod in approval at the choices. He did so again several more times as he watched her administer and apply them, and re-bandage his injuries.

The whole thing seemed to him strangely like a spot examination by one of his professors. Fortunately, she appeared to have passed with high marks.

The trip from Diana's estate had taken longer than he expected. It wasn't until mid-afternoon when he found himself walking up the hill to his family's home. The implosion of the hellgate had wreaked havoc between the docks and the start of the High City, and obliterated the great crossroads of Lannamon. In its place lay the surface of a circular lake that had formed as the firth waters rushed into the crater left by the gate's destruction. Many of the avenues he knew ended abruptly at its shores, and finding a way around had been time-consuming. Being stopped several times and forced to produce his orders for inspection had not sped his passage.

He looked at the sun and took stock of his options. He judged that he could make it back to the academy on foot in under two hours. Mountainset would be in a little over three. That gave him an hour to spend with his family before he would have to leave — and less, if he wanted to give himself a margin of error. That wouldn't be enough to do much to help them if they needed it, but it would be better than nothing. Or at least, he hoped it would.

He found the front door locked and barred from the inside. A sense of creeping dread began to grow in him as he walked around the house. The windows were tightly shuttered and no one seemed to be at home, but he thought he could hear animated voices in the distance.

He turned to the warehouse. The cargo doors were chained shut, but he saw several of his family's caravan guards standing watch at the side entrance. As he approached, he could hear that the voices were coming from there.

"Master Orion," one of the guards said. "Good to see you're well."

Orion smiled. "You too, Nolan. How is everyone?"

The guard shook his head. "Best you hear any news from them," he replied. "I'll let you in."

Orion's trepidation spiked as he walked through the small maze of offices that served as the planning center of the Deneri Trade and Import Company. They were deserted, but he could hear the voices more loudly now. They were coming from ahead, down the hall that led to the storerooms. His family was holding a meeting in the largest one.

He wasn't certain what made him approach with stealth, instead of simply walking in and greeting them. He came to the door and quietly opened it a crack. It was just wide enough to peer through, and to hear what was being said. He stood there, watching and listening.

"Dennis is still missing," his cousin Lemma said. "And Orion. What about them?"

"Your brother was at the docks working the shipment from Port Tiberax," his father replied. "Everyone there was killed in the massacre."

"And Orion was at the Grand Academy," his mother added. "He's either taken or dead."

"And Claudia?" Lemma pursued.

"There's nothing we can do for her," his brother Jeremy said angrily. "The Hellmen are serious about their rituals. She was swept up in this 'taking' of theirs and that's the end of it."

Orion shut his eyes. Claudia was his younger sister, and like most of his siblings, had never much cared for her scholar brother. She'd thought him stuffy and boring, and had often said so. Despite their lack of closeness, he felt an intense stab of empathy for her. Perhaps if he could find out where she was, he could come up with a way to rescue her ...

"There's more to it than that," he heard his father saying. "Trying to intervene for her would jeopardize the family's standing. Orion too, if he's even still alive. It would attract negative attention at the worst possible time. Our future prospects depend on being flexible, adaptable, and cooperative with Zomoran's new order."

There was a murmur of assent from the assembled group. Orion gripped the edge of the door, eyes widening in anger and disbelief.

"Edward is right," his mother said. "The coup is a golden opportunity for us. We need to seize it. Danor's reforms were about to gut our business, losing our family charters it spent generations acquiring. Zomoran will rebuild the Trade Guild. If we play our cards right, we can become an important part of it."

"How?" Jeremy asked. He sounded intrigued.

"By finding out who will be in favor in the new order," his father replied. "And exploiting — or making — contacts and alliances with them. And by distancing ourselves from whoever is not."

"How will we know which is which?" Lemma asked.

"It won't be hard to figure out," his mother said. Her voice was sly and confident. "Start by assuming that whoever was close to the old regime is out, and whoever they were in conflict with is in. Baronet Kuhl, for example. I've already heard through my contacts that he was the first of the High Council to swear to Zomoran. We've had profitable dealings with him in the past, and he knows he can count on us. That's an alliance we need to strengthen at once. I've already sent a courier to him with a message ..."

Orion let go of the door and stepped back. He was shaking.

They're going to ingratiate themselves with the Warlord's regime, he thought numbly. *They're actually working out a deliberate plan to sell out to the Black Magus and his demons.*

It was a moment of brutal clarity for him. He had felt like an outsider in his family for most of his young life. Up to now, though, he'd thought it due to a passion for scholarship that they didn't share. Despite his uneasiness at their frequent lack of scruples, he'd tried to respect what he thought was a legitimate dedication to the family business.

What he was seeing now was wholly different. It was the basest kind of dishonor, and it went far beyond a mismatch of interests. It was a profound clash of morals, and it stripped away the generous excuses he had made for them. And for the first time, he saw that *this* was the root of his lifelong disconnection from his family.

Eyes narrowed and convictions hardened, he turned on his heel and went back the way he'd come. Leaving his childhood home behind, he set out on a brisk walk toward the Grand Academy.

The New Curriculum

Orion sat in the classroom by the garden in the Grand Academy. He noted, with bitter irony, that it was the same one in which he'd begun his career as a teacher the day before.

He recognized many of those seated around him from the department of philosophy. Most were fellow instructors, and some had even been his professors. A few were among the more advanced students. They wore expressions with varying levels of unease, from haunted to clearly terrified.

An elderly Hellwoman in a professorial robe stood by the podium. As with the clerk he'd encountered earlier, it was a deep green. It differed only in the addition of a bright yellow trim around the collar and cuffs. It was also cut to be rather less modest than was customary for the Grand Academy.

"I am Dame E'lath," she was saying. "The new head of the Department of Philosophy. You will address me as 'Mistress.' Do you understand?"

She waited as the group exchanged nervous glances. Her eyes hardened.

"I said, do you understand?" she demanded. The menace in her voice was unmistakable.

This time, they did. "Yes, Mistress," they replied together.

"That's better. No doubt you are all wondering why you've been assigned to this meeting tonight. The answer is simple. You are the members of my instructional staff who remain after yesterday's Taking."

Her gaze swept slowly around the room as she spoke, settling on each of them in turn.

"Warlord Zomoran intends to return the Grand Academy to its rightful role as Carlissa's — and indeed, Kalara's — premier center of learning," she went on. "This will be done largely with new teachers, many from my people, who will be brought in to fill its now vacant roles. *You* are the members of the prior instructional staff fortunate enough to have been chosen to assist in that noble undertaking."

Her eyes again took on a hard look.

"This assignment is a great honor," she continued. Her voice was stern. "One that will afford each of you significantly greater privileges in the new order than will be enjoyed by your fellow Carlissans. As long, of course, as you act accordingly."

She smiled as expressions of relief washed across many of the faces around him. Orion forced himself to suppress the sick feeling in his stomach — and, slowly and deliberately, faked a similar expression of his own. As Diana had said, they would have to lie their way through whatever was expected of them, at least for now.

"My job, for the next few months, will be to see that you are trained in the new curriculum. Some of you, and particularly those instructed by Professor Zomoran, may already be familiar with a *portion* of the material that we will be covering. Because of the propaganda stranglehold your "Covenant" has had on Kalara's eastern continent for so many centuries, however, you will all require extensive re-education before being ready to assume your new duties."

Orion fought to keep his expression calm. Cautiously, he let a subdued look of curious interest show on his face. It was one of the most difficult things he had ever done. He had been a student in then Professor Zomoran's course on Society and Culture, and knew the outlines of what to expect from Dame E'lath's "re-education."

The memory brought a stab of pain as he remembered a classmate who had been killed the day before. Aron Killraven had been in that class with him. The prince had been in his last year at the academy, and Orion in his first.

Zomoran had made it a requirement that his students form teams with the responsibility to argue for both the Light *and* the Dark. They had been paired for the task, and had worked diligently together to prepare their case. And they had earned top marks by handily winning *both* sides of the debate.

Part of the reason had been due to Aron's overwhelming power as an orator. As the only freshman in the advanced class, Orion was certain that Zomoran had teamed them precisely to compensate for the prince's advantage. But the choice had underestimated them both. Aron had a first-class mind, in addition to being an outstanding speaker. And Orion had turned out to be a far better debater than his shy demeanor had suggested — even to himself.

They had rarely seen each other afterward, and he had never told the story to his family. Now he suddenly found himself wondering, for the first time, whether the experience had had anything to do with his subsequent career, and with the Archmage's interest in him as a student. Why *had* he received that unexpected invitation to apply to the Silver Star a year ago? Had he actually impressed the elder prince enough to tell his grandfather about him?

He shook his head to clear it. He would never know the answer to that now.

"Your new curriculum has already been planned," Dame E'lath continued. "And outlined for you. You will begin these studies right away, starting tonight."

She held up a book, and gestured around the room to where a copy of it sat on each of their desks. It bore a plain title on the cover: *Basic Curriculum in Philosophy for the Grand Academy of Lannamon*. The editions were brand new. Orion opened it and glanced at the pages, immediately recognizing the distinctive look and smell of a recent magical printing.

"You will each take your copy when you leave. Tonight, you will *carefully* read the first chapter. When we meet here again tomorrow morning, you will be prepared to discuss your understanding of that material *in detail*. Those of you *not* prepared to do so with the scholarly rigor expected of this institution will have cause to regret it."

Her eyes narrowed in a threatening expression.

"We will repeat these seminars with new reading assignments every day until we have covered this introductory course. At that time, you will take an exam to evaluate whether you are qualified to continue your studies. Those who show an ability to understand and embrace the new teachings will be permitted to do so. Those who fall short will be dropped from the program."

Her eyes glinted. A barely restrained smile broke across her normally harsh features.

"To encourage your commitment," she continued, "Lord Zomoran has declared that those who fail the exam shall be eligible for the Taking. As your instructor, I will have first pick of any who do. I trust that will give you a sufficient incentive to impress me with your scholarship and initiative. If you can do that, then you will have a valued place in our new order."

Her restraint vanished, and her smile broadened into a look of anticipation.

"If you cannot, then I look forward to carrying on your education in a different form."

A student to Orion's right — a shy young woman he'd remembered from one of his ethics classes — closed her eyes and shuddered. He saw Dame E'lath note her reaction with a casual glance and a flicker of amusement in her black eyes.

"Until you pass your qualifying exam, you will be quartered on the academy grounds," she concluded. "A space in the dorms has been designated for you. You will find your room assignment written in your coursebook. Go there now to begin your studies. You will report here tomorrow morning by the ringing of the ninth bell."

A New Friend

Katarina Dal Meara met her daughter when she arrived at the Cathedral Hospital. They embraced tearfully, heedless of the blood staining the older woman's surgical gown. When they parted, she took Diana's face between her hands and held it.

"Bran brought me word that you had returned home," she said. "And that you were hurt. Do you need me to see to your injuries?"

Diana tried to shake her head, without success. They both laughed.

"Later," she said. "They'll be fine for now. Father helped me re-bandage them. I was able to eat and bathe, and get a few hours of rest."

Her mother frowned. She didn't stop until Diana had described her injuries and how they had been treated. Then she looked deeply into her daughter's face.

"You had some good luck finding those medicines," Katarina said at last. "You look well, and your eyes are clear —"

They were interrupted by a scream as two men carried an injured soldier into the ward. Diana paled when she saw blood soaking his leg and abdomen.

"I'm fine, Mother," she said impatiently. "And the people here need our help. What can I do?"

Katarina smiled at her. "Yes, of course," she said. There was an unmistakable hint of pride in her voice.

"We've made a list of those in greatest need, and you're better trained than a lot of these Carlissan healers are. Come on. Let's get you prepared."

The hours that followed became a blur in Diana's memory. She and her mother worked tirelessly into the small hours of the morning, cleaning and suturing terrible wounds, fighting a too often fruitless battle to save the lives of the injured. Many were soldiers who had been mauled by rampaging demons, or cut down by the swords of the Hellmen. They raced against time to mix and apply a set of special medicines that only her mother knew how to prepare. There were never enough ingredients, and they sent a constant stream of messengers to scour the city with desperate calls for anyone who might have them.

It wasn't until four in the morning that she found herself with time to catch her breath. Her mother had left an hour earlier to return home to rest, her healing magic taxed well past the point of exhaustion. Diana had helped the doctors attend to the remaining patients who were in immediate danger, and had taken a short meal to refresh her strength.

She was beginning to feel light-headed, and knew that she would soon have to return home to rest as well. Before she did, though, she wanted to review the less urgent cases. She worried that some of them might be missed with the morning's shift change.

The third patient she checked was a young woman with red hair in a guard lieutenant's uniform. She was lying in a corner of the ward, and Diana realized the staff had overlooked her as they struggled to save the more obviously and gravely wounded. No one had tended to her injuries. Diana's eyes widened, and she cursed, when she saw the blood staining the bedding beneath her.

Then she was struggling desperately with the guard's unconscious body, trying to turn her over, to unbuckle and remove her armor. Her breath hissed when she saw a large welt on the back of the woman's head, and the leather on her back hanging in loose, bloody shreds. It looked to have been rent by the strike of an enormous claw.

She cursed again when she finally got the guard's clothes off. The entire back of her body from shoulders to thighs was bruised a deep blue, as though she'd been thrown by a giant against a stone wall. The only breaks in the dark coloring were the badly clotting punctures and lacerations that had started to flow again. They were already showing signs of infection.

She went to work. The woman had lost a lot of blood, and Diana marveled that she hadn't already bled to death. She had only a little of the medicines left that she and her mother had mixed, and she would need all of them to save the guard's life.

She washed and treated the gashes in the woman's back with the same mixture she had used on herself and Orion the day before. She saw her flinch in her sleep as the deathsbane seeped into the wounds, and sighed with relief. The guard was unconscious, but didn't seem to be insensate. That probably meant she was recovering from her concussion. She'd be all right once she was properly cared for ...

Diana was still working when the guard's eyes suddenly fluttered open. They settled on Diana with a disoriented look, and then spurted tears. The woman gasped.

"Easy," Diana said. "I know it hurts, but try to hold on. I'm almost done with your back, and then I can give you something for the pain."

The guard stared at her, wet eyes wide with fear and agony. She tried to nod, and then winced.

"Try to keep still," Diana said. Her voice was soothing. "You're pretty banged up."

"You seem young for a doctor," the woman croaked. Her voice was dry and raspy, and she could barely get out the words.

Diana chuckled. "You seem young for a guard lieutenant."

The woman tried to smile. "Fair point," she whispered, through gritted teeth.

Diana finished her work in silence. When she was done, she took a flask of liquid from a bag she was carrying. It was water mixed with regenera, the last she had. She added a brown powder and began to stir it.

The woman lay on her stomach, head turned to the side. She watched Diana with patient stoicism, tears streaming down her face.

Diana held up the flask when she was done.

"This will ease the pain," she said. "And help you heal. It's strong, and it'll need a few minutes to take effect. Then you'll get giddy, and start to feel *very* good. Don't be alarmed by it."

The woman smiled wryly. "Alarmed by feeling giddy, good, and not in pain?" she rasped. "You give strange warnings, doctor."

Diana grinned. "So what's your name, Lieutenant?"

"Clarissa Kay. Most everyone just calls me Kay."

Diana held the flask carefully to her lips. "Drink it slowly, Kay," she said.

Kay did, and grimaced. The medicine clearly tasted awful, but she drank it obediently.

"I'm Diana. I'm not a doctor, though. As you can imagine they're in short supply here today compared to the patients. Fortunately, I know enough about healing to help."

Kay gulped, slowly swallowing the medicine. Her brown eyes met Diana's green ones with a look of desperate trust.

"You're going to be *really* sore for a few days," Diana went on, "but I got to you in time. You're going to make it."

"Thank you," Kay said, when she'd finished the flask. "I thought I was dead."

Diana took a small cloth from her bag and started wiping Kay's tear-stained cheeks.

"No wonder, with wounds and bruises like that. What did you do, try to take on the whole horde by yourself?"

Kay closed her eyes, and a look of pain clouded her face. She choked back a sob.

"Something like that," she whispered.

Then her eyes opened again.

"What happened, Diana? I don't remember much after I was attacked."

"What's the last thing you do remember?"

"It was late afternoon," she said. "I was ... guarding someone. There was a demon, and then blackness ... Then everything became a blur. More demons, pain, crawling, trying to get away, trying to find somewhere safe. Then dreams. I heard music, and saw the Blood Moon ..."

New tears ran down Kay's face. Diana took her hand and held it tightly.

"There was a battle," she said quietly. "The Archmage appeared with the princess in the face of the moon. They fought the demons together with magic and song."

Kay shuddered. She was openly crying now.

"Then she made it," she sobbed. "I didn't fail her."

Diana's eyes went wide. She looked around, but no one was near enough to have heard. She bent down and put her face next to Kay's.

"Is that who you were guarding?" she whispered. "The princess?"

Kay nodded.

Diana's feelings had become numb from the stress of her long day in the trauma ward. Now, without warning, a stab of emotion welled up within her again. She found it difficult to keep from crying as well.

"They were magnificent," she whispered. "She stood with the Archmage as he wielded a powerful magic against the gate."

"Did they ..."

"They gave their lives to destroy it. The demons took the city, but no more of them will be coming to Kalara."

She sat there for a long time, holding Kay's hand as she wept. Finally, the guard raised her head and kissed her cheek.

"Thank you," she said.

Diana blushed. Then she slowly rose to her feet.

"I need to get you something to cover you," she said. "A blanket, and something soft against that bruised skin. Hang on a minute and I'll be right back."

She wasn't gone long. When she returned, she was carrying some bedding and a small folding cot. She found Kay grinning at her stupidly.

Diana set down the cot and began to cover her with a sheet. "Well, that didn't take long," she said with a smile.

"Nope!" Kay giggled. "Feeling much better, now!"

Diana laid a blanket over the sheet and tucked it carefully around her. Kay glanced at the cot.

"Are you going to bunk with me?" she asked.

"I am," Diana said firmly. "I've been working all night, and I'm too tired to walk home. And I want to keep an eye on you. You need to stay awake for a while, at least until I'm sure you're over that concussion. I thought we might chat a bit and keep each other company."

Kay laughed. "It'll be like a sleepover!"

Diana laughed too, despite herself. She lay down on the cot, drew up her blanket, and turned to her new friend.

"I had a bit of a run-in with a demon myself yesterday," she whispered. "How about I tell you my story, and you tell me yours?"

Chapter 3 - The Seeds of the Rebellion

In Search of Accomplices

Diana gently closed the dead soldier's eyes and drew the sheet over his face. He was the third patient she had lost since beginning her nights at the Cathedral hospital five days earlier.

She started to bow her head, to offer a prayer to the gods to guide his soul into the Light. Then she caught herself. Her eyes darted furtively around for the guards, or one of the supervisors that had taken to wandering the trauma ward.

She breathed a sigh of relief. No one was looking. No one had seen her lapse.

The supervisors had been a regular presence in the hospital since her arrival. Their job appeared to be to watch for behavior unacceptable to the new rulers of Carlissa, and to punish it swiftly and ruthlessly. Their first lesson had been that devotions to the former religion of Carlissa — to the Covenant, as taught by the Church of the Divine — were now acts of blasphemy, punishable by death.

They had made a show of "leniency" the first time it had happened. A nurse had been overheard saying the prayer for the dead over a lost patient, and they had taken her through the hospital and publicly beaten her in every ward. The beatings had been accompanied by warnings that the *next* such transgression would not be met with such tolerance. When they finished they had left her, broken and sobbing, on the floor of the main hall.

That was the *first* time. The second time, the guards, at a nod from one of the supervisors, had unsheathed their swords and killed the man offering the prayer.

There hadn't been a third infraction.

Diana gritted her teeth. They might forbid her from praying openly, but the privacy of her mind was still her own.

Go now into the embrace of the Divine, brave soldier, she thought fervently.

As if in response to her prayer, the Cathedral bells began to toll. One, two, three, four ... five strokes. It was five in the morning.

She picked up her clipboard and stood looking at it thoughtfully. Her eyes were becoming blurry with exhaustion, but she still had several charges to look after before the end of her shift. And she needed to work those around the meeting she'd planned in the supply room at half past the hour.

The first was a woman who had been beaten brutally during the massacre. Fits of terror had left her unable to sleep, and they'd been forced to sedate her every evening. Diana noted with relief that she finally seemed to be resting on her own. She gently checked the woman's pulse and breathing, made a note on her clipboard for her mother during her shift in the morning, and moved on.

Her next patient was a shopkeeper who had died in the night. He'd been gored during the battle by some kind of horned demon, and it was a miracle he'd lasted this long. She drew the sheet over his head, thought a silent prayer dedicating his soul to the Divine, made a notation on her clipboard, and moved on.

Her next two charges were more promising. The couple had suffered terrible burns, mostly on their legs, when a blaze was set around their block of homes. The Hellmen had come for them and their neighbors, and used the ring of flame to drive them into the open for capture. They'd risked the fire to escape the Taking and succeeded, hiding in a thicket until morning. They were recovering now, thanks to the salves that she had mixed for their treatment. They would have terrible scars for the rest of their lives, but they had escaped becoming slaves of the Hellmen.

The pair dozed lightly as they lay on their cots next to each other, hands outstretched so that their fingers touched. They woke as Diana approached, and smiled. They chatted warmly as she gently replaced their bandages, washing and applying a new coat of the balm to their burns. The ointment included an anesthetic, and she was glad to see the pain ease from their eyes as she treated them.

By the time she was done, urging them back to sleep and writing another note on her clipboard, she knew she was late for her meeting. Carefully, with as much nonchalance as she could manage, she made her way toward the corridor between wards. After a quick look around to check that she wasn't being watched, she ducked through the shadowed entrance and into a stairwell.

She held the banister as she descended the steps. There were no lanterns below, and the light dimmed quickly around her. Her heart began to race, but she didn't slow down. She'd known to expect this and was prepared for it.

The stairway turned sharply, went through an archway, and descended again. It didn't take long before she had entirely lost the already dim light from above. She continued on, stepping carefully and testing the steps as she went, her hand gripping the banister tightly. She'd been told to use it as a guide to the level of the basement supply rooms, and to follow it to her rendezvous.

She stopped when she reached the bottom of the stairs. She was completely enveloped in darkness.

"Hello?" she asked softly.

There was no reply. A shiver of unease crept up the nape of her neck. She felt suddenly exposed and vulnerable in the surrounding blackness.

The mysterious message had promised a meeting with conspirators against the Warlord's regime. She'd come eagerly — and now, she realized, with too little caution. If this were a trap ...

"You're late," a quiet voice said.

She turned, but she could see nothing in the pitch darkness. The words didn't seem to come from anywhere in particular, but from all around her.

He's good, she thought. She had sharp senses, and they had given her no hint of the man's presence. No scent, no sound, not even breathing.

"I know," she whispered. "I had to wait for a break in my rounds. It would have looked suspicious otherwise."

There was a long pause. She began to feel even more uncomfortable standing in the darkness. The silence around her was broken only by the sound of her own breathing, and the hammering of her heart in her ears.

"Sensible," the voice said at last. "But it's dangerous to keep a contact waiting. Dangerous for him, and dangerous for you. You need to work on your timing."

Diana smiled. The rebuke didn't unsettle her. It was mild compared to the ruthless criticism she was used to from her father.

"So you want to play rebel against the Dark?" the voice asked. It took on an amused, almost condescending tone. "Why should the resistance want your help? It needs fighters and spies, not spoiled noble girls acting out an adolescent rebellion."

Diana felt the heat rising in her face. She fought to control her anger, to keep her voice calm and reasoned. She didn't fully succeed.

"I watched good people die when the Warlord came," she whispered hotly. "And every day I tend others who were maimed in the massacre. I lost another a few minutes ago. You dare call me a spoiled girl for wanting to fight the monsters that did this?"

"You're a pampered ambassador's daughter," the voice said. It was openly mocking now. "You've read too many adventure stories that romanticize fighting the Dark. The reality will be nothing like that. You'll run home to your father's protection at the first sign of real danger."

Diana's hands balled into fists as she spun, angrily seeking the source of the taunting voice. She knew in that moment that if she'd found the man, she would have hit him.

"You know nothing about me," she said acidly. "Or what I'm prepared to do."

The voice chuckled. "And what is that?"

"Whatever it takes."

"Even kill?"

"Of course."

The flat coldness of her response seemed to silence him. Diana went on, practically spitting her words.

"I fought a demon in the city," she said. "It attacked the group I was with. It slaughtered them with magic and claws. *I* put a knife in its eye. When it was over, only two of us were left, and *it* was dead."

"Talk," the voice mocked.

"The only 'talk' here is from you," she retorted. "*I* have the scars to prove it. And if this is all you have to say, then you're wasting my time. Go away and *don't* contact me again."

She turned, groping for the handrail in the dark, stepping blindly to find the stairs.

To her surprise, her hand found not the banister, but another hand. The grip was strong and masculine, and it held hers firmly. She found herself suddenly aware of the man's presence — the sound of his breathing, the shift of his feet on the stone floor, the faint scent of cologne. She stopped, uncertain, and they stood together for a long moment.

"You have an angry fire in you, Lady Dal Meara," he said at last. "You will need to learn to control it better, and to be more careful, if you are to be of any use to us."

Diana relaxed. She should have known the taunting was a test. She felt suddenly foolish.

"What do you need me to do?" she asked.

"For now, keep your eyes and ears open," he replied. "And your wits and temper about you. Learn what you can about sentiments among the nobility, and your father's contacts."

"He won't confide in me," she said. Her voice was tight and bitter. "He's trying to protect me. Whatever he's doing to undermine Zomoran's regime, he won't let me help."

"There are other things you can do. Learn what you can, and keep your inquiries discreet. The Warlord has his own spies at court."

"How will I contact you?"

"Those details will be worked out in a series of meetings. You will belong to cell eleven. It will meet tonight. Bring any recruits you can, but only if you are *certain* that their hearts are fully with us."

She nodded as he gave her the address.

"I know who to bring," she said confidently. "What do we do when we get there?"

"It's a hall for music and dancing in the Upper City North," the voice explained. "The Warlord is lifting the curfew tonight, and has ordered revels to be held throughout Lannamon."

Diana made a disgusted noise.

"Yes, I've heard. He's going to a lot of trouble to try to buy our good will. After what he's done, I doubt much will come of it."

"Don't underestimate his plan. The people have been living in fear for their lives and stressed to the point of breaking. Like an abused child, many will try to convince themselves that their new ruler loves them, if he makes a show of it. And if his beatings are infrequent enough."

"The Carlissan people aren't children," Diana said tightly.

"Perhaps not. In any event we will take advantage of the opportunity. Many will venture out into the city for the festivities, and so shall we. The activity will give us cover to begin our plans."

"How? By going to a dance?"

"In your case, yes. Lord Kelson is sponsoring the party there. Can you convince your father to let you attend? Without arousing his suspicions?"

"He'll want a guard on me for certain," she said slowly. "But I can persuade him to choose one we can trust."

"Very good. The dance will begin at seven bells. Try to be on time, and blend in."

"And then?"

"When the time comes, we will contact you. Fare well now, Lady Diana. Good fortune to you — and to us all."

The hand released hers, and his presence was suddenly gone. There was no sound of steps walking away. She found herself alone again in the darkness.

Diana smiled as she made her way back up the stairs. Her father might not trust her to help, but she wouldn't let that stop her from making allies against the demons — and she had taken the first step.

Closure

Orion walked through the streets of the Upper City North. His mood, like the day, was overcast. The noontime sun hid in a gray haze that surrounded the valley of Lannamon.

After six days they had finally granted him leave. Dame E'lath had kept their course in session for nearly the entire time, allowing them to return to their dormitories each night only to bathe and to sleep. They had even taken their meals in class under her supervision.

He thought of the beautiful seminar room by the garden, and shuddered. When he had begun his first class as an instructor the week before, he'd thought it impossible to imagine a more perfect setting for learning. Now he couldn't think of a place he hated more in the entire world.

Dame E'lath's instruction had been harsh, demanding, and relentless. It had taken its toll, but it was finally over. The remaining students had stood for their qualifying exam that morning, and those who passed had received a full day off as a reward. As promised, she had taken her pick from those who failed. The rest had been reassigned to a less privileged position in the city's new order.

Orion had passed, and with distinction. He had despised every word of the Hellwoman's indoctrination, but he was still a first-rate scholar. He knew how to analyze and learn a system of philosophical thought, twisted and evil though it might be. And he knew that he would need to understand his enemies' ideas if he were going to fight them. It had been easy enough to grasp what was expected of him on the exam, and to provide it.

The experience had left him with an intense desire to bathe.

He'd done that on returning to his little apartment in the Lower City. Thankfully it had avoided the fires that had ravaged so many other buildings, and the running water from the aqueduct still worked. Afterward he'd cleaned up, disposing of the food that had spoiled during his long absence.

That had left him with a feeling of empty depression — and nothing to do.

He couldn't go home to his family. He had few friends outside the academy, and he found that the thought of returning there now repelled him. He wouldn't do it a minute sooner than his orders required.

There were supposed to be events in the city that evening, to celebrate the Warlord's new reign. The curfew had been extended for them from dusk until midnight.

He didn't feel like celebrating.

So he had taken to the streets. He hadn't thought where to go, and for a while he'd followed a meandering path through the Lower City.

Eventually, though, he found himself wandering east along the firth, and up into the first level of the northern terraces.

They had let him keep Jameson's sword. He still carried it belted at his side, along with an updated badge marking him as a soldier in the reserve. His new orders said that he was on assignment to the academy, as an instructor in training. It was a less than subtle reminder of the fate he would face if he balked at the expectations of his new job.

He thought of Diana as he walked. He hadn't seen or heard from her since they'd parted at her parents' house the day after the massacre. He'd been prepared for that, but he was still surprised that his resourceful young friend hadn't found a way to send word to him.

He had heard from her father, though. A letter had been waiting for him when he finally returned to his apartment and checked his mail. The ambassador's words had been concise, praising his courage and thanking him again for bringing his daughter home safely. They explained that a reward of a hundred gold sovereigns — a small fortune for a struggling academic — had been set aside for him to collect at a prestigious bank in the High City.

They had also made it clear that he did not expect to see the young scholar again. Orion, surprised and mortified, had understood the intended message.

It wasn't until he turned onto Tribute Street that he realized where his thoughts were taking him. Before long, he saw the sign of the Smiling Nymph ahead. It had escaped the devastation of the massacre, and to his surprise, the door was open. He went in.

The tavern looked eerily as he had left it a week earlier. A few groups of patrons sat scattered around the room. Most of them were talking quietly and drinking heavily. With a shock, he even saw Henry and the woman shopkeeper sitting at the same table where he had left them. They looked at him for a few seconds with haunted eyes, and then turned away.

A burly man with a noticeable resemblance to Jameson stood behind the bar. He watched Orion as he entered, eyes fixed openly on his hip.

"What can I get for you, stranger?" he asked.

Orion nodded as he came forward. He pulled out a stool and sat down.

"I don't drink much," he said slowly. "But I could really use one today. Whiskey, please. Neat."

The man took a bottle and glass from beneath the bar and began to pour.

"Nice sword you have there," he said nonchalantly.

Orion nodded.

"It belonged to the man who used to own this establishment. I was hoping to find someone who knew him. Family, perhaps."

The man looked at him carefully, and then slid the glass toward him. "You have," he said. "Name's Glen."

Orion took a sip. "Your brother?"

Glen nodded. "You have a good eye. What do I call you, stranger?"

"My name's Orion. Orion Deneri."

"Ah. That explains it. The instructor fellow from the academy. The one with the girl. I saw you making eye contact with Henry and Else when you came in."

Orion took a long, slow breath.

"Then you've heard about our escape attempt, the day of the massacre."

"I have."

Glen watched him silently. Orion took a slow pull from his glass.

"How did he die?" Glen asked at last.

Orion closed his eyes. He fought the tears that threatened as he recalled the events of that terrible day.

"A hero," he said at last.

Glen nodded. "Tell me."

Orion opened his eyes, and he told him. By the time he was done, he had lost the battle with his tears. He had never had time to mourn his companions from the Nymph, briefly though he had known them. He finally realized why his steps had led him back here — and why he had needed to come.

Glen reached out, and slowly, awkwardly, gripped Orion's shoulder.

"Thank you," he said thickly. "The demons piled the bodies of everyone killed in the massacre and burned them. If you hadn't come, we would never have known what happened to him. And to the others."

"It was the least I could do," Orion whispered.

"I know most of their families. I'll tell them."

Orion shook his head. "Most people would hate me for bringing news like this," he said cautiously.

Glen chuckled.

"Well, I'm not most people. And I knew my brother. He wasn't one to hide from a fight. Not if he thought he could help. What kind of fool would I be, to blame a man for the courage to stand at his side?"

Orion nodded gratefully. He reached down and began fumbling with the buckle of his sword belt.

Glen gripped his shoulder more tightly. "No," he said firmly.

"It was your brother's," Orion objected. "You should have it."

Glen shook his head. "I can't use it," he said.

"But —"

He released Orion's shoulder and tapped his badge.

"And even if I could, the city's been disarmed. I don't have a weapons license, and you do. And I don't want to get arrested."

Orion looked at him in astonishment. "I don't know what to say."

"Don't say anything. You used it to avenge my brother, by slaying the monster that killed him. You've earned it."

"Thank you, Glen. I'll do it — and him — honor. I promise."

Glen nodded. "That's all any man can ask."

Orion reached for his glass again, but Glen pulled it away. The bartender's gruff face cracked in a smile as he took another one, and a different bottle, from beneath the counter.

"Let me pour you some of the *good* stuff," he said.

The Good Stuff

Orion sat at the bar in the Smiling Nymph. He had nowhere else to go, and he found the little tavern comforting despite its painful memories. And the good stuff was *very* good. He and Glen said little, the bartender sensing that he needed some time alone with his thoughts.

The door opened. Orion glanced over his shoulder to see a young woman with short red hair walk into the tavern. A longsword was belted at her hip, and she wore a suit of black leather armor with a purple badge. He gave her an appreciative glance and turned back to his drink.

He heard boots walking across the floor, and the scrape of a stool being pulled out at his side. He turned to offer an awkward greeting as the woman sat down.

He found her looking right at him.

"I had a hunch I might find you here," she said.

Orion's eyes widened. *I've had a couple of drinks,* he thought, *but not enough to hallucinate about beautiful women approaching me in taverns ...*

He smiled tentatively. "Do we know each other?"

She shook her head. "Not yet."

She looked at his glass, and then at the bartender. "I'll have what he's having," she said.

Glen glanced at Orion. His gruff face was trying to suppress an uncharacteristic smile. He set out a glass for her and poured it, and she took a long swig. Then she put it down as a shudder of appreciation ran through her head and shoulders.

"Mmmm," she said. "What *was* that?"

Orion grinned. "That's the good stuff."

"Well, points for first impressions. You do know where to bring a girl. I'm going to have to remember this place."

Orion took another sip of his own drink. He suddenly felt as though he were going to need it.

"I'm Kay," she continued. "Clarissa Kay. Everyone just calls me Kay. You can too."

She extended a hand. He took it.

"Pleased to meet you, Kay. I'm Orion Deneri. The fellow behind the bar is Glen Rivers."

"Yes, I know. About you, anyway." She turned to the bartender. "Like your place, Mr. Rivers. Sorry about your ... brother?"

Glen nodded. "Yes. Thank you."

Orion let out a long breath. He'd finally made the connection.

"Diana sent you," he said.

Kay grinned. "She said you were bright. And after a couple of slugs of the good stuff, too. I like that."

Orion folded his arms and regarded her. Now that he understood why she was here, he was feeling a little less out of his depth.

"Are you messing with me?" he asked. "Or are you always such a flirt?"

Kay laughed.

"There it is. Just like she said."

"There what is?"

She shook her head. Her manner suddenly sobered.

"I'll tell you later. Right now I'm here with a message. Can we talk?" She glanced at Glen. "Privately?"

Orion nodded toward an empty table in the corner of the room. They carried their drinks to it and sat down.

"I assume you got her father's letter," Kay said.

Orion nodded, flushing suddenly with embarrassment.

"I think he got the wrong idea —" he began.

Kay burst out laughing. He glared at her, cheeks red.

"You seem to think it's funny."

"Very. I wouldn't take it personally, though. He'd have done the same with any man."

"Does Diana know?"

"Of course. I told her."

"I see. And you know, because ..."

"Her father told me. I'm the one who delivered the letter for him."

He shook his head. "I was right," he said. "You *are* messing with me."

She smiled. "Call it a weakness. It's how I compensate for being so damned serious most of the time."

"I don't suppose you'd consider being serious for a few minutes now?" he asked hopefully. "And telling me the story in order?"

Kay took another swallow of her drink. She looked at him thoughtfully.

"I was an officer in the city guard," she explained. "Badly hurt in the massacre. Diana saved my life in the hospital, and we've become friends."

"So now you're working for her father?"

"Yes. It was her idea, too. I was impressed with how she played him."

"How?"

"After what happened, he insisted on her having a bodyguard. All the time, everywhere she went. She protested, of course. Made quite a stink about not wanting some muscle-headed lout breathing down her neck. Kept mentioning someone named 'Kieran.'"

He nodded appreciatively. "Which made you the perfect compromise," he offered.

"Exactly. By the time I was released from the hospital, we were already thick as thieves. I have no family in the city, and Di asked if I could stay with them until I got on my feet."

"And her father agreed?"

"The ambassador checked my background. He liked what he found and made me an offer instead. Which is precisely what we wanted in the first place, of course."

Orion was intrigued. "What did he find?" he asked.

"My service record. I had two commendations for professional conduct under pressure. I was very proud of that. The last one got me my promotion to lieutenant."

He grinned mischievously. "That doesn't sound like the flirt I met a few minutes ago."

She looked at him levelly, brown eyes suddenly cold and hard. She patted the hilt of her sword. When she spoke, her voice was even, businesslike, and had a note of command to it.

"That's because you haven't seen me doing my job yet."

He smiled at her.

"That's true, I haven't. Something tells me you're good at it."

She returned his smile. There was a hint of abashed surprise in it.

"I am. And my record sealed the deal. Serious and reliable about my work. Loyal to Diana for saving my life. Better with a blade than his own bodyguard, as it turned out when he tested me. And a woman, so he didn't have to worry about my 'intentions' — perceived or otherwise."

"And no attachments, I assume."

She smirked at him. "None. Who wants to know?"

He chuckled. "There you go, flirting again. I thought you were going to be serious for a bit."

"If you want that, then stop giving me openings you could drive a caravan through."

"The clerks must have tried to conscript you back into the guard.

Did her father use his influence to release you to his service?"

"He *is* the Dorian ambassador," she said. "And the regime is trying to win his support. It was a small concession for them."

Orion looked at her thoughtfully. She was tall, almost as tall as he was. Her copper complexion was darker than he would have expected from someone with her distinctively red hair. Her black leather armor looked new, and it did little to hide the lines of a well-muscled physique.

"That explains the context," he said at last. "You said Diana had a message for me?"

Kay nodded. She reached across the table to take his hand, and turned his palm upward. She traced her finger along the scar that remained from the week before.

"She wants you to know that she hasn't forgotten her oath," she said. "And that she's very sorry about the letter. She didn't realize how her father would react. She's really angry with him right now. For several reasons, though this one's at the top of the list."

He shook his head. "I still don't get how he misunderstood. I mean, she's ... well ..."

"Seventeen," Kay said. "Yeah, I get it. It's hard to remember because she handles herself so well. But she *is* a lot younger than we are."

He watched her as she took another swallow of her drink. "How young aren't we?" he asked.

She chuckled. "There you go with that caravan again. I'll control myself, though. Twenty-four. You?"

"Twenty-three."

"About what she thought. She knew you'd be mortified by his letter, and she blames herself for it."

"Why?"

"Because she does have kind of a crush on you. Don't look like that, it's not romantic. It's more like the way a girl idolizes her big brother. She talked you up for days, and she thinks *that's* what gave her father the wrong idea."

He nodded slowly. "But you don't."

"No. I've known men like the ambassador. And I got a long talking to from him about his 'expectations' when he hired me as her bodyguard. I don't think it mattered if there was anything between you or not. You're just not part of his plan for her, and the letter was to let you know that. But he owed you a debt, and so he paid it. That's all it was to him."

"She's never really been allowed to have friends of her own, has she?"

"You mean, that she's chosen for herself?" She smiled. "No, I don't think so. We're a new experience for her."

Orion took another sip of his drink. He was quiet for a time.

"Well, the two of you seem to have worked out a way around it," he said at last. "And I'm glad she's got someone at her side she can trust. Please thank her for me for sending you. And thank you for coming. I'm sure I wasn't easy to find, and I enjoyed meeting you."

Kay quirked an eyebrow at him.

"Is that all you think this was about?" she asked.

"Why? Is there more?"

Kay reached for his hand and tapped his palm again. There was a faint look of exasperation on her face.

"Of course there's more," she said impatiently.

She looked furtively around the room. A few patrons had been watching them at first, but they'd eventually returned to their own business. Even Glen had gone back to wiping the bar and chatting with the other customers.

She leaned forward and gestured for him to do the same. Their heads were nearly touching when she finally spoke.

"A resistance is forming," she whispered. "Di's made contact with one of their agents. There's a meeting tonight to stand up our cell. It's being staged under cover of a dance in the Upper City North. She wants you to meet us there."

Orion's heart leaped. A week of Dame E'lath's indoctrination had left him feeling defeated and hopeless. Hot determination woke in him at the possibility of doing something — anything — to fight back.

The fierceness of it took him by surprise. He didn't hesitate before answering.

"When and where?"

She told him.

"I'll be there. I have leave until tomorrow afternoon, so it won't arouse suspicion."

Kay smiled. Orion suddenly found himself intensely aware that her lips were only inches from his. Her fingertips were still touching his palm.

"Good," she said. "I'm looking forward to it."

She leaned back slightly. He thought he sensed a hint of reluctance in her movements as she withdrew her hand from his.

"And after tonight?" he asked.

"We'll see. For now, at least, she thinks it's better if the two of you limit your meetings. I'll be your contact and go-between."

"You're in this too, then?"

She looked at him evenly. Her cheeks flushed, and he could see — and feel — the heat of anger in her face.

"Yes. I have my own score to settle with Zomoran and his demons."

They slowly drew back until they were resting comfortably in their seats.

"Sounds like I'll be seeing a lot of you, then," he said.

"Sounds like it," she agreed.

She lifted her glass. She frowned when she saw that it was empty.

"Damn. What time is it?"

"A little before three, I think."

Her face brightened.

"I have to head back soon," she said. "But I do have time for another drink first. Join me? We can talk some more. And this round's on me."

Orion watched her thoughtfully as she picked up their glasses and headed to the bar. Only a few hours ago he had been sobbing in his shower, feeling that he would never be able to wash the filth of the last week from his mind and soul. Now he felt a renewed sense of purpose. His oath wasn't hopeless, and he had friends — and allies — in keeping it.

The Defiance of the Light

The festivities were already in full swing by the time Diana and Kay arrived at the dance hall. Orion was waiting for them near the entrance.

Vendors, performers, and citizens in their finest were roaming the streets. Orion noticed that most of them were trying to project a feeling of merriment, and that some of the displays seemed forced. He nodded to himself in understanding. These were people desperate to find some cause for joy — or at least to fake it, for the span of a few hours' escape.

He waited until the women's carriage had driven off, and waved to them as they approached the door. Diana smiled radiantly in a tea-length dress of green chiffon, and he was relieved to see that she looked well. He found his widening eyes drawn irresistibly to Kay, though, as she walked at her side.

She was also wearing a tea-length dress. Hers was black, and the material wasn't as light as Diana's. In fact, he thought he could make out the firm outlines of something like leather underneath her bodice. Was that some kind of *armor*? Her skirt was attractively flared, and he suddenly found himself thinking that there was plenty of room to hide a weapon in its folds ...

They met as the bells began to stroke the seventh hour. He regained his composure in time to greet them, offering his most gallant bow. They responded with smiles and elaborate curtseys, and they went inside.

Most of the hour passed uneventfully. They chatted easily, catching up on the events of their lives over the last week. Light fare and refreshments were served, along with an announcement that dancing would begin at eight.

At seven thirty Diana was becoming impatient for her unknown contact to make his move. At seven forty-five she took a glass of punch from a servant and began to sip it.

Ah, finally, a voice said in her mind. *Are you and your recruits ready, Lady Diana?*

Diana started, but she composed herself quickly.

Yes, we're ready. You're my contact? I didn't expect telepathy.

If you knew what to expect then we wouldn't be very good spies, now would we?

I suppose not. What do you want us to do?

Share your drink with your companions. That will let them hear my voice as well. When the time comes, I will lead each of you to our meeting place. Do not be alarmed when I take your sight from you temporarily, so that you cannot see the others as they do the same.

But why —

All will be explained. For now, you must do this. If you would be one of us, then you must trust us.

Diana shared her drink with Orion and Kay. When the voice took her sight she let it guide her from the hall. It was thorough, telling her when to slow, when to turn, even when to nod and greet an unseen passerby.

She soon found herself walking blind and alone, giving herself wholly over to the mental voice. She realized as she did that this was the first test of her commitment, and one that not everyone would pass. The resistance needed agents it could trust, and it had to learn whether they could trust it as well.

She could tell little about the room she finally found herself in. She could hear and sense the presence of others around her, but not who or how many they were. When the cell leader spoke, she listened carefully.

You will be organized into groups with little or no knowledge of each other. This is so that if you are captured, you will only be able to compromise a handful of your fellows.

Each of you will receive a code name. Mine is 'White Shadow,' and it will serve as your first pass-phrase. You will be contacted periodically with new ones. You will use these to validate any orders or messages that you receive from us ...

Do not let the nightmare into which our world has been thrust break your spirit. The Church has defended the Covenant and its children for millennia, and it will not stop now. But it knows also that you cannot be expected to fight a hopeless battle against the Dark. I am here to give you the cause for hope that you will need to carry on.

Before his heroic death at the palace, King Danor ordered the Diaspora of Carlissa. This ancient order was given by rulers during the Grim Times, when a land was about to be overrun by the forces of the Dark. It instructed the Children to flee and establish a new realm, or to take their faith into hiding, working for the day when the invaders could eventually be defeated and repelled. They were always defeated and repelled — and they will be again.

Despite its losses, the forces of Light remain strong in our land. Thanks to the sacrifices of the royal family, the Archmage was able to prepare a last, devastating strike at the invading horde. He killed thousands of them, drove its demon lord from our world, and destroyed its hellgate. He taught us that our enemy is not all-powerful, and we must remember his lesson.

His heroism, and the battles at the palace and at the Silver Star, allowed the leaders of the Diaspora to escape the Massacre of Lannamon. The greatest of Carlissa's adventurers and warrior-priests now stand united against the Dark. They are the spearhead of the rebellion you are joining, led by our Captain-General, Augustus Darren. Do not despair that you fight alone in a battle against an unbeatable enemy. You have powerful brothers and sisters who will fight it with you.

The road ahead will be hard and dangerous. Believe and trust in yourselves, and in each other. You are the Defiance of the Light — and as long as your hearts remain true, then hope will never be lost in the land of Carlissa.

When Orion's sight returned, he found himself standing before the dance floor. The voice had walked him back from the meeting, just as it had walked him to it. And before it had left, it had given him his code-name: *Black Owl*.

He looked around. Kay and Diana stood at his side. The three exchanged glances and smiled.

"Well, that's done," Diana said.

They couldn't hear her, but they could read the words on her lips. The band was playing one of the more modern — and energetic — dance tunes popular in the Lower City. Little could be heard above the loud music and the delighted shouts of guests whirling on the floor.

"So what do we do now?" Orion yelled.

"Well, I know what I —" Kay began.

She was interrupted as a young man in a blue suit approached them. *A nobleman in his late teens*, Orion judged, with a quick look of appraisal.

"Lady Diana," he asked, with a formal bow. "What a delight to see you here! Would you do me the honor?"

Diana smiled like sunshine and gave him a full curtsey.

"I would love to, William!"

Before her companions could react she had given him her hand, and the pair were stepping onto the dance floor.

Kay and Orion watched her as they walked off. They started laughing.

"I knew this bodyguard job sounded too easy," she shouted.

"She's going to make you work for every penny of it," he agreed.

"Well, this is a problem. I can't guard her very well from all the way over here."

She looked at him, and their eyes met. Her lips curled into a smirk.

"This is the part where you ask me to dance," she added helpfully.

He extended his arm without a word. She took it, and together they followed Diana onto the floor.

Chapter 4 - The Muster of the Elves

Standoff

Lindas lifted the viewing tube to her eye. She swept the lens across the line of the firth.

Nianos turned to watch her. "What do you see?" he asked.

She scanned the water, slowly and methodically. The sky was overcast, and the air laced with a chill spray. She was silent for a long time.

"Another refugee ship," she said at last. "A small merchant ketch. Limping toward us as fast as it can, but it's torn to hell."

The elven scout paused, her glass fixed on a point out on the water.

"They're not letting it go," she added finally. "A flight of demons is moving to cut it off."

Nianos cursed. "How long until it reaches us?"

Lindas took a deep breath. "At least a quarter hour, I think."

"Let me see," he ordered.

She lowered the glass and handed it to him. He took it and sighted. Then he sighed.

"You're right. The mainmast's in splinters. They don't have sail left to reach us in time."

"They could," Lindas said cautiously. "If we called up a stronger wind."

Nianos lowered the glass. He shook his head slowly.

"You know that's against orders, Lin," he said.

"They're innocent humans," Lindas countered. A sudden note of anger and frustration broke through her composure. "And I saw at least one elf on board. One of our own people, Ni. If we do nothing, they're going to be taken, or slaughtered!"

Nianos turned to face her. His eyes were hard.

"Do you think I don't know that?" he asked sharply.

Lindas looked away. "Of course not. But Light! Half the refugee ships aren't making it across the firth. When I think of how many have already died ..."

Her voice trailed off, and she bowed her head. Nianos sighed.

"I don't like it either," he said gently. "But we have our orders. Take in and protect the refugees who make it across, but do nothing to provoke the demons. They've left our shores alone so far. We don't want to change that."

Lindas looked up as Nianos handed the glass back to her.

"I just feel so helpless," she said. "And so ashamed. That we're doing nothing —"

She stopped as a wind rose around them. Her long, black hair stirred, whipping around her face in the suddenly moving airs.

Nianos cursed again. "Is someone breaking the order and doing it, anyway?"

Lindas looked out over the firth. Her face was lit with sudden hope. The glass snapped up to her eye again.

"Yes," she said. She was grinning now. "Their remaining sails are at full billow!"

"It's Captain Rian," Nianos said. "She's standing on the pier, facing the water. Her arms are raised."

The pair watched as the ship raced toward the shore. The demons had seen it, too. One of them stopped, its wings beating steadily as it hovered above the waves. It raised a horn to its lips, and blew a loud note.

Nianos sucked in a breath. "We're in it now," he said.

A long minute passed. The ship continued its mad dash toward them. Its prow plunged and bobbed into the frothing current as it came. A loud cheer erupted from the soldiers lined along the shore. It was answered by distant cries from the deck of the ketch.

Then a shape dropped through the ceiling of clouds. A huge dragon fell toward the ship from above. Flame licked greedily from its mouth and nostrils as it plummeted like an arrow toward the water, its wings pressed tightly along the sides of its body.

The refugees had a few seconds to scream. Then the dragon's jaws opened, and a blinding gout of fire emerged from them. It raced ahead of the creature to stab into the ship like a jet of glowing white liquid.

The deck exploded as though a bomb had hit it. The keel snapped in two. Burning bodies flew from the sundered halves of the ketch as they slammed into the water like a pair of flaming meteors. In less than a minute, both had disappeared under the waves.

A quiet horror came over the elves as they watched from the shore. They saw the dragon unfurl its wings and turn its fall into a glide that skimmed the surface of the firth. Its teeth plucked a charred body from the water as it did, and swallowed it whole with a shake of its long, snake-like neck.

"No," Lindas whispered.

"Forget the dragon!" Nianos snapped. "We have company!"

Lindas looked. Another figure had emerged from the clouds above. This one was an enormous, man-shaped demon with wings of dark feathers. He wore an armor of black leather straps and carried a huge, glowing axe.

"Captain Rian!" Lindas screamed. "Look out!"

She drew her sword and sprinted across the beach. She was dimly aware of Nianos running at her side, crying out with her.

The captain shook her head. She had been staring at the dragon with an expression of numb horror. When she heard the soldiers' cries and saw them running, she looked up.

Her face went white. The demon's weapon was pointed directly at her heart. Crimson electricity played around the axe's blade, building for a strike.

The sorceress raised a hand to her mouth, and screamed.

Then a ray of blinding sunlight tore through the clouds. A figure appeared suddenly in the air before her: an elven woman in golden armor, astride a white pegasus. It seemed almost as if she had ridden the sunray itself down from the sky above.

There was a roar of wind and magic as the figure raised a hand.

The demon's lightning lanced toward them, and her mailed gauntlet seemed to pluck the bolt out of the very air itself. The electricity played around the metal for a few seconds, and then winked out.

The demon's wings beat steadily as he hovered before them. He regarded the newcomer for a long moment.

"You will not harm my people, monster," the woman in gold cried. "Withdraw from my land. If you do not, then I, Talina Starlight, *will* destroy you."

The demon chuckled loudly. When it spoke, its booming voice carried across the shore.

"Your threats amuse me, elf-queen," it said. "Since you have not yet had the honor, I will introduce myself. I am Incanus Thad, Captain of the Horde of Zomoran, the Black Magus. I have come with a message for you."

"State your message, then," the Queen responded. "And begone."

"You and your people live for now," Incanus Thad said. "At the sufferance of my master. He has ordered that your land and your people be spared the ravages of my horde. As long, of course, as you do not interfere with the Taking of Carlissa."

Talina gestured behind her to where Captain Rian stood. The sorceress had composed herself. A nimbus of glowing magic played around her hands as she stood, ready for battle. Lindas and Nianos had reached her and now stood at her side, weapons drawn. Other soldiers were racing across the beach to join them.

"You speak of a truce," the Queen said scornfully. "And yet, you attack my people."

Incanus Thad leveled his axe at the captain.

"This one reached out into the firth with her magic," he said. "She crossed the line. She interfered with our pursuit of a ship that sought, *unlawfully*, to leave our waters." The demon sneered. "She forced us to abandon capture and to destroy it instead. The blood of those spent lives is on her hands."

Talina shook her head. "My people are not responsible for your butchery," she said. "And we will not turn away refugees."

The dragon had completed its turn, and was gliding toward them. Two more had descended through the clouds to join it, along with several winged demons. They took position behind Incanus Thad, hovering or circling around him.

"You may take in those who near your shores," the giant demon said. "Within one mile. That is the line. If you cross it, you end the truce. If that happens, I will *personally* bring an army to raze your capital — and kill everyone in it."

Talina's eyes narrowed. "The Elven Citadel will not fall so easily," she said.

Incanus Thad laughed. "I am sure you will put up a gallant fight," he said. "But it will still fall."

The Queen was silent for a long time. "All right, demon," she said at last. "Your words have been heard. Now go."

Incanus Thad shook his head. He pointed his axe again toward Captain Rian.

"You will surrender her for punishment," he said. "You will do the same for any of your people who cross the line. That, too, is the price of the truce."

The captain's eyes widened, but Talina's face did not waver.

"The terms of your truce will not be honored retroactively," the Queen said.

Incanus Thad shook his head. He gestured to the demons and dragons that circled around him.

"You cannot keep us from taking her," he said. "You lack the power, and you know it."

"Perhaps," Talina replied. She gestured with her gauntleted hand. "And perhaps not."

There was another flash of white magic, and a dozen pegasus warriors materialized suddenly around her. Their wings beat slowly as they hovered, lances lowered and ready. Their bluesteel weapons and armor gleamed brightly in the shaft of sunlight that fell on them from above.

"I left orders not to provoke your forces," Talina said steadily. "My officer disobeyed them. *I* will punish her. You will leave her with me, and to *my* discipline."

There was another long silence. Then Incanus Thad grinned.

"Warlord Zomoran can be magnanimous," he said. "You will be allowed this infraction. Now that the terms of the truce have been given to you directly, you will *not* be allowed another."

The Horde Captain turned and flew away across the water. The demons and dragons followed him. They dwindled quickly to a set of specks in the distance and were soon lost to sight.

The Demon Advance

Lindas let out a long, slow breath. She suddenly realized that she'd been shaking.

Captain Rian fell to her knees and shuddered. Nianos kneeled at her side and laid a comforting hand on her shoulder.

Lindas looked up as Talina and the pegasus warriors turned from the retreating demons. She wasn't a rider herself, and she had always marveled at the way the winged steeds appeared to gallop on the very air itself. Their hooves seemed to touch ground that wasn't there as they floated or rode across the sky.

The group descended quickly to land in a circle around them. Talina dismounted and strode forward until she stood before the kneeling officer.

Captain Rian looked up. Her tear-stained eyes met the Queen's gaze.

"Thank you, Your Majesty," she said softly.

Talina watched her for a long moment. When she finally spoke, her voice was hard.

"Attention!" she barked.

Captain Rian and Nianos sprang to their feet. Lindas snapped into a disciplined military pose along with them. The soldiers and pegasus warriors who had gathered around the group did the same.

"You are relieved of your command," Talina said coldly. "Report to the stockade and surrender to the duty officer. You will remain there until I decide what to do with you. Dismissed."

Captain Rian swallowed. "Yes, my Queen," she said. She saluted stiffly and strode quickly away.

Talina turned to the other soldiers. "Who is second in command?" she asked.

"I am, Your Majesty," Nianos replied. "Lieutenant Nianos Tarvinien."

"I've come to see the camp," Talina said. "And to speak to the refugees. I need intelligence on what's going on in Carlissa."

Nianos turned to Lindas. "This is Second Lieutenant Lindas Ciela," he said. "She's been in charge of organizing the camps. She'll be your best guide to finding the information you seek."

Talina nodded. "Collect your company, acting captain," she said. "And give them my orders. You will aid any ships that come within fifteen hundred yards of shore. *No* help is to go beyond that, or to violate the demons' one mile line. Not by any means, and not under any circumstances. And explain to them that when I give an order, *I expect it to be carried out.*" The Queen arched an eyebrow. "Clear?"

Nianos nodded. His eyes were wide. "Clear, Your Majesty," he said.

"Good," Talina said. "Commander Ailos, you and your pegasus warriors will return to your patrols. Lieutenant Ciela, you're with me. The rest of you are dismissed."

The others withdrew to carry out the Queen's commands. Talina turned to Lindas, who gestured with one hand.

"The camps are this way, Your Majesty," the lieutenant said.

She turned and set off at a brisk pace. Talina fell in at her side.

"May I ask what kind of intelligence you're looking for, my Queen?" Lindas asked. "That might aid me in selecting individuals for you to interview."

"You've talked to many of the refugees, then?" Talina asked.

Lindas nodded. "And heard their stories. I've been trying to compile a report on what I've learned so far."

"Good work," Talina said. "When we're done, complete a draft and send it to me immediately. With daily updates."

Lindas gulped, thinking of all the tasks that she was already behind on. "Yes, Your Majesty," she said neutrally.

"I need to know about the movement of the Horde's forces in Carlissa," Talina continued. She paused. "And anything you may have on what happened in Lannamon during the attack."

"I can brief you on what I've gleaned about the tactical picture," Lindas said. "If you want to know what happened in Lannamon the day the demons came, though, that'll be more of a challenge. Only a few made it out of the city alive."

Talina sighed. "I was afraid of that," she said.

"There *is* one person you could talk to," Lindas continued thoughtfully. "She was in pretty bad shape when we picked her up yesterday, but she's recovering. I think she may have actually been there when the hellgate opened."

Talina nodded. "Take me to her, then. Now, tell me. What have you learned from the refugees about the Horde's movements?"

"It's a lightning strike," Lindas said. "Their strategy seems to be to penetrate into Carlissa as quickly and deeply as possible."

"How?" Talina asked. "What are they doing? Specifically?"

"From what I've been told, they'll enter an area, threaten and disarm the people, cause some damage, kill any defenders, and move on. They aren't doing anything to try to occupy, or to consolidate their position in, the lands they take. At least, not yet."

Talina smiled grimly. There was a look of understanding on her face.

"They want to engage military targets," she said. "They're trying to flush out and destroy any opposition. To kill anyone willing to fight back."

"That was my assessment," Lindas agreed. "They don't seem to care about the general population, or consider them a threat."

Talina shook her head. "*That's* a mistake."

Lindas smiled. "Yes, the Carlissans *do* seem to be rather attached to their weapons, don't they? And they have quite a tradition of maintaining a civilian militia."

Talina nodded. "It goes back to the Codex War," she said. "When Aldran Killraven led them in an uprising against the Dargon dynasty, and their corrupt allies in the Church."

They strode through an opening in the trees and into a wide glade. An enormous camp of hastily erected tents spread across it. Hundreds of them dotted the grass. Humans and elves labored to set up more.

The Queen glanced at Lindas. "The Horde will send a second wave," she continued. "Eventually. That won't be battle demons and dragons, though. It'll be Hellman clerks and thugs. To establish and enforce a bureaucracy." She sighed. "That's the ancient pattern of conquest by the Dark."

She paused. "It won't happen right away, though," she added thoughtfully. "They've got to have their hands full with a city as large as Lannamon. That should give the people at the leading edge of the advance some time to prepare. What are they doing with it?"

"Their forces are withdrawing toward central Carlissa," Lindas said. "To regroup and make a stand. The rest are hiding weapons and organizing. To be ready to rise up at the demons' rear."

They stopped before a small, canvas tent. A woman in a plain cotton dress sat in front of it. A bluesteel amulet hung on a chain from her neck, and there were burn scars on her left hand. Her dark brown hair was disheveled, and she stared forward with haunted eyes.

"Hello, Helena," Lindas said gently. "How are you? Have you had something to eat?"

Helena looked up slowly. "Yes," she said. Her voice was flat, without emotion.

Lindas nodded at her hand. "It looks like one of our healers treated your burns. Are they feeling better?"

"Yes," Helena said again. A tiny crease appeared in the lines at the corners of her eyes. It was as though part of her wanted to smile, but had forgotten how.

Her haunted gaze drifted to the Queen. Her expression didn't change.

"Helena, this is Queen Talina," Lindas said. "I know this must be difficult, but we hoped you could tell her what you told me yesterday? And any more, perhaps, of what you saw in the city? The day it was taken?"

Helena continued to look at the Queen. It was as though she were looking through her, at something a thousand miles away. Finally, she nodded.

"My name is Helena Dylan," she said numbly. "I'm a craftmage. I was in the central marketplace, shopping for artifacts. When it happened."

"When what happened?" Talina asked.

"An eruption of magic," Helena said. "In the amphitheater, right next to the jeweler's cart. Where I was haggling for this." She gestured to the amulet that hung from her neck."

"Do you know where it came from?" Talina asked. "The magic?"

"No. It seemed to come out of nowhere. A violet haze in the air that formed into a dome. I could see the demons' homeworld through it. A blasted, volcanic landscape."

She shuddered, and her eyes fell. Talina kneeled at her side. She pulled off one of her gauntlets and gently touched the woman's injured hand.

"Is that how you were burned?" she asked. "Were you holding that amulet when the gate formed?"

Helena nodded. "I ran when the demons started to come through it. I didn't stop until I'd made it out of the city. It was hours before I even noticed the burns, or the pain."

"How did you escape?" Talina asked.

Helena looked up. A hint of guilt played across her face.

"I'm not proud of that," she said. "I stole a horse in the Upper City North. I rode it like mad until I reached the east gate. I kept going through the towns and fields north of the firth. I don't know how long. When the horse collapsed, I kept running until I passed out."

"And then?" Lindas asked. She tried to keep her voice gentle.

Helena shrugged. "Eventually I reached the hills. I tried to make my way through them, and into the mountains."

Talina's eyes arched. "That whole area is a wildland," she said.

Helena looked at her quizzically. "A what?"

"A wildland," Talina repeated. "Not every part of the world was brought under the Taming. There are patches of wildland all across the continent. Areas that remain as untamed as they were thousands of years ago."

Helena shook her head. "I wouldn't know about that," she said. "I was raised a Homelander. I had a very provincial upbringing."

"I understand the way of the Homeland," Talina said. "My people lived by it for thousands of years. It was only the discovery of the Codex, two centuries ago, that began to change that."

"I was taught so little about the rest of the world," Helena said. She chuckled flatly. "I'd never even been outside the city before this."

"It's not uncommon for wildlands to lie between the realms of the Children," Talina explained. "Often they'll form the borders between them. Like those hills. Carlissa holds the north shore of the firth up to them, and everything east of them is part of Elde. The hills themselves, though ... "

The Queen's voice trailed off. She looked at Lindas.

"We found her wandering in the forest to the north," the lieutenant explained. "She was hurt, exhausted, and in shock, and her clothes were in tatters. But she'd crossed the hills. Alone."

Talina looked at the craftmage with new respect. Helena returned her gaze numbly.

"A 'wildland,'" she said, with another mute chuckle. "That explains a lot. The things I saw — and fought — in there ... I'll never forget."

"Did you see anything else as you fled the city?" Talina asked. "Anything that might help us?"

Helena shook her head. "I don't think so. I didn't pay much attention to what was going on, especially after I bolted from the Academy. I was in too much of a panic. Too busy riding, trying to get away ... "

Talina's brow furrowed as the craftmage's voice trailed off. "Why did you run from the Academy?" she asked. "Was there something there that frightened you?"

Helena nodded. "I'd heard the Horde Captain announce the invasion in his name," she said. "I realized that he'd go there. For revenge. That I needed to be far away before he came to take it."

"Who?" Talina asked. "Whose name?"

"Zomoran," Helena whispered.

The Queen's eyes widened. "Incanus Thad announced the invasion in Zomoran's name?" she demanded. "*Before* the demon lord had been banished?"

Lindas turned to look at her in astonishment. She'd heard a tremble in Talina's voice.

Helena nodded. "That was him, yes. A great demon with black wings and an axe. He was the first to come through the gate. When he did, he said he was Captain of the Horde of Zomoran, the Black Magus."

The Queen stood. "Thank you," she said absently. "This conversation has been very helpful. Get some rest now. My people will look after you."

Talina turned abruptly, and strode quickly away. Lindas saw that she was making her way out of the camp. She sprinted after her.

"Your Majesty!" she called. "What is it? What's wrong?"

"This is bad," the Queen said. "Very bad. Worse than I'd imagined!"

"Why?" Lindas asked. "What does it mean?"

"It means it's a trap."

Talina turned to face her. They were alone for the moment. No one was near enough to hear their words.

"I had assumed that the demons were controlling Zomoran," Talina said. "That he was their dupe, their puppet. That they were just using his name, once the Archmage had driven their demon lord back through their gate and destroyed it."

"Why would they do that?" Lindas asked.

"To pretend the Horde was led by one of our own people. A Kalaran. So we'd be more likely to make terms with it, and not fight to the death."

"But he's not?" Lindas asked tentatively. "Under their control?"

The Queen shook her head.

"This demon lord, Borr ... its name is known. From ancient texts dating back to the time of the Great War. Texts that only a few of us have ever seen."

"What do we know about it?" Lindas asked. Her voice was a whisper.

"It is one of three who joined to open the first hellgate," Talina explained. "It is powerful, cunning, and incredibly arrogant. And it would *never* have allowed the captain of its horde to use Zomoran's name. Not unless the magus had some leverage over it. Leverage that he could continue to wield in the demon lord's absence."

"All right," Lindas said. "I understand that. But why is that so much worse?"

"Because if Emil Zomoran is commanding this invasion, then it's being directed by his knowledge," she explained. "He *knows* Carlissa, and its culture. He *knows* that its soldiers would fall back from a lightning strike, and regroup. He *knows* that the people would organize behind the demons' advance. That they'd attack it from behind when the soldiers make their stand."

She took a deep breath.

"If he's doing it anyway, then it *has* to be a trap," she concluded. "I don't know how, or what kind. I don't know if we can warn the

Carlissans in time, but I have to try. Before it's too late. If it isn't already."

She raised a hand. There was a flash of light, and her white pegasus appeared suddenly in the air above them. A rush of magic surrounded her as she floated upward, and sprang onto the mount's back. She wheeled it around to the north, and was quickly lost to sight.

Winged Storm

General Barnes looked out over the battle. His lips were drawn into a thin, white line.

Captain Sand came to stand at his side. "What do you think?" he asked tentatively.

The general shook his head. "I think we're fucked," he replied tightly.

They stood at the top of the tower, in a fortress outside the city of Deal. It had been the Carlissan army's headquarters and command post for its stand against the invading horde.

Deal lay at the head of a shallow valley, near the center of the Kingdom of Carlissa. Thousands of soldiers fought on the plains below, or on the slopes of the hills to either side. A steady hail of arrows and catapult stones rained down on the enemy forces that advanced on them.

"We're badly outmatched," the captain agreed. "And I don't see any way to retreat from this."

Barnes shook his head. "Not since that brigade of Hellmen came up through the caverns behind us."

Sand chuckled mirthlessly. "Subterranea. Isn't that supposed to be a legend? Are we fighting myths, now?"

Barnes turned to him. "You realize that's an army of demons out there, don't you?"

The captain looked sheepish. "Yeah. Sorry. This is all hard to wrap my head around."

The general waved a hand in dismissal. "You and me both. Anything new from the scouts?"

"Nothing we weren't expecting. They confirm that we're

surrounded. Both our forces, and that militia army that formed up behind the demons' advance. We're in a lull for now, but it won't last long."

"The enemy commander's still positioning his forces," Barnes agreed. "He's in no hurry. He knows he has us."

He sighed. "It's obvious now that the lightning war was a trap," he went on. "They anticipated our response, and prepared for it."

"How?" Sand asked. There was a note of helpless frustration in his voice.

The general pointed out across the valley. "They set several contingencies in place. See those winged demons and dragons, moving in on the militia's rear? They were patrolling the firth to prevent refugees from reaching Elde. A feint. They were on a timetable to fly here, right when they'd be needed."

"The enemy never cared about stopping those refugees," Sand said. "That was just a show."

"Right. Bringing those Hellman and trolls up behind us through the underground realms was another move we weren't expecting. So was making pacts with the wildlands throughout northern Carlissa."

"We haven't had trouble with the lizard men in decades," the captain agreed. "Nor the harpies, nor the lycans. Now there's a force of each flanking us."

"All this couldn't have happened in just a week," the general said thoughtfully. "It had to have been planned out in advance. Long before the hellgate opened. We're in the endgame of a campaign we didn't even know we were fighting."

"So what do we do?" Sand asked. "Do we surrender?"

General Barnes shook his head. "The enemy isn't offering to take prisoners."

The captain blanched.

"They've got us trapped," the general continued. "Without hope of rescue or escape. They probably think it'll be less trouble to just kill us."

A horn rang out on the battlement. Distant notes sounded throughout the valley in response.

"This is it," General Barnes said. "They're starting their strike."

"Archers!" Sand cried, pointing. "Incoming! Prepare to volley on my order!"

The general looked out. An enormous wedge of flying demons and dragons was coming straight for them. The mass of red and black shapes nearly blotted out the sky as it approached. His eyes widened.

"They've committed half their air force," he said. "They mean to take out our command post in one, brutal stroke." He shook his head. "Well, at least it'll be quick."

A tense minute passed as they waited for the enemy to reach them. Captain Sand raised his hand.

"Prepare to fire on my mark!" he cried. "Wait for it … and … loose!"

A rain of arrows flew from the battlement. Bluesteel points gleamed in the sunlight as they sped toward the infernal forces.

A shimmering barrier of red and blue flame appeared before them. Dragon breath and demonic magic struck the fusillade in mid-air. Flaming shafts fell from the sky and into the valley below. The enemy continued to close, its ranks unscathed.

The captain cursed. "You said we were fucked," he said. "Looks like you were right."

General Barnes drew his sword and raised his shield. "All hands, brace!" he cried.

And then there was light.

It burst like a shower of fireworks over the battle in the valley. A thousand points of light, shining with a radiance that rivaled the sun. And in the center of each light, weapons glowing with elven magic, a mounted pegasus warrior appeared, dropping like a falling star onto the demonic force.

The monsters never saw them coming.

Spears, arrows, and magic rained down from above. In the distance, General Barnes saw the same thing happen to the fliers closing on the militia. Hundreds of them fell, pierced, blasted, or disintegrated by the sudden onslaught.

A deafening cheer rose over the valley. It drowned out the screams of panic from the stunned and dying monsters. The assault, which a minute earlier had looked as though it would be a death stroke, was turning into a rout.

General Barnes lowered his shield and stared. "What the hell," he said.

"Greetings," a voice said behind him.

He turned to see the image of an elven warrior's face. It hovered in the air before them, on the platform at the top of the tower. Wind seemed to whip the elf's black hair around him, as though he were standing in a gale.

"I am Prince Nimrod Acheron," he said. "Son of Tarnas Acheron, the Peregrine King of Mount Cassandra. The pegasus warriors have come to defy the Horde of Zomoran. We stand with the soldiers of Carlissa!"

Comfort

Captain Rian lay in her cell with her face to the floor. Nothing meant anything to her any longer. She had failed her queen.

She heard soft footsteps outside her door. Were the guards bringing her another meal?

"Leave me alone," she mumbled.

A key turned in the lock, and the door's hinges creaked as it swung open. She heard steps, and sensed a figure at her side.

"Please go away," she said. "I don't want anything to eat."

"Do you think that's wise?" a voice said. Its timbre was strong and confident, but its tone was gentle. "It wouldn't do to be fainting from hunger when your liege calls you back into service, you know."

The captain twisted and looked up, and her eyes went wide. Talina was kneeling at her side.

She tried to rise, but the Queen put a firm hand on her shoulder. "At ease," she said. "Valira."

Valira struggled to keep her tears from flowing again. She held her breath, not daring to move.

"I am ready to accept my punishment, My Queen," she said softly. Somehow, she kept the tremble in her soul out of her body, and her voice. "For failing you."

Talina sighed. She sat on the ground next to her. She moved her hand from the captain's shoulder to touch her cheek.

"Your punishment is over," she said gently. "And it was too harsh. I regret it terribly, but it had to be done. The others needed to see an example made, or it might have happened again."

"I disobeyed your orders," Valira said.

"And could have started a war," Talina confirmed. "That would have destroyed the Elven Citadel."

"I'm not fit to serve you," Valira whispered.

Talina shook her head firmly.

"One of my best officers acted out of compassion," she said. "How could I believe that would make her unfit to serve me? Would that not make *me* unworthy of her loyalty?"

Valira met the Queen's gaze. She felt the tears, and the trembling, threaten to break through her resolve.

"Do you think I don't know what was in your heart?" Talina went on quietly. "When you tried to save those people? That I haven't felt the same, since this terrible invasion began?"

Valira's resolve shattered like a dropped vase. To her astonishment, the Queen took her in her arms and held her as she cried. When her tears had finally stopped, they sat together on the floor.

"I should have come to you sooner," Talina said. "I meant to, that first day, but something came up. I needed to act swiftly."

"What happened?" Valira asked. She was relieved to hear that her voice had returned to normal.

"I received intelligence from the refugees," Talina explained. "It convinced me that the Carlissans were planning a counterstrike — and that they were being set up. And I was right. A few hours after our standoff with the Horde Captain, he and his entire force of demons and dragons flew away to the south."

"What did you do?"

"I ... had Commander Ailos follow them."

Valira's eyes arched, and she smiled wryly. "And you say *I* nearly started a war?"

"Ailos is a mage," Talina explained. "And one of the few who can cast a strong cloak. He also volunteered. He understood that if he were caught, I would have to disavow and surrender him. To preserve the truce."

"You wouldn't surrender me," Valira said softly.

Talina shrugged. "I gambled that I could save you," she said. "But none of that matters, because the whole thing was a farce. Zomoran was only pretending to care about catching refugees. That was a ruse to park half his air force here. To mislead the Carlissans into thinking they'd be elsewhere when they were ready to make their move."

Valira's eyes went wide. "Oh, no," she breathed. "Then they were all killed?"

Talina shook her head slowly. Her eyes were lit with anger, but strangely, she was smiling as well.

"That hotheaded husband of mine," she said, through gritted teeth. "The arrogant, infuriating, noble madman that he is, took *all* of Mount Cassandra's pegasus warriors into the fight." She chuckled. "He must have been jealous of the bloody nose Lenard gave them in Lannamon, and wanted to even the score."

"Did he?"

"Oh, yes. He saved the Carlissans from being wiped out, but the battle ended in a stalemate. For now, at least, Zomoran's invasion has stalled in the center of the kingdom."

Talina rose to her feet. She held out her hand.

"Are you ready to resume your duties?" she asked.

Valira took her hand and stood up slowly.

"I am," she said. "I'll check in with my company now."

Talina shook her head. "No," she said. "I want to reassign you."

Valira swallowed, and her heart sank. She nodded.

"Of course," she said. "I understand if you don't trust me to return to my command."

Talina frowned. "No, that's not it," she said.

Valira held herself at attention. She said nothing, waiting for the Queen to continue.

"I rule the largest elven realm in the world," Talina explained. "And sometimes, that requires making hard choices. Hard decisions. *Very* hard. With a demon horde right on our border, that will only get worse."

"That strength is what makes you our Queen," Valira said. "It's why I ... why your people would give their lives for you."

"That hardness takes a toll," Talina warned. "On one's soul."

She looked suddenly into the captain's eyes.

"Do you know why I was so furious with you when you tried to save that ship?" she asked.

Valira shook her head.

"It's because I was jealous. So *very* jealous. Of your courage. To risk so much, out of compassion. To do what's right, and *damn* the consequences. As a queen, responsible for the lives of my people, that's a compassion I can't always afford. But I mustn't let myself lose it, either. Or I'll become a monster."

She took a deep breath.

"My aide-de-camp is overdue for a new assignment," she continued. "So I have an opening. For someone with the courage, and the heart, to help me temper the ruthlessness with which I sometimes have to rule."

She arched an eyebrow. "Would you like the job, *Major* Rian?" she asked.

Valira straightened. She lifted her head high as she met the Queen's gaze.

"I am at your service, My Queen," she said. "Always."

Talina smiled. "Good. Now let's get some food in you, and then you into a warm bed. I'll want you rested and ready when you report for duty tomorrow morning."

Chapter 5 - The Headmaster's Last Student

Awakening

Lenard Killraven opened his eyes.

He stared upward for a long time, familiarizing himself once again with the sense of sight. He saw a white plaster ceiling, crisscrossed by beams of rich mahogany. A splash of sunlight streaked in from a skylight in one corner of the room.

He heard sounds, and marveled at the sense of hearing. Birds were chirping pleasantly outside, and trees rustled in a gentle wind.

He felt a soft blanket drawn up over his chest, and rediscovered the sense of touch. There was a slight chill in the air, but he was warm and comfortable.

His sense of smell was next. He thought he could detect the scent of honeysuckle on the cool breeze, and the hint of a fire.

He looked around. He knew where he was. It was his room, in his hidden home, in his hidden valley. He was at Blackwing Lodge.

He slowly pushed away the covers of his bed, and tried to swing his legs onto the floor. He rediscovered another pair of sensations: weakness and pain. He knew these, didn't he? Wasn't he old? Yes, he was, but had he ever felt them like this?

He carefully got to his feet. He looked up, saw an open door, and remembered. The opening led down a short set of steps to his laboratory. He couldn't see into the room, but he could hear sounds of movement coming from it: footsteps, pages being turned, a woman's voice muttering softly …

He walked shakily to the door. His legs were wobbly and he could barely stand, but he managed to grip the rail and make his way down the stairs.

He was near the bottom when he began to feel dizzy. The world spun, and his head drooped. He found himself suddenly looking at the floor …

But he didn't fall. He heard a suppressed curse, and a rush of steps. Then he felt a shoulder under his arm, supporting him.

"Grandfather," a voice said. It sounded both exasperated and relieved at the same time.

Slim, strong arms lifted his frail body and carried him into the room. He felt himself being set down on a couch. A moment later a figure sat on the edge of it next to him, and took his hand.

"Grandfather," the voice repeated. "You're awake!"

He opened his eyes and saw his granddaughter's face.

"Randia," he breathed. "You're alive!"

Tears sprang suddenly into Randia's eyes.

"Of course I'm alive," she laughed. "I'm not the one who just woke from a week on the edge of death!"

He looked at her. The world was still spinning, but it seemed to be slowing now that he could focus on her.

"Is that how long?" he asked. "I … lost my way. Lost track of time. Almost didn't make it back."

She kissed his cheek.

"And almost broke your neck on the stairs when you did," she said. "Didn't it occur to you to try calling for help?"

He smiled at her. "No," he said simply.

"Well, next time, do. Now, how are you feeling? Can I get you anything?"

He lay for a while, looking into her eyes. He took deep breaths, waiting for his dizziness to clear. As it did, his memory started to return.

"The battle," he said finally.

"What happened, Grandfather?" she asked. "After you destroyed the gate? After she … died?"

Lenard's eyebrows rose. "You know about that?"

She nodded.

"When you cast the spell that linked her to my magic, we kind of … merged. She could hear my thoughts, and I could see through her eyes. Even from here. It was like … when Windheart died."

Lenard nodded slowly. "Of course. I should have known. Your grandfather's magic."

"You mean Grandfather Acheron."

"Yes. The Peregrine King. You've inherited his power, or at least some of it. As your mother did, and your uncle Nimrod. And your brother Aron."

"Is that what gave me the strength to help you destroy the gate?"

He looked at her thoughtfully.

"Perhaps, in part," he said at last. He reached up and gently touched her face. "Your magic is stronger than you realize, Randia."

For a time they sat together in silence.

"That *was* you, then, wasn't it?" he asked at last. "When she convinced me to draw on your power?"

She nodded.

"I could see that you needed me. She knew what I thought and felt, and she echoed it."

"And after? When the power had burned out her body?"

She smiled. "We saved the world, you and I," she quoted.

He shook his head. "She seemed so real in that moment. As though she really *were* you."

"She was," Randia said quietly. "Her last words were from both of us."

"I felt … as though I had killed you."

"You nearly did. Don't look horrified, Grandfather. We both know it was necessary. And it was the right thing to do."

"What happened to you? After we arrived here?"

"I laid you down on the couch. Then I watched as the battle unfolded."

"And when I drew on your power …"

"Pain, like I've never known. It felt like my body and soul had caught fire. When you finally severed the link, I lost consciousness."

"How long?"

"A little over a day, I think. We were both in pretty bad shape when I woke. You were barely breathing, and I was so weak … I could hardly move."

He patted her hand. "You seem to have recovered, though."

She smiled awkwardly.

"Blackwing Lodge is well stocked with curatives. It's impressive what chugging regenera can do for a ravaged body."

He looked at her carefully. "And for a ravaged spirit?"

She paused.

"That will take stronger medicine," she said at last.

She stood up slowly. Her eyes made clear that it was time to change the subject.

"Are you well enough to eat something? I was able to get you to swallow broth and juice while you were unconscious. And some of that nutritional powder of yours, mixed with water and regenera. It kept you alive, but just barely. You're not going to recover unless you start taking food again."

Lenard smiled. "I feel like I could eat a horse," he said.

"Sorry, we don't have one of those handy. But we do have some stew that I made last night. That ought to get you started. Let me help you sit at your desk, and I'll bring you some."

A New Name

Lenard stepped out the front door of Blackwing Lodge. A week of rest — and of Randia's cooking, which was still as good as he remembered — had done wonders for his condition. His wiry frame had never been muscular, especially in his later years, and his body had wasted badly during his long unconsciousness. Now he was putting on weight again, and feeling much stronger. Soon he would be up to facing the challenges he knew were ahead of him …

Don't delude yourself, old man. That casting nearly killed you. And your granddaughter. She's young, though, and she'll recover. A shadow passed over his face. *Or at least, her body will.*

He sighed. He had pushed himself past limits that no mortal should have been able to survive. Was he too old now to ever regain his full strength? He didn't know.

And he had no time to think about it. There was too much to do.

The sun was shining brightly into the small cleft between ridges of the Nurian Mountains that was his "Hidden Valley." The trees around the lodge were flowering in full color, and he could hear the buzzing of bees and the chirping of birds. A gentle breeze touched his face, along with the warmth of the mid-morning sun.

He saw that Randia was already up. She stood in the clearing next to the front path, and Flamebane was in her hand. She was practicing a series of fencing moves: blocks, thrusts, dodges, and pirouettes. A blanket had been set out on the grass nearby.

She was concentrating so intently that she didn't see or hear him when he came out. He watched her for a long time until she finally noticed him.

"Good morning, Grandfather," she said. She continued her practicing. "How are you feeling today?"

He walked over to stand next to the blanket. A skin of water, a pen, and a sketchbook were lying on top of it. The book was open, and he saw that the page was filled with notes: names, fragments of hand-drawn maps, arrows indicating the strategic movement of forces …

"Your basic technique is fairly good," he said finally.

She stopped herself at the point of a lunge and looked up at him.

"Aron tutored me," she said, holding her pose. "For my part in that play a couple of years ago. There was a fencing scene, and I needed my moves to look authentic."

"Yes, I remember. They do *look* good, and you have excellent control."

She released the pose and stood up. She met his eyes.

"But they just *look* good," she said. "All I really know is how to put on a show. They won't help me much in a real battle."

He shook his head. "No, they won't. There are half a dozen counters for the forms you're practicing. An experienced fighter would have already used them to kill you."

She nodded. Her expression was thoughtful.

She's changed so much, he found himself thinking. *So carefree before. And so serious, now. So focused, so intent …*

He looked down at the book. "I see you're planning a campaign."

She sheathed her sword and walked to his side.

"Just some thoughts," she said. "Ideas for alliances, and where to try to build resistance cells."

"Isn't that premature?"

"How can it be premature? Zomoran is going to take Carlissa. We need to prevent him from consolidating his hold on it, and from spreading his power further."

He shook his head.

"I meant, premature for you. Augustus is leading the Diaspora. And there is no better man left alive than he to take on that task."

She took a deep breath.

"I know. But I can't just sit here and do nothing. I need to act."

"We will. But for that, we need to prepare. For now, we've done all that we can. We need to trust others to take up the sword we've left them — until we're ready to rejoin the fight."

She turned away and shook her head. "I don't know if I can do that," she said.

"You need to have patience, Randia."

She whirled to face him. "Patience for what?" she demanded.

"To *think* before we leap," he said sternly. "The world believes we are dead. Even Zomoran and his demons believe it. That gives us an unprecedented opportunity."

"To do what?"

"To watch and to plan. To observe, and to learn our enemy's weaknesses. To prepare our moves against him — so that when we make them, they truly count."

She took a deep breath, and he could see her biting back her anger. Finally, reluctantly, she lowered her eyes.

"Just as you did," she said softly. "The day of the attack. You hid — and prepared the only possible counter-strike that could save the world."

He nodded sadly. The hard look in his eyes slowly faded, until all that was left was a haunted stare.

"And the price of that choice was the life of nearly everyone I loved."

She looked up at him. Her eyes were brimming with tears.

"Grandfather," she sobbed. "How can you bear it?"

Then she was buried in the old wizard's arms, hugging him tightly. He closed his eyes as he held her.

"I can't," he whispered.

She slowly released him and stepped back.

"I'm sorry," she said.

"As am I, Granddaughter."

She turned and walked away from him. She stood alone looking at the walls of the valley for a long time.

"I can't just live here," she said at last, "while you study our enemies for weakness. I need a focus, a purpose."

He smiled. "You sound like you have something in mind."

She nodded.

"You were right when you said I've done all I can — for now. Song and theater won't defeat Zomoran and his horde, and Carlissa doesn't need a princess bard. It needs a warrior princess."

She turned to face him. Her eyes were alight with determination.

"Teach me, Grandfather," she said. "To fight, with steel and magic. You're the world's greatest living adventurer. Take me as your student. Help me become the weapon I will need to be to defeat our enemies."

"Ah, Randia," he said. He looked at her sadly, and his eyes were filled with bitter regret.

"I would have given my life to spare you this fate. Do you truly want to set out on this path?"

She nodded eagerly. "You know I do."

He bowed in acquiescence.

"Then let the Silver Star live on, here in the sanctuary of Blackwing Lodge." He smiled. "The headmaster will don his robes for a last, long semester — and a class of one."

She returned his smile. "Thank you."

She walked to her blanket and sat down. She picked up and unstoppered her waterskin, and took a long drink.

"You know," she said thoughtfully, "I've been mulling over this whole idea of letting the world think we're dead. If we're going to do that properly, we'll need new identities."

Lenard sighed. "You and your passion for playing parts. I think you're going to have more trouble giving up the princess bard than you realize."

She shook her head. "Then I'll use it. Leverage it, make it a part of what I become. And you're changing the subject."

"I suppose you're right. Do you have a suggestion?"

"Well, we should start with names. A new surname will be easy enough. 'Blackwing Lodge' should belong to the Blackwing family, after all." She looked up at him. "An old man and his granddaughter, living a quiet and peaceful life in the mountains of southern Carlissa."

"All right. I hope we won't have much need to use the story, though. Neighbors coming by for tea every Thursday will defeat the purpose of living in a 'hidden' valley."

"True. Now we need a name for you. How about 'Reynard?' Or 'Frederick?' No, those sound too pompous. How about —"

"Allen," he interrupted.

"Allen Blackwing," she mused. "Yes, I think that works."

"And you?"

She was silent for a long time.

He smiled. "Difficult decision?" he asked.

She looked at him pointedly. Her lips quirked into a wry grin.

"Don't rush me," she said.

She was still thinking when she heard a rustle of wings in the tree above her. She glanced up to see a robin light on one of its branches. It cocked its head and began to sing cheerily.

"Robin Blackwing," she said slowly.

And then she smiled.

The Fate of the Sanctum

Robin Blackwing stepped into her grandfather's laboratory. He sat at his desk, working intently on a collection of scattered papers. Magical formulas littered the pages, many of them crossed out and corrected.

"Working on a new spell?" she asked.

"Yes," he said absently.

"Well, it's time to take a break. Dinner's ready."

He looked up at her. "Have you finished your exercises?"

She nodded. "And the written assignments. You can grade them after we eat."

He sat back in his chair. "You're doing well in your studies," he said.

She shook her head. "I'm just getting started. And flattery won't get you out of coming to the table on time."

He smiled. "No, of course not."

He stood slowly. He leaned on the desk a little as he got to his feet.

"Grandfather," she asked suddenly. "What happened to your staff?"

"Gone," he said. "It was destroyed in the battle."

"You never told me how that ended."

"There's little to tell. Your simulacrum collapsed. Mine stood over her body and fought until the enemy was about to overwhelm him. I made sure the image of that last stand appeared in the Blood Moon for everyone to see."

She grinned. "Nicely staged. You could make a dramatist yet."

"I hope not," he said fervently.

"And the end?"

"When they were closing in for the kill, I finally abandoned possession of my duplicate. He used his last reserves of power to create an explosion. The blast vaporized what was left of our simulacra, the sanctum, and its artifacts. And a good bit of the southern cliff in the process too, I think."

"The ring as well?"

"I'm afraid so. Now you go on. I need to wash up, and then I'll meet you at the table."

She nodded and walked toward the door. She paused on the stairs and turned.

"The legendary Sanctum of the Archmage," she said wonderingly. "And now it's gone. A small price to pay to save the world, I suppose. But still, what a shame."

He heard her footsteps receding as she climbed the steps and left the room. He smiled as he watched her go.

"Ah, Granddaughter," he said quietly. "Surely you didn't think I had only one?"

GLOSSARY

Aquaphilic

Having a love of, or affinity for, water.

Archmage

The title reserved for the greatest wizard on the Eastern Continent.

Blood Moon

One of the two moons of the world of Kalara. Its name comes from its distinctively reddish hue.

Blue Moon

One of the two moons of the world of Kalara. Its name comes from its distinctively bluish hue.

Codex War

A Carlissan civil war that took place approximately two centuries before the events of *Dawn of Chaos*. It followed the rediscovery of the ruins of Janthala by the adventurer mage, Aldran Killraven. [Read more about *the Codex War* on the Kalaran World history timeline at https://sanctum.andarian.net/world/history/codex-war.]

Craftmage

A mage skilled in the art of creating magical items.

Dweomer

The pattern of magical energy, or "algorithm," constituting a spell. Often used colloquially as an informal synonym for "spell," it also denotes the form in which an enchantment is invested by a craftmage in a magical item. [Read more about *Dweomer Technology* on the Kalaran World history timeline at https://sanctum.andarian.net/world/history/dweomer.]

Eastern Continent

That part of the continent of Kalara lying east of the Calihan River and the Northern Plains. It is typically considered to include the lands of Elde, Carlissa, and Rayche, and the Nurian Mountains.

The Grim Times

A period in the ancient history of Kalara that preceded the *Taming*. It was marked by constant warfare between Light and Dark, resulting in a descent by both sides into a barbaric dark age. The great knowledge of the *Age of Legends* was completely lost during this time. [Read more about *the Grim Times* on the Kalaran World history timeline at https://sanctum.andarian.net/world/history/grim-times.]

High City

The terraced westernmost part of the city of Lannamon. It lies beneath the face of Mount Cascade, between the palace and the crossroads adjacent to the great amphitheater. It is the most exclusive part of the city, and mostly home to the mansions of the greater nobility.

Lower City

The flat and non-terraced part of Lannamon lying around the tip of the Firth of Fajang. It is home to most of the city's people who lack great wealth or noble rank.

Magus

The highest designation of accomplishment or "rank" among wizards, save for the singular title held by the Archmage. It denotes a mage of exceptional power and skill.

Mountainset

In Lannamon, the time when the sun descends below the shoulder of Mount Cascade to the west. The time between mountainset and full sunset creates an extended dusk-like period in the city.

Scry

The use of magic or telepathy to find, sense, or generate images of something distant or hidden, such as with a crystal ball.

The Taking

A ritual practiced by the Hellmen upon conquering a land. It involves the taking of spoils, especially slaves, from among the defeated people.

The Taming

A period in the history of Kalara that followed the *Grim Times*. It refers to the long, slow victory of the Children in the ancient conflict between Light and Dark. Their many separate realms grew in strength during this time, "taming" the wild lands of Kalara around them. They allied at its end for the first time since the Great War to defeat the Dark, driving its remnants into the mountains and wastes to the north and west. Read more about *the Taming* on the Kalaran World history timeline at https://sanctum.andarian.net/world/history/the-taming.]

Upper City

The terraced northern and southern arms of Lannamon, lying between the Lower City and the bluffs that ring the valley. The more affluent and influential of the capital's inhabitants tend to live there, including the merchant class and the lesser nobility.

Preview: *Wrath of the Peregrine King*

Dawn of Chaos will continue in *Wrath of the Peregrine King*, the next book in the *Sanctum of the Archmage Saga.*

> *In the occupied capital of Lannamon, Orion, Diana and Kay work in secret for the growing rebel movement. And the princess, now calling herself Robin Blackwing, continues her studies in the Hidden Valley with her grandfather, Lenard the Archmage.*
>
> *As Carlissa falls and the Warlord threatens the Eastern Continent, the leaders of nation after nation, fearing conquest by his infernal army, sue for treaties of peace. Only one leader stands, alone, to defy the horde: Tarnas Acheron, the Peregrine King of Mount Cassandra. Consumed by wrath over the murder of his daughter and her family, the lord of the mountain elves has sworn vengeance against the Black Magus and his demons.*
>
> *But can he survive their attack when even his wife, Queen Talina of Elde, fears to stand at his side? And will Robin and the resistance remain in the shadows while the Peregrine King fights a lone war against the Dark in their name? Or will they risk a final defeat by coming out of hiding to join his cause?*

Wrath of the Peregrine King will be the first book in *Crucible of Heroes*, the second volume in the *Sanctum of the Archmage Saga.*

About the Author

I'm *Tony Andarian*, and I'm the author of the *Sanctum of the Archmage* epic fantasy novels and games. They are published by my personal imprint, *Andarian Publishing*.

Invested from a young age with an overactive imagination, I've had a lifelong love of science fiction, fantasy, computer games, and writing. In my career as a computer scientist, I've worked in areas ranging from data visualization and machine learning to quantum computing.

I'm also an indie computer game developer. As *Andarian* in the Neverwinter Nights gaming community, I released two award-winning, Hall of Fame "adventure modules" based on parts of the *Sanctum* saga. Their success helped convince me to explore my passion for storytelling in today's new world of self and e-publishing.

For more information about my writing projects, visit my website at *publishing.andarian.net*, find me on social media at *publishing.andarian.net/social*, or sign up for my monthly email newsletter at *sanctum.andarian.net/subscribe*.

About the Editor

Samantha Rosalbo has a degree in English Literature and lives in New York City. The written word is her lifelong passion, and she's always looking for new worlds to jump into. You can find her at *samantharosalbo.wordpress.com* or at *twitter.com/SamanthaRosalbo*.

Please Leave a Review

Thank you very much for reading *Dawn of Chaos*. I hope you enjoyed reading it as much as I enjoyed writing it. If you did, would you be willing to write a short review?

Reviews are incredibly important to help indie authors become known and recognized for our work. Without them, we are essentially invisible to the community of readers who might otherwise find and enjoy our books. They are also one of the best ways for us to get the kind of feedback we need to grow and improve as writers.

Just a line or two of honest feedback can make a huge difference, so I hope you'll be willing to help.

Andarian Publishing - https://sanctum.andarian.net/sota-doc/ap
Goodreads - https://sanctum.andarian.net/sota-doc/goodreads
Amazon - https://sanctum.andarian.net/sota-doc/kindle
Apple Books - https://sanctum.andarian.net/sota-doc/apple
Barnes & Noble - https://sanctum.andarian.net/sota-doc/BandN
Kobo - https://sanctum.andarian.net/sota-doc/kobo
Other Review Sites - https://sanctum.andarian.net/sota-doc/ubl

Even if you don't leave a review, I hope that you'll tell others about the book, and look for the upcoming works in the saga. And thank you very much again for reading!

Sincerely,

Tony Andarian
Andarian Publishing